The gorthling sneered. "I've been looking for you, Sorceress."

"And I you," Gabria replied, studying the creature before her. He looked like Lord Branth: brown hair, tall, muscular build, everything perfectly normal and human. Only his presence was different. There was a cold glint of merciless cruelty in his eyes and an aura of hostility in his every move.

"Go back to the realm of the dead," she said at last. "You don't belong here."

"It's too late, Sorceress. I am here to stay." Even as the words left his mouth, the gorthling fired a bolt of the Trymian Force at the woman.

It came so fast Gabria was taken by surprise. However, the Hunnuli mare she rode upon had been waiting for just such a move. The magical horse reared high to protect her rider, and the blue bolt struck her full on her chest.

Other TSR Books

STARSONG
Dan Parkinson

ST. JOHN THE PURSUER:
VAMPIRE IN MOSCOW
Richard Henrick

BIMBOS OF THE
DEATH SUN
Sharyn McCrumb

RED SANDS
*Paul Thompson and
Tonya Carter*

ILLEGAL ALIENS
*Nick Pollotta and
Phil Foglio*

THE JEWELS of ELVISH
Nancy Varian Berberick

MONKEY STATION
*Ardath Mayhar and
Ron Fortier*

THE EYES HAVE IT
Rose Estes

TOO, TOO SOLID FLESH
Nick O'Donohoe

THE EARTH REMEMBERS
Susan Torian Olan

DARK HORSE
Mary H. Herbert

WARSPRITE
Jefferson P. Swycaffer

NIGHTWATCH
Robin Wayne Bailey

OUTBANKER
Timothy A. Madden

THE ROAD WEST
Gary Wright

THE ALIEN DARK
Diana G. Gallagher

WEB OF FUTURES
Jefferson P. Swycaffer

SORCERER'S STONE
L. Dean James

THE FALCON RISES
Michael C. Staudinger

TOKEN OF
DRAGONSBLOOD
Damaris Cole

THE CLOUD PEOPLE
Robert B. Kelly

Lightning's Daughter

Mary H. Herbert

LIGHTNING'S DAUGHTER

All characters in this book are fictitious. Any resemblance to actual persons, living or dead, is purely coincidental.

This book is protected under the copyright laws of the United States of America. Any reproduction or other unauthorized use of the material or artwork contained herein is prohibited without the express written permission of TSR, Inc.

Random House and its affiliate companies have worldwide distribution rights in the book trade for English language products of TSR, Inc.

Distributed to the book and hobby trade in the United Kingdom by TSR Ltd.

Cover art by Fred Fields.

DRAGONLANCE and FORGOTTEN REALMS are registered trademarks owned by TSR, Inc. TSR and the TSR logo are trademarks owned by TSR, Inc.

First Printing: December 1991
Printed in the United States of America.
Library of Congress Catalog Card Number: 90-71516

9 8 7 6 5 4 3 2 1

ISBN: 1-56076-078-8

TSR, Inc.
P.O. Box 756
Lake Geneva, WI 53147
U.S.A.

TSR Ltd.
120 Church End, Cherry Hinton
Cambridge CB1 3LB
United Kingdom

To Jeannie,
one good dedication deserves another!

For Roy,
the story continues!

Mary H. Herbert
Dec. 1991

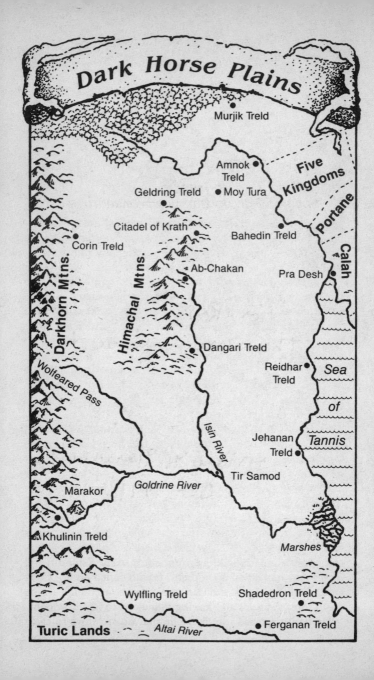

Prologue

ord Branth slid into the shadowed entrance of a storage tent just as several enemy warriors dashed by. He drew a long, ragged breath and, for a moment, savored the warm darkness of his shelter.

Events were happening so fast. He could hardly believe he was hiding in the middle of this huge encampment—a camp that up until a little while ago had been the center of a victorious force of clan warriors and mercenaries under the iron-fisted command of Lord Medb. Now, the camp was nothing more than a place of chaotic retreat.

Branth cocked his head to listen to the sounds outside the tent. He could still hear the clash and yells of battle from the broad valley beyond the camp. His fingers curled tighter around the dagger he held.

The fools! he thought to himself. The Wylfling clan was still fighting. Didn't they realize the day had been lost when the sorceress had destroyed Lord Medb? Had they missed that stunning duel of magic?

Even now the forces of Medb's enemies, led by the Khulinin chieftain, Savaric, were sweeping over the valley into the big camp to destroy the army.

Branth shrank back into the tent while more clan warriors ran by. Their gray cloaks identified them as Amnok. The Amnok had been Medb's allies until the fury of the Khulinin and their forces had fallen upon them. Branth curled his lip. Cowards, all of them! His own clan, too, had betrayed him, laying down their weapons and leaving him alone to face his doom.

He had not stood idly by while that doom strove to catch

him, however. Branth was Medb's second-in-command and would be executed without question if he were captured by Savaric's men. He was also practical and self-serving, a man who did not believe in wasting energy and blood on a lost cause.

No sooner had his clan abandoned him in the valley, than Branth had decided it was time to grab what he could and leave. He had already packed a saddlebag with his own gear and two bags of gold taken from another chieftain's tent.

There was just one more thing Branth wanted before he left, a thing that would ensure the prosperity of his future. He wanted Lord Medb's *Book of Matrah*. The book was an ancient compilation of two hundred years of arcane study. The knowledge contained on its pages was priceless. Lord Medb had kept the book under close guard, but Branth knew where it was and he wanted to get his hands on it before it was discovered by anyone else.

Branth had a strong feeling that he had the inborn talent to wield magic, and, with the tome, he could learn the forbidden arts of sorcery. He would then exact his own revenge on the clans and the sorceress, Gabria, for the defeat and dishonor he had suffered this day. All he had to do was get the book and escape before anyone found him.

Escaping was not going to be easy. He shifted an eye cautiously around the edge of the tent flap. The way was clear for the moment, so he ran, zigzagging between the black felt tents toward the biggest dwelling in the encampment.

More enemy warriors raced by, and several groups of Medb's mercenaries ran past, heading for the horses picketed at the east end of the camp. Branth avoided them all and kept moving until he reached the circle of tents around Lord Medb's big shelter.

He stopped abruptly and swerved behind an open tent flap. Five warriors were standing by Medb's tent, watching another man take down the chieftain's brown banner. Branth swore furiously in a barely controlled whisper. The warriors wore the gold cloaks of the Khulinin.

One of the men turned sideways, and Branth recognized the handsome, hawk nosed profile of Lord Savaric, the man who had stood up to Medb's unlawful bid for rule of the Ramtharin Plains.

Branth's curses died on his lips as he studied the chieftain and the tent where the book lay hidden. Savaric obviously felt the victory was his, for his sword was sheathed and only five of his hearthguard, his personal bodyguard, were with him. Branth could not see anyone else close by. He pressed back into the shadows and wondered what to do. There was very little time left.

Suddenly a great roar of victory resounded through the valley. Branth glanced out toward the mountains where the ruins of the ancient fortress of Ab-Chakan sat on its hill, overlooking the valley of the Isin River and the encampment of Medb's army. He could not see the valley floor, where the battle was being fought, but he could make out the remnants of the four clans, who had taken refuge in the ruins, standing by the walls and cheering. He glanced back at the six Khulinin and saw that they, too, were watching the spectacle. One man, a respected warrior named Bregan, was standing close to Lord Savaric.

At that moment, a commotion snared the warriors' attention. Several mercenaries were riding furiously through the tents toward Lord Savaric. It was unclear if they meant to attack or surrender, for their swords were drawn, but the blades were behind their backs. The hearthguard took no chances with the riders' intentions. They drew their own weapons and ran out to head off the mercenaries, leaving Savaric temporarily alone.

Branth did not waste a second. As soft-footed as a stalking cat he ran across the space between the tents and slipped up behind Savaric.

The Khulinin chieftain sensed his enemy's presence too late. As Savaric started to turn, Branth rammed his dagger into the man's back and up into his heart.

The chieftain grunted, a hard, surprised sound, and sagged

to the ground. Branth jumped over the body, ran into the tent, and snatched the book from its hiding place. He was out and running before the other warriors realized what had happened.

His pleasure in the murder was confirmed when he heard Bregan's agonized cry, "Lord Savaric!" In a matter of moments, Branth found a saddled horse and was galloping out of the valley toward the east. A vague idea formed in his mind as he rode. He would leave the plains for a while, until the clans' emotions cooled and the events of this battle were mere memories. Maybe he would go to the city of Pra Desh in the kingdom of Calah. There he could study his book and perhaps sell his services to wealthy Pra Deshians willing to overlook the laws forbidding sorcery.

In time he would return to the Ramtharin Plains and remind the clans that their troubles had not ended with the death of Lord Medb.

1

abria stood motionless on the hard-packed floor and watched the faces of the clanspeople crowded in front of her in the chieftain's hall at Khulinin Treld. Many she knew had come to the trial, and some of those she loved. Piers Arganosta, the healer of the Khulinin; Cantrell, the great bard; and Lady Tungoli, widow of Lord Savaric and mother of the new chieftain, were seated in the front rows, their faces creased in worry. Sadly, too many other faces in the crowd did not show worry. They wore looks of confusion, hostility, and unhappiness.

To her left, Gabria could see eight men and women seated on benches against the whitewashed walls of the hall. Their expressions were deliberately blank as they attempted to watch the proceedings with open minds. Thalar, priest of the god Surgart, stood before the Khulinin and exhorted the chieftain and the people to reject the foul heresies of magic and to cast the evil sorceress out.

"Sorcery is an abomination!" he shouted. The priest was a short, squat man who made up for the inadequacies of his height with the volume of his voice.

Thalar had been shouting for some time now, and Gabria could sense Lord Athlone's mounting rage and frustration. Unfortunately the chief was behind her on his dais, and she was forbidden by the laws of the *getyne* to look at him. She must face her accusers and leave the chieftain free to act as an impartial judge.

Gabria sighed and shifted her weight a little to ease her stiff back. The doors of the huge earthen hall were closed, and the heat from the crowd and the fire in the central hearth was growing uncomfortable. The smell of resin from the numerous torches overwhelmed the smells of leather, wood smoke, and sweat that usually permeated the meeting hall. Gabria badly wanted a drink of water, but she was not permitted to speak during the *getyne*, so she tried to ignore her thirst and concentrate on the faces before her.

This ordeal is all too familiar, she thought. Half a year ago, at the start of spring, her clan had been massacred by followers of Lord Medb. Without family or friends, she had come to Khulinin Treld and stood before the chieftain to ask for acceptance into the clan. Instead of revealing her identity as a woman and risking rejection, she had disguised herself as a boy and brought with her a legendary and rare Hunnuli horse she had rescued from wolves. The Khulinin had reluctantly chosen to take her in on Lord Savaric's recommendation.

Now, months later, the Khulinin had to chose again, but this time they knew the full truth of Gabria's identity and her powers as a sorceress. Under normal circumstances, clan law prescribed death for a woman found guilty of hiding her sex in order to join a werod, the tribes' fighting units. The penalty for practicing the heretical arts of sorcery was also death. Yet in Gabria's case, the circumstances were far from normal. She had been the only person in the eleven clans able to face Lord Medb's sorcery and she had saved them all from annihilation or slavery. In thanks, the council of chieftains had released her from the punishment due a sorceress, but only under the condition that she not use magic again until the laws were revised. However, they did not release her from punishment within her new clan for her other crimes.

The new chieftain of the Khulinin, Lord Athlone, had made his feelings for Gabria known to his clan and had already paid the bride price to the priestess of the goddess, Amara. The Khulinin knew they could not anger their chieftain or ruin the honor of the clan by putting Gabria to death. Nevertheless, the ancient laws could not be maintained if Gabria was allowed to go unpunished. Some penalty had to be meted out to calm the anger and resentment of the clanspeople. Many of them, incited by Thalar, wanted Gabria exiled. Others wanted her tongue cut out so she could not speak the words needed to cast spells. Still others, though only a minority, felt she deserved a mild sentence. The controversy raged through the Khulinin during their trek home and continued even as they prepared the treld for the coming winter.

The emotions grew so high, Lord Athlone had finally stepped in to put an end to the furor. As chieftain, his powers were bound by the limits of clan law. He could have simply released Gabria from any judgment, but he was the son of a chief and had been wer-tain, commander of warriors, for several years. He knew when it was time to acquiesce to the demands of his people. Reluctantly, he had agreed several days past to hold a *getyne*, a form of clan trial in which a *tyne*, or jury, of eight decided the accused's guilt and punishment.

To Priest Thalar's fury, Lady Tungoli had insisted that the *tyne* be composed of four men and four women. Women did not usually serve on a *tyne*, but the lady reasoned that, since Gabria's crimes encompassed so many issues, it was only fair that clanswomen should help judge her. Lord Athlone had agreed. And so four men—two elders, a warrior, and a weaver—and four women—the priestess of Amara, two wives, and a grandmother—gathered on a chilly autumn afternoon to decide Gabria's fate.

The sorceress shifted her weight again and pushed a strand of flaxen hair out of her eyes. The heat was growing worse. Beads of perspiration gathered on her forehead, and her long skirts hung on her like a heavy blanket. She wished the people would hurry and get this over.

Particularly Thalar. The priest's voice was still ringing loudly through the hall. With a small frown, Gabria tried to concentrate on what he was saying.

"I do not condemn the council of chieftains for releasing this woman from her justifiable execution," he cried, his voice thick with righteousness. "The chiefs were overcome with joy and relief at their release from the evil ambitions of Lord

Medb. But they did not see then that they had only traded one evil for another. *This* magic-wielder—" he pointed a finger at Gabria "—still lives! The responsibility of wiping out this heretic has now fallen into our hands. We have a gods-given opportunity to show the clans of the Ramtharin Plains how we deal with magic-wielders. We do not tolerate them!" Thalar's voice rose to a thundering shout. "Khulinin, we must blot out this stain of sorcery before it spreads. Fulfill the penalty of death. Kill the sorceress!"

The words were barely out of the priest's mouth when the healer, Piers, leaped to his feet and demanded the right to speak.

"No! I am not finished," Thalar shouted. He had the crowd's attention and wanted to press home his point.

Lord Athlone, however, had had enough of Thalar's rantings. "We have heard you for some time, Priest. Give the right to someone else. Piers, you may speak."

The healer, ignoring Thalar's infuriated glare, turned to face the *tyne*. His pale skin and light, graying hair looked almost colorless in the dim light of the hall, but there was nothing lackluster about his speech. The old healer loved Gabria like a daughter and would have done anything to save her. "Khulinin, I realize that I am not a blood member of this or any other clan. I am a foreigner to your ways and laws. Yet in the eleven years that I have been with you, I have never seen you act with anything but honor, courage, and loyalty. This young woman who stands before you has those same qualities in full measure.

"When Medb's men massacred her clan, Gabria did not crawl away in fear to die. She took the only way open to her to seek justice for the murder of her people. When she learned she had the talent to wield magic, she did not hide her power, she used it to save all of us. Gabria's methods were wrong by the strictures of your law, but they were the only methods available to her and she acted on them with courage and honor. The council of chiefs has released her from death for her use of sorcery. Can we now turn our backs on their wisdom and justice and kill her for striking back against an enemy stronger than even the warriors of this clan? She does not deserve death for that, she deserves our respect."

For a moment the healer looked at each member of the *tyne* as if to seal his words in their thoughts, then he smiled at Gabria and sat down.

The watching clanspeople shifted and murmured among themselves.

Lady Tungoli rose next and claimed the right to speak. As widow of Lord Savaric and the mother of Athlone, Tungoli held one of the highest positions of status and respect among the Khulinin women. Everyone listened quietly as she nodded to the *tyne* and began to talk. "I would like to speak for myself and for several witnesses who are not in this hall today," she said. She did not raise her voice, yet her firm words were heard clearly throughout the hall. "For myself, I will only note that I agree wholeheartedly with the beliefs of those I am here to represent.

"The first is Lord Savaric. I knew my husband well enough to say with complete confidence that he would never have ordered Gabria's death under these circumstances. He respected her for her courage, her intelligence, and her determination. If he were here today, he would examine her deeds, her motives, and her strength of character, as well. He would want you to do likewise.

"The other witnesses I wish to include are the Corins. Gabria's clan did nothing to earn their fate. They were pieces in Lord Medb's game, pieces he discarded when they would not turn against their fellows. Gabria did not accept that fate. She fought back to redeem her clan's memory and to win justice for the murder of her family. The Corins would not have expected anything less, and neither should we."

"Perhaps there is another witness we should take into account," added a man from the crowd, the Khulinin herdmaster. He looked toward Lady Tungoli, who nodded and relinquished the right to speak. "I mean the Hunnuli mare, Nara. Clanspeople have always loved and revered the ancient

Hunnuli breed. We believe that Hunnuli cannot tolerate evil in any form. And yet, if that is true, why does Nara love Gabria and stay with this admitted sorceress? Does the horse know something we do not about the quality of magic? I think the mere fact that a Hunnuli horse trusts and obeys Gabria says more for her heart than any of the guesses we can make." The herd-master quickly sat down.

Finally the bard, Cantrell, stood and turned his sightless eyes toward Gabria. His rich bass voice rang through the hall, capturing everyone's attention. "The herd-master has brought up an interesting incongruity. For years we have been told in song, story, and decree that magic is heretical. We have believed in its ultimate evil and in the despair and grief sorcery can cause. In that we were right: Sorcery is evil." Many of the onlookers gasped and stared at the bard in shock. He smiled, and his fingers lightly touched the strings of the harp at his side. A soft melody lifted on the air and enticed the peoples' imaginations.

"But what we forgot was that magic could also be as beautiful as a Hunnuli horse, as good as a healing stone, as intricate as an ancient riddle, and as strong as true love. Magic is only what people make of it. It has been a part of the plains since the birth of the world, and it was said, before the Destruction of the Sorcerers, that the ability to wield magic was a gift of the gods. It is time we accept our heritage once again. I ask you to accept Gabria. She has a great gift that should be protected, not destroyed." He turned toward the *tyne* and lifted his harp toward them. "Be fair in your decision, Khulinin. We may need Gabria again some day."

The clanspeople stared at the old bard as he sat down, and his words hung in their thoughts. When no one else moved to speak the members of the *tyne* huddled together and discussed their problem. Gabria stood alone in the space before the chief's dais and waited. A heavy silence fell on the watching people.

Sweat dripped in beads down Gabria's forehead as she remained still, her head up and her face calm. How would they decide? she wondered. All she really wanted was peace, rest, and time to build a normal life again. This past year she had suffered more than most people would in a lifetime. Gabria wanted fervently to get through this trial so she could put the memories behind her.

She glanced down at the splinter of the Fallen Star gleaming under the skin of her wrist. It was too bad she could not put away her sorcery as easily as her memories. The talent to wield magic was an integral part of her, as natural as breathing. It was not a power she had wanted, but she had learned to use her talent to survive. She knew now she would never be able to ignore or forget the magic. Neither would anyone else in the clans.

At last Gabria heard Athlone stand. The edge of his sword clanged against his stone seat, and the sound rang through the quiet hall. The members of the *tyne* left their benches and stood.

Athlone, his feet planted on the stone dais and his arms crossed, searched the faces of his people. A golden torque of rank glittered on the chest of his leather shirt, and gold bands encircled both of his arms. He had recently cut his hair, and Gabria thought the shorter, dark brown locks and thick mustache enhanced the clean lines of his features. "What is your decision?" the chief asked without preamble.

The elder, a gaunt, silver-haired man, spoke. "We have heard the accusations against Gabria. We all know the truth of her deeds and her courage. Because she has given us our lives and our freedom to be Khulinin instead of Medb's slaves, it is our decision that she be freed from the penalty of death and exile. She has earned a place among the Khulinin."

Thalar sprang to his feet, his face dark with anger. "Never!" he shouted.

Athlone raised his hand to still the priest's outraged interruption. "Continue."

"However," the man went on. "We feel the laws of the clans cannot be put aside even for this. Therefore, we order that Gabria be pronounced dead for a period of days equaling the time she spent in her disguise—a passage of six months, by our reckoning. During banishment, no person may speak to her or acknowledge her in any way, and Gabria must retire to the temple of Amara beyond the treld. There she will serve the goddess in penance. At the end of six months, Gabria may return to the clan and be accepted as a permanent member."

Surprised, Gabria gripped her hands together to still their trembling. The sentence was harsh, for she would be alone and unaided through the winter. Most women would die under such difficult straits. On the other hand, Gabria knew—as Athlone must—that she stood a good chance of surviving the ordeal. Unlike other clan women, she could handle a bow and a sword. She might go hungry now and then, but she would not starve.

Thalar stepped forward, his expression wild, his eyes burning into Gabria with all the hatred of a priest for a heretic. "This is outrageous! That woman is profane! A creature of evil. If she is allowed to enter the holy temple of the Mother Goddess, our whole clan will be cursed!"

At that Piers jumped up to protest. The healer, the herdmaster, and several others crowded around Thalar and began to argue. Others joined in until the entire hall was filled with shouting voices. The noise crashed around Gabria like an avalanche. She gritted her teeth and silently watched the uproar.

"Silence!" Athlone bellowed. "Enough!" He crossed his arms as the shouting ceased, and every face turned toward him. "Priest Thalar has a valid argument. Perhaps the members of the *tyne* could explain their decision and put the clan's mind at rest."

This time the priestess of Amara stepped out of the group. Her long green robes were a bright contrast to the more somber colors of the men. She was an older woman, past forty-five summers, and equal to Lady Tungoli in the honor and respect of her clan. Her gray hair was swept back in a long braid, and her startling green eyes seemed to pierce through Thalar. "It was I who made the suggestion to the *tyne* to send the sorceress to Amara's temple."

"You!" Thalar exclaimed in surprise.

Gabria, too, was startled and watched the woman as she paced forward in the light of the lamps and torches to face the priest.

"I believe I know more of the goddess's ways than you do, Thalar. A man who follows the god of battle and death cannot begin to comprehend the power of life and birth. It is my belief that Gabria has the favor of Amara. Her survival and her success against overwhelming odds are indications to me that the goddess is watching over her daughter. If this is the case, then Cantrell's arguments for magic are more than the artful words of a skilled bard." She paused as Cantrell chuckled.

"I suggested sending Gabria to the temple," she continued, "to learn the truth of the goddess's will. If the sorceress is blessed with Amara's grace, then she will live and thrive to return to us. If she is not, the mother goddess will punish her as no mortal can imagine."

For a long moment the Khulinin stared at Gabria. No one moved or said a word. At last, Lord Athlone raised his hand. "So be it. Lady Gabria's sentence begins at moonrise tonight. She may return to the clan in six months, marked by the rise of the full moon." He turned on his heel and strode to the chieftain's quarters in the back of the hall. The tapestry fell closed behind him, signaling the end of the *getyne*.

Thalar snorted in disgust and stamped to the entrance. As the guards pulled the doors open for him a cold gust of wind swirled into the hall. The chilly air seemed to rouse the crowd from their astonishment. In ones and twos they averted their eyes from Gabria and left the hall until only the sorceress and Cantrell remained.

The young woman took a deep breath and stepped away from the fire. She sank down on the dais steps. "We have been back in the treld but ten days and already they are getting rid of me," she said with bitter sadness.

The old bard did not answer her immediately. Instead he gently strummed the strings of his harp. Cantrell had lost his sight the previous summer, when Lord Medb had slashed his face in a fit of rage during an ill-fated clan gathering. The bard had fled the sorcerer's camp and found sanctuary with the Khulinin. Since then, Cantrell's ancient harp had rarely left his hands. His eyes were gone, but the music of his harp and his songs had kept his life full.

He played his instrument now, letting the notes flow into the new ballad he was creating about Gabria. The clans loved heroic tales, and it would not hurt to remind them of the courage in Gabria's deeds. For a while he simply played to her, knowing the music would say more than his voice. He brought the tune to an end with a strong flourish and listened as the notes passed into silence.

Cantrell stood and laid his harp carefully by his stool. "I am pleased you will not be far away. We will be waiting for you to come home."

"Home," Gabria repeated sadly. "I am a sorceress. The only home I had is now a ruin. I doubt I'll ever be allowed to find another." She climbed to her feet and looked miserably at the door through which Athlone had disappeared. She hadn't even been given a chance to say good-bye to him.

Cantrell felt for her arm. He pulled her close and held her tight. "You will survive this, child. And more to come. Be ready."

Gabria smiled into his blind face. "Is this one of your prophecies, Bard?"

"No. It is something I feel—like the coming of night. It will be moonrise soon. You had better go."

Gabria picked up her golden clan cloak from the steps, threw it around her shoulders, and walked toward the big double doors. Behind her, the bard resumed his seat and ran his fingers along his harp. The soft music followed her toward the doors. Just as she was about to leave, a familiar voice called to her. Gabria turned and saw Athlone hurrying to her with a bundle in his hands. The emotions of the past few hours swelled within her, and she ran to meet him before the fears and angers could tear apart her flimsy control. She wrapped her arms around him and buried her face in his neck.

The chieftain hugged her fiercely. "I could not let you go without a word."

As he held her is his arms, she looked up and said forlornly, "Six months is a long time to be away." She dropped her eyes again. "I have never been alone for so long."

"I don't like it either," Athlone replied, "but the law must be upheld or we will never have peace." He looked down into her deep green eyes. "Besides, you will not be totally alone. Nara will be with you, and while I cannot visit, I'll watch and guard you as much as I can."

His face suddenly lit with laughter and he added, "The goddess must look after you, too. I have already paid the bride price. Will you marry me when you come back?"

She looked away. "You may change your mind in six months."

Athlone cupped her chin in his hand and gently turned her head to look at him. "I'd sooner change my clan. I will be waiting for you. In the meantime, take this." He thrust a bundle in her hands, then kissed her deeply. "And take my love." A final hug and he was gone, striding back to his quarters.

The sorceress watched him go, her heart heavy. Finally she stepped past the entrance and looked down through the deepening twilight at the wintering camp of the Khulinin. The chieftain's hall was built into the side of a large, treeless hill overlooking a broad valley in the foothills of the Darkhorn Mountains. To the north, the Goldrine River tumbled out of a deep canyon and spread out to water the fertile valley. Here, in this natural shelter, the Khulinin spent every winter, caring for their herds and gradually losing their nomadic habits.

From the promontory where she stood, Gabria could see the entire encampment of black felt tents, corrals, and scattered permanent buildings that dotted the banks of the river. Beyond the Goldrine, large herds of horses and livestock grazed on the lush grass of the foothills. The Khulinin were a large, wealthy clan, and Gabria had hoped to make a home with them. Now she was not so sure. Two hundred years of hatred and suspicion of sorcery ran too deep in the beliefs of the people to be put aside in a few months. Gabria doubted the clans would ever completely accept magic—at least in her lifetime.

Even Lord Athlone could not help her cause. He had admitted at Gabria's trial before the gathered chieftains that he, too, possessed the talent to wield magic—but only because that admission would help sway the council in its deliberation of her crimes. Yet he had never used sorcery before his people, and they seemed content to ignore his talent so long as he never utilized it. Gabria, on the other hand, was not only the sole survivor of a massacred clan, she had the audacity to train as a warrior and the temerity to openly display the forbidden powers of magic. She was too different to be acceptable.

There was but one creature who totally accepted Gabria for everything she was: Nara.

The woman raised her fingers to her lips and blew a piercing whistle. The guards on either side of the doors ignored her, but they could not ignore the magnificent mare that neighed in response to the whistle and came galloping up the main road through the treld.

The mare was a Hunnuli, a rare, wild breed of horse that had once been the steeds of the ancient sorcerers. Like all Hunnuli, Nara was larger and more intelligent than other horses and impervious to magic.

Gabria's sad face slowly broke into a smile as the huge black horse galloped to the hall and slid to a stop. The young woman knew every clansperson nearby was watching the beautiful mare, and her heart warmed with gratitude and joy as the Hunnuli reared before her rider in the timeless obeisance of respect and honor.

Gabria pulled herself onto Nara's broad back.

Are we leaving? Nara asked in Gabria's mind. The Hunnuli's telepathic thoughts were gentle, and full of love.

"I am to go to the temple of Amara. The Khulinin want me out of sight for a few months," Gabria replied irritably.

The mare dipped her head. *It is better than death.*

Gabria's lips twisted in an ironic smile. "Yes, I guess you're right." She paused to secure Athlone's bundle to her belt, then said, "I must leave by moonrise, but I would like to stop at Piers's tent first. They did not say I had to go empty-handed."

We'd best hurry, then. The moon has already reached the mountaintops.

Nara trotted down the path to the edge of the treld and the spot where Piers kept his shelter. The healer's tent had been home to Gabria for the past six months. Piers had discovered her hidden identity shortly after she had joined the Khulinin, but he had kept her secret despite the danger to himself. He had offered her sanctuary, security, and friendship when she needed them most.

Gabria slid off the mare and walked into Piers's tent. The large, dark shelter was quiet and empty; only a small lamp burned on the table. The girl looked around in relief. Piers was not there. By law, the healer would have to shun her if she came near him, and she knew neither one of them could bear that.

She found her old pack, the one she had salvaged from the ruins of her home at Corin Treld, and began to gather her belongings. There was not very much: a few tunics, a leather jerkin, boots, a blanket, a small wooden box with her precious flint and steel, and a sheath for her father's dagger, though she had lost the weapon itself. She borrowed a cup, a pot, and a few cooking utensils from Piers's hearth. Last of all she collected her bow and sword.

When Lord Medb had fallen at Ab-Chakan, Gabria thought she was through with the pants, the sword, and the skills of a warrior. Now she realized she would need them again to survive her banishment. She took off her full skirts and put on a pair of heavy winter pants, which would be warmer and more practical than a skirt. Then, reluctantly, she belted on her short sword. She would be alone through a long, cold winter, and even though she would be near a treld, wolves, bears, cave lions, and other creatures were known to prowl the valley and the hills. She would feel safer with a weapon at hand.

Gabria was about to leave when she noticed a full leather sack lying near the coals of the hearth fire. A red cloth was fastened to the sack—red for Clan Corin. She peered into the bag and smiled. Piers had found a way to say good-bye. The bag was packed with food: dried meat, beans, horsebread, dried fruit, and a flask of Piers's own favorite wine. There was enough food to satisfy her for many days. Gratefully she took the bag and gathered her loose belongings into two bundles.

Outside the tent Nara waited patiently. When Gabria appeared and began arranging the bundles over the mare's withers, Nara nickered softly. *The priest watches.*

Gabria surreptitiously glanced around Nara's chest and saw Thalar standing in the shadows of a nearby tent. He was watching them with obvious anger and disgust.

"He does not obey Lord Athlone's command," she replied, annoyed.

He is not the only one who watches.

The sorceress sprang onto the horse's back and tightened the golden cloak around her neck. "Then let's show the Khulinin how a Hunnuli and her rider leave camp."

Nara trotted back to the main path. She paused for a moment to sniff the chill evening breeze, then lifted her head and neighed a challenge that rang throughout the camp. The unexpected noise brought people running out to look. The stallions in the far pastures answered with their own clarion cries, and the dogs in the treld barked furiously.

Nara proudly neighed again and reared, her powerful front legs pawing at the pale stars. Gabria felt her own joy soar to meet the Hunnuli's. She drew her sword and answered Nara's call with the Corin's war cry.

The mare leaped forward. Her eyes ignited with a golden-green light as she galloped down the road through the treld. Her hooves pounded the hard ground.

Gabria clung to the mare and raised her sword above her head. "Farewell, Khulinin!" she shouted to the dark tents and the people who stared after her.

From the hall's entrance high on the side of the hill, Lord

Athlone smiled as he watched them go. He should have known Gabria would not slink out of the treld. He raised his fist in a silent salute, which he held until the horse disappeared into the deepening night.

* * * * *

It was fully dark by the time Gabria and Nara passed the Khulinin burial mounds and found the tiny stone temple of Amara nestled in a copse of trees atop a hill. Because the temple was used only a few times during the year, it was small and very plain. A rectangular stone altar sat across from the only door, and above the altar a large circular window faced the east and the rising moon.

Gabria left Nara outside to graze, carried her bundles into the temple, and built a small fire in one corner away from the window. Chewing on a piece of dried meat, she curled up in her blanket and cloak. For a long while she stared at the fire and tried not to shiver. A cold draft blew through the window and made the fire dance.

Though Gabria was apprehensive, she was not frightened or worried about Amara's reaction to her presence in the temple. Despite Thalar's warnings, she had always felt secure and accepted by the Mother Goddess. Nothing had changed that, but this temple was so quiet and strange! She could hear Nara grazing among the trees, and she thanked Amara with all her heart for the black mare. Gabria was used to noisy, bustling camps and the constant company of people. This silent solitude was frightening. She could not imagine being alone for a long period of time, and without the Hunnuli for company, Gabria doubted she would be able to bear this banishment for six months.

It would be six very long months without Athlone, too. Gabria cuddled deeper into her blanket and let her thoughts wander to the Khulinin lord. When they'd first met, Gabria had hated Athlone. He was a wer-tain then, commander of the Khulinin warriors, and his father's most trusted adjutant.

He, too, had befriended a Hunnuli, a stallion named Boreas who later died at Lord Medb's hand. Gabria quickly learned that Athlone was a forceful, commanding, sometimes impetuous man whose sole loyalty lay with his clan. He had been immediately suspicious of Gabria's disguise, and when he discovered the truth of her identity, he nearly killed her. It was only through the unexpected help of magic and the support of Nara and Boreas that Gabria was able to fight him off and eventually convince him to help her. What had begun as mutual animosity and distrust, grew to respect and love.

Unfortunately, their love was not being given much of a chance to blossom. The deep feelings they shared were very new to both of them and had not been fully explored. Gabria worried that a six-month separation might prove too rocky for the tenuous roots of their new love.

Thinking of Athlone reminded Gabria of the bundle he had given her. She had not yet opened it. Quickly she pulled the wrapped parcel out of her pile and untied the leather thongs that held it together. Several small items tumbled onto her lap, each one hastily wrapped in large pieces of woolen fabric.

The young woman was pleased to see that each scrap of fabric was large enough to cut for mittens or to piece together for a small blanket. Best of all, a packet of bone needles was tucked into one of the parcels. Gabria began to unwrap the packages and found a little stone oil lamp, its wick hole plugged with wax to hold the oil, a pair of mittens lined with rabbit fur, a hatchet, and a warm cap.

Last of all, she found a long, narrow package bound with a golden armband. The band was small and solid, traced with an interwoven design of fanciful horses. It slipped over her hand and settled comfortably on her wrist. Armbands were a favorite gift among betrothed couples, and Gabria sensed the band was Athlone's way of reassuring her of his love. The thought pleased her.

Finally she uncovered the narrow package. The gold wool fell away, and a dagger slid into her hand. Gabria gasped. The dagger blade was forged from steel, a rare, valuable metal crafted only in the city of Rivenforge in the kingdom of Portane. The handle was braided silver, formed to fit the hand and inset with small rubies and topaz. Red for the color of the cloaks of the Corin clan, gold for the Khulinin.

Tears formed in Gabria's eyes as she turned the dagger over in her hands. The weapon was a priceless gift given from the heart. Women did not usually carry such weapons, but she had owned another dagger once. It had been a gift to her father from Lord Savaric, and she had found it in the smoking ruins of her home. It had been her only physical remembrance of her dead father. Unfortunately, on that afternoon when she faced Lord Medb in the duel of sorcery, she had transformed her father's dagger into a sword to slay her clan's murderer. The weapon had been destroyed with Medb's body.

She realized then that Athlone understood how much the old dagger had meant to her. The armband was his gift of love, but the jeweled weapon was his gift of hope that she could build a new life.

Gabria wiped the tears from her eyes with a scrap of wool and carefully laid the gifts aside. She found her empty sheath, slid the dagger in, and fastened it to her belt. The weight of the weapon felt good on her side. She curled up in her blanket once more and watched the fire die to embers.

As the coals' glow dimmed, Gabria promised herself that she would endure this exile. She would go back to Khulinin Treld in the spring and do everything in her power to build a good relationship with the clan and with its chieftain. She owed herself nothing less.

abria did not realize how much the events of the previous summer had drained her emotionally and physically until she had time to relax. After only a few days at the temple, she caught a cold and came down with a fever and racking cough. For days she stayed in the small temple, curled up on her crude bed, lost on the paths of her thoughts. She had barely enough strength to eat or fetch water and firewood. Nara kept watch over her and waited worriedly for the illness to pass.

One cold night as Gabria tossed in a feverish, restless doze, she thought she heard the sound of Nara's hooves galloping up to the temple. There was the soft thud of footfalls, then she sensed another person close by. She struggled to wake until a cool hand soothed her forehead and a familiar voice spoke softly to her. A cup filled with a warm herbal drink was brought to her lips. She drank without opening her eyes and settled down into a peaceful sleep.

Piers stayed with her through the night and slipped away at dawn, leaving behind a stack of wood, a filled water jug, and a simmering kettle of soup. He did not come back after that night—he did not need to. His herbal drink eased Gabria's symptoms and his brief, comforting presence revived her interest in survival. Gabria was not sure how he'd known of her illness. She could only thank her goddess that the healer cared enough to risk the visit.

The food Piers had given Gabria sustained her through the days of her malaise. However, as her illness eased and she regained her strength, she realized the supply of food was dwindling rapidly. She would need more than a few beans to keep herself alive. One cold, cloudy afternoon she forced herself to take her bow, mount Nara, and hunt in the hills for meat. To her pleasure, her skill with the bow had not diminished. She brought down a small deer, and that night she feasted on venison.

The exercise and the meat were just what she needed, and Gabria felt stronger than she had in days. After that she went out every afternoon to ride Nara, or to hunt, fish, or gather food in the hills. Her health and her good spirits returned in full measure. She was pleased to notice that, as she grew stronger, her intense grief for her family began to ease, taking with it the bitterness and anger that had burned within her during her struggle for revenge. She was left with a growing sense of contentment and release.

As the last days of autumn passed, Gabria began to enjoy the solitude of the little temple, the peace of her thoughts, and the quiet companionship of the mare. She felt closer to Amara in this place, and each day she knelt by the altar in the light of the rising sun to give thanks to the Mother Goddess for sustaining her.

Nara, too, seemed to thrive in the peace of the temple. The foal within her, sired by Athlone's Hunnuli stallion, Boreas, grew steadily and filled out Nara's sides as she grazed contentedly on the dried winter grass of the hills.

Although no one came to visit them, Gabria often saw Athlone at a distance, keeping a watch on her. His vigilance meant a great deal to Gabria, and she always acknowledged him with a wave.

The only thing that began to bother Gabria as the time passed was boredom. She spent many hours every day gathering food and turning the stone temple into a more comfortable dwelling. But there were times when she had nothing to do. Then loneliness would creep in, and she would long for the distractions of a busy treld. She wanted to find something that would keep her busy during those lonely, dull times.

Then one rainy, cold night she found the answer. An autumn storm had blown in suddenly as Gabria was collecting firewood. By the time she'd made it back to the temple, she was soaking wet and chilled to the bone. She dumped the wet wood in a corner to dry and quickly laid some kindling in the small hearth she had built. To her annoyance she realized she had not banked the morning coals, and the fire was dead. Gabria tried to light the kindling with her flint and steel, but her hands were trembling with cold and she could not draw a spark. Her frustration grew with every failed attempt.

All at once, an idea flashed in her head: she was a magic-wielder. She could use a spell to start a fire. All it would take was a single word.

Gabria hesitated for just a moment. She had promised the council of chiefs that she would not practice sorcery, and under normal circumstances she would have kept her vow. Now, however, she was banished from the clans and dead in the eyes of her people. What she did during the time of exile was her own concern.

She spoke the word of her spell, and a warm, cheerful flame leaped out of the pile of kindling. Gabria grinned like a mischievous child. At that moment, she decided to use her time to practice her sorcery. She had only learned the basic skills and rules of wielding magic from her teacher, the Woman of the Marsh, and had found little opportunity to use her powers since then.

Gabria decided to begin her practice by perfecting one spell. After some thought, she chose a spell of transformation. Magic could not be used to create something out of nothing, though it could alter forms or change appearances. Gabria had used a wild version of a transformation spell to transform her father's dagger into a sword during her fight with Medb. That experience had taught her how powerful that enchantment could be.

When her evening meal was over, Gabria found a pinecone and began to practice changing its shape. Her teacher had stressed that a spell had to be perfectly clear in the magic-wielder's mind or disaster could result. Gabria was a little clumsy at first. Her concentration would waver, the image of the spell would not focus in her mind, or she simply did not try hard enough. At those times, the pinecone would warp and twist from the image she had chosen for it. Sometimes she could not make it change at all.

That night and for many days after, she practiced her spell until she was able to change the pinecone into any shape, size, or color she desired. In the process of her learning, a deep respect and curiosity for the endless powers of magic were awakened in her soul. Delightedly she took the next step in the progression: to transform the essence of an object, not just its appearance, into something different. Once again she chose a pinecone and began to try transforming it into her favorite fruit, a sweetplum.

*   *   *   *   *

It was a few days before the end of the year when Gabria began to notice the gifts.

The year, and three months of Gabria's banishment, would end on the night of the winter solstice. By clan reckoning the new year always began on the day when the sun resumed its journey back to the north. During the last days of the year, it was customary to present gifts to the clan priests and priestesses as thanks for special blessings that had been received during the year. Women usually gave gifts to the priestess of Amara in gratitude for a healthy child, a pregnancy, a loving husband, or a fruitful herd. The gifts were small—food or handmade items that were given from the heart. The priestess used these gifts as part of her livelihood.

One evening Gabria came back from checking her snares and found a bowl of eggs and a beautifully wrought leather belt lying on the threshold of the temple. Curious, she picked them up and looked around. The clearing and the temple were empty. She carried the things into the stone room and laid them on the altar. She could only imagine someone had brought the gifts for the goddess and had been afraid to enter the temple because of her. It's strange, Gabria thought as she cleaned a rabbit, gifts such as these are usually given to the priestess in person, not left in front of the temple.

To Gabria's surprise more gifts were left by the door the next day while she was gone: a jug of honey, a pair of wool slippers, and a loaf of bread. Gabria gazed hungrily at the honey. She had not had anything sweet in months, but she placed the gifts on the altar by the others and ate her meal of rabbit soup.

Seeing the gifts gave Gabria an idea. She owed her goddess a huge debt of gratitude for preserving her life and sheltering her these past few months. There was very little she could give as a gift, but as she stared at the pile of furs and skins on her bed, an idea formed in her head.

The next night was the Night of Ending, the last night of a very eventful year. Snow fell heavily that day, so Gabria spent much of it working on her gift for Amara, cutting pieces of soft leather and stitching them together into the shape of a horse. She worked late into the night to sew a mane and tail, stuff the little body, and color it black with soot from her fire.

When she was finished she set the horse on the altar and knelt to voice her thanks. It had been a very long year, and she hoped the next one would not be as difficult. As she raised her hopes to Amara, a cold gust of wind swept through the window, setting Gabria's fire leaping. She shivered. Hurriedly she banked her fire and crawled into her warm coverings. At dawn the priestess would be coming to the temple to perform the ceremony of prayers for the new year. Gabria did not want to make the situation uncomfortable, and she planned to be away before daybreak. She fell asleep to the sound of the wind humming around the temple.

Gabria had only been asleep a few hours when Nara's thoughts brought her bolting awake. *Gabria, the priestess comes.*

The sorceress frantically leaped to her feet and grabbed for her boots and cloak. Outside she heard Nara neigh a greeting to the Khulinin priestess and her acolytes. Gabria saw through the window that a faint golden light rimmed the hills to the east and glimmered on the snow that blanketed the ground. She stuffed her feet into her boots and shoved her belongings into the corner. She was about to dash out when the priestess and two young women entered the temple.

The women's eyes widened when they saw Gabria. The priestess's gaze was turned only to the altar and the window facing the rising sun.

Gabria knew she should slip out now, for most priestesses did not allow the uninitiated to attend this ceremony, let alone a woman under banishment. Yet she hesitated, drawn by the grace and beauty of the priestess at her altar.

At that moment the priestess, without turning around, said, "Stay."

The acolytes looked shocked when they realized who she was talking to, but the priestess had already begun the prayers and they did not dare interrupt.

Gabria was pleased. She pressed back into her corner and knelt as the acolytes knelt.

Softly at first, like the light that began the morning, the priestess chanted her prayers to Amara the Mother, goddess of love, life, and birth. As the light intensified and the stars dimmed, her chants grew clearer, more joyful. The priestess's green robes glowed in the morning light and swayed gently with her body while she sang. Her long grizzled hair flowed loose to her waist, like a maiden's.

The fiery rim of the sun edged over the plains, and its pure light poured directly into the stone temple. The priestess's voice rose to a song of greeting, and the acolytes' voices joined hers with triumph.

Although Gabria did not know the words of the prayers, she felt their meaning sweep through her mind and carry her to the heart of her feelings. As the light of the sun warmed her face, she raised her hands and hummed the tune of the invocation, sending her own thoughts of gratitude to the goddess who nurtured her.

The prayers came to a last song of hope when the sun parted from the far horizon. Only then did the priestess lower her

arms. Standing in the blaze of sunlight, she turned to face the
other three women, her wise face still glowing with her joy.
She gave a slight nod to the sorceress kneeling in a corner lit by
the sun.

"Thank you, sisters, for your help," she said to the acolytes,
then added, "Lady Gabria, Amara shines her light upon you."

The acolytes gasped, and one said, "Mistress, remember the
law."

The priestess lifted her hands to the sunlight. "Here in Amara's temple I am the law. Please go outside and wait," she told
them. "I will join you in a moment."

The two women walked out, keeping their gazes firmly on
the ground.

Gabria slowly stood. "Thank you for asking me to stay."

"I'm pleased you did. This only confirms my belief that you
hold the goddess's favor." The priestess paused to study
Gabria from head to foot. "You are looking well."

"I am feeling fine," Gabria said eagerly, "although I was ill
for a while. It was miserable. I didn't have the strength to
leave my bed. I think I remember Piers coming once, but that
time is rather blurred." She broke off, and her eyes went to the
round window where the light was pouring into the room.
"It's strange. It seems more than just a fever was healed within
me. I feel as if a great weight has gone from my mind."

The priestess nodded. "Your experiences last summer
would have exhausted a seasoned warrior. I knew you were
worn thin when you left the treld. Your voice was full of bitterness and defeat. I do not hear that any more."

"I don't feel it. It's ironic. The time I've spent in the temple
was supposed to be a punishment. Instead, it has been the
best healing I could have had."

"Lord Athlone will be pleased to hear that," the woman
said, her eyes were warm with pleasure. "He has worried constantly about you and misses you sorely."

Gabria smiled to herself. "And I him." She colored slightly
and said, "I'm sorry. I didn't mean to talk so much. It's just
nice to see another person."

"There is no need to apologize. I am glad to listen."

"Before you go, could you tell me how the clan is faring?"

The priestess caught the faint note of loneliness in Gabria's voice. "The clan does well. This mild weather has been a blessing. The herds are healthy and everyone is keeping busy." She paced to the window and looked out at the snow.

"I haven't seen much of Lord Athlone lately," the priestess went on. "He has been working with Lord Koshyn of the Dangari and Lord Sha Umar of the Jehanan to restore clan unity." Her wise face looked troubled. "Lord Medb did more damage than he ever imagined when he tried to conquer the twelve clans. Our people were not meant to be ruled by a single overlord. We're too different from one another. Now the people who sided with Medb are fearful and defensive, the ones who fought against him are angry and resentful, and those who ran are ashamed. Lord Athlone is worried that all of this will tear the clans even further apart. He has been communicating with every chieftain on the plains to help sooth the angry feelings. It has kept him quite busy."

"I hope they can resolve some of these problems before the clans gather this summer at the Tir Samod," Gabria said.

"So do I. We do not need another war." The priestess stopped as something else occurred to her. "There was another piece of news I heard. It's only a rumor, but Branth may be in Pra Desh."

"Branth!" Gabria spat the name. "That murderer. I had hoped he was dead."

"Apparently not."

"Has Athlone said anything about Branth's whereabouts?"

The priestess replied, "Not that I know of. He might be waiting for more reliable information."

Gabria shook her head absently and stared at the floor while she pondered the priestess's news.

After a moment, the priestess went to the altar and studied the gifts lying to the side. A knowing smile touched her mouth. She picked up the little black horse. "Yours?"

Gabria looked up. "Nara is pregnant."

"Indeed. Then I shall take this and add the mare to my prayers."

The sorceress walked over to the altar. "Aren't you going to take the other gifts?"

"Those, young woman, are for you."

"Me!" Gabria gasped.

"There is a small but growing belief among the women that you are the blessed of Amara. There have been five births this season and all have been successful. Some women attribute that to your continued presence in the temple. They have brought these gifts to you."

Gabria was amazed. "But you are Amara's priestess. These gifts should be for you."

The woman's smile widened, and she shook her head. "I do not need them." She paused, her eyes boring into Gabria's. "But the clan needs you whether it knows it or not. Stay in the light of Amara's grace, and you will weather all the hatred and suspicion the unbelievers throw at you." She came to stand in front of Gabria. The girl tensed, waiting for the rest of the warning.

"Step out of the light," the priestess continued, her voice low and adamant. "And I promise you, the goddess will destroy you."

Gabria nodded once in understanding. The priestess examined her face for a long moment before she stood back, satisfied with what she saw.

"You will be home in three months, in time for the celebration of the Birthright. I will look forward to your return."

The Birthright was the ceremony of thanksgiving to the goddess, Amara, for a fruitful birthing season. It was a vital part of the clan's duty to the Mother of All. Gabria could not help but wonder if the rest of the Khulinin would look forward to her return at that time.

The priestess strode to the entrance. "If the Hunnuli needs help at the time of her birthing, call for me."

"Thank you, Priestess," Gabria said with gratitude. She went to the door and watched the three women walk down the path until they disappeared among the trees.

For many days after the priestess's visit, Gabria mulled over her words. After so many months of rejection and suspicion, she found comfort in the knowledge that a few clanswomen were beginning to accept her basic goodness and her loyalty to the gods. Sorcery was believed to be a heretical evil and a perversion of the gods' powers. Gabria had believed that herself until she came to understand her powers. Perhaps now the clanspeople were beginning to question their old beliefs, too. That was an encouraging thought.

The only part of the priestess's news that worried Gabria was the rumor about Branth. She wondered if he really was in Pra Desh and if he had the *Book of Matrah*. She turned cold at that possibility. Everyone believed the Geldring chieftain had stolen the book of spells, so it was very possible that he could be trying to use the knowledge captured within its ancient covers. Gabria hoped with all her heart that he was not, because Branth was as cruel and ambitious as Lord Medb. The gods only knew what kind of trouble the Geldring could devise with his power.

Gabria wondered, too, what Athlone might do when he learned where Branth was hiding. Clan law granted Athlone every right to seek Branth and exact justice for the murder of his father. But Athlone had responsibilities to the clan to think of. Besides, if Branth had become a practicing sorcerer, Athlone would not have a chance against him.

Gabria finally shook herself and set aside her disturbing thoughts. She still had several months left of her banishment, and it seemed senseless to waste her time worrying about a rumor she could not confirm. She brought out her pinecones and returned to her practice of sorcery.

As the winter days passed, Gabria grew more adept at her spells. Her first attempts to turn the pinecone into a sweet-plum were dismal failures. Her plums were either too hard, too sour, or too strange to eat. Finally, one evening, she envisioned exactly what she wanted, spoke the words of her spell, and changed the prickly brown pinecone into a perfect sweetplum. She laughed with delight when she took a bite and the delicious juice ran down her chin.

The sorceress practiced a few more times until she had a bowl of different kinds of fruit, then she went on to the next step: changing an organic substance into something inorganic. By this time her senses were more attuned to the process of bending magic to her will. In only a few days she was able to transform the pinecone into stone or any object she desired.

Gabria was so busy hunting for food and practicing her magic, she did not notice immediately that winter was giving way to spring. The weather had remained dry and mild so the changes came gently to the land. The fifth full moon of her exile had come and gone before she realized that the air was not as chilly and the days were growing longer. She had less than one month left before she could return to Khulinin Treld.

To her surprise, Gabria had to admit that she was not completely happy about going back. She had grown to like the freedom to use her magic. It would be difficult to give that up—even with the possibility that the council of chiefs would change the laws forbidding sorcery when the various clans gathered later that summer at the Tir Samod.

But that was not the only reason she was reluctant. As much as Gabria liked Khulinin Treld, she did not feel at home there. The only home she knew in her heart was a broad meadow far to the north, where the Corins had once made their winter camp. She had not been back since that day of the massacre, almost a year ago.

One night, when the half-moon rose above the plains, Gabria lay on her pallet in the dark, cramped temple and thought about her family long into the night. After a while she dozed, drifting in and out of sleep. Her dreams crowded in and jostled with her memories of her father and brothers. She tossed and turned as the dreams grew more vivid, and the phantoms of her old terrors gathered like shadows in her mind.

In the blink of an eye, her thoughts cleared. A vision came

to her then, as real as the first time she had experienced it. It was the same vision she had dreamed that previous summer, just before her first meeting with Lord Medb.

Gabria saw herself standing on a hill, looking down at the ruins of a once-busy camp. The sun was high and warm, and grass grew thick in the empty pastures. Weeds sprawled over the moldering ashes and covered the wreckage with a green coverlet. A large mound encircled with spears lay to one side, its new dirt just now sprouting grass.

Gabria jolted awake. The vision faded, but the image of the burial mound remained clear in her thoughts. She had no idea if the mound was real. When she found Corin Treld after the massacre, she had been alone and unable to do anything but leave her people where they had fallen. It was all she could do to save herself.

Gabria mulled over the vision for several days, and in that time her desire to see her home again became a powerful yearning. The more she thought about it, the more important it became for her to see for herself if her clan had really been buried. There had been no chance to say good-bye to her father and brothers on that horrible day. Perhaps now, while she still had about eight days of exile remaining, was a good time to go. On Nara she could cover the distance to the treld in three or four days and be back before anyone missed her. No one would have to know she had left the temple.

When Gabria told the Hunnuli mare of her idea, Nara agreed. *To see your home once more will give you strength,* the mare told her. *We will go.*

They left the next morning in the cold, misty hour of dawn. Nara cantered east beyond the foothills to the plains and gradually swung north to avoid the Khulinin scouts. By sunrise they were well to the north of Khulinin Treld and following the Sweetwater River. Nara settled into an easy, flowing canter that would carry them for hours over the open leagues of grass.

Gabria relaxed on Nara's broad back. It felt wonderful to be on the plains again, away from the temple, the hills, and the people who would not come near her. Here on the wide, treeless grasslands she could see from horizon to horizon, feel the wind that tugged at her hair, and rejoice in the eternal blue sky that arched over her head. She threw her arms wide and laughed happily at her freedom.

Nara neighed in reply. The black horse stretched out into a gallop, her muscles moving effortlessly as she raced the wind for the sheer joy of running. Her black mane whipped into Gabria's face. Her hooves pounded the hard ground.

Gabria laughed again. She felt the power of the Hunnuli flow beneath her as quick and hot as the lightning that marked the horse's right shoulder. All at once she was overwhelmed by love, gratitude, and wonder. As long as she had Nara, she knew she would never be alone. She would always have an empathetic companion who would stand by her no matter how often her own people rejected her. She flung her arms around Nara's neck and pressed her cheek against the soft hair.

The mare slowed to an easy canter. *Are you all right, Gabria?*

The young woman sat up, smiling, and rubbed the horse's shoulder. "Stay with me, Nara, and I will be."

Always, the Hunnuli replied.

Silently they went on. There was no need to say more.

They traveled north for three days through the wide, grassy Valley of the Hornguard. To the east, the snowy peaks of the Darkhorn Mountains towered into the sky, their white mantled heads crowned with clouds and their gray ramparts hidden behind veils of wind and snow. To the west, the smaller range of the Himachal Mountains bordered the valley like an old, crumbled fortress wall. The valley was a fertile, green land where antelope, wild horses, and small game flourished. Both the Geldring and the Dangari hunted in the Hornguard, and, since Gabria had no desire to meet anyone from the clans, she and Nara stayed to the eastern side of the valley among the foothills of the Darkhorns.

To Gabria the journey felt strange, yet half familiar. They were traveling back the way they had come almost a year ago.

The mountains and hills looked much the same: barren, gray-brown with winter, and patched with snow. Only Gabria was different. She felt a lifetime older and wiser; she was no longer a simple, terrified, girl. The realities of war and magic had changed her.

Her problem was that her experiences had not erased her memories. The closer they came to Corin Treld, the more nervous Gabria became. Time and again she remembered that hideous day when she had stumbled into the ruins of her home and found her murdered family. She had thought that she would be calm and able to deal with the memories, but the feelings of terror, grief, and confusion boiled out of her mind like a turbulent flood.

As hard as she could, Gabria fought down the turmoil within her and pushed on, refusing Nara's suggestion to stop and eat or rest. The Hunnuli was not bothered by the constant traveling, but she grew worried about her rider. Gabria was obviously lost in her own thoughts. She was no longer alert or attentive to her horse and their well being.

On the third day from Khulinin Treld, Nara cantered over a hill and down into a bowl-shaped gully. She paused at the edge of a half frozen, muddy pool.

Do you remember this place?

Gabria stared down at the dark pool. "Very well. I still have the scars on my hands." She ran her hand down Nara's neck. "A small price to pay for the gift of a friend."

In one motion, they both looked up to the top of a nearby hill where a small cairn of rocks could still be seen on the crest. It was there that Gabria had buried Nara's first foal.

She had come across the wild Hunnuli trapped in the mud and fighting for her life against a pack of wolves. Gabria had driven off the marauders and spent two days digging out the pregnant mare with her bare hands. She had tried to save the foal, but it had died during birth. She had laid it to rest among the rocks.

Thinking of the foal, Gabria belatedly remembered Nara's current condition. The mare was almost ten months into her pregnancy. Shamefaced, she ran her hand down Nara's silken neck. "I'm sorry," she said softly.

Nara nickered. *There is no reason to be so.*

"Let's camp here tonight," the young woman suggested.

The mare tilted her head and looked at Gabria with her wise eye. *There are still several hours of daylight left. We could be in Corin Treld by nightfall.*

Gabria shook her head. "We need to rest. Besides, I want to face the treld in the light of day."

They found shelter in a shallow overhang in the side of one of the hills. Nara went to graze while Gabria built a small fire, ate her meal, and lay down on her blankets. Darkness came quickly, for the sky was overcast and the air was heavy with the threat of snow. Gabria closed her eyes and tried to sleep.

She was very tired, and she knew tomorrow would be a trying day, but her thoughts could find no rest. Her mind kept returning to the reality of the massacre and the dream-images of her clan's grave mound. What would she find tomorrow? Had her family been buried with honor or were the bodies still there, rotting into the grass? She tossed and turned as her imagination envisioned every possibility, then jumbled the imaginings together with the real memories of the carnage. Phantoms drifted through her mind with half-remembered faces and voices silenced by death.

Outside Gabria's meager shelter, Nara came to stand against the cliff wall. The horse's eyes reflected the firelight, glowing like gems against the darkness.

Gabria remembered lying in the dark that night long ago, watching the eyes of the wild, trapped mare and wondering what would become of both herself and the horse. She never imagined the incredible events that were to follow. Now, she and Nara were going back to the place where the chain of events had begun.

Gabria sat up and leaned back against the rock. No, that's not quite true, she thought. The chain of events led back to Medb and his greed, and even farther back to the generations of clanspeople who had zealously avoided magic. It went back to the Destruction of the Sorcerers, to the blossoming of the magical city of Moy 'Tura, to Matrah who compiled his great tome, to the early magic-wielders who had experimented with magic, and as far back as Valorian, the hero-warrior who had first used magic to defeat the evil gorthlings of Sorh. Gabria was only a small part in a story that actually had begun centuries before and would continue long after she was dead.

The woman laughed. Seen in that perspective, her worries and inner turmoil were merely threads against a vast tapestry of clan history and human events. All of her frightened imaginings would change nothing about the treld or her dead clan. What was done, was done. She would simply have to wait until morning to settle her personal fears. She lay down again, pulled her cloak up to her chin, and let her thoughts relax. This time she drifted off into a peaceful, dreamless sleep.

Snow was falling the next morning when Gabria awoke. It was a light, fitful shower that patterned Nara's dark coat with tiny stars and dusted the ground with powder. The mountains were completely obscured behind a wall of cloud. Gabria shook the snow off her belongings, ate a quick meal, and mounted Nara. They left the gully without a backward glance and trotted slowly north through the swirling snow. Corin Treld was not far by horseback, but Gabria did not want to miss it in the billowing storm.

Fortunately the snow shower did not last long. A little before noon, as Nara crested a ridge near the treld, the snow stopped and the clouds began to break.

Gabria felt her heart pounding. "It's not far," she said. "It's just across that stream and up the next hill."

Nara broke into a canter. She went down the ridge, leaped the stream without missing a stride, and ran up the slope of a long, treeless hill. Suddenly the sun broke through the clouds and poured down on the land. The Hunnuli reached the top of the hill and stopped.

For a breathless moment, Gabria wondered if they were at the right place. The area looked similar to the home she remembered: the broad meadow surrounded by trees on two sides and backed by the dark, tree-clad mountains; the small stream that clattered along its stony bed; and the pile of boulders by the copse of trees where children used to play. With a stab of pain, Gabria realized this was the same meadow, it just looked different without its once-thriving treld.

Gabria flung up her hands and cried with relief and joy. Her vision had been right; there, in the broad field, stood a new mound, crowned with spears and shining with a dusting of snow in the morning sun. She slid off the Hunnuli and ran down the hill. Halfway down, she unpinned the Khulinin cloak and dropped it in the grass, then she drew her sword and shouted the Corins' cry of victory. Her voice sang through the empty meadow. The young woman raced up the slope of the mound and through the ring of spears to the very top. She brandished her sword high.

"Corin!" she shouted. "I did it, Father. You are avenged!"

The silence of the ruined treld rose to meet her. Head thrown back, she listened to the wind in the grass, the cry of a hawk overhead, and the music of the stream. It almost seemed as if beloved voices would sound then, acknowledging her heroic feats, but there was no one left to answer her. She looked around, half expecting to see her father, her brothers, or someone standing by the mound.

The meadow was empty, and only the wind walked in the treld.

Gabria's joy died within her as quickly as it had come. Beneath her feet lay the hundred-odd members of Clan Corin; her father, Lord Dathlar; her three older brothers; and her twin brother, Gabran. They were long gone, beyond the earthly lands they had once walked. Her family was in the realm of the dead now, in the presence of the gods. They might know of her victory over their killer, Lord Medb, and the price she had paid to earn her revenge, but they could not share in her glory. They were gone, forever beyond her reach.

Gabria's eyes filled with tears as she looked down. The new growth of spring was beginning to cover the mound; the earth was gently settling down around the buried bodies. The girl noticed the spears were already sagging, so she walked around the circle and straightened each one. When she was finished, she climbed down from the mound.

For most of the afternoon Gabria wandered around the treld, remembering the places she had loved so well: the site of her father's tent, the chieftain's hall they had proudly built with logs, the pens and corrals, the tents of her brothers and her friends. Everything had been burned by the marauders during the attack, but Gabria found many traces of what had been. The foundation of the hall sprawled in the weeds, its interior crisscrossed with a few charred logs. Bits and pieces of personal items lay in the grass. The charred remains of the tents stood rotting into the blackened earth.

At last Gabria came to a level place by the edge of the treld. There was only a broad, burned patch on the ground to mark the spot, yet Gabria would never forget this place. She had dragged her father's body from the front of his hall to this open ground and laid her brothers beside him. Then she had built a makeshift pyre and burned them as was befitting for honored warriors. It was all she could do alone.

Whoever had come later and buried the clan had also buried the remains of Dathlar and his sons, leaving no trace of the pyre. It was as it should be, and Gabria gave thanks to the unknown benefactors who had worked so hard to honor her people. She stared at the ground for a long time, remembering the faces of her family. This time her memories brought her warmth and peace. The anguish was gone. At long last her old terrors had been laid to rest.

She walked back through the treld a final time. Near the ruins of the hall she paused and looked around. Except for the burial mound and the scattered, decaying ruins, the meadow looked much like it must have before the Corins came to winter there. She smiled with bitter sweetness. That was the wonder of it: no matter how much blood was spilled on the grass, the plains remained constant and unchanging. This land could not be altered by human feelings.

"Farewell, Corins!" she called. "Rest well."

Sadly she walked back up the hill to Nara. She pinned on her Khulinin cloak and mounted the Hunnuli. "We can go. There is nothing here for me now."

The mare turned to face the burial mound in the meadow below and, with a trumpeting neigh, she reared high in the Hunnuli's gesture of honor and respect. When her feet touched down again, she and Gabria looked at the treld for one last time. After that, Nara turned south and cantered away.

wo days later, Nara and Gabria came to the hot springs in the foothills of the Darkhorn Mountains near Wolfeared Pass. They had stopped there the year before to rest and bind the wounds gained both from the wolves and during Nara's rescue from the mudhole. Once again Gabria gave in to the temptation of warm water. They found a warm pool among the bubbling springs and twisting vapors, and both woman and horse spent the afternoon soaking away the dirt of their journey. It was delightful. By the end of the day, Gabria felt more relaxed and peaceful than she had in a year.

As she dried herself she thought of Athlone and the Khulinin, suddenly realizing she was excited to see them all again. Her banishment would be over in two nights, and she could rightfully return to the clan. For the first time she felt as if she were going home. Smiling to herself, she put on her pants and tunic and fastened her golden cloak. In two days she would be home—at last.

Gabria made camp that night at the edge of the springs, upwind of the mineral-laden pools. Nara stayed close, grazing on the sweet grass. The woman was just settling down to sleep when the mare threw her head up and sniffed the night breeze.

The young woman sat up. "What is it?"

Do not worry, Gabria, Nara told her. *I will be back soon.* Without another word, the horse galloped into the darkness.

Surprised, Gabria shouted, "Wait!" She jumped to her feet and ran after Nara, but the mare was already gone.

The girl stood perplexed, staring into the night. What had

gotten into Nara? The mare did not usually go off alone without an explanation. Surely she could not be going into labor. It was too soon, and she would have told Gabria. Neither did Gabria think there was any immediate danger lurking in the night. Nara never would have left her rider unprotected.

Gabria returned to her blankets and tried to put her concern aside. Nara had said not to worry, but the sorceress found that that was impossible. She could not close her eyes, and sleep stayed far away through the long night.

Just before dawn, Gabria heard Nara's hoofbeats pounding into the little valley. She bolted to her feet and ran to meet the horse. She could barely see the black mare as Nara materialized out of the darkness.

Nara snorted. Her flanks were heaving from her exertion. *We must go,* she demanded.

"Go!" Gabria shouted. "Go where? Why did you leave?"

I must take you to the mountain. To the Wheel. Someone wants to see you.

"Who?"

The mare stamped her hoof, clearly agitated. *Gabria, please! You will see.*

Gabria stared at the horse in astonishment. If the demand had come from anyone but Nara, Gabria would have insisted on an explanation before she went anywhere. Instead she shrugged, gathered her belongings, and silently mounted the Hunnuli. She would trust Nara to keep her safe wherever they were going.

Nara galloped out of the valley of the hot springs and headed deeper into the mountains. The night was still quite dark, but the Hunnuli raced over the rough terrain as if her path was lit by the sun. Gabria held onto the horse with every ounce of strength she had as Nara lunged, jumped, and twisted higher and higher into the heart of the Darkhorns over a trail only the mare could see.

"Nara, slow down," Gabria cried.

The Hunnuli flattened her ears and ran faster. *We must be there by dawn.*

•   "Be where?"

The Wheel, was Nara's only reply.

The Wheel. Gabria had never seen that strange place. She had only heard it mentioned in the old tales told by the bards. The Wheel had been built in the mountains by Valorian, somewhere near the pass where he had led the first clansmen from the west to the grasslands. No one knew where the Wheel lay or even what it was; the tales had grown vague with time, the pass forgotten as the clansmen had turned their lives to the plains and let go of what had gone before.

Gabria gritted her teeth and clung to Nara. It took all her concentration to stay mounted against the jolting violence of the Hunnuli's gallop. She would find out soon enough what this place was and who wanted to see her.

Nara continued to run ever higher up the steep, rocky valleys, through forests of pines and dark spruce, and around thickets of heavy underbrush. She plunged over rock falls, raced past high alpine meadows where deer grazed, and galloped over the rough clearings left by avalanches or forest fires. The dry winter was especially evident this high in the mountains. There was only a few feet of snow where normally the drifts would have stood over Gabria's head. Nara was able to find her way through the low patches of snow without much difficulty.

By dawn they were high in the mountains, nearing the twin peaks of Wolfeared Pass. There were fewer trees on the upper slopes, and the undergrowth was thin and sparse. Nara finally slowed to a trot. Her breath came hard and fast, vaporizing into clouds in the cold, thin air. Her body was steaming from her efforts.

Gabria patted the horse's neck. She was worried, for Nara should not be running like this in her condition. Wherever we are going, she thought, it is important enough to Nara to endanger herself and her unborn foal.

We are close now, Nara told her.

The sorceress sighed with relief. She was surprised to see the early morning creep into the mountains with a soft light that dimmed the stars and revealed the peaks' rugged faces.

Nara struggled up a rocky incline, past a few stunted pines and clusters of boulders, to the edge of a broad plateau. There she stopped and snorted in satisfaction.

Mystified, Gabria looked about. The plateau lay like a huge plate on the side of the northernmost of the two peaks, its bare, flat ground swept clear of heavy snow. It seemed empty at first, and Gabria asked curiously, "This is it?"

Nara lifted her head to the peaks. Gabria followed her gaze and saw the distant pass that cut between the two pinnacles.

The Wheel is here. Go see. They will come soon.

"Who are 'they?' " Gabria demanded.

Nara did not respond. She remained gazing at the peaks as if waiting for something to appear. Her ears were perked, and her nostrils flared in the cold air.

Gabria shook her head and slid off the mare's back. Her legs and hands were stiff from clinging to Nara; it felt good to stretch her muscles and walk on her own feet. She took a deep breath of mountain air, savoring the sharp, rich smells of frost and alpine trees. For a moment she stood at the edge of the plateau and looked down to where the land fell away into the rugged highlands of the Darkhorns. Her eyes followed the land downward over the slopes as the sun rose higher and spread its light over the distant plains below. The endless leagues of the Ramtharin Plains were slowly revealed to Gabria in lightening hues of indigo, purple, and lavender. From her high promontory she could look far to the east, where the grasslands of her people rolled beyond the horizon.

A smile lit Gabria's face. It was no wonder Valorian's people had looked down on those lands and rejoiced. The plains were vast and beautiful and held everything the clanspeople needed to survive. Whatever they had left behind could not have compared to the grasslands.

Gabria turned away from the edge and studied the big plateau around her. At first glance it seemed strangely empty. There were no trees or shrubs or large boulders to break up the tableau, only a few scrubby, tough plants and some blotches of lichen on the flat ground. The only thing that caught her in-

terest was a low pile of rocks lying in the center of the plateau.
She was perhaps thirty paces away from the pile when she saw
something else. On the ground in front of her were two lines
of smooth, round, grayish stones. One line curved away to the
right and left in a huge arch; the second line intersected the
first and ran directly to the pile of rocks.

Gabria followed the straight line of stones to the rock pile.
She saw immediately that the pile was a cairn, carefully shaped
into a circle about two paces across and as high as a horse's
knees. Radiating out from the cairn were other equally spaced
lines of stones. Gabria followed a second line out; the curved
trail of stones circled the cairn and united each straight line
into— Gabria nodded her head—into the shape of a giant
wheel. She walked around the entire circumference of the huge
design, marveling in the perfect curve of the circle and in the
arrow-straight lines of the spokes. It was a remarkable creation.

If this is Valorian's Wheel, Gabria thought, it has to be over
five hundred years old. Despite weathering and time, the
Wheel was in very good condition.

She shook her head in wonder at the dream behind the
Wheel. Lord Valorian was a man known to many civilizations,
for tales of his deeds had spread far beyond the limits of the
plains. He was a hero-warrior and a chieftain, a man believed
to be half-god. He traveled to Sorh in the realm of the dead to
fight the gorthlings for Amara's crown; he bred the Hunnuli
from his own stallion and taught them to communicate with
magic-wielders; he was the first human to tap into the powers
of magic, and he led his people out of the miseries of their old
land to a new home beyond the mountains. After his death,
his twelve sons spread out across their new land and formed
the twelve clans of Valorian, preserving their father's heritage
and passing on the talent to wield magic.

Gabria smiled and thought Valorian might be pleased to
find one of his descendants had come back to see his wheel.

Without warning Nara neighed a cry of welcome. *They
come!* she trumpeted.

Gabria turned in astonishment. She had never heard Nara

sound so joyful. Her eyes followed the horse's gaze to the high
pass where the light of morning was streaming onto the mountain face. A herd of dark horses galloped down between the
peaks, their manes flying and their tails raised like royal banners. Snow flew from their hooves, and the thunder of their
coming rumbled over the plateau.

With the sun reflecting off the rocks and the snow, it was
difficult for Gabria to clearly see the horses; then she rocked
back in astonishment. She clambered up to the top of the
cairn for a better view. As they drew closer, she recognized
them immediately, for the horses were huge and black. They
were all Hunnuli.

They galloped onto the plateau where Nara pranced to join
them, and the entire herd neighed their welcome to the mare
and the woman. They flowed into a circle around Gabria, following the curve of the wheel.

She tried to count them, but there were too many and they
raced by her in a boisterous, wild run. Their black coats
gleamed in the sunlight, and a blazon of white lightning
marked each horse at the shoulder. Her mouth slightly open,
Gabria stared at the magnificent mares and stallions. Her
heart sang with their delight.

At last the Hunnuli slowed down and stopped. They wheeled to face the woman, their breath billowing in clouds around
them. A stallion broke away from the ring, trotted forward,
and nodded his head to Gabria.

He was huge. Even on the cairn of stones, the woman's head
barely reached his nose. She realized immediately he was the
King Stallion. His great strength was molded in the muscles of
his neck and legs; his eyes glowed with a deep, abiding wisdom. White hairs of age covered his muzzle, yet his step was
powerful. A regal courage showed in his every movement and
toss of his head.

We greet you, Sorceress, he told Gabria. The stallions
thoughts to her were proud but kind.

She swept back her cloak and bowed low to the majestic
horse.

We have waited a long time for the magic-wielders to return, he continued. *The Hunnuli were bred and born to be the companions of humans with the ability to use the powers of magic wisely. We have missed them. You are the first in a long time to return to the arts. For that we are greatly pleased.*

Gabria stared at the stallion, her eyes huge. She had no idea what to say to him. Sensing her confusion, Nara left the circle of Hunnuli and came to stand beside her.

The King Stallion turned his dark eyes to Nara. *Serve her well,* Gabria heard him tell the mare. *She must continue her work if sorcery is to return to the clans.*

The mare agreed with a neigh.

Gabria spoke up, "Nara has been my friend beyond all imagining. She has served me very well indeed."

And so shall her sons, the stallion replied. Then he dropped his head down to Gabria's height, arching his massive neck, and looked at her through the long hairs of his forelock. *Sorceress, we have asked you to come to Valorian's Wheel so we can warn you. Someone, some human, is tampering with magic beyond their control.* He shook his mane angrily.

You know the Hunnuli cannot be harmed or altered by magic, but we are innately sensitive to it and to any change in the forms of magic. Lately, we have sensed strange vibrations emanating from the east. These frighten us, for we believe the powers of magic are being abused.

Gabria looked away, her eyes thoughtful.

The stallion snorted. *You know who it is?*

"Possibly. An exiled chieftain may be in Pra Desh. We think he has the *Book of Matrah*."

Then, Sorceress, you must go. Find the source of this tainted magic before something terrible happens that you cannot challenge or reverse.

Gabria paled. "Do you know what he is doing?"

The Hunnuli lifted his head to the east, his nostrils flaring. *That is unclear to us. The only thing we know is this magic-wielder is unskilled in handling the powers he is trying to use. He must be stopped.*

Gabria felt her heart sink. Oh gods, not now, she cried to herself. To the stallion she forced her reply: "I understand."

Good. The stallion neighed a command, and a smaller, younger male broke away from the herd and joined Nara. The stallion bowed his head to Gabria.

It would be wise if you took other humans with you, the king told her. *Particularly the chieftain, Athlone. He would be a great help to you. Eurus will go with you. Lord Athlone will need a mount befitting his talent.*

Gabria eyed the young stallion doubtfully. "I don't mean to be ungrateful, but Athlone is very reluctant to admit his powers. Now that his stallion, Boreas, is dead, he may not accept another Hunnuli."

The King Stallion snorted, a noise that sounded much like laughter. *We will let Athlone and Eurus work out their own relationship. I'm certain the chieftain will come to his senses.*

The woman's mouth tightened, for she knew Athlone's stubborn nature. "I hope so," she muttered.

With a toss of his head, the king signaled his herd. The horses neighed and pranced forward.

Farewell, Sorceress, he said to Gabria. *We will come if you need us.* Then he wheeled and galloped back up the plateau, the other Hunnuli falling in behind him.

Before Gabria could draw another breath, the horses were gone. The thunder of their hooves echoed on the peaks and faded. An empty quiet fell on the plateau. She gazed at the twin peaks, wishing the Hunnuli would return, wondering if she would ever see their like again.

Nara nickered to her softly. *When Valorian brought the clans over that pass and built this wheel to celebrate their journey, they had over two hundred Hunnuli in their midst. Now our herd has barely thirty. Our numbers are dwindling rapidly, Gabria. Without magic and magic-wielders to give us purpose, our mares and stallions do not always mate. Our breed will disappear.*

Eurus snorted in agreement.

"May the gods forbid that ever happening!" Gabria said

vehemently. She vaulted onto Nara's back. "Let's go home."

The two Hunnuli fell in side by side and made their way down the mountain at a more careful pace. By late afternoon they had reached the foothills and turned south toward Khulinin Treld.

* * * * *

Two days later Gabria and the Hunnuli arrived at the Khulinin camp, just as the horns were blowing to send the evening outriders off on their duties. She rode Nara past Marakor, the tall summit that guarded the entrance to the valley, and waved to the startled outriders standing guard nearby.

She smiled to herself as one of the guardians galloped toward camp to warn Lord Athlone. Nara trotted placidly along the path to the treld, Eurus close by her side. By the time the two Hunnuli reached the training fields by the camp, Gabria could see activity at the chieftain's hall. A moment later a horseman came galloping down the hill to meet her. It was Athlone.

Even from a distance Gabria could see his anger. His body was rigid on the horse, and his face was dark with fury. He reined his stallion to a halt in front of Nara.

"In the name of all the gods," he shouted, his eyes on Gabria. "Where have you been?"

Before the startled woman could answer, Eurus came around behind Nara and snorted at the chieftain.

Athlone stared at the second Hunnuli, his anger retreating a little before his surprise and curiosity. "Who is that?"

I am Eurus, brother of Boreas, the young Hunnuli replied.

By this time the members of the hearthguard and the other warriors had caught up with their lord. They gathered close by him, their faces interested but wary. Other clan members clustered around, staring and pointing at Gabria and the two Hunnuli.

Casually, Gabria glanced at the clanspeople to gauge their welcome. She was relieved to see they showed no overt hostility, only curiosity. The priestess of Amara stood at the back of the crowd, a wise smile on her face as she nodded a welcome. Athlone seemed to be the only one disturbed by her return. This time, however, she was not troubled by his reaction. The chief was a volatile man, and Gabria sensed his anger was fed mostly by concern. Instead of rising to meet his rage, she merely asked, "How did you know I was gone?"

Athlone tore his eyes away from Eurus. "Piers went to find you five days ago. He told me you had left. There was no sign of where you were going, when—or even if—you would return."

She smiled. "You should have known that I would return."

Athlone nodded once, sharply, unwilling to give up his anger that easily. "Where did you go?"

"Heretic!" someone suddenly shouted from the edge of the crowd. Thalar shouldered his way through the people and planted himself in front of Nara. "Be warned. Your exile is over, but this clan will not tolerate your evil magic!"

Nara snorted menacingly, but the furious priest ignored her and shook his fist at the young woman. "Your presence curses us, Sorceress, and your foul heresies bring our doom. Leave us in peace!"

"Thalar!" the chieftain said sharply.

Nara, however, had had enough. Her head snaked forward, and she snapped at the priest, her teeth coming dangerously close to his head. The crowd gasped as Thalar stumbled backward, his eyes wide with shock.

"That will be enough," Athlone demanded.

Thalar started to say something, but the Hunnuli mare flattened her ears, and he stepped hastily back. Glaring ferociously, the priest withdrew to the edge of the crowd.

The sorceress ignored him. She patted Nara and said to Athlone, "Please, Lord, could we go to the hall? The Hunnuli are hungry, and I am very tired. I will tell you everything over a hot meal."

The chieftain nodded and said with genuine relief, "Welcome home." He glanced back at the hall with a strange expression of regret. "There is someone else who has been waiting for you."

"Oh?" Gabria asked. She felt a tug of foreboding, but Athlone dismounted without a reply and handed his reins to a warrior. Gabria, too, slid off her horse. The mare gently nudged her rider before she and Eurus trotted back to the meadows.

Gabria watched them go. Standing beside her, Athlone studied the sorceress's features and marveled that a face capable of showing such love could also have such strength.

The crowd began to disperse to their own tents and cooking fires. Athlone, Gabria, and several hearthguard warriors walked up the hill to the entrance of the hall.

Twilight was settling into the valley. Once inside the open doors of the hall, Gabria noticed the lamps were lit and a fire was burning in the central hearth. A haunch of meat had been set to the side of the fire, ready for the chieftain, his family, and any other warrior who wanted to eat in the hall. Lady Tungoli and her serving girls were setting up the trestle tables before bringing in the meal.

Gabria said softly, "It's good to be home."

The chieftain overheard her, and the quiet pleasure of her words evaporated the vestiges of his anger. He offered her his arm, and they walked into the hall together.

As Gabria and the men ate their meal and talked, Piers, Cantrell, and a stocky, ruddy-skinned man Gabria did not recognize came to join them. Other clanspeople sat close by, listening. Lady Tungoli organized her serving girls and also joined the group to hear the talk. No one bothered to introduce Gabria to the stranger in their midst.

Sitting beside Athlone's dais, Gabria told them all about her vision, her journey to Corin Treld, and the burial mound she had found there. She did not mention her own catharsis, but those who knew her well sensed the new peace and assurance in her manner. She went on to describe the Wheel and her meeting with the Hunnuli. Her listeners sat spellbound as she told of the black horses and their king.

When she repeated the King Stallion's warning about
Branth, the stranger sucked in a breath through his teeth.
"Lord Athlone, I—" he began.

The chieftain waved him to silence. "A moment, please,
Khan'di." He turned back to Gabria. "You haven't told us yet
why you have a second Hunnuli."

Gabria lingered over her cup of wine for a moment before
answering. "The King Stallion sent him."

"Why?"

"He thought you needed a mount befitting your abilities."

Athlone looked up at the ceiling, the lines on his face taut.
"I have a good mount. One befitting a chieftain."

The warriors around him stared at their chief in surprise.
Any among them would have traded their swordarms for a
Hunnuli to ride, but Gabria looked into Athlone's face and
understood his refusal. She sipped her wine and let the subject
drop. The King Stallion's advice was wise. She would let Athlone and Eurus work out their difficulties.

Athlone, meanwhile, settled back into his seat and acqui-
esced to her silence. He had no wish to push the subject further. Instead he poured more wine into his cup and passed the
silver ewer to the stranger. "Khan'di Kadoa, now you know
why we have been unable to find Lady Gabria," the chieftain
said with a twist of wry humor. "Perhaps now you would tell
her why you are here."

Gabria finally got a good look at the stranger when he rose
from the table and bowed to her. She guessed he was about
fifty years old, for his short-cropped hair was gray and his
heavy face was deeply lined around the mouth and forehead.
He was dressed simply in a pair of leggings and a knee-length
hooded shirt, but there was nothing simple about the massive
gold seal ring on his index finger. He met her scrutiny with a
sharp, interested gaze of his own, and Gabria recognized immediately that this man was no fool.

"Lady, I am Khan'di Kadoa, a nobleman and merchant
from the great city of Pra Desh, capital of the kingdom of Calah," he said smoothly. "I have come to talk to you about this

exile, Branth. As I have told your chieftain, Branth has been in Pra Desh over six months now and has been causing nothing but trouble."

Gabria shifted in her seat. "What has he been doing?"

"He has an old book of spells and the ability, however feeble, to use them." The man leaned forward, his dark eyes piercing under a line of bushy eyebrows. "When he first arrived, he ignored our laws forbidding sorcery and tried to sell his services. Then, he simply stole or conjured what he wanted. Before long he had the entire city in an uproar. He became such a problem that the city guards tried to arrest him. He killed them all. Then the ruler of our city, the fon, captured him."

A note of suppressed rage hardened the nobleman's voice. "The fon is an ambitious woman. She not only wants to rule Pra Desh, but Calah and the other Five Kingdoms, as well. She has already laid her plans to take over the rest of the country and invade our neighbor, Portane, in just two months' time. Somehow, she has coerced this Branth into serving her. She uses his book and his power to strip our fine city, all to build her armies. She will lay waste to Pra Desh just to satisfy her insatiable lust for power." Khan'di paused. When he spoke again his voice was calmer.

"Lady Gabria, Branth's presence has become intolerable. I beg of you, please come to Pra Desh and remove this man before the fon fulfills her plans. I know I am asking a great deal, but if you could just take him away, the people of Pra Desh—nay, of all Calah—would rise up and deal with the fon themselves."

The hall went very quiet as the clansmen waited for a response. Gabria looked at Athlone's stony face, then at the splinter of the Fallen Star, the mark of a magic-wielder, glowing redly just under the skin of her wrist.

Sadly, she touched the bright spot. After the Hunnuli's warning and this news from the Pra Deshian, Gabria felt that she had no choice. She would have to try to find Branth before he wrecked havoc on the city or returned to the clans to take

Medb's place. She knew, too, what she would have to post-pone her marriage to Athlone. It wouldn't be right, begin-ning their life as husband and wife under such difficult circumstances.

"Athlone," she said into the silence. "He's right. I must go to Pra Desh as soon as possible."

At first the chief did not respond. He sat and stared into the fire for several long moments, his expression showing no trace of the conflict that warred within him. Finally he seemed to reach a decision, for he tossed out the dregs of his wine and slammed his cup on the arm of the stone seat. He did not no-tice that the horn cup split from the force of the blow.

Rising, he said tersely to the men around him, "It is late. We will make plans for the journey tomorrow. Gabria will go to Pra Desh."

His companions were startled by the abruptness of his dis-missal. They stood and began to leave the hall.

"Bregan," Athlone called to one of the warriors. "Stay. I need to talk to you."

Gabria gazed at the chief's back, trying to hide her hurt. He had accepted her decision without a word; perhaps he didn't care after all. Since her return from the temple, she had found Athlone to be angry, irritable, and interested only in the news she could give. She began to wonder if she had misread him earlier. He was not worried that she was missing, simply angry that she had disobeyed his command by leaving the temple to go to Corin Treld. Perhaps in six months he had already changed his mind about her. She rose to go, her heart heavy. She looked up when Piers touched her sleeve.

The healer read the look in her eyes and understood. "Don't take his rudeness to heart. The responsibilities of a chieftain weigh heavily on him tonight," he said gently.

She looked up at her old friend and squeezed his arm. "It's not very often you defend Athlone."

The healer's pale eyes met hers with sympathy and caring. "I'm fond of you both. Don't worry. Athlone will come around as soon as he straightens out his own thoughts."

Wearily she nodded, more hope than conviction in her heart, and the healer took her arm. "Come," he said. "I have your old sleeping place ready for you."

He led Gabria out of the hall and down the path toward his tent. She looked back at the hall entrance, hoping Athlone would call to her, but the lord was talking to a warrior and did not even seem to notice she had left. She bowed her head and hurried on with Piers.

In the hall, Lord Athlone paced back and forth by the fire pit. The hall was momentarily empty, save for Bregan. The warrior was standing silently by the dais, waiting for his chieftain to speak.

Bregan was twenty years older than Athlone and a handspan shorter. His dark hair, worn short, was graying, and a black and silver beard trimmed his square face. He was dressed in a warm tunic and pants with none of the ornamentation or gold jewelry that was the privilege of a warrior of his experience. His features were well-defined, but in the past winter a deep sadness had left permanent lines on his forehead and face. Bregan watched his lord despondently, for he knew what Athlone was going to ask him and what he would have to answer.

Lord Athlone finally stopped pacing and said, "Bregan, I have asked you twice to be wer-tain and both times you refused. I have to ask you again. I need you as commander of my warriors."

Bregan shifted uncomfortably. "Lord, you know I can't."

Athlone held up his hand. "Before you refuse again, hear me out. I am going to Pra Desh with Lady Gabria."

The warrior did not look surprised. "Good. Branth must die," he said flatly.

"And Gabria must not," Athlone muttered. He put his hands on the older man's shoulders. "I understand how you feel, but I am chieftain now and I must leave this clan in capable hands. The journey will take months. You have the wisdom to rule in my stead, and you still hold the respect of the werod. There is no one else I trust as much."

"Lord, you do me great honor, but please choose another! I

cannot go back on my vow."

Athlone studied the man before him and saw the adamant refusal in Bregan's eyes. Of Lord Savaric's five hearthguard warriors who had been with him the day of his murder, only two still survived. Two of the warriors had chosen suicide instead of facing the shame and dishonor of their failure. One warrior had died of an illness on the way back to Khulinin Treld—some said he had lost the will to live. The fourth withdrew from the werod and each day drank himself into a stupor. Only Bregan remained a warrior. After Savaric's death, he voluntarily stripped himself of his status and the gifts he had won for distinguished service, then placed himself in the bottom rank with the young warriors in training. He would begin again, he had told Athlone, and work to regain his lost honor.

The chief shook his head. He could respect Bregan's choice, but it did not help him solve his dilemma. He had not yet chosen a wer-tain for the clan in the hope that Bregan would eventually accept. Now he had to decide on someone else quickly. He dropped his hands from Bregan's shoulders and resumed pacing.

"Do you have any suggestions?" he asked.

"Guthlac would serve you well."

"He's too young."

Bregan's mouth lifted in a slight smile. "He is several years older than you were when you became wer-tain."

Athlone stopped pacing, his face thoughtful. "I will think about it."

"He is a good warrior, and the others approve of him. He has been an excellent mentor for the younger men."

"Isn't he also your cousin?" Athlone asked, his eyebrow arched. The older man smiled, then the chieftain found himself mirroring the expression. "I will think about it," he repeated.

Bregan stepped forward. "Lord, will you consider something else?"

Athlone turned slightly, surprised by the note of pleading in the warrior's voice.

"Allow me to come with you," Bregan said. "I failed your father, but I swear by my life I will not fail you. You will need guards. Let me be one of them."

"This will not be an easy journey. Gabria goes to face a sorcerer."

"I know that. Lady Gabria will need protection, too."

"Pack your gear," Athlone ordered.

"Thank you, Lord." Bregan saluted the chief and withdrew, leaving Athlone in the chaos of his own thoughts. The young lord paced for a few more minutes, then left the hall and walked up a path to the top of the hill overlooking the camp. A large, flat rock lay among some scrubby bushes at the edge of the slope. It was Athlone's favorite place, for it afforded a view of the entire valley.

He gathered his cloak close against the night wind, sat on the rock, and studied the glorious clouds and patterns of stars breaking the monotony of the black sky. In front of him, a full moon sailed high above the plains. He looked down on the encampment. The black tents melted into the darkness, but here and there pools of firelight gave shape to the sleeping camp.

Usually this view of Khulinin Treld gave Athlone solace and strengthened his sense of purpose. Tonight, it only made his confusion more acute. Duty to his clan had always been his sole obligation. When his father had been alive and Athlone was only wer-tain, that duty was clear and simple: defend the chieftain and the clan with his strength of arms and his battle-wit. Now he was chieftain and his sense of duty was split. He still had to care for and defend the Khulinin, but he also had to avenge his father's murder, sustain the honor of the clan, and struggle to maintain peace with the other clans on the plains. To make matters more complicated, he loved a heretical sorceress more than life itself and feared for her safety. He was still ambivalent about sorcery, especially his own talent, yet his love for Gabria was undeniable.

Athlone looked up at the deep black firmament and prayed he had made the right decision to go to Pra Desh. He would choose Guthlac to serve as wer-tain while he was gone. Hopefully the clan gods would watch over the Khulinin until he could return.

The chieftain shook his head and stood up. The decision was made; nothing could be served by worrying the matter to death. There were problems to settle, plans to make, and a journey to begin. For good or ill, he was going to Pra Desh with Gabria.

Calmer now, he strode back down the hill and returned to his quarters in the hall. He thought about going to Piers's tent to see Gabria, but the night was late and she had suffered from the long journey. He decided to wait until morning, when she was rested. He knew he hadn't given her a very pleasant welcome that evening; in the morning he would apologize and make up for his bad temper.

With a yawn, Athlone laid his sword by the bed and settled down on the wool-stuffed mattress. He was asleep in moments, dreaming of Gabria.

4

abria was glad to be back in Piers's tent, lying on her own pallet and listening to the familiar sounds of the sleeping camp. Her body was tired, and her thoughts were weary of spinning over the same paths. She wanted to sleep, but she could not. A strange restlessness coursed through her mind and kept her tossing and turning. The girl could not identify the cause of her uneasiness. It did not seem to spring from her own worries. It was a vague anxiety that stirred the deepest levels of her consciousness and kept her on edge throughout the night.

It was near dawn when Gabria was brought upright by a pain that lanced through her abdomen.

"Nara!" she said aloud.

Gabria! The call came clear in her mind. *Please come. It is time.*

The woman paused only long enough to pull on her boots and grab her belt and dagger. She bolted from the tent and ran down to the pastures. Nara was waiting for her by the river. Gabria recognized immediately the signs of approaching delivery. The foal had dropped down toward the birthing canal, and Nara's sides were wet with sweat from her labor.

Without a word, the two walked out of camp and into the hills. They found shelter in a small glade at the bottom of a wooded valley.

Gabria rubbed the black horse's neck and spoke quietly to her as the labor progressed. "The baby is early," the woman said after a while.

Nara breathed deeply before replying, *By a turn of the*

moon. I should not go running in the mountains before my time. She trembled while a long contraction rippled through her body.

Gabria's fingers tightened on the black mane as the tremors of pain reached her. "Is it all right?" she asked.

I think so.

They lapsed into silence again, waiting for the natural progression of life. Just before the sun lifted over the hills, Nara laid on the ground. Unlike her first pregnancy, there was no difficulty with the birth. A small, black colt slid neatly out of his mother and lay squirming in his wet sac. Gabria cleared the birthing sac away from his body, wiped out his nostrils, and cut and tied the umbilical cord. Nara climbed to her feet and began to lick him vigorously.

Gabria stood back, tears streaming down her face, and watched in sheer delight as the black foal began to struggle to his feet. The sun rose over the hill, and sunlight poured through the trees. Its warmth invigorated the baby Hunnuli. He tottered to his feet and nuzzled close to his mother for his first breakfast.

Gabria cleaned the glade and went away to bury the remains of the birth and to give Nara time alone with her baby. She smiled to herself as she worked. The baby was alive and Nara was well! The words sang in Gabria's mind. She had not realized how strong her worry had been until it was gone. Happily she returned to the glade. She was so tired, she decided to lie down for just a moment. The woman was asleep in a heartbeat.

In the treld not far away, the hornbearers blew their welcome to the morning sun and the clanspeople began another day. Athlone, dressed in his finest shirt, overtunic, and pants strode down the path to the healer's tent. He jingled the small bells that hung by the entrance.

"Come!" Piers shouted from within. The healer was struggling with a pan of fresh bread when the chieftain entered. Muttering, Piers fumbled the hot pan to the table and dumped a heavy, flat loaf onto a wooden plate. The bread tipped off and fell to the floor.

Laughing, Athlone picked the loaf off the carpet and dropped it back on the plate.

"Thank you," Piers said. He poked at his handiwork. "Look at that. It would break teeth. I will never learn the knack of baking."

Athlone sat on a stool, still chuckling, and said, "You need a woman of your own."

The healer grimaced. "I've had one. They're more trouble than baking my own bread."

The younger man nodded vaguely as his eyes searched the tent for Gabria. Piers took one look at Athlone's gaze and the finery he wore, and realized immediately that this was not a casual visit. He turned back to his hearth and tried to appear natural as he spooned some porridge into a bowl.

"Where is she?" the chief asked.

Piers cast a worried glance at the chief. He poured two cups of ale, brought his bowl to the table, and sat down before he answered. "I don't know. She left in the middle of the night."

Athlone slammed his fist on the table. "Someone is going to have to nail that girl's foot to the ground!"

Piers picked up a spoon and dipped it in his porridge. "Her gear is still here."

"Well, maybe she'll come back for *that*," Athlone replied, glaring at his ale.

Piers glanced up at him. "She always comes back."

"Hmmm. I just wish she'd tell me once in a while where she was going." He sat morosely and watched Piers eat his meal. He was always fascinated at the neat, almost ritualistic way the healer consumed his food. His eating habits and his social manners were the only two things that Piers had not left behind when he had fled Pra Desh eleven years ago. Athlone had never been to the great city, and he had the feeling there was a lot to learn about the people and their customs before he arrived there.

Piers looked up and caught Athlone's eyes. Deliberately he put his spoon down and straightened his thin shoulders. "I have a favor to ask," he said with some effort. "I would like to go with you."

The chief was astonished. "You have sworn more times than there are hairs on a horse's back that you would never return to the city."

Piers nodded. "I know. However, I think your gods would forgive me if I changed my mind. Gabria may need my help. Besides . . ." He shrugged and looked away. "She has taught me a thing or two about facing memories. It is time I go back."

Athlone leaned forward, stunned. As far as he knew, Piers had never told anyone, except perhaps Savaric, why he had left Pra Desh. He had appeared at a clan gathering one summer and followed the Khulinin home. They had been happy to have the skilled healer in their clan and had not pried into his past.

"What about the clan? They will need a healer while you are gone," Athlone said.

"I will ask the healer of the Dangari to send one of his apprentices. He has a man ready to pass his rites."

Athlone stood and rubbed his chin thoughtfully. "All right. You are welcome to come with us." He paused. "How did you know I was going?"

"You could not do otherwise."

Athlone snorted. "And what of the clan I am leaving behind, O wise sage?"

"They will be fine," Piers replied. "It is us I would worry about."

The chieftain laughed without humor and went to the entrance. "We will leave in two days . . . provided Gabria returns in time." He turned and strode out.

Piers watched him go. He missed his friend, Savaric, very much, yet through Gabria he had found some common ground with Athlone. Now the son was becoming as good a friend as the father. The old healer sighed to himself. He could hardly believe he had asked to go to Pra Desh. Even after eleven years he was not certain he was up to facing the old memories and emotions. At least Gabria and Athlone would be with him. He would not have to endure the ordeal alone. He forced down his rising apprehension and went to find a rider willing to take a message to Dangari Treld.

In the meantime, Athlone returned to the hall and the business of planning for the journey. He met with the elders and warriors and told them of his decision. A few were concerned about his leaving, but the majority understood the necessity of finding Branth and avenging the murder of Lord Savaric. Quite a few men volunteered to go with him. He chose Bregan and three other seasoned warriors as an escort and ordered the remainder to stay and obey Guthlac, who he named wer-tain.

As the meeting continued, Athlone and the elders discussed clan problems. They made plans for the approaching birthing season, when the herds would be having their young, and for the Khulinin's departure for the Tir Samod. Guthlac made several astute suggestions, and Athlone was relieved to see the elders and the warriors listened to the new wer-tain with respect. At least, the chieftain thought, I can feel secure about leaving the clan in Guthlac's capable hands.

By late afternoon, the entire clan knew that their lord was going on a long journey and that Gabria was missing again. Everyone was buzzing about Pra Desh, magic, Branth, and the absent girl. The priest, Thalar, stole from group to group, trying to convince the clanspeople that Gabria's evil was spreading and that she was going to destroy their chief. But the priest's lies were overshadowed by the tale of Gabria's meeting with the King Stallion. Those who had heard the tale the day before spread it all over camp, embellishing the story with every telling. People flocked to the meadows to stare in awe at Eurus, who contentedly grazed before his audience. The speculation grew that Gabria had left to see the Hunnuli herd again. Perhaps, the people said to one another, she would return with more of the horses.

The truth became clear late that afternoon in a way no one quite expected. The clanspeople had not known of Nara's pregnancy before Gabria was banished and had seen little of the mare since her return, so they had not noticed her bulging sides. Thus it was that the news of Gabria and Nara's return swept through the camp like a whirlwind.

Athlone was the first to know of their coming. He was talking to Piers about supplies for the journey when he suddenly stiffened. "Eurus?" he gasped. His eyes went wide, and his handsome face broke into a grin.

"Piers," he cried in delight. "She's coming back. Eurus told me. Nara has had her foal!"

The two men ran through the camp just as an outrider came from the edge of the treld, shouting the news. Clanspeople gathered in the fields to see Gabria, Nara, and the long-legged foal come out of the hills and cross the meadows. Never in the recent memory of the Khulinin had anyone seen a baby Hunnuli.

The foal stared wide-eyed at the crowds, his small ears perked and his whisk-tail twitching. He trotted forward to sniff noses with Eurus. The stallion nickered gently; the foal whinnied in reply. As the three Hunnuli gathered around Gabria and walked with her to the camp, the clan watched, caught up in the wonder of the moment.

Athlone met them on the training field. He swept Gabria into his arms and kissed her soundly. "Don't ever leave me again without telling me where you're going."

Happily she hugged him. "Hello to you, too."

"And you!" the chieftain said, turning to Eurus. "Why didn't you tell me where they were?"

The stallion tossed his head. *You did not ask.*

Gabria laughed. "You'll have to get used to having a Hunnuli around again, Athlone."

The chieftain chose to ignore her remark. He stood with Gabria as the three Hunnuli trotted off to the river and the crowd of excited clanspeople slowly dispersed.

"We're going to leave in a day's time," Athlone said after a while. "Is the foal strong enough to travel?"

Gabria looked at him sharply. "We?"

"I am going with you. So is Piers."

"Piers, too? Blessed be Amara!" She grinned, the relief plain on her face. "Thank you, Athlone. I was afraid I'd have to go alone."

"You've been alone long enough," Athlone replied.

"But what about the council this summer?"

"If Branth and the fon do not cause too much trouble, we'll have enough time to return for gathering at the Tir Samod." He hesitated, then he drew Gabria close. "Will you marry me before we go?"

She leaned into him, her eyes almost level with his. Her finger gently traced the strong line of his jaw. She had been dreading this question. "Not yet, Athlone. I love you so much. But this journey will be long and dangerous. I'd rather begin our marriage on happier omens. Besides, I want you to be certain of your choice. You are chieftain of the most powerful clan on the plains. I am a convicted sorceress. This journey may give you a chance to know who I really am." Gabria felt her fingers trembling, and she clasped them together tightly behind Athlone's back. "You might change your mind by the time we reach Pra Desh. You should have that chance."

"I know who you are," he protested.

"Are you certain you can spend your life with magic and all of the uncertainty, hatred, and suspicion that go with it?" Gabria asked quietly. Her face was pale and set.

Athlone hesitated, and in that moment Gabria saw the faint shadow of doubt in his eyes. Although she hated to wait, she was glad now she had made that decision.

He looked away, aware that she had seen his doubt. "All right," he said. "I'll wait. If only to satisfy you."

She hugged him again, and the two walked through the camp toward Piers's tent. "What about the colt?" Athlone asked when they stopped by the tent flap.

"I wondered about that, too. He is premature, but Nara says he can easily keep up with your Harachan horses. She insists on going with me."

Athlone glanced away, trying to be casual. "What about Eurus?"

"Oh, he's coming, too," Gabria said, hiding a smile.

"Good. He can help look after that foal. Does the colt have a name?"

"Not yet. Nara told me the foal will name himself when he is ready."

"A son of Boreas," Athlone said with a proud grin. "I can hardly believe it."

The woman looked up into his smiling face, and her hand reached out for his. They went into Piers's tent for the rest of the afternoon.

*　*　*　*　*

Clouds were moving in from the northwest and the wind was freshening on the morning Gabria and her party left Khulinin Treld. They gathered in the training field just after daybreak to bid farewell to the clan. Khan'di astride his chestnut arrived first, then Piers on his favorite brown mare and Gabria with the three Hunnuli. The chieftain and his four hearthguard warriors came last with the pack horses. Bregan rode his gelding, Stubs, and Athlone was mounted on his gray Harachan stallion.

Every member of the party was dressed in plain, unadorned clothing and cloaks of undyed wool. Khan'di had stressed the importance of secrecy, warning the chief that the fon's spies must not learn of Gabria's journey to Pra Desh. Athlone agreed, for he knew how fast news could travel on the plains. Even the golden banner that usually went with the chieftain whenever he ventured from the treld was left behind.

When the travelers were gathered together, the entire clan came to see them off. Only Thalar was conspicuous by his absence, though the priest of Sorh and the priestess of Amara came to bless the people leaving the treld.

Lord Athlone rode before the Khulinin and raised his arms until the crowd fell quiet. In the customary speech to the clan, he reminded them of Savaric's murder and his duty as Savaric's son to seek wier-geld, or blood money, for the murder of his father. Since he wanted to minimize the taint of sorcery on his journey and leave his people in a propitious mood, he told the clan only of the fabulous city he would be visiting and of the tales he would have to tell when he returned. No mention was made of the *Book of Matrah* or Branth's more recent crimes.

Cantrell stepped forward and sang a boisterous song of leave-taking that had the Khulinin singing and clapping as the party rode out of the valley. Many of the men rode with them for a time, calling out their farewells, while the rest of the clan stayed behind and cheered them on their way.

Before long, the travelers passed the last of the foothills and came out into the open country. A light rain began to fall, and the accompanying riders turned back for home. The party pushed on in single file, their cloaks pulled tight against the cold wind and rain. The pleasant leave-taking was behind them, and each person was lost in his or her own thoughts of the journey ahead.

By afternoon the rain eased, and the clouds raced south across the sky. Gently sloping hills, clad in gray-green grass, unfolded under the horses' hooves and rolled endlessly beyond the horizon. The riders shook out their cloaks and relaxed a little on their mounts.

They were riding northeast, following the Goldrine River. They planned to parallel the Goldrine as far as its junction with the Isin River, then strike east to intersect the old caravan route that ran north along the Sea of Tannis.

The caravan route ran north and south, and dated back to the days before the clans roamed the plains. It had been made by the invading armies of the Eagle, the same men who had built the fortress, Ab-Chakan. It was still used as a major overland route between the clans' trelds, the Turic tribes in the south, and the Five Kingdoms in the north. At the end of the road lay the golden city of Pra Desh.

Gabria had never been to Pra Desh, though she had heard about the city from her father, who had visited there once, and from Piers. She knew that Pra Desh was the capital city of Calah, one of the Five Kingdoms in the Alardarian Alliance and that a person titled "the fon" ruled the city's government. She knew little else.

Piers had told Gabria once that the latest fon had poisoned her husband and had pinned the blame on Piers's daughter. His daughter had been tortured and executed as a sorceress. Sick at heart, Piers had turned his back on Calah and Pra Desh. He had never returned to his homeland or the city of his birth, and his sense of rage and injustice had been deeply buried behind a facade of resigned sadness.

Gabria studied Piers's back as he rode ahead of her. Then she nudged Nara forward to walk beside the healer's horse. The old brown mare nickered pleasantly to Nara, who towered over her, and the Hunnuli answered in kind.

Piers smiled wanly at Gabria. He hated getting wet. "I suppose it is too late to change my mind."

"Not if you don't mind a long ride back to the treld."

He glanced over his shoulder to the dark line of stormclouds and rain that could still be seen behind them. "I don't think so. It's drier here."

"For now." Gabria studied her friend for a moment before she asked, "Piers, what is the city like?"

He grimaced, surprised by her question. "What, Pra Desh?" He gestured to Khan'di ahead of them. "Ask him."

The old anger and grief were very clear in his voice. Gabria was startled by the intensity. "Do you know him from before?" she inquired.

"Yes, and he knows me." Piers glared at the man's straight back. "He is the son of one of the wealthiest merchant families in Pra Desh. He was a courtier and my good friend. He is also cunning, ambitious, and clever. He was supposed to be the fon's taster, but on the night the fon was poisoned, Khan'di fell conveniently ill. I was nursing him instead of dining with the fon." Piers's fingers tightened around the saddle horn. "I could have saved the fon if I had been there." He shook his head sadly. "I've always wondered if Khan'di deliberately feigned his illness."

"I'm sorry," Gabria said, knowing how useless that sounded.

The healer shook himself and laughed. "Why? It is I who should be sorry. I came on this journey to face those people, to remember my daughter, and to banish my inner hatred. I am off to a poor start." He fell silent.

Gabria thought Piers had forgotten her question. She was about to repeat it when he drew out a small wineskin and took a long swallow. He slammed the stopper back in and looked up at Gabria. His pale gray eyes were twinkling.

"You asked about Pra Desh?" His hands flew out in a grand gesture. "The queen of the East. There is no other place like it in the world. It is huge, sprawling, magnificent! It is a city of incredible squalor and unbelievable wealth; of palaces, teeming wharves, markets, bazaars, and tenements."

Gabria stared at the healer, surprised by his sudden change of mood. She rarely saw Piers so animated.

"Pra Desh is the center for all trade and commerce in the East, you know," he noted. "Every road, caravan route, and shipping lane leads to Pra Desh. You can find anything available in the known world in that city. There are schools of great learning, libraries, academies of art, and theaters. The city is rich with artisans, philosophers, explorers, merchants, seamen, teachers, noblemen—and overflowing with slaves, peasants, and criminals." Piers laughed. "Gabria, you have never seen anything like it."

The girl tried to form a picture of this incredible place in her mind. "It sounds so . . . big," she said lamely.

"You have nothing to compare to it, nothing that could help you fathom its size. The entire population of the eleven clans would be lost in the old part of the city."

Gabria's mouth went slack. It suddenly occurred to her that, not only was she riding into a hornet's nest, it was much bigger than she expected. How could *she* do anything useful in a city so big? "Well, if they have all of those people, why do they need me?" she asked, exasperated.

"Ask him," Piers replied, pointing at the nobleman again. "He's the one who made the demands."

"Khan'di!" Gabria shouted. The other men looked around

in surprise, but the Pra Deshian pretended he had not heard.

Piers looked annoyed. "I'm sorry. In Pra Desh, women must always address a man by his full name. To do less is to show a lack of respect."

Gabria gritted her teeth. "Khan'di Kadoa, may I please speak with you?"

At that, the nobleman half-turned and nodded once.

While Nara trotted forward to join the other rider, Gabria tried to put on a pleasant and sociable expression. She knew very little about this man, and what she did know she was not certain she liked. He was of medium height with a stout figure turning to fat. A mustache hid his thin mouth, and his shrewd eyes were almost lost in the folds of his ruddy skin. He was often polite to the point of arrogance and had the confidence of a man who was used to being obeyed.

Gabria could not help but wonder what his true motives were for asking her to come to Pra Desh. Was he setting an elaborate trap, vying for his own power and influence, or was he truly concerned for the welfare of his city? His hidden motives would not change her decision, but Gabria would be happier if she knew what to expect from him.

Since Gabria did not know how to salute the emissary and it was difficult to bow on horseback, she inclined her head politely to the man. Khan'di looked up at the sorceress on the huge black horse and returned her greeting.

She threw her hood back and let the wind tug at her hair. "I was talking to Piers a moment ago," she said. "He told me how big your city has become."

"It is the largest city in the Five Kingdoms, perhaps in the world," Khan'di answered proudly. "I've heard that Macar is bigger, but that was several years ago, before their tin mines began to decline. Since then their trade has fallen slightly. Pra Desh, of course, has widened its influence throughout the Sea of Tannis. Our merchant fleet is the largest and . . ."

Gabria sighed to herself as he talked on. It was the most she had heard him say in four days. She smiled and held up her hand. "Khan'di Kadoa, excuse me, but you are speaking beyond my experience. I know little about Pra Desh or its shipping."

"Oh, of course. Forgive me," he said. "Was there something in particular you wanted to know?"

"I was curious," Gabria continued. "Why, in a city so large, could you find no one to remove Branth? Why did you ask me?"

"Because," Khan'di said, irony edging his words, "sorcery is forbidden in Pra Desh just as it is on the plains. We do not have the clans' intense hatred for the arcane, but it was more convenient and safer to outlaw it. To outlaw such practices keeps magic-wielding foreigners from coming into the city and disrupting the trade."

Gabria straightened and gazed at the man in surprise. "Foreigners? I thought your people could use sorcery, too."

"No. Only the clanspeople or those with clan blood in their ancestry have the power to cast spells. Many wise men have studied this unusual inherited trait, but no one has discovered why only the clans have such power." He lifted his hand eloquently. "To put it bluntly, you were the only one available."

"Wonderful," Gabria muttered. "All right. If I am to go to Pra Desh as a sorceress, what guarantees do I have for a safe passage? Will I face Branth with my magic, only to be put in prison if I win?"

Khan'di reached into his saddle bag and pulled out a scroll sealed with the stamp of his family. He held it up. "The fon rules the roads of Calah, but within Pra Desh *I* am patron of the powerful merchants' guild and head of the most respected and influential family in the city. If you are successful in routing Branth, you will be paid handsomely from my treasury and escorted with honor back to the borders of Calah. I give you my word as a Kadoa."

Gabria was skeptical. "What of your fon? She will not be pleased to lose her personal sorcerer."

Khan'di laughed once, a sharp, bitter bark. "Leave her to me."

Gabria studied him for a long moment. It was still possible

the Pra Deshian was leading her into a trap. If not for the warning of the King Stallion, she might not have accepted Khan'di's plea so readily. Now, as she examined his fleshy face and watched the way his hands tightened around the reins in suppressed anger, she thought that he was probably telling the truth, at least as he saw it.

"That will have to do," she finally answered. "Do not go back on your word." She plucked the scroll out of his fingers, nodded once again, and turned Nara away.

The man watched her go, his mouth pulled tight. The woman was ignorant, but she was not stupid. He would have to tread carefully with her. And her Hunnuli. Khan'di could not swear to it, but just before the big mare turned, he thought he saw an almost human glint of warning in her dark eyes.

or five days the party followed the Goldrine River as it flowed northeast then east across the grasslands of Ramtharin, toward its junction with the Isin River. Ignoring the cold winds and incessant rains, the riders traveled fast from dawn to dusk, stopping only at noon to eat and rest the horses. True to Nara's word, the foal had no trouble keeping up with the other horses and seemed to thrive on his mother's milk and the constant exercise. The people slowly settled into the routine of the trail, too, as their muscles adjusted to the long hours of riding and their minds grew accustomed to each other's constant company.

Gabria divided her time between Athlone, Piers, and Khan'di. Although she did not care for the nobleman from Pra Desh, he enjoyed talking to her and was a fountain of information and advice. While Piers told her about Pra Desh's history, culture, and society, Khan'di filled her in on the changes that had been taking place in the government, economy, and politics during the past few years.

"The kingdom of Calah is ruled by a king," he explained one afternoon, "but the capital city, Pra Desh, is ruled by the fon."

"The king allows that?" Gabria asked in surprise.

Khan'di chuckled. "He usually doesn't have much choice. The fon controls the vast flow of goods to and from the Five Kingdoms, so he or she holds more wealth and power than the king. It is not the easiest of situations. There has been constant feuding between the king and the fon for generations."

"Where is your king now?"

The nobleman's brow lowered in anger. "About eleven years ago, the king of Calah died in a mysterious accident, leaving a son too young to rule. Fast on the heels of that disaster, the fon was poisoned. His body wasn't even cold when his wife snatched control of the city *and* the kingdom. She still holds them both—in the name of the young prince, of course."

"Why hasn't the prince reclaimed his throne?"

"No one knows where he is. The fon held him prisoner for a few years, but we have not seen him recently. I'm afraid she may have disposed of him."

The nobleman fell silent after that and rode with his expression frozen and his eyes as hard as rock.

The next day, during another talk, he told Gabria more about Branth's arrival in Pra Desh.

"The man was a fool," Khan'di said in disgust. "He ensconced himself in a big house in one of the wealthiest districts of the city and began flaunting himself in the highest social circles. He made no secret of his talent as a magic-wielder, but he was smart enough not to use his power openly. Then odd things began to happen. Gold was stolen out of locked safes, gem shipments disappeared, and ships sank in the harbor for no apparent reason. Men who angered Branth were financially ruined." Khan'di shook his head. "By the time someone tied the crimes to Branth it was too late. The fon sent a detachment of her own guards to arrest him, but he'd had plenty of time to set up his defenses. His house was fortified and his power too great to overcome. He blasted the captain of the guard with a strange blue fire."

"The Trymian Force," Gabria said softly.

"The what?"

"It's a force drawn from the magic-wielder's own energy." She grimaced. "It can be very deadly."

Khan'di nodded. "It certainly was. Branth wiped out an entire company of heavily armed men with it."

"How did the fon finally capture him?"

"The way she takes anything—through guile. She played

on Branth's vanities and lured him to the palace with the promise of an alliance." The man broke off and surprised Gabria by glancing over his shoulder at Piers riding behind him. She thought for just a moment there was a flicker of regret in his dark eyes.

"I suppose the healer told you," Khan'di continued, "that the fon is an expert at poison?"

"He mentioned it," she replied carefully.

"Well, she used a special poison of her own concoction to gain control of Branth's mind and render him helpless. He still has his talent, but she has the book and controls his actions."

Gabria looked pale. She despised Branth, but it was hard to imagine the powerful, ambitious chieftain trapped in the grip of an insidious poison. It gave her the shivers. "Can she make him do anything?"

"The man is a total prisoner."

"What will happen to him if we take him away from the fon and her poisons? Will he regain his will?"

"I don't know or care. Just remove him or kill him." Khan-'di twisted his mustache, a habit that showed when he was agitated. "We *must* get him away from the fon before she invades Portane. If she attempts that, the entire Alardarian Alliance will shatter. Pra Desh will be ruined! I—"

Nara suddenly tossed her head, interrupting him. *Gabria, someone comes.* The mare whirled and faced a hill they had just passed. Eurus neighed a warning to the men, and the party drew in close to Nara and came to a halt.

At that moment, a lone horseman appeared on the crest of the hill and waved to them in apparent excitement. He was too far away to recognize, yet they all saw he was not a clansman. He was a Turic tribesman from the southern desert. Gabria glanced worriedly at Athlone, and the hearthguard gathered around their lord, their hands resting on their swords.

The horse came toward them at a full gallop, his ears pinned back and his tail flying. The man leaned back in his stirrups and greeted the party with a wild, high-pitched ululation. The afternoon sun glittered on the great curved sword by his side, and the burnoose he wore flew out behind him like a flag.

He reined his horse to a snorting, prancing stop directly in front of Nara and Gabria and swept off his hood. "Sorceress!" he cried. "I have been looking everywhere for you!"

Gabria was so surprised she could only stare down at the man. He was young and lean, with the dark skin and brown eyes common to Turic tribesman. His black hair was worn in an intricate knot behind his head. His face was clean-shaven, revealing the strong, narrow lines of his jaw and cheekbones. Gabria thought he was compellingly handsome, and he met her confused stare with a bold, masculine look of pleasure.

He ignored the other men, who were watching him with varying degrees of curiosity and wariness, and dismounted from his horse. He came to stand by Gabria's foot. "You are Gabria of Clan Corin," he stated, looking into her face. "I know it. I am Sayyed Raid-Ja, seventh son of Dultar of Sharja. I, too, am a magic-wielder. I would like to travel with you and learn your sorcery."

Gabria felt her jaw drop.

"Absolutely not!" Athlone thundered.

"Why not?" Sayyed asked reasonably, turning to the chief for the first time. "Lord Athlone, forgive me. I was so pleased to find the sorceress that I forgot my duty to you. Greetings!"

Athlone nodded curtly. He had taken an instant dislike to this man, and he did not appreciate the way the Turic was looking at Gabria. "Good day to you, son of Dultar. Please stand aside. We must be on our way."

"That's impossible," Gabria mumbled.

"What?" Sayyed and Athlone said at once.

The woman quickly gathered her wits and turned to the tribesman. "How can you be a magic-wielder? Only clan blood carries that talent."

Sayyed flashed a grin at her. "My mother was of Clan Ferganan. She was captured one day near a waterhole by my father. He sought a slave to sell in the market that day, but it was he who became a slave to a wife and twelve children."

"You are half-clan?" Piers exclaimed.

Khan'di shrugged. "It is enough."

"How do you know you are a magic-wielder?" Athlone demanded.

A mischievous twinkle danced in Sayyed's glance. He stooped down, picked up a handful of dirt, and tossed it into the air. The earth and stones flew high, then exploded into a cloud of shimmering blue butterflies.

The unexpected fluttering startled Khan'di's gelding. It snorted in fear, spun around, and slammed into Athlone's stallion. The Harachan horses picked up the gelding's panic and leaped into a frenzied attempt to escape.

"Of all the stupid things to do," Athlone yelled from the back of his bucking stallion. "Get rid of those things!"

Sayyed spoke a command and the butterflies vanished. He tried to look contrite as the riders calmed their mounts.

He is a magic-wielder, Nara told Gabria, *though how much use butterflies will be against Branth I cannot say.*

"All right," Gabria said, trying not to laugh. "You are who you say you are. Why do you want to come with me?"

Sayyed threw his arms wide in excitement. "To learn! My father has enough sons to bother with, so I can do what I want. I want you to teach me about sorcery."

"It looks like you know enough already," Khan'di remarked dryly.

"Only a trifle I have learned by accident. I want to know more."

"No," Gabria said. She was thoroughly taken aback. "I can't teach you, I hardly know enough myself."

"Well, then, I might help you. They told me at Khulinin Treld that you are going to battle another sorcerer. Let me come. If you can't teach me, maybe I can help."

"I don't think . . ." Gabria began.

"Isn't sorcery forbidden by the Turic?" Athlone interrupted in annoyance.

Sayyed locked his gaze with Athlone's and said, "Yes. And since I have been outlawed from my people, I decided that I should die doing what I was born to do."

His words and their obvious sincerity touched Gabria to the
core, stirring the similar feelings she had about magic. To hear
another person state a desire for sorcery so honestly was all she
needed to win her trust. The King Stallion had advised her to
take other humans with her. Why not another magic-wielder?

She held out her hand palm up. "Come, Sayyed Raid-Ja. If
you're so certain, maybe I can use your help."

"No!" Athlone snarled, but his protest was lost in Sayyed's
shout of glee as he clasped Gabria's hand to seal the deal.

Nara began to move, and the whole party fell in beside her,
leaving Athlone fuming on his mount. The chieftain kicked
his horse forward and caught up with Gabria. To him, her expression looked maddeningly pleased.

The chief gritted his teeth. Unless the Turic changed his
mind and left, it looked like they were stuck with him. The
man had already swung his horse in behind Nara and was
whistling a tune to himself. Short of driving him off at sword-
point, there was nothing Athlone could do about him.

"What possessed you to invite him along?" Athlone said
coldly to Gabria. "You don't need his help. And we don't
have time to mollycoddle an irresponsible boy."

Gabria was stung. Her eyes flashing dangerously, she leaned
over and snapped, "The King Stallion told me to bring others
with me. I am following his advice."

"Why him? He's a Turic. He'll just be in the way," Athlone
replied, his fury mounting.

Gabria glared at him, hurt and angry. On this journey she
needed all the support and trust Athlone could give her. She
could not understand why he was being so vehement about
this stranger. "Because he sought me out. Because he cares
about what he is. Because he is a magic-wielder and I may
need him!" Her last word broke off sharply, and she lapsed
into silence.

Athlone studied her for a long time, watching the way her
blond hair curled around her ear, how her small nose turned
up slightly at the end, and how the freckles on her cheeks

stood out when she was angry. She was so lovely it made his
heart sing and yet, sometimes she was so strange and distant to
him; he did not know how to reach her. All he could do was try
to understand, but that hardly seemed enough.

The chieftain let out a long breath. "Perhaps you're right,"
he told Gabria, his voice still sharp with anger. "Not all
magic-wielders are willing to use their powers. One like the
Turic might be useful."

"You have the talent, too, Athlone," she said quietly.

"And no desire to use it." The chief shifted his weight and
kicked his horse forward. For the rest of the afternoon he rode
the point, well ahead of Gabria, Sayyed, and the others.

Gabria and Athlone had little chance to bridge the rift over
the next few days. Gabria felt she was in the right in their dis-
pute over the Turic's presence and did not try to approach the
chieftain with apologies or contrition. Athlone, in turn, had
few opportunities to talk to her. Every time he tried, he was
called away by the warriors or interrupted by Piers or Khan'di.

Sayyed did not help matters, either. The young Turic made
himself at home with the company. He laughed and joked
with the warriors—Secen, Keth, and Valar; helped Bregan
hunt for meat; talked medicine with Piers; and discussed the
merits of fabrics and spices from the South with Khan'di. But
he saved the best of his attentions for Gabria. He used every
chance he had to be near her, whether Athlone was there or
not.

The sorceress was resting upon Nara's back one afternoon
while the mare paused for a drink. Seeing an opportunity to
talk to Gabria alone, Athlone waved his men on and went to
join her and the Hunnuli on the riverbank. She looked at him
curiously and a little warily, as if expecting the outbreak of another argument.

"Gabria, I—" he began. Then he stopped, for it dawned
on him that he really did not know what he wanted to say to
her.

"Lord Athlone!" Bregan yelled. "Secen is signaling."

The chieftain cursed under his breath and looked for the

warrior, who was riding the point. Secen was atop a far hill,
signaling the presence of other riders. Athlone left Gabria and
hurried to investigate. By the time he checked the two riders
Secen had spotted and made sure they had not seen his party,
Gabria had joined Sayyed.

The chief's face darkened with anger as he watched the two
of them together. Sayyed had found some early wildflowers
and had made a crown for Gabria. They were talking and
laughing like old friends as she fastened the ring of flowers in
her hair.

Athlone spurred his horse away so they could not see the
doubt and anger on his face.

* * * * *

On the evening of the twelfth day, Gabria and her companions reached the Tir Samod—the name given to the holy joining of the Goldrine and Isin Rivers—where the clans of
Valorian had gathered every summer for countless generations. They arrived before sunset and made camp in the grove
of cottonwood trees near the place where the council tent usually stood. To the clansmen the meadows looked empty and
strange without the big camps, the bustling market, the huge
council tent, and the throngs of people, dogs, and horses that
crowded the site every year. Except for the ripple and rush of
the two rivers and the wind sweeping through the bare trees,
the place was quiet and peaceful.

For the first time in several days the sky was cloudless and
the sun set with the promise of another clear day. After the
evening meal, the warriors settled down by the fire to clean
their weapons and tack. Piers examined his medical supplies to
see if any had been spoiled by the intermittent rains of the
past twelve days. Khan'di sat on his cushion and cleaned his
nails.

For a short time, Gabria watched Nara and her baby as the
colt frolicked in some shallow water. Beyond the horses, the
gold light of sunset illuminated the circle of standing stones

on the holy island of the gods in the middle of the rivers. Gabria looked at the island and then beyond to the far banks.

Every year when the clans gathered, each one encamped on the same site. The Corins had always made their camp to the north of the island on a wide, grassy bend of the Isin.

With little thought, Gabria took off her boots and waded across the gentle rapids of the Isin to the opposite side. She climbed the low bank and meandered slowly toward the trees that identified her clan's ground. As in the treld far to the north, there was little here to mark the passing of the Corins: a few old fire pits, a refuse pile that would last only until the next flood, and some cut trees. Like the Corins' meadow, there was also a burial mound. It had been left by the Khulinin when they camped on the Corin ground the previous summer.

Gabria wandered to the mound and stood gazing at the one spear and helmet that still adorned the single grave. The rustling of the grass alerted her to the presence of someone else in the campsite. She turned, smiling, thinking it was Athlone.

"Someone you know?" Sayyed asked.

The woman shook her head and pushed her disappointment aside. She had wanted Athlone, but Sayyed was good company, too. In the few days she had known him he had already become a close friend, someone with whom she felt comfortable and happy. She crossed her arms and said, "I didn't know him except by name. He was Pazric, second wertain of the Khulinin. He was the first to be deliberately murdered by sorcery in over two hundred years."

"Oh? I hadn't heard about him. Tell me."

"Lord Medb killed him during a council meeting of the chiefs last summer. It was the first time Medb displayed his powers."

Sayyed stared down at the mound. "That must have been terrible," he said with sincerity.

Gabria turned away. All at once she was overwhelmed by memories of that harrowing, event-filled day—the day Pazric had died; the day she had attended the council to accuse

Medb; the day Savaric had forced Lord Medb to reveal his sorcery. Her throat tightened, and she blinked as the light of sunset blurred and shimmered through sudden tears.

Quickly Sayyed put his arm around her waist. He was rather
short for a Turic and Gabria was tall for a clanswoman, so their
heads were level as he pulled her close. She leaned against him
and drew solace from the comfort of his strong arms and the
warmth of his presence.

Her sadness slowly disappeared until her mouth curved up
in a faint smile. "You remind me of my brother, Gabran."

Sayyed masked a grimace with a chuckle. "Why?" he
asked, hiding his disappointment. "Was your brother handsome?"

She laughed. "Yes, and kind, as strong and cunning as a
wolf. He could also make me laugh." She sighed softly. "I
loved him very much."

He tightened his arm around her. They stood for a long
while in the afterglow of twilight, silhouetted against the pale
gold luminescence that hung in the western sky.

From his place by the fire, Athlone watched the two distant
figures and felt his heart grow heavy. The Turic was intruding
deeper and deeper into Gabria's life. He had only been with
the travelers for seven days and already she was fascinated by
him, this energetic tribesman who plainly worshiped her. A
boil of jealousy erupted in Athlone's mind, fed by his pride
and uncertainty.

To the chieftain, the most frustrating thing was his own confusion. His relationship with Gabria was still new to him—
they never seemed to get a chance to let their feelings develop
without something getting in the way. Now this Turic was with
them, and Athlone was no longer sure where he stood. Worst
of all, he didn't know what to do about it! Gabria was intelligent, self-reliant, and determined. She had proven her courage and worth ten times over. If she wished to give her love to
Sayyed instead of him, then Athlone felt she had earned that
right. Gabria had suffered enough heartache and pain without being forced into a relationship she no longer desired. Of

course, that did not mean Athlone had to like being put aside.

He slammed the sword he was cleaning into its scabbard and strode out into the darkness. It was easy to tell himself that he could let her go if she chose to leave, but the thought of losing her was tearing him apart. Without thinking, he wandered to the small field where the horses grazed. There he stood, staring into the night, searching for the familiar shape of his old friend, Boreas.

The search was futile, and Athlone knew it; Boreas had been slain in the final battle with Medb the previous summer. That didn't lessen the chieftain's need for his old steed, though. Just as Nara was Gabria's friend and confidant, Boreas had been his companion and advisor.

Athlone frowned and readied himself to return to camp, but something moving in the darkness stopped him. It was the great black bulk of a Hunnuli, a stallion like Boreas. The chieftain's heart leaped with hope and fear. *His ghost, perhaps, returning from the dead to aid me when I most need his advice?*

The Hunnuli came to his side, but it was not Athlone's long-dead steed. An unfamiliar pair of wise eyes gleamed at him, and a deep, soothing voice said, *I am not Boreas*, Eurus told him. *But I am here.*

Thankfully the man leaned against the big horse and ran his hand through the stallion's long, thick mane. He stood, stewing over his problem, his mind working like a boiling pot with bits of thought and feeling bubbling to the surface faster than he could follow them. He loved Gabria and did not want to lose her, yet he did not know how to win her back.

On the heels of those thoughts came the guilty notion that, perhaps, it would be better if he didn't win her back. She was a sorceress. She should be with other magic-wielders, people like Sayyed who would appreciate and support her talent. Athlone was chieftain of the largest and most respected clan on the plains. Even if Gabria survived this journey and the clan chieftains changed the laws forbidding sorcery, there would always be suspicion, distrust, and hatred for magic-wielders. He was not completely sure he was ready to accept the controversy and the constant battle for acceptance.

With that thought, a bubble of remorse boiled out of his mind. *He* was a magic-wielder, too. But it was so much easier to ignore that truth, to let Gabria go, and to live peacefully as a mere chieftain with his clan—like his father and his father's father before him.

Athlone twisted the black mane into his fingers. He knew full well he couldn't take that path and live with himself. No, winning Gabria's heart was the important thing; somehow he would have to find a way to reconcile himself with his talent. If only he knew what to do.

He shook his head in frustration and pushed himself away from the Hunnuli.

The black horse nudged Athlone's chest. *Sometimes the heart speaks clearer than the mind, lord chieftain.*

Athlone laughed humorlessly. "And sometimes they argue unmercifully." He patted the horse and went back to the camp. After a word with the sentry, he retired to his small traveling tent. For Athlone, it was a very long night.

abria and Nara stood in rippling grass on the point of a high bluff and looked down on the green plains below. The woman shielded her eyes from the noon sun and peered downhill to the caravan trail that wound over the rolling grasslands like a giant snake. The route was not like the stone road near the fortress of Ab-Chakan. It was really nothing more than a dirt path worn into the ground by years of constant use. Nevertheless, it was wide and well marked, and the hooves of countless pack animals had pounded the surface to a rock-hard consistency. In some places the wagons and traders' carts had cut wheel ruts several handspans deep.

Even now, as Gabria looked up the road, she could see the dust kicked up by a distant merchant caravan heading north toward Pra Desh. She glanced toward the south. The semi-arid high plains had gradually dropped down in elevation as Gabria's party had journeyed east, and the rough grasses and shrubs had given way to lush meadows, scattered copses of trees, and small sparkling streams.

Coming up beside her, Bregan sat back in his saddle and stretched his legs. "It's good to see that road," he commented. "We should be about half way to Calah."

"We are," Khan'di noted as he joined them. "But we need to be closer. We've got to get to Pra Desh within twenty days."

"Are you tiring of our journey already?" Piers asked in an icy tone.

Gabria glanced irritably at the healer as the rest of the men came up the hill. Piers and Khan'di had remained bitterly po-

lite to each other, but their poorly hidden animosity was beginning to annoy her. She sighed and leaned her arms on
Nara's mane. After twenty days of constant traveling they all
needed a change—especially Athlone. Gabria shot a look at
the chieftain.

It was obvious something was bothering him. He was cool
and distant to her, spoke to Sayyed only when he had to, and
was short to everyone else. Gabria had tried several times to
talk to him, but it was difficult to find time for privacy on the
trail, and Athlone seemed to avoid her in night camp. After
days of being ignored, Gabria was hurt and confused. It was
much easier to deal with Sayyed. He was always there, warm
and comforting with his ready smile and his easy wit.

Gabria could not help but wonder if Athlone had decided
at last that he did not want her. The thought made her half-ill
with dread. She had given him time to make up his mind, but
deep in her heart she had always believed he would finally
come to accept her for everything she was. Now she was not so
certain. She fought down the queasy feeling in her stomach
and tried to dredge up some hope.

The one good thing to come out of the journey was Athlone's friendship with Eurus. Little by little, the man was
spending more time with the horse, grooming him, feeding
him special tidbits, or just talking to him late at night. The
special bond between a Hunnuli and its rider was beginning to
form. Gabria was pleased for Athlone's sake. She decided it
would be better if she did not interfere. Eurus knew what he
was doing.

She pulled her cloak closer about her shoulders. The sun
was shining, but the early spring winds were cold and damp
with approaching rain. Far to the northwest a gray line of
clouds was forming along a storm front that would bring rain
by nightfall.

Piers looked at the clouds and shivered. He had a bad cold,
despite all of his precautions. "I wish we had time to stop at
Jehanan Treld. I would like to be under a real tent before that
rain hits," he muttered.

The company urged their horses downhill and joined the great caravan route to the north. With luck, Gabria thought, we will be in Pra Desh in another fifteen to twenty days.

A few hours later, the party was riding through a narrow creek bed lined with eroded gullies and budding trees. Bregan suddenly held up his hand and brought the party to a stop. Athlone cantered his horse forward. The others stayed back and watched as Bregan pointed to a far hill where a group of horsemen were coming down the slope.

The chieftain rode back, smiling for the first time in days. "We have visitors," he told them cheerfully.

Bregan trotted ahead to meet the seven riders cantering toward the road. They were led by a horseman holding aloft the dark red banner of the Jehanan chieftain, Sha Umar.

The two groups met along the road. Sha Umar and Athlone greeted each other like old friends while the Jehanan warriors accompanying their lord saluted the Khulinin and stared in surprised awe at the three Hunnuli.

Lord Sha Umar grinned through his neatly trimmed beard at Gabria and saluted her. "Greetings, fair lady. I see you have increased your number of black horses."

The sorceress returned his smile. She had always liked the Jehanan chief, for he had been one of the few lords to support her at the chiefs' council after Medb's death. She noticed his arm was still stiff from the wound he had received in the battle at the fortress, but his strong, tanned face was as healthy as ever, and his robust voice left no doubt as to his power and authority.

"Athlone," he boomed. "You should have sent word you were coming! When one of my outriders told me he had spotted you on the road, I didn't believe him. I had to come out here to see for myself."

Athlone laughed. "My apologies, Sha Umar, but we're traveling fast. We hadn't planned to stop."

"At least stay the night. The treld is not far. Besides—" he pointed to the sky "—there's a storm coming."

The Khulinin chief followed his gesture to the dark clouds.

"I suppose we could use some supplies and a good night's sleep."

"Done!" Sha Umar exclaimed. He beamed with pleasure. "We don't have time for a feast, but I can promise you a good meal and a dry tent. Come."

The two chiefs rode ahead, side by side, and the others fell in behind.

Sha Umar lowered his voice so only Athlone could hear. "You are riding fast and without your cloaks. Your mission must be important."

"Yes," Athlone stated flatly.

"Would it have anything to do with Branth?"

Athlone assessed his friend for a moment before he answered. "Perhaps. But we do not want our journey to become common news."

"That's what I thought. Good. We can't leave Branth loose with Medb's old tome."

Athlone agreed. "The clans couldn't stand another war."

"Exactly. What can we do about that blasted book?"

"What do you mean?" the Khulinin asked carefully.

Sha Umar slapped the horn of his saddle. "That tome! It's caused nothing but trouble from the day it was found. What if you take it away from Branth and someone else gets his hands on it?" He paused as if embarrassed. "What would Gabria do if she had it?"

Athlone froze. "What are you implying?" he demanded, his voice harsh.

"Magic can corrupt, Athlone. It's simply a fact of human nature. That much power could lead even the purest to stray into greed, selfishness, cruelty, or vanity. Gabria is controlling her powers now, but what if that book of knowledge fell into her hands? How would she react? What would she do?" He looked at his friend. "More to the point, what would *you* do?"

Athlone was silent for a long while. When he finally answered, his voice was deeply troubled. "By the gods, I don't know."

"You'd better think about that on your way to find Branth," said Sha Umar.

The Khulinin chief looked away, and the two men, without another word, left the road and led the party east toward Jehanan Treld. The winter camp of Clan Jehanan was only a few leagues away, sheltered in a wide, green valley not far from the Sea of Tannis. The Jehanan numbered several hundred, and their clan was rich in pride and tradition. Although their treld was close to the sea and they often fished and gathered food in its waters, they remained stock breeders and horsemen who followed their herds across the plains in the summer. They were fiercely loyal to their chieftain, devoted to each other, and hospitable to guests.

The Jehanan happily greeted Athlone and his companions, and they recognized Gabria from the summer before. Because of their gratitude to her for their survival, they stifled their fears and suspicions of her powers and welcomed her as befitted the lady of Clan Corin. They gave her the finest guest tent and a serving girl to tend to her needs. A bag of the clan's best oats was their gift for Nara. They were all amazed by the black colt and clustered around him in a distant but admiring circle.

Gabria was pleased by their efforts and, for her part, she hid her weapons, put on her skirts, and tried to blend in with the jovial crowd.

That night the travelers joined Sha Umar in the chief's big hall, a long, low building crafted of local stone and driftwood. The Jehanan chieftain was still unmarried, so his sisters served as hostesses and skillfully supervised the serving girls and the food.

The lord stinted nothing for his friends and had his finest wine brought out and the best of his remaining delicacies set before his guests. Because it was early spring, there was very little fresh food to offer. Still, the larders and storerooms of the treld yielded dried fish, sugared fruits, honey, bread, cheese, pickled gulls' eggs, and shellfish brought from the sea that day.

Gabria was delighted with the fare. Her clan had never traveled near the Sea of Tannis and had no access to seafood. She happily feasted on clams, crabs, and gulls' eggs and washed her meal down with the fine white wine.

As soon as the chief's meal was cleared away, other clan members gathered in the hall. They pushed the benches and trestle tables aside and cleared a space in the center of the hall. The clan's bard brought out his pipes and invited several other men to join him with their drums. The torches and lamps were lit as the dancing began.

For a while, Gabria watched the dancers and clapped her hands to the music. For the first time in days, she felt comfortable, warm, and full. She drank wine freely, nibbled on the sweet cakes and dried fruits that were being passed around, and relished every note of the exciting, happy music. Then, before she realized what he was doing, Sayyed pulled her to her feet and whisked her into the boisterous dance. She barely had time to be surprised at the Turic's knowledge of the clan's dances before he whirled her away to the rhythm of the pipe and drums.

From his seat by Sha Umar's dais, Athlone leaned back and watched the pair dance the intricate steps. He had been drinking the Jehanan's strong wine steadily and was unaware that his pain and his feelings were plain on his face.

Sha Umar glanced at his friend and followed Athlone's stricken gaze to the fair young woman moving through the crowd of dancers. The Khulinin had been closed-mouthed and irritable all evening. Now Sha Umar was beginning to understand why.

"You have not married the Corin yet," the Jehanan chief said bluntly.

Athlone shook his head and drained his cup to the dregs. He held the horn cup out for more. "She was banished from the clan for six months. When she returned, we left for Pra Desh," he replied.

Sha Umar filled the cup. "You picked up that young Turic pup along the way, I hear. He seems pleasant enough."

"Huh," Athlone grunted. "A half-breed."

"If he bothers you," the Jehanan commented, "you should send him on his way."

"Gabria asked him to come."

"Ah." The truth became abundantly clear, and Sha Umar smiled. "Athlone, as a warrior there is none better in the clans than you. As a lover you have a lot to learn."

Athlone glared at his friend, his brown eyes rock hard. "What is that supposed to mean?"

"Look at her! Is that the face of a girl madly in love with her dancing partner? She likes him, yes, but she has been watching you all night. Her heart is as plain as day when she looks at you." Sha Umar leaned over and slapped Athlone's shoulder. "Don't worry about her! Let her dance and enjoy. Come, talk with me while we have a quiet moment. When we are finished you can sweep her off her feet."

The Khulinin stared at the older man for a long moment. Sha Umar's words made sense. Maybe his friend could see the problem clearer; he could understand what Athlone could not. For just a heartbeat the Khulinin lord almost accepted the truth of Sha Umar's words, then he saw Sayyed pull Gabria into his arms. The smile that lit Gabria's face brought Athlone's doubts pounding back. But before he could react to his anger, Sha Umar took his arm and pulled him away to the chieftain's quarters, where the two men talked long into the night.

By the time they were finished discussing the problems of clan unity and their plans for the upcoming gathering at the Tir Samod, the music had stopped and the main hall was quiet. In the dim light of the dying fire, Athlone saw only some bachelors without tents of their own asleep on pallets along the walls. Piers and a few companions were still deep in their wine cups in a far corner. Gabria was nowhere to be seen.

Swallowing his disappointment, Athlone walked with Sha Umar to the entrance and looked out over the camp. The wind had begun to gust around the tents, and the first drops of rain splattered on the ground.

The Jehanan chief put his hand on Athlone's shoulder. "I'll

have your supplies ready for you at first light, my friend."

Athlone nodded his thanks. Sha Umar bid him goodnight and returned to his chamber. The Khulinin drew on his cloak and stepped into the wind and rain.

The treld was quiet and dark; only a few dogs and the night outriders would be out on a stormy night like this. Ducking his head to the wind, Athlone made his way toward the men's guest tent. Just as he reached the entrance he paused, pleased to see Eurus, Nara, and the colt standing nearby, sheltered from the wind by the canvas. He was about to go inside, then changed his mind and made his way toward the smaller tent that had been set aside for Gabria. It was very late, but he could see light shining through the tent flap. Perhaps he would have a chance to talk to her. In private, he could learn the truth of her feelings.

Athlone was about to call to her when he heard a sound that froze his heart: Sayyed's voice. The man was in Gabria's tent. They were talking very softly, so softly that Athlone could not hear their words, but he did not need to. Their low, private tone was enough to breathe life into every dread he had imagined.

The chieftain clenched his hands into fists. Sha Umar was wrong; Gabria had indeed turned to another man. It took every ounce of his will to turn around and walk quietly back to his tent. Like a man half-dead with cold, Athlone lay down on his pallet and clenched his eyes shut. Although he tried to sleep, nothing he could do would erase the memory of those seductively whispering voices from his mind.

The rain began to fall harder.

Gabria raised her head and stared toward the tent flap. "Did you hear something?"

Sayyed half-closed his eyes and leaned out of the lamplight into the shadows. "Tis the wind and the voices of the dead as they ride the steeds of Nebiros," he said in a low, dismal voice.

The sorceress smiled lopsidedly. "Oh, good. It might be the Corins. They would love to be out on a night like this."

Shaking his head, the Turic chuckled. He rose and fastened

the tent flap tight against the wind. "I forget sometimes that you have already had your life's share of death and pain. Your next life should be one of ease and happiness. Perhaps as the spoiled wife of a wealthy man?"

Gabria wrinkled her nose and leaned back against one of the cushions strewn on the floor. "Why do you Turics delight in punishing yourselves with talk of many lives? I like our clan belief of paradise. I would rather go to the realm of the dead, a place where you can ride the finest horses and feast with the gods."

She filled her cup from a wineskin, drained it, and filled it again before passing the skin on to Sayyed. Her head felt light with wine and music, and the heat of the dancing still burned on her cheeks. She was delighted by the joy of the evening and by Sayyed's attentive company. Tonight she wanted him more than she cared to admit, and yet, even as her body yearned for the young, handsome Turic, her thoughts wandered to Athlone. She had waited all evening for the chieftain to dance with her, but he had disappeared with Lord Sha Umar. Only Sayyed had remained.

For his part, the Turic was well aware of the effect he was having on Gabria, and that made his heart surge with hope. Smiling, he sat down on the floor beside her, poured his wine, and picked up the handful of polished stones they were using for a game of Rattle and Snap. "Reincarnation is difficult for some to understand, but it seems clear enough to me. How else can a soul attain perfection? One lifetime is not enough to learn the grace and wisdom of the One Living God."

Gabria sipped her wine and laid her head back on a cushion. "And what does your god have to say about magic-wielders?"

"Our holy men preach against magic for the same reasons yours do," Sayyed said. "Magic and sorcery are an abomination of the Living God's power."

"Do you believe that?"

"No. My father does, though. He was the one who banished me. Now I am like you. I have no tribe. No family." He waved his hands in the air in a mock spell. "Only magic."

Gabria shifted a little on her cushion so she could see his face. Her eyes were not focusing very well. "And you still want to learn?"

"I cannot ignore what I am as long as there is a chance of doing something good with my talent. I believe magic is a gift of the Living God." He held a finger up. "Or gods, if your people are correct."

"I think it's a gift, too," she whispered.

"That's why I sought you out. You are the only one who can teach me the laws of sorcery." He glanced at her and caught her watching him with a slightly puzzled frown. "What is it, fair lady?" he asked, but she only shook her head and looked away. He was surprised to see tears sparkling in the corners of her eyes.

Quickly Sayyed leaned down beside her. He cradled her face in his hands and tilted her head up so she had to look at him. The tears brimmed and spilled down her cheeks.

Gabria touched his jaw and smiled blearily at him. She was about to pull his head down to kiss him when suddenly her vision blurred. The lightness in her head turned to a dark, heavy fog, and she slowly sank back into the cushions. "Sayyed, I can't . . ." she began to say when her eyes closed. She was asleep before she could finish the sentence.

The young Turic looked down at her for a long while and the need for her rose in him like a tide, pulling at him with an almost irresistible force. Yet he fought it down. He had fallen in love with Gabria that first afternoon, when he saw her sitting on the back of that magnificent Hunnuli mare. Since then he had come to realize that Gabria was a woman to be won, not conquered. He also knew full well that she had not yet given up her love for Athlone. The Khulinin chieftain had a hold on this woman that was not easily broken.

Sayyed sighed and sat back on his heels. He prayed to his god that someday she would chose him over the irritable lord. In the meantime, he had sworn his undying loyalty to her and he fully intended to fulfill his oath—no matter what.

Gently he pushed the curls off her face and traced the line of her cheek with the tip of his finger. Then he covered her with a woolen blanket and went to the tent flap. Outside the rain came down in torrents, blown into sheets by a powerful wind. Sayyed looked out toward the tent where he was supposed to sleep and shook his head. This tent was just as comfortable and did not require a long walk through a heavy storm.

He found an extra blanket and laid down on the rugs across from Gabria. Just before he fell asleep, a grin lifted the corners of his mouth as he imagined what Athlone would think if he knew who was keeping Gabria company in the dark hours of the night. The Turic went to sleep with the grin still on his lips.

Sayyed had slept only a few hours when a strange sound brought him instantly awake. His hand went to his dagger as he leaped to a crouch and poised, waiting for a repetition of the noise. It came again, low and terrified, a moan of pain and sorrow.

"Gabria?" Sayyed cried. He sprang to her side and laid his hand on her cheek. Her skin was as cold as ice.

She moaned again, and the sound tore at his heart. He had never heard such despair. He shook her carefully to waken her, but she seemed to be trapped in the depths of a hideous dream. Her face was contorted by terror and her hands clenched around his arm with maniacal strength.

"No!" she shouted suddenly. "You can't! Don't do it." Her cry rose to blood-chilling screams that tore out of her throat in uncontrollable terror.

"Gabria!" Sayyed shouted frantically. He shook her hard, but she shrieked and struggled, still locked in the visions of her dream. Finally he slapped her. The stinging pain seemed to rouse her, so he slapped her again and again until at last her screams stopped and she fell sobbing into his arms.

Voices called outside the tent, and people crowded into the entrance. Athlone was the first one in, his face ashen. He took one look at Gabria in Sayyed's arms, at the crumpled blankets and the empty wine cups, and his mind went numb. He wanted to step forward and comfort Gabria himself, but he could not force himself to move.

Just then Piers pushed his way in through the onlookers. He took a quick, speculative glance around before hurrying to Gabria. Her look frightened him. She was shaking violently, and her face was deathly white. She let go of Sayyed and clung to her old friend. Neither of them saw Athlone by the tent flap or the look of pained fury on his face.

Slowly Gabria calmed down enough to speak, and the haunted look faded from her eyes. "By the gods, Piers," she gasped. Her voice was hoarse from screaming. "They're really trying to do it!"

"Who is?" he asked, confused. "Do what?"

She grabbed the front of his tunic. "Branth! That woman! I saw them. In some dark room Branth was forming a summoning spell around a golden cage. Something was there for just a moment. I saw it, Piers. It was hideous! I looked into its eyes!"

The onlookers gasped and edged away. Gabria scrambled to her feet, her face wild. "The King Stallion is right! Branth is trying to summon something horrible. We have to go now!"

Outside the tent the three Hunnuli neighed in response to Gabria's emotional summons.

The strident calls broke Athlone's numbness, and he strode forward, relieved to be able to do something. "It is almost dawn. Sayyed, tell the men to saddle their horses. Piers, stay with Gabria until we are ready to go. I will tell Sha Umar that we are leaving."

Gabria's fear galvanized them all and everyone leaped to obey Athlone's commands. In a matter of moments, the company gathered their gear, mounted, and bid farewell to the surprised Jehanan. In the darkness and pouring rain, they urged their horses after Nara as she cantered northwest once again to meet the caravan road.

7

 n the darkness of the dank palace storeroom, Lord Branth sank down on a stool and tried to light the oil lamp on the table beside him. His hands were shaking so badly that it took several attempts before he could bring the fire to the wick. When the flame leaped up, he leaned forward and rested his head on his arm.

The tall, thin woman behind him crossed her arms and stared at him in disgust. "You fool," she hissed.

The spell had failed. They had been so close this time. Branth had performed the opening ritual flawlessly, and they had even seen the creature begin to appear in the small, specially reinforced cage. The summoning had been going well until Branth had hesitated in the completion of the spell, and, in that vital moment, the creature had slipped away.

The fon paced around the table in fury. Branth had practiced the spell dozens of times. He had all of the proper tools—the oil lamp, the golden cage, the collar of gold to put around the creature's neck—yet he had still failed. The woman's deep-set eyes narrowed to slits, and she wondered if he had deliberately spoiled the incantation. She had noticed of late that his body was becoming resistant to her mind drug. He tried to disobey her occasionally, and his eyes showed brief flashes of willfulness. She decided to increase the drug to ensure that Branth remained her slave.

Unfortunately the man was too exhausted to try the spell again tonight. It was infuriating to have to wait, but the fon realized she should not force Branth to attempt the incantation a second time until he was fit and rested. He had to be at his utmost strength to control the being she sought.

The fon calmed down as she thought about this creature. Gorthlings, as some named them, were quite tiny in stature and rather mild in appearance. Nevertheless, they embodied great evil, and, according to Matrah's book, their essence greatly enhanced the powers of a sorcerer strong enough to capture one and pull it from the realm of the dead to the world of mankind. More importantly, to the fon's mind, gorthlings could impart the power to wield magic on a human who did not have the inborn talent. In his tome, Matrah had explained the dangers inherent in summoning a gorthling, but the fon paid little attention to that. There would be no danger, because she was certain she could control the creature.

The fon smiled to herself. Once the gorthling bowed to her command, she could take the next step in her plan. She would use her sorcery and the armies of Pra Desh to quell any unrest in Calah and conquer the other four kingdoms of the Alardarian Alliance. From there it would be an easy step to conquer other realms to the north and the east, and with the might of the East in her grasp, she could swoop down on the barbarian clans and add the rich Dark Horse grasslands to her domain.

All at once, the fon threw back her head and laughed. An empire would be hers—not a mere city, but a world! She sobered as her glance fell on the exiled clansman staring blankly at the floor. She would have to watch him closely after this failure. When the gorthling was hers, Branth would go to the deep, natural pit in the dungeon where she often rid herself of inconveniences.

The only threat the fon could imagine was the other clan magic-wielder. One of her spies had picked up a rumor in court that Khan'di Kadoa had secretly sent for the sorceress to rid the city of Branth. The woman snorted. She hoped the sorceress would come, though she had not decided whether it would be more beneficial to kill the clanswoman or capture her for her power. She wanted to study that problem a while longer, but there would be time for such pondering later. Her primary concern now was to capture a gorthling.

Irritably, the fon put away the makings of the spell. She hid the golden cage and the *Book of Matrah* in a secret compartment she had constructed beneath the floor of the old storeroom. The room was forbidden to the palace inhabitants on pain of death, but she was taking no chances with her precious book or the golden cage.

As soon as Branth was completely rested they would try again. Until then, she would have to tighten her security and continue to lay her plans for the invasion of Portane, the first of the neighboring kingdoms that would fall to her might. With a snap of her fingers, she ordered Branth to move to his pallet of straw by the wall, where his chains hung. The man ignored her, and she was forced to yank him to his feet. For just a moment, his eyes flashed hatred.

"Branth!" she said, her words cold and deadly. "Go to the wall."

The emotions snuffed out of the man's gaze. He shuffled to his place like a whipped dog. The fon chained him with the shackles, left him some food and water, and locked the heavy door of the storeroom.

Although it was night and the palace inhabitants were probably asleep, the fon took the precaution of using hidden passages to reach her private rooms on the third floor of the palace. With a chuckle of pleasure, she stepped out onto the balcony of her bedroom and looked down on the sprawling city of Pra Desh. The harbor was a silver crescent in the moonlight. Her glance found the reflection of the Serentine River and slowly followed the water's path north through the city and beyond into the rich farmlands of Calah. The river's trail vanished in the darkness, but the fon followed it onward in her imagination, past the borders of Calah to Portane and the other lands of the Five Kingdoms.

"Soon," she whispered to herself. "Very soon."

* * * * *

"Gabria!" The shout came from a long distance behind her, its urgency clear over the sound of galloping horses.

The young woman tried to ignore the call. She knew what the shout meant: they had been riding for hours and the men wanted her to slow down. But the memories of her dream still burned in her mind and urged her on. She had to keep going. She had to get to Branth before it was too late.

The call came again. "Gabria!"

Gabria, this road is treacherous. We must slow down, Nara said in her thoughts. *The others cannot keep pace with us.*

"Then leave them. I don't need any of them," the woman cried. Although Nara continued to run, Gabria could feel the mare's reluctance breaking her smooth stride.

I know the men are causing you confusion, but you cannot leave them. You need them with you.

Gabria's hands tightened on the horse's mane. She had a wretched headache from both the wine and the vision, and her thoughts were a whirlwind of frightening, half-seen dreams and tangled memories of Athlone, Sayyed, and the night before. She was angry, confused, and in no mood to be reasonable. "No. I don't need them. They're making me crazy."

Nara nickered, the sound like gentle laughter. *So I have noticed. Still, we cannot go on like this. My son cannot keep up.*

Gabria turned to look back and saw the small, black form far behind, struggling gamely through the mud to catch up with his mother. Eurus was staying with him, and farther behind were the seven men and the other horses. She said, "Oh, Nara, I'm sorry."

The Hunnuli immediately slowed to a walk, and in a moment, Eurus and the colt cantered to her side. Their black coats were spattered with reddish mud, and their hooves were caked with the stuff. The colt was so tired he could not even nicker his relief.

The men caught up shortly. Their horses were muddy, too, and sweating heavily. Atop his steed, Piers looked thoroughly miserable.

Athlone, who looked much less put out by the hard ride,

started to say something, but Gabria glared at him, turned her back on the company, and rode ahead up the trail—this time at a more manageable pace. The men glanced at one another, yet no one spoke their thoughts. They were a very silent group as they followed the road north in the wake of the sorceress and her Hunnuli.

The rain ended shortly after midday, and a warm wind from the south pulled the clouds apart and cleared the huge sky. By late afternoon, the green-gold hills basked in the warm sun, and a verdant smell of herbs and grass rose from the damp earth.

The comfortable heat of the spring sun dried the travelers' cloaks and hoods, their packs and horses. It also warmed their spirits. Gabria slowly felt her tension and frustration melt away in the mellow sunshine. Although her dream still bothered her and urged her on to Pra Desh, she slowly realized that much of her inner turmoil was caused by the men. They were making her crazy.

She was already worried and nervous about a confrontation with Branth and the fon. Now her emotions were being torn apart by the two men she cared for more than anyone. She still loved Athlone, but he did not seem to want her. Sayyed, on the other hand, obviously adored her, but she did not know if she wanted him. She was being pushed and pulled in too many directions.

The other men were not much help, either. Piers, her usual counselor and supporter, was either miserable with his cold or arguing with Khan'di. For his part, the merchant was constantly urging the party to keep moving toward Calah as fast as they could go. Bregan never let Lord Athlone out of his sight long enough for Gabria to talk to the chief, and the other three warriors never said a word to her.

This journey would be enough to try the patience of Amara, Gabria noted silently. Nevertheless, she knew Nara was right. She did need the men to help her reach Pra Desh and find Branth. Without them she would be lost. The young woman took a deep breath and let it out in a long sigh. It would do little good to antagonize her companions with her bad temper. She would have to calm down and find a way to deal with her tangled feelings.

By the time the company stopped to camp by a watering hole, Gabria had rejoined the men. Her earlier frenzied anger was apparently put aside. She laughed and talked with Sayyed and Piers, chatted with Khan'di, and teased Bregan about his short-legged horse. She tried to talk with Athlone, without much luck. The chief was taciturn all evening and seemed to have his thoughts a thousand leagues away.

For the next several days the company continued on their northern route, riding fast on the heels of Gabria and the Hunnuli. She pushed them all hard, for the sense of urgency that had awakened during her dreams grew stronger by the day. They were losing precious time. They had to reach Pra Desh before Branth attempted his spell again.

Although Nara and Eurus tried to keep a pace the smaller Harachan horses could tolerate, the constant, hard traveling began to take its toll on the weaker horses.

One afternoon, four days from Jehanan Treld, Bregan's horse tripped in a rodent hole at the side of the road and fell heavily on his head. Gabria, riding beside the warrior, heard a sickening crack as the horse went down and saw Bregan thrown violently to the ground. She slid off Nara immediately and went to the warrior's side. His head was bloodied, and his eyes held a vague, dazed look. He tried once to get up before he fell back in her arms.

The other men dismounted and came running. Piers examined the injured warrior, then looked up at Athlone with obvious relief. "He's cut and bruised. He might even need stitches, but he should be all right."

"Stubs won't be," one of the other warriors said glumly.

They turned to look at Bregan's gelding, still struggling on the ground. The three Hunnuli were standing beside the stricken horse, their muzzles close to his to quiet and comfort him. Everyone could see the shattered, bloody end of his foreleg.

Athlone cursed. He knew how much Bregan loved his

horse. Silently, Athlone drew his sword and knelt beside the gelding.

"No! Wait!" Bregan pulled himself painfully to a sitting position. Blood poured down his face from the deep cut on his forehead. He struggled to focus on his horse and, as the realization hit him, tears mingled with the blood on his face. Slowly he crawled to Stubs and cradled the horse's head in his lap.

The gelding nickered once and relaxed in Bregan's arms. Without a word, the old warrior gently pulled the horse's nose up until the base of the throat was exposed. Athlone drove the point of his sword through the soft throatlatch, deep into the brain. Stubs died instantly.

Bregan, blinded by blood and tears, closed the gelding's eyes and passed out.

They removed the bridle and saddle and erected a cairn of rocks over Stubs's body. Piers and Secen gently lifted Bregan onto the healer's mare. It was almost dark by the time they rode on, so they soon stopped in a sheltered, wooded valley only half a day's travel from the winter camp of the Reidhar clan.

While the other hearthguard warriors set up the small traveling tents and Gabria started a cooking fire, Piers tended to Bregan's injuries. The warrior had roused from unconsciousness and was muttering between his clenched teeth as the healer gently cleaned the wound on his forehead. That done, Piers began to stitch it closed with a tiny bone needle and horsehair thread. Athlone and Khan'di came to sit beside them.

"The blow to Bregan's head is serious," Piers said without preamble. "He's going to need at least a day of rest."

The chieftain glanced an inquiry at Khan'di. The nobleman rubbed his mustache and said, "There is not much time left. If the fon stays with her original plan, she will invade Portane in fifteen days."

"My lord, I . . . Ouch!" Bregan flinched away from Piers's needle.

"That's what happens when you move! You're worse than a child," the healer admonished. He pushed Bregan's head around so he could see the gash better in the firelight.

"If you were about to say that you don't need the rest," Athlone told the old warrior, "forget it. All of us could use a respite from the road." A look of concern crossed his face. "We could also use several new horses and some supplies."

Piers looked sharply at the chieftain. "Do you intend to stop at Reidhar Treld? Is that a good idea?"

"No. But they're close, and we have little choice."

Khan'di asked, "What is wrong with the Reidhar?"

"There's nothing particularly wrong with the clan," said Piers, tying off a stitch on Bregan's forehead. "The trouble is their chieftain, Lord Caurus. He hates sorcery, and he's suspicious of the Khulinin's wealth and influence. Last summer, when Medb threatened the clans with war, Lord Caurus would not side with Medb, but he wouldn't side with Lord Savaric either. He took his clan back to their lands and waited to see what would happen."

"I don't know what he expected to do there," Bregan commented. "His clan would never have survived an attack by Lord Medb if the sorcerer had survived the battle at Ab-Chakan."

Athlone chuckled. "Caurus still can't believe my father and Gabria destroyed Lord Medb without his help."

"He won't be happy to see us," Bregan said, frowning.

"He will abide by clan hospitality," Athlone stated flatly. "We will receive the supplies we need to continue."

Piers finished the stitching and began to put away his tools. "Will he include Gabria in that hospitality?" he asked carefully.

Khan'di turned to watch the sorceress as she helped Sayyed fix the evening meal. "She travels with us. Doesn't clan law make it clear that she must be included?"

"Caurus might not pay attention to the details of the law, but I don't intend to give him a choice." Athlone replied.

Bregan and Piers exchanged glances at the stone-cold tone

of the chieftain's voice. "I hope you're right." Piers said. "Gabria needs rest more than any of us."

There was a pause. The chief shifted slightly and said, "Why?"

"I think this confrontation with Branth is affecting her more than we realize. She has been pushing herself too hard."

Athlone's eyebrows went up. His cold, dark eyes softened a little, and he nodded once to himself. "We have all been pushing her," he said quietly. He slapped Piers on the shoulder and went back to work.

After the meal, Athlone passed the word of their destination to the rest of the party. Gabria's heart sank. She did not like Lord Caurus. He was loud, arrogant, and very unpleasant to anyone who annoyed him. He had also made it clear last summer that he despised sorcery—an attitude he had impressed upon his clan.

While the men settled down for the night, Gabria went for a long walk beside the creek that meandered through the valley. She took only her thoughts with her and tried to find solace in the solitude of the spring night. She did not have much success.

On her way back to camp, she passed the meadow where the horses grazed and saw Athlone standing in the grass with Eurus. The chieftain was brushing the Hunnuli's ebony coat with a steady, unconscious stroke.

For a time the young woman stood in the shadows and watched the chieftain. She wanted to talk to him, to ask him what was wrong, to learn if he still loved her. But an uncomfortable reluctance to know the truth made her hesitate.

Her heart pounding, Gabria finally walked out of the trees to Eurus's side. The big horse nickered a welcome, and Athlone started, dropping his brush. To hide his nervousness, he slowly leaned over to retrieve it, then took the time to clean it of dirt.

Nara came to join them, and Gabria leaned gratefully against the mare's warm side. "Athlone, I . . ."

The chief did not seem to hear her. He resumed brushing

Eurus and immediately said, "Tomorrow, when we ride to the Reidhar camp, I want you to wear your skirts. Put your sword away and keep quiet."

Gabria straightened and felt her face begin to burn. "I had already planned to do so," she replied, her words frosted with anger.

"Good. We need the Reidhar's cooperation. And another thing," he went on, "all of us have been expecting a great deal from you. Too much, I think, and our feelings have only been getting in the way. We need to remember the priorities of our journey."

Athlone glanced at her form in the shadow of the Hunnuli. It was too dark to see her face or the hurt confusion in her eyes. "Gabria," he said, brushing Eurus harder, "I came on this journey to help you, not get in your way. From now on I will stand behind you and allow—"

Gabria pounced on the last word. "*Allow!*" she cried, coming around beside Eurus. "Don't patronize me with your pride-riddled speeches, Athlone. I don't deserve it!" She glared at him. "What are you really talking about?"

For days Athlone had been wondering what he would say if he had time alone with Gabria. Now he had that time, but nothing was coming out as he had planned. He wanted to gather her in his arms and feel her warmth and love. Instead all he could see in his mind was her slim, strong body in Sayyed's embrace, and the more the image played in his head, the greater his anger waxed. The jealousy grew until all of his rehearsed speeches and truest desires were burned in its heat. His days of frustration, anxiety, and confusion suddenly crested in a flooding wave of anger and confusion that came sweeping out in a reckless torrent.

"I'm talking about Sayyed!" he shouted at her.

"Sayyed!" Gabria gasped in surprise. "What does he have to do with this?"

"Everything. You love him. You had him in your tent the other night. All right! If he's the one you've chosen, then take him. I will not hold you to our vow."

Gabria was shocked. She did not know whether to laugh or cry. Of all the things that had gone through her mind in the past few days, she had never imagined Athlone could be jealous. How could she have missed it? She stepped toward him, raising her hands to implore him. "My tent. Yes, I did—"

But he was angry beyond reason. "No. I've heard enough. Our betrothal is broken." He turned his back on her and strode swiftly into the darkness. The wind swirled his cloak like a gesture of farewell, and he was gone.

Gabria started after him. "Athlone! Wait! You haven't heard anything," she cried, only she was too late. Her hands clenched into fists. "The gods blast that man!" she shouted with frustration and hurt. For just a moment, a pale blue aura glowed around her hands in the darkness.

Gabria, Nara warned softly.

The sorceress glanced down and saw the telltale glow, the first sign of the Trymian Force building within her. The force was a powerful spell that fused the energy within a magic-wielder into one destructive force. It could sometimes appear as an instinctive reaction in times of strong emotion. Gabria had learned well the idiosyncrasies of the Trymian Force when she'd accidentally killed one man and almost killed Athlone the summer before.

Quickly she hugged her arms around herself and forced her emotions to calm. The blue aura faded and, with it, her anger.

Gabria shook her head. She should have known better than to approach Athlone when he was tired and worried about their stop at Reidhar Treld. Now their situation was worse. Athlone had exploded in one of his rages and broken their vow of betrothal. Gabria felt cold.

She pulled her cloak tightly about herself and glared at the night, toward the spot where Athlone had disappeared. She could not go on like this, with her emotions in constant turmoil. For the sake of her survival she would have to put her life in order. She would concentrate on her journey and the confrontation with Branth, and deal with Athlone and Sayyed later. As much as they meant to her, they would simply have to wait. Her survival came before the demands of her heart. Perhaps afterward, if she was still alive, she would have the freedom and the time to settle such affairs of the heart. Until then, she would avoid close confrontation with the two men. There was no other way.

With a heavy step, Gabria walked alone toward the creek. The sheltering shadows of the night gathered around her like a suit of black armor.

* * * * *

Piers was still awake, sitting alone by the fire, when Gabria came back from her walk. She knew the healer was waiting up for her, but this night she did not want to talk. Instead, she bent over his shoulder, gave him a quick hug goodnight, and slipped away to her tent.

Piers watched her go. He understood the fears she faced and the uncertainties with which she wrestled. He knew how much her love for Athlone and her friendship for Sayyed were troubling her. He just wished she would talk to him about all of it. He might not have the right advice—how could you advise a sorceress? Yet he could listen and be a friend if she needed one. He knew more about her than anyone else alive.

Piers shook his head and began to bank the fire. Perhaps he had been foolish sitting out here in the damp, waiting for her to come back to camp and talk to him. As much as he knew about Gabria, there was so much more he did not know. In the strange, difficult year since her clan's massacre, she had learned the skill of reticence, to keep her own counsel, and to do as she decided on her own. Those were traits she had acquired to survive.

The healer went to his tent and crawled into his warm coverings. No, he decided, the waiting was not wasted. His gesture told Gabria he was there if she needed him, and he knew her well enough to realize she would be grateful for that.

* * * * *

The travelers broke camp the next morning in a haze of golden sunshine. High clouds dotted the deep blue sky, and a light wind whisked the leafing trees.

Bregan had had a restless night. The old warrior was stiff and aching from his fall, and he grumbled under his breath as he helped load the packhorses. He tried not to look grief-stricken when the other men brought in their mounts to be saddled.

Athlone watched stonily from the back of his gray stallion. His dark eyes were ringed from lack of sleep, and his mouth was drawn tight with a hidden sadness. The shadow of his morning beard made his face look gaunt.

Gabria watched him with mingled sadness and regret. The pain of their argument still ached in her mind. Yet when Sayyed, who deftly read the expression on her face, winked at her, she could not help but smile.

She looked over the rest of her companions as they mounted. The group was heavily armed, dirty, travel-worn, and weary. They looked more like a rabble of thieves and exiles than a nobleman and the finest of the powerful Khulinin clan. Gabria hoped the Reidhar were in a generous mood that day.

She pushed down her nervousness and rode Nara in behind Piers's mare. Keth, carrying Bregan behind him, and the other riders fell in line with Athlone. The travelers left the caravan road and struck northeast at an easy canter. If all went well, they would be at Reidhar Treld by midday.

8

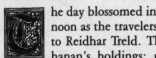he day blossomed into a glorious, warm spring afternoon as the travelers followed the faint trail that led to Reidhar Treld. The land was much like Clan Jehanan's holdings: gently rolling hills, patches of woods, open meadows, and lush valleys. Like the Jehanan, the Reidhar had their winter camp near the sea, but unlike their neighbors to the south, the Reidhar had given up many of the ancient nomadic ways and were turning more often to the water. Year by year their herds of horses dwindled and more and more of the clanspeople chose to stay at the treld during the summer to fish the teeming waters of the inland sea or mine the rich veins of copper in the hills nearby. More than any other clan, the Reidhar had lost the ways of Valorian.

Evidence of the changing social patterns were quite visible to Gabria as Nara crested a ridge that looked down over the Reidhar settlement. She had never visited the Reidhar clan at their treld, so the differences between her own clan and this one were startling. The Corins had been a small group and one of the most nomadic of the twelve original clans. The Reidhar clan was larger, and its roots went deep into the place they called home. A huge, ornately decorated stone hall graced the center of the treld, and many stone buildings replaced the usual tents. There were permanent structures housing the clan artisans, as well as storehouses and barns. A wide, shallow stream meandered down the valley's center, past the meager herds of stock animals, and flowed a short distance to the sea.

From her vantage point, Gabria could look down the valley to where the creek flowed between two gentle bluffs and tumbled out to a white beach. Even from the ridge, she could see the boat sheds, drying racks, and docks that crowded the sands. Beyond those, the small fleet of tiny fishing boats bobbed on the sparkling water.

"No wonder their horses are such poor beasts," Keth, the warrior in front of Bregan, said aloud. "The clan is nothing but a bunch of fisherfolk."

"They can still fight, so keep a civil tongue in your head," Athlone reminded him sharply.

"They couldn't last summer," the warrior muttered.

Lord Athlone ignored him. Fisherfolk or no, the Reidhar were still clan and kindred in blood and spirit, and despite Lord Caurus's refusal to fight Lord Medb the year before, Athlone felt that the Reidhar still deserved the respect due any clan. Lord Caurus was a great warrior and fiercely devoted to his people. It was not cowardice that had forced him to leave that disastrous gathering, it was his own independent nature and an unfortunate distrust of the Khulinin.

Athlone nodded to his companions, and the party rode downhill toward the busy treld. On a rise nearby, an outrider drew a horn and sounded a warning to the camp below. At the edge of the treld, another rider left his post and galloped down the valley to find the chieftain. By the time Gabria and her party reached the fringe of the encampment, Lord Caurus and his hearthguard were gathered on horseback in the middle of the path. Behind them clustered other warriors and clansmen, until the entire way was blocked. Their faces were wary as Athlone and Bregan spurred their horses forward to meet Lord Caurus.

The Reidhar chieftain was obviously startled by Lord Athlone's sudden, unexpected arrival at his treld. Caurus made no attempt to hide his suspicious, angry expression, but he remembered enough of his manners to greet Athlone first. He raised his hand. "Hail, Khulinin. Welcome to Reidhar Treld."

"Greetings, Lord Caurus," Athlone replied evenly. He eyed the heavily armed men around the chief. "This doesn't look like much of a welcome. Were you expecting someone else?"

"We were expecting no one. Least of all you."

Athlone shrugged. "I did not have time to send messengers. Our mission is urgent. We had not planned to stop, but we are in need of supplies and extra horses."

"We have no extra horses," Caurus said belligerently.

The Khulinin chief clicked his tongue. "Lord Caurus, do I need to remind *you* of the dictums of clan hospitality? Just last spring you were rumored to be the most generous host in the clans. Have you forgotten in one short year?"

"I have not forgotten." Caurus shifted in his saddle, his ruddy face wary. "You are welcome, Lord Athlone, but we cannot allow that sorceress to enter our treld."

With difficulty, Athlone swallowed his rising anger and stared coolly at the red-haired chieftain. "Why not, Caurus? She has been welcomed by other clans. We will not leave her at the edge of camp."

"We are about to celebrate our Birthright ceremony. If that heretic were to enter our treld, Amara would curse our clan forever."

The other Reidhar warriors muttered in agreement. The clan wer-tain kicked his horse forward and deliberately dropped his hand to his sword hilt.

Inwardly, Athlone groaned. He had expected reluctance and suspicion, but not outright refusal. It was their bad luck to have arrived so close to the clan's Birthright ceremonies.

"Gabria," Athlone called over his shoulder. "Come here and bring the foal."

The startled Reidhar fell back a step, and a hint of fear passed over Caurus's face as Gabria rode Nara forward to stand by Athlone. The colt and Eurus came with her.

A long moment passed before anyone spoke. The men of the Reidhar stared in open amazement at the fair woman and the magnificent black horses.

Finally Athlone asked, "Would Amara bless Gabria and her Hunnuli with a healthy colt if she were displeased?" His tone was deceptively pleasant.

This possibility stunned Lord Caurus. His face grew as red as his hair as he struggled to find a solution to the dilemma Athlone had thrust on him. He never imagined the sorceress could be anything but evil. And yet, if that were true, how could she now have three Hunnuli, one a baby? The Hunnuli despised evil and avoided it at all costs. Still . . .

Caurus suddenly threw up his hands in disgust. "The sorceress and her Hunnuli may stay. But—" he glared at all of the party "—only for one night."

Athlone barely nodded in reply. "Your generosity is overwhelming."

The Reidhar wer-tain slammed his fist on his sword. "Lord Caurus, you cannot allow this!" he shouted. "That . . . female is a magic-wielder! I don't care how many Hunnuli tag after her, she's a profaning heretic. The goddess will never forgive us for bringing her into camp."

"Gringold," Caurus said in annoyance, "I have made my decision. Abide by it!"

"As wer-tain of this clan, I cannot let her evil endanger our people."

"And as chieftain of this clan, it is *my* decision to make," Lord Caurus thundered. "I will not dishonor the Reidhar by refusing aid to another chieftain."

With a snarl on his lips, the wer-tain backed down, but he savagely reined his horse over to Nara and leaned forward, his eyes blazing like a wolf's. The wer-tain was a big man with heavy muscles and the overbearing attitude of a bully. He bore the scars of many battles and carried a full array of warrior's weapons.

Nara pinned her ears back and snorted a warning. Gabria remained still, her expression cool and unruffled as the wer-tain shook his fist at her.

"Lord Caurus has given you one night, Sorceress. If you do anything that reeks of magic, I'll slit your throat."

"Thank you, Wer-tain Gringold, for your gracious welcome," Gabria said with all the politeness she could muster.

"Gringold," Caurus snapped. "Return to the treld and prepare quarters for our guests."

They all breathed a sigh of relief when the wer-tain saluted his lord, spurred his horse away, and disappeared into the treld.

A very dangerous man, Gabria thought to herself. Her mouth tightened to a thin line, and she sadly remembered the Jehanan. She knew full well the Reidhar would never offer her companions a welcome like the one Sha Umar's clan had provided.

She was quite right. Escorted by Lord Caurus and the warriors of the clan, Gabria and her party were led through the treld to the stone huts at the edge of the camp that were used to house guests. The huts were cold, damp, and sparsely furnished with a few cots and a fireplace. As soon as the party reached the huts, the Reidhar left them for the rest of the afternoon. No one came to talk, offer wine, or bring food or firewood, and no one brought blankets or the barest necessities due to a guest. The Reidhar blatantly ignored them all.

After a while, Piers found the clan healer and talked him into giving them enough firewood to light a fire in one of the huts. Two warriors, Secen and Keth, filled the water skins at the stream, and Gabria and Sayyed unpacked the bedrolls. After a great deal of trouble and effort, Athlone and Bregan found a trader willing to deal for several horses.

The trader was from Calah and spent his time traveling the plains and dealing in horseflesh. He had stopped at Reidhar Treld for a few days and had been disappointed with the trade so far. He was pleased to barter with the Khulinin for their pure-blooded Harachan.

Several hours later, Athlone and Bregan returned to the guest huts with three new horses. Lord Athlone was pleased with the deal, for the trader had taken the three Khulinin pack horses in an even exchange for three Calah horses. Athlone knew the trader had gotten the best deal, because the clan horses had better breeding and training and only needed a little rest and food to be back in shape. Still, the Calah horses were sturdy, strong, healthy, and available. Even Bregan had not been displeased. He had chosen a black gelding with long legs for his mount.

It was dusk by the time Athlone and Bregan had settled and fed the horses and made their way to the huts. Both of them were hungry and looking forward to the evening meal. By the unwritten clan code of hospitality, it was the chieftain's duty to feed his guests. If the guest was a visiting lord, then he and his escort were always invited to share the host chief's meals. Thus Athlone fully expected an invitation to Caurus's evening meal awaiting him when he returned. But when he inquired about it, Piers shook his head.

"My lord," the healer replied, "there is neither food nor a message from Caurus. We are as good as forgotten."

"This insult shall not be ignored," Athlone snarled. He slammed his sword and scabbard on a cot beside him. "Remove your weapons," he told his men. "We are going to the hall to eat with Lord Caurus. All of us." He waited impatiently while Sayyed and the warriors left their swords, bows, and daggers on the cots. Slowly the chief brought his temper under control. It would not help their problems if his fury got the best of him.

When everyone was ready, he nodded once to his men and turned to Gabria. She was standing by the fire dressed in her long skirt and over-tunic. He was surprised to see she was wearing the armband he had given her and carrying her jeweled dagger in a scabbard under the sash of her skirt.

"Caurus may not feed you if I come," she said. Her words were spoken half in jest, but her eyes were shadowed with worry.

"Caurus will have no choice," Athlone retorted. He crossed his arms, and his lips curved upward in a harsh smile. "I'm sure he has done this deliberately to show his anger at me for bringing you to his treld. The clans will never learn to accept magic-wielders if we let chieftains like Caurus get away with these insults."

Gabria looked at his face, and for a moment she saw something there she had never noticed before. That cold, calculating smile was exactly like his father's. Lord Savaric had been a deliberate, controlled, cunning man who had often harnessed his anger to fire his actions. He had always sought for ways to turn difficulties to his advantage.

Gabria sighed to herself. Athlone was going to need every scrap of his father's wiles and self-control tonight.

The treld was peaceful as the travelers left their hut and walked down the path toward the hall. The sun had dropped below the hills, leaving the plains to the approaching night. The smells of cooking food and wood smoke mingled in the treld with the usual smells of animals and people.

As the party approached the chieftain's hall, Bregan took the lead and the other hearthguard warriors gathered around their lord. Piers, Khan'di, and Sayyed drew close to Gabria. Without asking to enter, they walked past the startled guards and strode under the flapping yellow banner above the doors into the large stone hall.

Lord Caurus, his wer-tain, a few hearthguard, and several bachelors were grouped around a long, wooden table near the center of the hall. Caurus's wife, Lady Maril, and two girls were busy serving the men from a platter of roast meats and a kettle of stewed vegetables.

The entire group fell silent as the Khulinin chief and his companions entered the hall. Lord Caurus, for once, went very pale.

"Forgive me, Caurus," Athlone said, his voice amiable. "We seem to be late."

There was nothing for the Reidhar to do, short of openly insulting the Khulinin, so he accepted the party's presence. With an ill-tempered look and a grudging gesture, Lord Caurus ordered the bachelors to another table and had places cleared for Athlone and his party. Lady Maril hastily set eating knives and plates for the guests and poured wine. The Reidhar warriors did not utter a word.

The serving girls brought more meat and vegetables and laid out baskets with thick slabs of bread. Gabria thought the meal would have been quite good if the silence and tension had not been so palpable. As it was, she found it very difficult to ignore the hostile looks of her hosts. Even Lady Maril, who sat beside her lord to eat her meal, remained grimly quiet.

Finally, the silence became too much for Lord Caurus. He pushed away his platter and said to Athlone, "I heard you found some spare horses."

Athlone continued to eat for a few minutes before he answered. "Ah, yes. A trader from Calah had a few strong horses he was willing to part with. Unfortunately, he only had three. The rest of the stock we saw was quite poor." He took a bite of bread and did not bother to look at Lord Caurus.

Caurus colored slightly and leaned back in his carved chair. "Your horses seem weary. You have been traveling fast?"

Athlone nodded. "As fast as we could." He was not going to give this ill-mannered boor the satisfaction of an easy answer. He gestured to a girl for another helping of meat.

"Your business must be urgent."

"Yes," the Khulinin chief replied casually.

"Where are you going?" Caurus pressed.

"Hunting."

At the other end of the table, Sayyed choked back a laugh, and Caurus turned fiercely on him. "And you, Turic, what are you doing with clansmen?"

The young tribesman stood up and bowed. "I am Sayyed Raid-Ja, son of Dultar of Sharja. I am traveling the Ramtharin Plains to compare the hospitality of the clans."

"And you, Pra Deshian," Caurus rapped at Khan'di. "Where are you going?"

The stocky nobleman raised and lowered his eyebrows as if he had just been asked a stupid question. "With them," he said, waving his hand at the table in general.

"I see." Caurus twisted his mustache in anger. His expression was thunderous, and white showed around the edges of his mouth. He felt it was bad enough that the Khulinin had come without warning, stampeding through his camp with their sorceress in tow, and now they wouldn't even tell him about their journey.

"By the way," Athlone broke in pleasantly, "we still need a few supplies. Trail food. A new water bag. Grain. Some leather to repair our tack."

"To go hunting," Caurus said sarcastically.

Wer-tain Gringold suddenly slammed his eating knife on the table. "Lord, I wouldn't give them a used horseshoe."

"We don't need horseshoes," said Bregan as reasonably as he could manage.

The wer-tain turned to the Khulinin beside him and studied Bregan for a moment until a flicker of recognition lit in his narrow eyes. He curled his lip. "It's a good thing your chief is only going hunting. With you as a guard, he's going to need better luck than his father."

"Bregan!" Athlone's voice cut like a whip across the silence and stopped the warrior in mid-lunge.

The wer-tain chuckled as Bregan forced himself to sit down again.

"Now," Lord Athlone said to Caurus, "about those supplies."

Caurus scowled. "We have little to spare. This has been a bad winter."

Khan'di looked amazed. "A bad winter? We didn't know. I'd heard you had a prosperous summer last year, since you weren't involved in that unpleasantness with Lord Medb. Besides, the weather has been quite mild this season."

Athlone raised his hand to forestall the Reidhar chief's angry retort. "Caurus, look. We need those supplies badly. I cannot tell you exactly why or where we're going because your treld is too close to the caravan road. Word can spread fast, and we need the element of surprise. Just know our mission is very important. If we had not needed new horses so badly, I wouldn't have bothered you."

Caurus's anger subsided a little, and he shifted his heavy frame in the chair. For the first time he looked directly at Gabria and asked, "And what of the sorceress? Is she a part of your important mission?"

Gabria had been quiet during the meal, trying to stay out of the conversation and not exacerbate the raw emotions in the room. At Caurus's question, she looked up and met his stare with a cool expression of her own. "I am only a part of this troupe, Lord Caurus, and I can promise you that I have controlled my sorcery and kept my vow to the chiefs."

"Huh!" Gringold said harshly. "What is a vow to a magic-wielder? They twist and turn their promises like nests of snakes until no one knows where the words begin or end. Remember Lord Medb and his silky promises? You are just like him, treacherous and evil."

"She saved your clan, you miserable slug," Secen, the Khulinin warrior, snapped.

Gabria, amazed by the warrior's quick defense, smiled at him with gratitude.

"Since none of you had the guts to fight," Bregan added.

This time it was Gringold who leaped to his feet. His golden wer-tain's belt glittered in the firelight as he reached for his eating knife.

"Gringold!" Caurus shouted as the other warriors jumped up. "Sit down."

The big wer-tain was too angry to obey. He snatched a heavy platter from the table and brought it down hard on Bregan's head. The older warrior slumped sideways on the table, dazed and bleeding from his reopened head wound. Without a pause, Gringold slashed at Secen with a knife and caught a third Khulinin warrior in the stomach with the platter. Then, before anyone could stop him, he lunged across the table and grabbed Gabria's wrist. "Viper!" he shouted at her. "You saved nothing but your worthless neck."

Athlone, at the end of the table, snarled a curse and leaped toward the wer-tain. Before the chief could get there, Sayyed desperately grabbed for Gringold's knife arm, and Bregan tried to block the wer-tain's body on the table. To their dismay, Gringold was a powerful fighter. He swept them off and tried to wrench Gabria over the edge of the table.

However, he had forgotten Gabria's past and her own training as a warrior. Instead of being the screaming, struggling female he had expected, the woman fought back. She snatched a heavy goblet from the table, smashed it into his face, and twisted her wrist out of his grasp.

Swearing, Gringold covered his bleeding nose and looked up to see the sorceress poised in front of him, her dagger drawn and her green eyes blazing. At that moment, Athlone reached him, and a furious blow to the jaw sent the wer-tain reeling. Even that did not stop the man. He staggered upright and went after the chieftain.

Lady Maril abruptly jabbed her husband in the ribs, jolting him out of his shocked inactivity.

"Gringold, that's enough!" Caurus shouted belatedly. "You men hold him."

The Reidhar warriors, who had not moved during their wer-tain's attack, now scrambled after Gringold and pinned his arms to his sides.

"My apologies, Lord Athlone," Caurus said with some sincerity.

"No!" Gringold yelled. "No apologies. I demand the right to defend my honor by battle."

"A duel?" Caurus exploded. "Whom would you challenge?"

The wer-tain glanced at Bregan and the other Khulinin warriors, then he shook off his men and pointed at Lord Athlone. "I challenge you, Chieftain. To the death."

Caurus looked aghast. "Don't be a fool, man," he gasped, rising from his seat.

Gringold disregarded him. "What do you say, Khulinin?"

For a moment, Athlone did not answer. If he accepted and was badly wounded or killed, his loss could jeopardize their mission. On the other hand, if he did not accept, his refusal to duel with a man of lower status would seriously harm his influence in the clans and cloud his own honor. He looked about him—at Bregan leaning against the table while Piers tried to staunch the blood on his forehead; at the other warriors, one nursing a cut on his arm and one bent double over his bruised abdomen. Athlone glanced at Sayyed and Khan'di, and finally he looked at Gabria. The woman had sheathed her dagger and was standing quietly nearby.

The sight of her ignited a powerful mix of feelings within Athlone. He knew he still loved the sorceress in spite of their arguments, and he was furious with Gringold for assaulting her. If that was not enough to fuel his temper, his anger, jealousy, and hurt pride from the past days still hammered at his patience and self-control. He felt ready to explode.

Lord Athlone grinned wickedly to himself. He would never admit it aloud, but what he really wanted was someone to vent his rage upon. Gringold had just volunteered. "Your challenge is accepted," he murmured. "You have been rude and insolent. You have insulted and attacked my men. Worst of all, you assaulted a woman of our clan. For the sake of our honor, I will meet you in the morning. May Surgart bless my sword."

Lord Caurus groaned and sank back in his seat. Without another word, Athlone gathered his people and left the hall.

* * * * *

By dawn the next day, word of the duel had spread through every corner of the treld. Because the sky was clear and the sun shone with the promise of a warm, comfortable day, the clanspeople began to gather early around the chief's hall. Duels were exciting to watch, but rarely were two such excellent antagonists matched in a battle to the death. Wer-tain Gringold was big, heavily muscled, and well-trained with the short sword, while Lord Athlone, although lighter, was reputed to be the finest swordsman on the plains. The clan could not wait to see the outcome.

While the Reidhar gathered by the hall, Lord Caurus paced in his quarters and cursed the rashness of his wer-tain. Individual dueling was a common clan practice used for settling arguments, ending blood feuds, or claiming weir-geld, and its rules were strict and rigidly adhered to. Combatants were required to fight with only a short sword and without a shield or mail for protection. A man needed every advantage of strength and ability to survive, so challenges were restricted to the initiated warriors of the werod.

Normally Lord Caurus would not have objected to a duel. The battles were usually fought until one opponent surrendered, and he would have enjoyed seeing Athlone taken down a notch or two. A battle to the death, however, was an entirely different matter. Athlone's death could have serious repercussions throughout the clans. The other chiefs would be furious with Caurus and blame him for the killing. The powerful Khulinin would be without a chieftain and *they* would be enraged. And that sorceress . . . Caurus shuddered to think of the problems she could cause.

As for the other possibility, he would hate to lose his wer-tain. Gringold was a hot-tempered fool at times, but he was an excellent leader to the clan's warriors. He was Caurus's cousin, too.

All in all, the outcome of this duel looked grim to Caurus.

Unfortunately, not even a chieftain could call off a challenge if the combatants were determined to fight. Caurus had tried to talk to Gringold that morning to no avail. The wertain was adamant; the duel would be fought.

On the other side of the treld, as Caurus paced back and forth in his hall, the travelers joined Athlone in the meager hut to help him prepare.

Gabria watched the men for a short while, then slipped outside. Athlone had all the help he needed, and she wanted to be alone to compose her feelings. She was very worried. Athlone was an experienced, highly trained swordsman who could easily hold his own in duel. But Gringold was a brutal, powerful fighter, and battles between two well-matched antagonists were often unpredictable. Gabria swallowed hard to banish the nervous flutters in her stomach.

For a few moments she paced anxiously by the door until, finally, to take her mind off her worries, she retrieved the horse brushes from the baggage and carefully brushed the dust off Nara and Eurus until their ebony coats glistened. She combed their manes and tails and brushed the colt's scruffy coat. When she was finished grooming the horses, she leaned against Nara and tried to be patient.

Abruptly the wooden door of the hut swung open and Athlone strode out, followed by his four hearthguard, Piers, Sayyed, and Khan'di. Gabria stared at the Khulinin lord with pride. He wore only a pair of tight-fitting breeches, and he carried his sword in one hand. His muscles, while not as bulky as Gringold's, were well-formed and as dangerously sleek as a mountain lion's. His skin had been rubbed with oil to make it difficult for his opponent to hold him; his hair was tightly bound.

Gabria recognized the concentrated look of resolution in his eyes. He had withdrawn from everything but the battle at hand. "My lord," she said softly. "Your mount is ready."

Athlone looked at her, then at the great Hunnuli stallion that stood watching him with those deep, intelligent eyes. He hesitated for a breath while his reluctance to ride a sorcerer's steed gave way to his common sense. He and Gabria knew the horses only accepted magic-wielders, yet the rest of the clans only knew that a man who could ride the magnificent horses was a man to be honored and respected. His appearance on Eurus would make a valuable impression on the minds of the Reidhar and hopefully unnerve his opponent.

Athlone vaulted to Eurus's back, raised his sword, and shouted, "Khulinin!"

The four hearthguard warriors repeated his cry, and their shouts reverberated through the valley. They immediately took their positions beside their chief, and the others fell in behind. Nara walked with Gabria, for the sorceress did not want to distract the Reidhar's attention from Lord Athlone. To her relief, Piers laid her hand on his arm and walked beside her while Sayyed stayed close behind.

On Eurus's back, Athlone looked out over the Reidhar camp and saw the clanspeople swarming to the path to watch his approach. He grinned with pleasure and held his sword, blade down, as a gesture of peace to the Reidhar clan. The people cheered their approval. They did not care if he was an opponent to their wer-tain. All they saw was a proud clan warrior astride a great Hunnuli, his sword gleaming in the sun, his body ready for battle. In that moment, Athlone became a thrilling embodiment of the clans' hero, the legendary warrior, Valorian.

They cheered as the group approached the hall, then fell silent and gathered in a ring around the wide, open space before the building. Lord Caurus and the wer-tain were waiting by the entrance. Gringold's body was oiled like Athlone's and laced with scars from many fights.

Athlone paused for a moment to run his hand down Eurus's neck. He felt so alive, so natural, sitting on the back of this Hunnuli. He was as comfortable and at ease with this horse as he had ever been with Boreas. It was like coming home to an old friend.

Eurus twisted his head around and looked at Athlone through his long forelock. *His reach is longer than yours, but he only uses his sword in his right hand.*

The chieftain chuckled. "You know him well?"

Merely observant. Keep your head down.

With a laugh, Athlone slung his leg over Eurus's withers and slid to the ground. He saluted Caurus.

The Reidhar chief returned the salute, as one lord to another. He tried to appear calm, but his face was grim, and his red beard fairly bristled with his agitation.

"Lord, a moment," Gringold said. "I must ask a favor."

"What is it?" Caurus asked impatiently.

The wer-tain turned and pointed to Gabria. "The sorceress. She must not interfere. Keep her at sword point."

Before anyone else could move, Sayyed drew his long curved blade and planted himself before Gabria. "Do not try it," he said flatly.

Athlone caught Sayyed's glance, and the chief gave a slight nod of approval. Sayyed grinned.

The Reidhar warriors edged forward, waiting for their lord's command until Caurus waved them back.

"Lord Athlone, tell her she is not to interfere."

"I do not need to, Caurus. She would not do so."

"So be it. Begin the duel."

The Hunnuli and the travelers withdrew to the edge of the ring of people as Athlone and Gringold approached each other. The two men faced off silently and raised their swords above their heads until the two points touched. Gringold's anger had hardly abated from the night before. His rugged face was twisted into a sneer of rage. Athlone was almost expressionless, and his eyes watched the wer-tain with the calculating calm of a hunter.

Into the silence stepped the clan priest of Surgart. He raised his arm. "God of war, god of justice," he shouted. "Behold this contest and judge these men. Choose your champion!" At his last word, the priest swung his arm down and the two men brought their swords clashing together.

Eurus's observation was right; Gringold held his sword only in his right hand, but he used his left to punch, gouge, and grab, and his reach was several fingers longer than Athlone's. His strength was greater, too, and he bore down on the chieftain with the power and fury of a bear.

Athlone met Gringold's sword attack blow for blow. He soon realized, though, that without a shield, he could not keep up his guard against the brute strength of the wer-tain. He ducked to avoid a punch to his head, slipped under Gringold's arm, and, switching his sword to his left hand, nicked the man in the ribs. The wer-tain roared in rage and doubled his attack.

The sounds of clashing swords rang through the treld as the men fought in wordless fury. Time and again Gringold tried to beat down Athlone or crush him with his greater strength, but the chieftain was faster, more agile, and used his sword with either hand. Neither man could force a killing blow on the other, so they both struggled to wear the other down and catch a weakness or a fatal slip.

Before long, the men were sweating heavily. Gringold was bleeding from several cuts and nicks from Athlone's sword. Athlone's jaw throbbed from a well-landed punch, and his muscles were aching. He drew back a moment to wipe the sweat from his eyes.

"Too much for you?" Gringold sneered. "Would you care to kneel here and let me end it? I'll kill you swiftly."

Athlone jeered with contempt, "You couldn't hit a dead horse, you lumbering oaf."

Gringold charged the Khulinin, his sword swinging in a vicious arc. Athlone dodged and slashed at the man's legs as he passed. The blade caught Gringold's right thigh and cut deep into the muscle. The man staggered.

At that moment, Gabria heard Sayyed mutter a strange phrase, and she saw Gringold pitch forward to land heavily on the ground. To everyone else the wer-tain appeared to have fallen because of his wounded leg, but Gabria knew better. Her hand clamped around Sayyed's arm.

"Stop that, now!" she hissed.

The Turic shrugged like a boy caught in mischief. "Do you want Lord Athlone to lose?" he whispered.

"Of course not. But he has to win this alone. He would not tolerate our help."

"All right, but if you change your mind . . ."

They turned back to the duel in time to see Athlone press his attack on the fallen man. Gringold barely avoided the chief's sword by rolling under the blow and deliberately tripping Athlone with his legs. The chief fell on top of him, and Gringold took the opportunity to land several punches on Athlone's face.

The Khulinin chief, his head reeling, struggled out of the way and climbed to his feet. He faced the wer-tain with his sword in both hands. He could taste blood in his mouth, and his eye was beginning to swell. He drew some deep breaths as the wer-tain staggered to his feet. They glared at each other through their blood and sweat.

Swinging his sword in short, wicked, slashes, Athlone feinted toward Gringold's wounded leg just enough to force the man's sword down, then he cut upward for the throat. The Reidhar's reflexes were not fast enough to parry the jab, so he slammed his fist into the chief's stomach. The blow deflected Athlone's arm just enough to throw off the blade. The sharp edge cut the skin of Gringold's neck and slid by.

The heavy punch threw Athlone off balance, and he stumbled, gasping for air. Instantly the wer-tain jumped after him and jabbed his sword toward the chief's upper body. Athlone saw the blade coming. He tried to twist out of the way, but the point caught him in the hollow of his right shoulder. He snarled in pain, wrenched away from the blade, and fell heavily on his side. His sword was jarred out of his hand. It landed in the dirt a few feet away from his outstretched fingers.

Gringold shouted in delight. The wer-tain, his neck and leg running with blood, slashed his blade down at Athlone's head. The Khulinin twisted away from the blow and reached for his weapon.

"Oh, no, you don't," Gringold cursed. Unable to reach Athlone's fallen sword himself, he tossed aside his weapon and jumped on the chieftain. He wrapped his hands around Athlone's throat and grinned at the delight of killing a man with his bare hands.

"Gabria, please!" Sayyed whispered fiercely.

The sorceress clenched his arm. "No."

Athlone's world suddenly closed in around him in a red vise of pain. He struggled desperately to dislodge the heavy wertain sitting on his chest and to pull off the hands that were slowly strangling him. He might as well have tried to move a mountain. Inexorably the agony increased. The blood roared in his ears, and the used air burned in his lungs. His strength drained away.

Unbeknownst to him, the power of his sorcerer's blood began to build in every fiber of his being. In his last moments of lucid thought, he remembered his sword lying only inches away from his fingers. He gave a frantic, tremendous lunge that brought him close to the weapon. He stretched every muscle and tendon in his arm to reach the hilt.

Gringold paid no attention to the heaving of his victim. He was too certain of victory. The Khulinin would be dead in seconds. He closed his eyes and bared his teeth as he squeezed harder.

All at once, Athlone's fingers touched the cold leather wrapping the hilt of his sword. In that moment, his rage and desperation fused with the magic within him into a furious surge of power. A faint aura of blue, so dim it could not be seen in the morning sun, glowed around his fingers as he clamped onto the sword. The energy burst outward from every muscle and nerve ending, and galvanized into one mighty effort. He brought the sword up and over, hacking into the curve of Gringold's unprotected neck. The blade cut into muscle; blood splattered over both men. Unseen, a pale burst of blue sparks exploded out of Athlone's hand as the magic power seared into the wer-tain's body.

Gringold died instantly. He jerked once and slowly toppled over Athlone, his dead face twisted in a grimace of surprise and rage.

Athlone gasped a lungful of air. He felt the pain and roaring in his head recede into darkness. A blessed quiet stole over him, and, as his sword fell from his hand, he passed into unconsciousness.

9

 shocked silence hung over the crowd for several moments while everyone stared at the two men lying in the dust. Then the quiet was shattered. The clanspeople broke loose in excited talk, sporadic cheers, and wailing from Gringold's relatives.

Gabria drew a long, ragged breath and slumped against Nara. She tasted blood in her mouth where she had bitten her lip.

He lives, Eurus told her, and she nodded gratefully.

Piers and the Reidhar's healer stepped out of the crowd at the same time and hurried to their men. They pulled Gringold's heavy body off Athlone and checked the two warriors. The clan healer glanced at Lord Caurus and shook his head.

Caurus gritted his teeth. The duel was over. Surgart had chosen his champion.

The ring of clanspeople began to break up. Several men approached the wer-tain's body and bore him away to his family. The travelers gathered around Athlone.

"He's not badly hurt," Piers assured them. "He has mostly bruises and flesh wounds."

"Then why do I feel like a stampede just ran over me?" Athlone croaked. The chieftain opened his eyes and squinted at the anxious faces around him.

Sayyed flashed his bright grin. "A stampede did run over you. A very large and ugly one."

Carefully, with Piers's help, Athlone sat up. "He's dead?" They all nodded.

"I had the strangest feeling when I struck him. I thought I . . ." Athlone stopped and looked at his hand.

Piers and Gabria exchanged wondering glances.

"Most men have strange feelings when they're being strangled," Bregan said.

Piers quickly stanched the bleeding in Athlone's shoulder, and he and Bregan helped the chief to his feet.

Athlone breathed deeply in the warm spring air. "Saddle your horses. We're leaving." His words were hoarse from his bruised throat, but his tone was adamant.

"My lord," Piers protested, "you can't possibly ride."

At that moment, Lord Caurus joined them. Most of his belligerence was gone, replaced by a modicum of concern and regret. "Lord Athlone, surely you will rest here tonight."

The Khulinin chieftain glared at him. He was aching, his shoulder was on fire, his face was battered and bruised, and he was utterly exhausted. He was in no mood to placate this bad-mannered lout. "You said one night, we stayed one night. I will *not* remain in this treld another hour."

Caurus's face flamed bright red. He started to say something, but Athlone straightened, let go of Bregan, and walked away without another word. The others followed. Caurus made no effort to go after them.

While Athlone sat on a stool and Piers fussed over him, Gabria and the men packed their gear, saddled the horses, and prepared to leave. When they were ready to go, Athlone turned his gray stallion over to Bregan and mounted Eurus. Gabria hid a smile of joy and relief. Since none of the Reidhar came to bid them farewell, the party left the treld without fanfare and rode west up the valley to rejoin the caravan road.

They had traveled only a few leagues from the treld before Piers took a close look at Athlone's pale face. He called an immediate halt and ordered the chieftain to rest. Ignoring Athlone's protest, the party stopped and made camp along the banks of a small stream. Gabria arranged the chief's blankets on a soft mat of leaves and grass; Piers gave him a mild concoction of poppy extract and wine. Athlone decided he was too weary to argue further. He drank the wine and was asleep in moments.

Bregan, too, lay down to sleep in the warm sun, and Valar and Keth went hunting. The others stayed near camp and relaxed.

Gabria changed from her woman's skirts back into her pants and warm tunic, which were more practical and comfortable than skirts on a journey like this. She had learned to enjoy the easy movement and the lighter weight of pants. She pushed back her hair and went to start a cooking fire. She hoped the hunters would find something. The supplies were dwindling fast.

"Rider coming," Secen shouted. The travelers drew together and watched warily as a horseman, leading a pack animal, came up the valley. The man, who wore the yellow Reidhar cloak, stopped at the edge of camp and saluted respectfully. He did not seem surprised to find them so close to the treld.

"Lord Caurus ordered me to bring you these supplies and to offer his apologies. He hopes that when the Khulinin visit again he will be able to prove his hospitality."

"I hope so, too," Secen muttered.

Piers stepped forward to take the packhorse's lead rope. "Thank you, rider. Please take our greetings to Lord Caurus."

The man nodded civilly and left the way he had come.

Gabria, Piers, and Sayyed unpacked the horse, and after hobbling him with the rest of the string, examined what Lord Caurus had sent.

"For a man who claimed to have had a bad year, he certainly was generous," Gabria said, holding up a nutcake.

Sayyed looked over the parcels and bundles. "He sent everything Lord Athlone asked for."

"And then some," Piers remarked. "Oh, look at this." He held up a carefully wrapped cask of Reidhar's famous honey wine. "I could almost forgive him his rudeness."

"Do you suppose the man is feeling a little guilty?" the Turic asked in heavy sarcasm.

"Guilty as a horse thief," Gabria replied with satisfaction.

She and Piers repacked the extra gear while Sayyed fed the horses. Next they laid out the delicacies and set about preparing the evening meal. Shortly before sunset, the two warriors returned with several rabbits and a small deer. The plain, meager meal Gabria had expected was transformed into a feast.

The smell of roasting meat awakened Bregan and Athlone and lured both warriors to the fire. The chieftain sat down and leaned back against a fallen tree trunk while Gabria poured a cup of wine for him.

"You're a sight," she said, studying his battered face. She wanted to say more, to tell him how relieved she was that he was alive, but the words stuck in her throat. She had made her vow to avoid further difficulties with Athlone and Sayyed until later, and she was going to stick by her decision. She handed him the wine cup and watched as he drained it, then she filled it again.

Athlone tried to grin, but the pain of his swollen face made him wince. He said nothing, for talking still bothered his throat, and watched Gabria return to the fire. The wine warmed his stomach, and the evening breeze was pleasant on his face. An unexpected contentment stole over him. For the first time in many days, he did not worry or grow angry or morose. He was too happy to be alive and in the company of these companions. Even Sayyed.

The young Turic was sitting nearby, keeping an eye on the roasting meat and repairing some tears in the sleeve of one of his robes. Athlone noticed that even though Sayyed poured his attention on Gabria, she was keeping her distance from both of them. She had hardly spoken to either man in two days.

Perhaps there was some hope, Athlone thought to himself, that Gabria's relationship with Sayyed was not what he imagined. Perhaps he had jumped to conclusions too soon. Already he regretted his precipitous ending of their betrothal the night before last. He had not planned that, and he had not given Gabria a chance to talk. Now she might never tell him how she felt out of injured pride and hurt. Athlone sighed. He had made a serious mistake by getting so angry; he had set their relationship back almost to the beginning. If he ever wanted to let her go, now was the time to do so. However, Athlone knew he could not give her up so easily. Even if she loved the Turic, the chieftain wanted to try to win her back. He slowly drank his wine and watched Gabria as she helped prepare the meal.

When the food was cooked, the travelers gathered around the fire to enjoy a hot meal and the gifts sent by Lord Caurus. They ate so much stewed rabbit, roast venison, cheese, fresh bread, winter squash, and nutcakes that no one bothered to move after the meal was over. Everyone lounged by the fire, redolent with food and wine. Athlone was still weak from loss of blood, but the bone-deep exhaustion was gone, and he propped himself by the tree trunk and relaxed in the tranquil evening.

Keth brought out a wood whistle he had made and piped tunes to the rhythm of the dancing flames. Sayyed uncovered his gaming stones to take his chances with Bregan. Gabria stayed by Piers, watching and listening to the men around her.

Sayyed, sitting across the fire from Gabria, played the stones and smiled at her with barely concealed hope and yearning. He was not the least upset by her sudden withdrawal from their increasing intimacy. She had not shut him out completely, and the caring that still lurked in her smile and her eyes fed his hope. He would simply bide his time.

A pale moon hung over the camp, and the night was cool with a mild breeze. An owl hooted nearby. Athlone was about to return to his blankets when all at once, Gabria sprang to her feet.

"Athlone, someone is near the camp!"

The chief sat up, and the men jumped to their feet, their hands reaching for their weapons. Beyond the firelight, Nara neighed in the darkness. Her call sounded to Gabria more like a greeting than a warning.

They peered into the darkness around them, until Bregan pointed to an indistinct, pale form on the edge of a grove of trees near the camp.

"Come forward," the old warrior shouted.

A cloaked figure shuffled hesitantly into the farthest reaches of the firelight.

"Are you the Khulinin party?" a muffled voice called.

Athlone struggled to his feet. "Who wants to know?" he answered.

"I am looking for the Corin girl. The one they call 'sorceress,' " came the reply.

Before Athlone could stop her, Gabria stepped forward. "I am here." She sensed no danger from this person, but she was glad when the three Hunnuli appeared out of the night and gathered around her.

The shrouded figure gasped and stepped back at the sight of the huge, black horses.

"I am Gabria of Clan Corin," the sorceress said gently. "Don't be frightened. What is it you want?"

The stranger seemed to take courage from Gabria's calm voice and edged into the firelight. "I saw you at the treld, but you left before I could talk to you." With trembling hands, the stranger pushed back the hood of the bright yellow Reidhar cloak and revealed the face of a woman. She was not a beautiful woman and never had been. Years of toil and living out in the dry wind and sun had taken a hard toll on her thin, angular face. She was well past middle age, gray-haired, and she wore no jewelry or ornaments to mark her as a member of the higher social ranks of her clan.

"How did you know we were here?" Bregan demanded.

"I overheard the outrider who brought the supplies tell Lord Caurus where you were camped." She glanced warily at the men and turned back to Gabria. "I have something I must give you, Lady," the woman said nervously. "It is very important." She pulled at something hidden behind her. "Come on!" she cried and yanked harder. A small grubby girl stumbled out from the folds of the yellow cloak. The girl tried to clutch her companion's skirts, but the woman thrust her toward Gabria.

"This is Tam. She is ten summers old. My sister died giving birth to her," the clanswoman told Gabria desperately. "She is

a magic-wielder like you. Please, take her with you. With you
she will be safe. I can't hide her talent much longer, and if
Lord Caurus finds out he will kill her."

Gabria was astounded. She looked speechlessly from the little girl to the clanswoman.

"We can't take a child with us," Khan'di began to say, but
Athlone cut him off with a gesture.

"How do you know she can wield magic?" the chief asked.

The woman gestured nervously. "She can! She does things.
She . . . she's different."

Gabria laid her hand on Nara's neck. "Is the child a magic
wielder?" she asked the mare.

Yes. The mare answered. Her foal whinnied in agreement.

The sorceress knelt down to look Tam in the face. The child was
dirty and disheveled. Her ragged clothes were obviously hand-
downs from a larger child, but her features were pretty and her
unkempt hair was thick and black. Her enormous eyes had an
intense, wary gaze that seemed much too old for her years.

Gabria felt her heart melt. Khan'di was right, they did not
need a child along. This journey would be long and dangerous, and the chances of survival were questionable. Still, as
Gabria studied Tam's troubled face, she felt no doubt. This
little girl was a kindred spirit, a magic-wielder, and as such she
should be nurtured, protected, and taught, not left to the
questionable mercy of someone like Caurus.

"Would you like to come with us, Tam?" Gabria asked.

"She can't talk," the woman cut in.

"Can't or won't?" Piers inquired.

The clanswoman shrugged. "She hasn't spoken since her
father died five years ago. My husband says she's a weakling."

Gabria gently pushed a strand of dark hair away from Tam's
eyes. "Did your husband also say how she got this?" She turned the little girl's head toward the firelight and pointed to a
large, purplish bruise on her temple.

The woman sidled back, her expression a mixture of fear
and sadness, and said, "That's why you've got to take her. She
won't last much longer with me."

"I don't know how safe she'll be with us," Gabria said.

"At least she'll have a chance," the woman pleaded. "Tam's your kind. You'll take care of her. I can't!" Before anyone could stop her, she tossed a small bundle on the ground, turned, and fled into the darkness.

The warriors started after her, but Athlone stopped them. "Let her go." They came back, sheathing their weapons.

Khan'di, his heavy face frowning, came forward. "Lord Athlone, I must protest. This is no journey for a child. We can't lose any more time by dragging her along."

Piers knelt beside Tam and ran his long fingers over the bruise on her head. "She seems healthy, if undernourished. She should be able to stand the journey."

"Besides, we can't just leave her here," Sayyed said.

"Or take her back to Lord Caurus," Keth added.

Athlone quirked an eyebrow at the sudden rush to defend this little girl. He agreed with Khan'di's protest, but at the moment, they did not have much choice. "She'll have to go," he decided. "The Hunnuli can look after her, and we can spare enough food for one more small mouth."

Gabria smiled at Athlone gratefully and, for a moment, the pain in his heart receded under the warmth of her relief and pleasure.

Tam had not budged during the departure of her aunt or the exchange between the men. She stood as if rooted to the ground, too frightened to move. Gabria was surprised by her total silence. The little girl did not cry or speak or even whisper. She just stayed in the place where her aunt had left her and stared fixedly at the sorceress in front of her. Gabria slowly held out her wrist where the jewel splinter glowed red under her skin.

"Tam," she said softly. "I am Gabria. I am a magic-wielder, too."

Tam did not respond. Her small face was pale under the dirt, and her hands were clenched at her sides.

The sorceress cast a glance at the men. Only Piers, Athlone, and Sayyed could see what she was doing, so she picked up a stone the size of her fist. She smiled at Tam. "Watch." The months of practice in the stone temple came to Gabria's aid, and with just a single word, she transformed the stone into a perfect sweetplum.

Tam's eyes grew huge. The men around her started in surprise.

"How did you do that?" Sayyed asked eagerly.

Gabria looked up at Athlone, the hint of a smile in her eyes. "Practice." She pressed the plum into Tam's hand and watched as the girl tasted it.

Tam tried a tentative bite, and her body seemed to relax a little. Plum juice ran down her chin as she devoured the fruit.

Lord Athlone said nothing at first. He was not sure what he should say about Gabria's display of sorcery. To be honest with himself, he had to admit her skill at changing the stone to a fruit intrigued him. It looked so simple, so useful. He watched Tam wipe her hands on her tattered skirt and, for the first time, the chief smiled at her. "Now that you have her attention," he said to Gabria, "why don't you give her a real meal. She looks famished."

Tam suddenly nodded eagerly, and she held out her hands imploringly.

Piers smiled. "There's certainly nothing wrong with her hearing."

All at once, Tam's eyes widened. Whirling around, she put her fingers to her lips and blew a piercing whistle. To everyone's surprise, a dog barked far down the valley. Gabria's mouth opened, and Athlone and Sayyed started in disbelief.

"Did you hear that?" Gabria gasped incredulously.

Bregan glanced around. "What? The dog?"

"I thought I heard—" She stopped.

"What?" Piers asked, puzzled.

The dog barked again, closer this time, and Gabria, Athlone, and Sayyed heard the words in their heads. *Tam! Tam! I'm coming. I am free, and I am coming!*

Suddenly the Hunnuli neighed, and a huge, mottled dog charged into the firelight, barking with frantic joy. A frayed rope dangled from his neck. He leaped on Tam and knocked her flat, licking her and whining with delight. The girl hugged him fiercely.

Gabria stared at the dog in amazement. "I can understand him!"

"The dog?" Khan'di frowned.

"Yes!" Sayyed agreed excitedly. "He is barking, but in my head I can hear his meaning."

Piers said, "Well, I don't."

"I do," Athlone said, astonished. He sank back down to his seat.

Khan'di crossed his arms. "That's ridiculous. It's just a dog. A scruffy looking one at that."

"It's a Tesser," Bregan told him. "A hunting dog from the northern forests. The Murjik breed them. These dogs are white in the winter and brown in the summer. He's shedding."

"Tesser or not, it's still a dog and dogs do not talk," Khan'di insisted.

Gabria shook her head. "No, he doesn't talk as we do, but something is translating his voice to us. I don't understand it. I've never heard of anything like this."

The dog in question sat down beside Tam and wagged his plumed tail. His lips pulled back in a wolfish grin. Carefully, Gabria held out her hand to let the dog sniff it. He woofed.

Hello, the magic-wielders heard. *I am Treader.*

"Treader," Gabria repeated in wonder.

Tam's pale face lit with a brilliant smile as if someone had just discovered her most wonderful achievement. Silently she tapped her chest then touched the dog.

"Ah," Gabria muttered, studying the child and the dog together.

Athlone caught her thought. "Tam did it?"

"She must have. Somehow she has put a spell on him to translate his voice, and because she used magic . . ."

"We can understand him, too," Sayyed finished.

"So why can't *we* hear this remarkable dog?" Khan'di asked.

"Tam's magic must be limited," Gabria answered. "Her spell was probably intended to translate Treader's voice only to a magic-wielder. She didn't know she was going to meet more of us." Gabria fingered the frayed end of the rope tied to the dog's collar. "I wonder whose dog it is?"

Secen said with a smirk. "Lord Caurus's, maybe?"

Tam shook her head and pointed to herself.

"I doubt it's hers," Bregan remarked. "It's a valuable dog. Should we take it back?"

At that, Tam leaped to her feet and flung herself on the dog's shoulder. Treader rose, barking furiously.

Athlone smiled lopsidedly. "Ah, no. He says he goes with Tam whether we like it or not. Besides, we don't have the time to go back."

"Think they'll come looking for it?" Sayyed asked.

The chieftain shrugged. He was exhausted again and ready for his blankets. "Probably not tonight," he muttered. "And we'll be leaving at dawn." As Piers came to help him, he waved a hand at Tam. "Feed the child." In a moment, he sank into his rough bed with deep relief and was asleep before the others returned to the fire.

Khan'di grumbled something about troublesome children and retired to his tent. The rest of the group gathered around the fire and brought out the remains of their meal. The Hunnuli foal tagged along.

Sayyed grinned as he watched Tam dive into a bowl heaped high with bread, meat, and cheese. "She's so small. Where is she putting it all?"

"She acts as if she hasn't eaten in days," Valar said.

Bregan nodded. "Maybe she hasn't. She certainly doesn't look well cared for."

"Her kinswoman didn't even say good-bye," Gabria said.

"No," agreed Piers. "But Tam doesn't appear to be upset about it."

The little girl listened to them all and kept her thoughts hidden behind her bright eyes. When she was finally finished, she laid her plate down and smiled her thanks.

The night was late by that time, and one by one the men went to their beds to sleep. Gabria collected the bundle of Tam's meager belongings and nestled her down in a small traveling tent. Nara and Eurus returned to grazing, but the foal stayed near Gabria's tent.

Early the next morning, in the dim moments before the sun rose, Gabria awakened and found Tam's bed empty. Hastily she donned her pants and tunic, and ran outside, only to stop and smile with relief. Tam had not gone far. She slept curled up beside the Hunnuli foal, her head pillowed on his warm side, her hand resting on his leg. The dog lay at her feet, and Nara stood protectively over them all.

The mare turned her dark eyes to Gabria. *The child will do well. She has already tamed her Hunnuli.*

Gabria was pleased to agree.

* * * * *

The travelers prepared to leave their camp soon after sunrise. Athlone was much stronger after a night's sleep, and he swore he could ride Eurus with no difficulty. Piers tried to convince him to rest another day, but the chieftain knew that they should not waste any more time. Although Gabria had said nothing, Athlone sensed her restlessness and recognized the way her eyes constantly turned to the north. Khan'di, too, was growing impatient. The danger in Pra Desh would not wait.

So they packed their gear, obliterated their camp, and rode out of the Reidhar's valley. If anyone from the treld missed a dog, they did not bother to chase the Khulinin party.

As they trotted over the line of hills marking the valley, Gabria glanced back at Tam riding behind her on Nara, and she wondered if the little girl was unhappy to be leaving her home. To her relief, Tam did not seem to be upset. The girl wagged her fingers at the Hunnuli foal trotting by her foot and stared out over the plains with a shy look of delight. Whatever Tam was leaving behind would not be missed.

In the days that followed, Gabria had no reason to change

her mind about Tam or regret that she had accepted the little girl. Tam was an intelligent child who tried to be helpful. She learned quickly not to annoy Khan'di, and she was wary of Athlone and the warriors, but Sayyed could bring a shining smile to her face and Gabria held her trust. She settled in to the difficult routine of the journey, and the steady food and attentive care soon filled out the hollows in her cheeks and erased the dark circles around her eyes.

The humans in the party quickly discovered Tam would be no trouble for them. True to Athlone's word, Nara and Eurus guarded the little girl like one of their own offspring. One or both of them were always close by to keep her from harm. Nara's colt helped in his own way, for he tagged after Tam constantly, making it easier for his elders to guard them both. The dog, Treader, stayed with his mistress most of the time, but he liked Sayyed, too, and once in a while the Turic would take him hunting. Treader's catches helped supplement their supplies and more than made up for what he and Tam ate.

For all these happy achievements, Gabria could not overcome the little girl's silence. She never made any noise at all. Even if she was a mute, Gabria thought Tam should be able to make some sound—a cry, a groan, or a whimper. But the girl was totally silent. She was so still the men often forgot she was there. When someone spoke, she sometimes flinched before she realized who was talking to her, then she would look at the ground and nod politely. Only when no one seemed to be paying attention to her would Tam lift her eyes and watch everyone with her grave, fascinated gaze.

While Tam liked Gabria and seemed to be happy, she did not become deeply attached to any of the people in the party. Gabria thought the little girl had been so neglected in her past that she had withdrawn into the sanctuary of herself, a place where only pure and gentle creatures like the dog and the Hunnuli were allowed. Gabria could not help but wonder if any human would ever be able to draw her out from behind her walls.

10

everal days after leaving Reidhar Treld, the travelers abandoned the caravan trail and struck across country for Calah. The traffic on the caravan route had increased with every passing league until the party found it impossible to avoid detection. At Khan'di's urging, they left the easy trail and sought a faint, seldom-used path that was shorter and much rougher than the caravan route. Here the grasslands and meadows gave way to higher hills, rock-strewn valleys, and thicker woods of oak, juniper, and pine. The tall prairie grass was replaced by brambles, brush, and vines. The Ramtharin Plains had come to an end in the Redstone Hills, the boundary between the grasslands of Valorian's clans and the rich farmlands and forests of the kingdom of Calah.

The travelers pushed on as fast as they could, the warmer winds of advancing spring coming swiftly on their heels. The closer they drew to Pra Desh the more Khan'di urged them on. He knew if the fon stayed with her original plan for the invasion of Portane, the party would arrive in Pra Desh with very little time to spare. There was also the possibility that the fon had changed her plans or plotted some new outrage for the city. Khan'di had been gone from Pra Desh for over two months, and he was frantic to get home to lay plans of his own.

Gabria, too, felt the urgency of the passing days. The memory of the terrible vision played in her memory time and again, driving her on toward Pra Desh like a goad in the hands of an unseen but brutal taskmaster.

One afternoon, as she rode Nara along the rugged slopes of the Redstone Hills, Gabria thought again about her confrontation with Branth. She was not looking forward to that encounter. With luck and some cunning of their own, the company might be able to find the renegade chieftain and slip him out of the city before the fon realized he was gone. Unfortunately, Gabria could not pin her hopes on things going that easily. Branth's magical powers were not only the fon's greatest weapon, but her greatest peril, as well. She was certain to have him imprisoned and guarded like a dangerous animal.

Gabria allowed herself a sigh. She was not ready for this confrontation. She had learned the basic skills of sorcery from the Woman of the Marsh in a hurried lesson that had lasted only two days. There had been no time to practice or prepare before she'd met Lord Medb for the duel, and her victory over him had been founded on tenacity and luck. Since that time she had only been able to practice during the months of her banishment—months that now seemed brief indeed. To all intents and purposes she was still an apprentice. Yet everyone expected her to face a sorcerer who was better prepared and had the *Book of Matrah*.

She shot a look at Athlone and Sayyed on the trail ahead of her. It was too bad she did not feel ready to teach them the rudiments of sorcery. Athlone had the strength to wield his talent well. Gabria did not know about Sayyed's natural abilities, but if his determination and personality were any indication, he could be as powerful a sorcerer as Athlone. If only she felt capable enough to teach them!

Her thoughts were still on sorcery and the future when the party crossed over a high, craggy ridge into the kingdom of Calah and looked down on the valley of a broad river.

"There is Pra Desh," Khan'di told his companions, pointing down the valley to the south. The city was still leagues away, but from their vantage point, the travelers could make out the high towers, the white walls, and the vast harbor of the huge city.

The river in the valley, the Serentine, flowed from the forests far to the northwest. It ran east across the northern plains, past Amnok Treld, Bahedin Treld, and three of the Five Kingdoms, gaining substance and changing from a tumbling stream to a wide, majestic river. At the end of its long journey, the Serentine swept past the feet of the Redstone Hills and into the finest natural harbor in the Sea of Tannis.

Here, at this propitious meeting of river, land, and sea, the people of Calah built their capital and nourished it into the richest and most powerful maritime city on the Tannis. Their fleet controlled the northern and western coasts and roved the sea to its farthest reaches. The merchants of Pra Desh traded everything in the known world from raw materials such as grain, timber, and ore to livestock, slaves, and finely wrought crafts. They shipped silk, wool, and cotton, jewelry, spices, wines, pottery, weapons, and carpets. They brought anything that could be bought to the marketplaces of Pra Desh and filled their coffers with the gold coins of many realms.

After a moment, Khan'di pointed to the right, and the travelers saw where their path wound down out of the hills to the valley and joined the caravan route as it paralleled the river to the city. They rode on to the last heavily wooded hill before the path dipped down to the open farmlands. There, Khan'di led the party into the shadows of the trees.

He turned his horse around and addressed the others. "Pra Desh is only three leagues away, and I want to get you into the city unnoticed. The fon's spies are on every street of Pra Desh and at every gate. They have orders to report *anything* unusual."

Gabria sadly ran her hand down Nara's neck. She knew what she was about to say would be painful, but she had thought about it for days and there was no other way to maintain the party's anonymity. "We will have to leave the Hunnuli," she said quietly.

Khan'di bowed his head to her in mixed respect and relief. "Lady Gabria, you have saved me the pain of asking that favor. Unfortunately, there are no other Hunnuli in my country, and as far as anyone knows the only one in the clans belongs to the great Corin sorceress. You would not be safe for long on the streets of Pra Desh."

The young woman nodded unhappily. Although she had made the suggestion, the thought of leaving Nara behind made her very uncomfortable. "Do you mind?" she asked the black mare.

Of course I do, Nara answered. *Leaving you goes against everything I am. But you are right. It must be done.*

If you really need us, we will come, Eurus added.

"Thank you," Gabria replied.

"All right," Khan'di said. "Listen. We will separate here. I should not be seen with clansmen. It might also be best if you split up and enter the city in small groups." He dismounted, found a stick, and drew a detailed map in the dirt.

"This is the Serentine River," he explained to his listeners, pointing to the relevant marks with his stick. "This is the harbor, this the Redstone Hills. Here is the old city wall on the west side of the river. It extends around the fon's palace here on Second Hill, the temple of Elaja on First Hill, and the older residential districts, warehouses, and merchant offices. This is the arsenal where the fon's guards live and the weaponry is stored.

"The city, of course, has long outgrown these walls, and you will find the markets, the auction houses, and the shipwrights' yards here, here, and here." He pointed to each spot on his map. "The rest of the city spreads out this way to the north along the river and up the slopes of the hills. The land to the east is swampy and often floods. Only the poorer peasants, criminals, and runaway slaves live there. Do you understand so far?"

The fascinated clanspeople nodded in unison.

"Good. Now, there is a row of warehouses here in the old city. Follow this caravan road through the gate called the Sun Door. If you look for the tall buildings with the different colored flags on their towers, you will find the warehouses. Go to the fifth one in the row. It is a wool house and will be flying an orange flag. There is a wooden sheep hanging above the doors. Go there and wait for me. Do not wander around. Do not ask questions."

"What will you be doing?" Athlone demanded.

"Seeking information." Khan'di's heavy face broke into a scheming grin. "I have spies on every street, too."

"Whose warehouse is it?" Piers asked coldly.

"My cousin's. He pretends to be a supporter of the fon, but he has been helping me." The Pra Deshian actually rubbed his hands together and chuckled. It was obvious he was delighted to be back in the midst of the intrigue and political scheming.

"What do we say if we meet anyone at the warehouse?" Gabria asked.

"Say nothing." He glanced at the sun through the tree branches. "By the time all of you get there, the warehouse will be empty except for my cousin. He usually works late. He will know who you are."

Athlone grunted. "Do you trust this man?"

"Totally. His daughter is my son's wife. He knows what I will do to her if he betrays me."

The travelers were quiet for a time as they studied Khan'di's map. The Pra Deshian mounted his horse. "Remember. The fifth warehouse." He spurred his horse back to the path.

"Be careful, Khan'di Kadoa," Gabria called after him.

He glanced back, hiding his pleasure at the concern in her voice. "You, too, Sorceress."

Reluctantly Athlone, Gabria, and Tam dismounted from Eurus and Nara. The chieftain wiped out Khan'di's map with a leafy branch while the others unloaded one of the packhorses and secreted most of the traveling gear and tents in a dense thicket.

Gabria was wearing her riding skirts that afternoon, so she brought out a long, cotton scarf and wrapped it like a veil over her head and across her mouth and nose. In her travel-stained garments, she would pass as a simple clanswoman. While she gathered a few belongings out of the packs for herself and Tam, someone bumped into her. Gabria turned and came face to face with Athlone.

The chief was as dirty and travel-worn as she and still bore the evidence of his recent battle. His face had lost its swelling, and he could see out of both eyes, but the bruises were colorful shades of blue, green, and yellow.

Gabria decided his bruises and his newly sprouted beard gave him a raffish look. Hesitantly she touched his arm. "You look like a border ruffian," she teased.

For a moment, he almost gathered her in his arms. He turned toward her, lifting his hands to caress her face, then he saw Sayyed standing close behind her with a strange glint in his black eyes. Athlone's impulse faltered in a rush of renewed doubts. His hands fell back to his sides.

To hide his confusion, he patted Eurus, then swung up on his gray stallion. "Mount up, you motley plains rats. Let's ride." His warriors grinned at him and sprang to obey.

"Bregan, you and I will ride with Lady Gabria. Piers, you go with Tam, Sayyed, and Secen. You two," Athlone said to the last warriors, "are on your own. Go first. Don't get lost and don't stop to chase the women." The two warriors saluted and trotted out of the woods.

Gabria threw her arms around Nara's neck. The world suddenly shimmered through the blur of her tears. "By Amara, I am going to miss you," she whispered to the mare.

Nara gently pressed her head against Gabria's back, enfolding the woman in the curve of her neck. *And I you.*

"I don't want to do this. It doesn't feel right."

I will be close. You only have to call.

Gabria sniffed and smiled lopsidedly. "Like in the marshes?" she asked, remembering that awful day she'd been forced to leave Nara behind to seek the Woman of the Marsh alone.

Yes, but this time you have friends with you. Trust them. They love you. I will be waiting when you are ready for me.

Gabria nodded. Lovingly she traced the white lightning mark on Nara's shoulder before she patted her again and stepped away. A sharp nudge almost knocked her over. She twisted around and found the foal nearly stepping on her feet, Tam hanging onto his wispy mane. Treader sat beside her, his ears drooping.

"Good-bye to you, too, little fellow," Gabria said.

The colt whinnied shrilly in reply.

Gabria was about to take Tam's hand, but the girl's stricken expression made her pause. The child's dark eyes were huge, and a trail of tears had blazed tracks through the dirty smudges on her cheeks.

She doesn't want to leave us, a light, childlike voice said in Gabria's mind.

The sorceress started in surprise; this was the first time the colt had sent his thoughts to her. She knelt by Tam. "You must understand," she said to the girl, "we are going to a big city. We cannot take the Hunnuli. It would be too dangerous for them, and for us, as well."

Treader barked. *She thinks she'll never see the horses again if she goes away.*

"They will wait for us," Gabria explained patiently. "When we return from the city, they'll come down from the hills and greet us." She took Tam's chin and lifted her head up until the girl had to look at her. "All you'll have to do is whistle and they'll come." She smiled. "You can whistle, can't you?"

The little girl grinned through her tears and nodded.

She wants to know if we will be gone long, Treader growled.

"No. Only a few days. All right?"

The colt bobbed his head, Treader woofed loudly, and Tam let go of the Hunnuli's mane to take Gabria's hand.

"That was some conversation," Athlone remarked as Gabria settled Tam on Piers's horse.

"Do you know what's really amazing? Tam never once opened her mouth. She can send her thoughts to these animals just like the Hunnuli do."

"Good gods," Athlone exclaimed. "Is that a natural part of her talent or something she learned to do?"

"I don't know," Gabria said. "I hope we can find out one of these days. It certainly is a useful ability."

The little girl sniffed loudly and wiped her nose on her sleeve, then she waved good-bye to the Hunnuli and settled comfortably against Piers's back.

Gabria touched the healer's knee. During their preparations he had sat on his horse without speaking or moving. Now, as he glanced down at Gabria, she was startled by the haunted expression on his face. His normally pale skin was deathly white; his thin features were pulled tight with tension. His hands were clenched around the saddle horn.

"Are you all right?" Gabria asked worriedly.

He nodded and drew a long, ragged breath. "I did not expect to feel my memories so sharply."

Gabria understood completely. "Face them," she whispered, "and you will find they are only ghosts." She waited while the healer considered her words, then he relaxed a little and took his hands off the saddle horn.

He squeezed her hand. "I'll see you at the warehouse." He reined his horse around, and he, Tam, Sayyed, and Secen took the two remaining packhorses and rode off through the trees. Treader ran ahead of them.

Reluctantly Gabria threw an extra saddle blanket over the withers of the pack mare and mounted. It felt so strange to sit astride such a small, thin horse. She gathered the reins and cast one last look at the Hunnuli, then she followed Athlone out of the trees and back to the path without a backward glance.

Before long, they trotted their horses over the last rise and down into the fertile Serentine Valley. Here, this close to the sea, the valley was so wide that the travelers could barely make out the hills on the opposite side. The land was so fertile almost every square acre was used for crops, pasturage, or vineyards. Huts, cottages, barns, sheds, farmhouses, and outbuildings of every kind were scattered on both sides of the river. The closer the riders drew to the city, the more numerous the cottages and houses became. Inns, hawkers' stands, and shrines appeared along the road. The caravan trail soon changed to a stone-paved road as other trails and paths met and joined it.

The flood of people, carts, wagons, and animals on the road

increased with every step closer to Pra Desh. Gabria and her companions had seen several caravans and small groups of riders on their journey, but they were not prepared for the crowded, swarming populace that lived in Pra Desh. The clanspeople had never been to a city this size, and the largest group of people they had ever seen in one place was at their own clan gatherings. This city was mind-boggling. Even Piers, who was a native Pra Deshian, had lived on the open plains long enough to be taken aback by the throng that rushed purposefully back and forth. They crowded into the markets, crushed into the streets with a seemingly endless tangle of animals, pedestrians, and conveyances, and shouted, sang, talked, and bellowed in every known language.

Gabria tried not to let her mouth hang open as they followed the road into the city, but she could not hide her wide-eyed amazement at everything she saw. There were so many new things to look at!

Pra Deshians were fervent in their worship of their one god and his prophets, and built shrines and temples at every wide spot by the road. There were also open markets, shops, tenements, stables, and huge houses all along the great caravan route.

The road passed through the outskirts of Pra Desh, past a guard post at the official city limits, and into the city proper. Customs officials were checking loaded wagons and collecting taxes from irate drivers. A squad of five guardsmen in purple tunics helped enforce the collection. They were too busy to notice the small groups of dusty clanspeople that rode by. Gabria breathed a sigh of relief as she, Athlone, and Bregan passed the guard and were lost to sight in the crowded streets.

They stayed close together in the streets, following the road as Khan'di had instructed. It still paralleled the river into the heart of Pra Desh's market district. They passed the huge fish market, the meatmongers' street, and the livestock market. One street seemed to be dedicated to the leather trade and another was obviously for bakers.

Along one particularly busy street, Bregan reined his horse closer to Athlone's and leaned over. "Lord, I don't think this city is at war yet." he said over the noise of wagons and pedestrians.

Athlone glanced around. He had come to the same conclusion. "You're right. But have you noticed the number of armed men in the crowds? The city looks like a fortified camp. The fon's invasion must be coming soon."

"So we have come in time," Bregan replied.

Gabria, riding close by, said, "I don't think there's much time left. I've been watching the people and they seem to be in an ugly mood. They don't like all the soldiers in their midst."

"I wonder how much cooperation the fon is getting from the Pra Deshians," said Athlone.

"We'll find out tonight from Khan'di," Gabria said.

The chieftain nodded once. "If he comes."

The travelers rode on in silence. After a while, the road curved away from the river and left the busy market streets behind. The riders passed through an entertainment district of theaters, libraries, and a huge amphitheater to a quieter residential area. The houses here were two-story stone and wood edifices set back from the streets behind privacy walls. The houses were older and showed signs of age, but most of them were well-maintained and their gardens overflowed with flowers.

The road began to rise up a gradual slope until abruptly the riders reached the old city wall. There was a wide gap between the houses and the towering wall, and Gabria felt vulnerable as she rode across the open space to the gate. The Sun Door was a high, arched entrance with two tall gatehouses to either side. A rising sun was carved on the huge wooden door that stood open to allow traffic to pass. More soldiers, these wearing the red of the fon's own guard, stood on both sides of the entrance and carefully scrutinized those who passed through. They ignored the glares and the ugly remarks hurled at them by the city people who went by, but they kept their hands on their swords at all times.

As unhappy as she was to leave Nara, Gabria was glad now the Hunnuli mare had stayed behind. The guards would have noticed the huge black horse instantly. As it was, they still paid more attention to Gabria and her companions than she cared for as she and the two men rode by.

Athlone nodded to one guard and passed under the arched gateway as if he'd done it all his life. Bregan and Gabria were quick to follow. The road led them deep into the maze of crowded, crumbling houses and dark alleys of the old city. Then, unexpectedly, the road split. The right hand way led uphill, and the left gradually dropped down toward the harbor.

Athlone reined his horse to a stop in the middle of the fork and studied each road.

"Which way, Lord?" Bregan asked, coming up beside him.

"Khan'di said to look for the tall buildings with the flags," said Gabria. "But I don't see any."

The three gazed at the city around them. To their right and atop a huge hill sat the temple of Elaja, its white columns and facade shining in the late afternoon sun. On a neighboring hill to the south was the magnificent palace of the fon. Even from a distance the riders could see the palace's multi-storied wings and the crenelated wall that surrounded the huge edifice.

Several buildings close by seemed to be barracks, and Athlone thought there was a dangerously large number of soldiers about. The presence of so many armed men around them alarmed him, so thinking quickly, Athlone spurred his horse to the left fork and trotted downhill. To his relief, the way opened up after a block or so, and he saw the full expanse of the busy harbor. At the bottom of the hill, just outside the city walls, were rows of tall buildings, each flying a different colored flag. Beyond those were the teeming wharves and the great crescent-shaped harbor.

Athlone allowed himself a grin of relief. He had not fancied the idea of asking a guardsman for directions. By the time the riders reached the rows of warehouses, the sun had sunk below the tops of the hills, the sign for laborers and workers to end their day. Athlone, Bregan, and Gabria found Keth and Valar loitering in the shadow of an alley between two warehouses. From there they watched the wool house and kept track of the workers as they left.

"Where's Piers?" Athlone asked when he dismounted.

Keth shrugged. "I don't know. We haven't seen him or the Turic."

"You don't think he's lost," said Valar.

Athlone scratched his beard. "I doubt it. Piers knows this city better than any of us."

"Maybe he went to find old ghosts," Gabria said, as if to herself. The men glanced at her in surprise.

"Well, we can't look for him. He'll have to make it here on his own," the chieftain noted. He took his place in the alley and waited for the remaining workers to leave the warehouse.

Twilight settled into the streets of Pra Desh, and the warehouse workers slowly filtered out and left. No one noticed the five riders waiting in the heavy shadows between the buildings.

At last the street was empty. Athlone was about to approach the warehouse when three horses, two packhorses, and a dog jogged down the street. The chief stepped out to meet them.

"Where have you been?" Athlone demanded.

"Gathering information of our own," Piers answered. He helped Tam down from the horse.

Athlone crossed his arms. He had been more worried than angry. "You could have been betrayed to the guard."

"Not by the people I talked to."

"You really don't trust him, do you?" asked the chieftain.

"Khan'di?" Piers's shoulders shifted slightly under his healer's robes. "Yes and no. I trust him only as long as we are useful to him."

Athlone agreed. "All right. Listen to him tonight and tell me afterward what you think."

The healer nodded with satisfaction. He had dreaded the

possibility that Gabria was walking into a clever trap set by the
fon, a trap that sported Khan'di Kadoa as bait. Two magic-
wielders would be an invincible weapon in the fon's hands.
But after what Piers had heard this afternoon from old friends
and connections in the Healers' Guild, he doubted Khan'di
was planning to betray Gabria.

It was common knowledge around the city that the Kadoa
family had suffered severe financial losses because of the fon.
Khan'di's wife and son were in hiding, and several other family members had been arrested and had subsequently disappeared into the depths of the palace. The powerful Kadoa
family had no reason to love the fon and every reason to dis-
pose of her. Several contacts had even hinted to Piers that
Khan'di, as the most influential nobleman left in Pra Desh,
stood a chance of assuming the coronet of the fon if she were
removed. Piers knew his former friend well enough to know
that possibility alone would be enough to ensure Khan'di's
trustworthiness. The healer patted his mare thoughtfully. He
would be very interested in hearing what Khan'di had to say
tonight.

At a word from Athlone, Piers handed his reins to Sayyed
and followed the chieftain toward the fifth warehouse. The
others stayed behind to wait.

The huge timbered building loomed above them, dark and
strange in the deepening twilight. The warehouse's big wood-
en sign creaked in the night breeze. Athlone stifled a shiver as
he looked up at the building. Its unfamiliar size and blank
walls made him distinctly uncomfortable.

He was about to knock on the warehouse entrance when the
door was whisked open and a short, portly man rushed out.
The man was going so fast he did not see Athlone and
slammed full force into the big Khulinin. Both men grunted
and staggered back. The stranger would have fallen if Piers
had not caught him.

The man gasped at the sight of the two strangers at his door
and threw his hands up in alarm. The hand lamp he was carrying swayed wildly.

"It's all right," Athlone hastened to explain. "Khan'di sent us."

The sound of that name seemed to reassure the man, for he straightened up and looked closely at the two men in the light of his lamp. When he saw the healer's face, he lit up in amazement. "Piers Arganosta! I thought you were dead!"

Piers grimaced. "I've heard that a lot today."

"You probably don't remember me," the Pra Deshian said with a grin. "I was quite a bit thinner in those days."

The healer studied the other's face for a moment, then he smiled in recognition. "Lord Athlone, this is Sengi Kadoa, Khan'di's younger cousin and a page to the fon."

"The old fon," Sengi corrected, his voice edged in anger. "Today I am a wool merchant and—" a devious look flashed across his features in the lamplight "—a spy. That woman on the throne looks to me for mercantile advice." Sengi looked around and ushered the two men into his warehouse. The door opened into a room obviously used as an office. He lit another lamp, and in the increased light the two men were able to get a closer look at their host.

Sengi bore a strong resemblance to Khan'di in the shape and density of his body frame, the heavy lines of his features, and in the ruddy coloration of his skin. But where Khan'di's eyes were sharp and calculating and his expression readily showed his cunning intelligence, Sengi's face was placid and his eyes were framed by skin crinkled from laughter.

The merchant straightened his rumpled robes with nervous hands and flicked his eyes from one man to the other. "Did Piers say 'Lord Athlone?' " he asked after a hesitant pause. "You are a clan chieftain?"

"Of the Khulinin," Athlone replied shortly.

The Pra Deshian's expression melted in obvious relief. "Did you bring the sorceress? Is she here?"

Athlone jerked his head toward the door. "Outside."

"Ah, praise Elaja!" Sengi clapped his hands. "Please, bring her in. The warehouse is empty. She will be safe."

"What about our horses?"

"There is a closed shed in back I use for the dray horses. There is enough room and grain for yours. Grain, ah!" He smacked his forehead. "I'll be back." With that, he bustled from the office, deeper into the warehouse.

Piers met Athlone's eyes and shrugged slightly. "He's always been like that. Busy. But he's an honest man to his friends. He'll do what he can."

In a short time, the travelers settled their horses in the shed behind the warehouse and gathered in the office to wait for Sengi. He came back carrying a bottle and a tray of food. His eyebrows went up at the sight of all the people, their gear, and the dog.

"Goodness. I did not expect so many." He looked over them all, especially Sayyed and the little girl, and was rather puzzled. "Is the sorceress with you?"

Gabria stepped forward to meet him. She untied her scarf and lowered the veil from her face. "I am Gabria."

Sengi blinked at her, then he smiled with welcome and relief. "Your disguise is good, Lady. It hides your fairness like a leather bag can hide a jewel. Please, come."

The merchant, still carrying his tray, led the party into the main warehouse. Even in the darkness they could sense the vast size of the room and hear its echoing emptiness.

"My stock is low at the moment," Sengi said, directing them toward the building's rear. "The fon has not interfered with my business as she has with Khan'di's, but she has imposed heavy taxes on all of us to finance her plans for war. I expect more wool soon from the north country." He shook his head. "But that bloodthirsty woman will suck up all of my profits. If we do not act soon, she will destroy the economy of this city, and without the merchants . . ." He let his sentence trail off, then ducked into a narrow gap in a pile of big bales. The pile reached up out of the range of the lanterns, into the darkness that clung to the high ceiling.

From the smell, the clansmen realized the bales were wool fleeces packed and tied together. One by one, the travelers followed the merchant through the gap and into a narrow space as wide as two men side by side and twenty paces long. The wool bales and the warehouse wall surrounded them.

Sengi set the tray and his lamp down on a wooden crate. "I created this space two months ago after Khan'di left for the plains. I thought it might be useful. My workmen will be here tomorrow, but if you are quiet and stay out of sight during the day, you can stay here as long as you need to. I will care for your horses."

The men looked around the space dubiously. "Is all of this secrecy really necessary?" Bregan asked.

The wool merchant glared at him. "If the fon hears even a rumor that the sorceress is in the city, she will tear Pra Desh apart to find her."

Athlone nodded once and set his gear down. The others followed his example. Sengi looked around to be sure all of his guests understood his warning. "Now then, I must get some more food." Again he rushed away into the warehouse.

While the merchant was gone, the travelers piled their weapons and packs out of the way and settled down to wait.

Piers picked up the bottle, uncorked it, and sniffed the contents. "Andoran Wine," he said in delight. He found his own horn cup and poured a full measure.

The wine was being passed around when Sengi returned. More bread, cheese, sugared dates, and another bottle of wine filled his arms. Khan'di followed in his wake.

The others stared in amazement at the nobleman as he stepped into the lamplight. His travel-stained knee-length robes and leggings had been replaced by resplendent robes of brilliant blue and gold, trimmed with white furs and embroidered with gold threads. Rings clustered on his fingers, and a heavy gold chain with the dolphin emblem of the Kadoa family hung about his neck.

Khan'di smiled at their reaction. "I've been to court this afternoon to pay my respects to the fon. That is only right, since I am newly risen from my sick bed."

Athlone cocked an eyebrow. "Sick bed?"

"Before I left Pra Desh I had my seneschal spread the word

that I had fallen ill with a contagious disease. My healer has convincingly kept up the lie for all these weeks. Now, at last, I am well. The fon seemed disappointed."

"Was it wise to reveal your return to health now?" Piers asked.

"It was the only way I could learn what I needed to know." He rubbed his hands together. "We have come just in time." He waited for a few minutes while Sengi bustled around, bringing a jug of water, a couple of leather stools, and another lamp.

When the wool merchant was satisfied, he nodded farewell to his guests. "Until tomorrow. And, Piers, I hope you will tell me how you came to be among the clans. Good night."

When he was gone, Khan'di lifted the hems of his robes and sat down on a stool. The travelers helped themselves to the food and wine and gathered around him.

Khan'di hesitated another moment before he began. "The fon has accomplished a great deal while I was gone," he said. "The entire kingdom of Calah is now completely in her grasp. No one has seen the young prince for days. It is rumored she had him thrown in the pit beneath the dungeon. She has either beggared, bribed, or destroyed many of the old noble Pra Deshian families, and the merchant guilds are almost bankrupt."

There was a deep undertone of anger and sadness in his voice, and as Gabria listened to him, she began to understand that Khan'di's motivations were not totally selfish. He truly cared for his city and its well-being. He wanted to protect his power, influence, and wealth, but he also wanted to protect Pra Desh. Perhaps Khan'di had earned Piers's distrust those many years ago in the old fon's court, but now he was striving to save his city—not just himself—from the ravages of a merciless ruler.

Khan'di went on. As he talked, he restlessly employed his hands to emphasize his words. "As you may have noticed, the fon has not yet begun her invasion of Portane. She has delayed in order to gather more draftees and mercenaries for her army.

I haven't heard yet when she plans to strike."

"In about four days," Piers said quietly.

"Where did you hear that?"

"In a tavern. It was full of soldiers. They were complaining about leaving home."

Khan'di drew a deep breath. "Four days. That doesn't give us much time."

"Does the fon still have Branth?" Gabria asked.

"As far as anyone knows. No one has seen him, and there has been no sign of any sorcery."

"He's preparing," she said, her voice strangely distant. The memory of her dream-vision flared up in her mind, and she shuddered.

Athlone set his cup down and leaned back against a bale. "Preparing for what?"

"The strike against Portane?" Bregan suggested.

"Quite likely," said Khan'di. "I have arranged a meeting for tomorrow with the masters of the city's guilds. I am going to try to stage a distraction that will help you enter the palace unnoticed. There you should begin your hunt for the exiled chieftain."

Athlone looked at Gabria. Her face looked so pale, it worried him. "How do we get into the palace?" he asked the nobleman.

"I am working on that, too," Khan'di replied. "I have an idea, but I need to locate someone whose help we need."

"So what do we do in the meantime?" Athlone demanded.

"Wait. A day or two at most. We must move before the fon attacks Portane. If she breaks the alliance of the Five Kingdoms, the whole region will go to war. But we have to lay our plans well. The fon is no fool." He rose to go, his fine robes gleaming in the lamplight. "I will be back tomorrow if I can." He hesitated, his dark eyes on Gabria's face. "If I don't come back within two days, please try any way. We cannot leave a sorcerer in the fon's hands."

Wordlessly Gabria held out her hand, palm up. The nobleman nodded and placed his hand, palm down, atop hers.

They locked fingers in the clan gesture of sealing a vow.

Khan'di, satisfied, left their hiding place.

Athlone waited until he heard the warehouse door shut before he turned to Piers. "Is what he said true?"

The healer put his empty cup down and spoke with regret. "Unfortunately, yes. Perhaps even worse than he told us. The city is on the verge of open rebellion. The people here are terrified, but they've been abused as much as they're likely to stand. One spark will set them off."

Athlone looked thoughtfully at the gap where the Pra Deshian had disappeared. "Do you think Khan'di is about to provide that spark?"

"Undoubtedly."

"I just hope we don't get caught in the flames," Bregan muttered. The others could only nod their agreement.

11

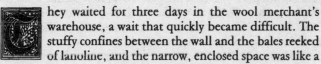hey waited for three days in the wool merchant's warehouse, a wait that quickly became difficult. The stuffy confines between the wall and the bales reeked of lanoline, and the narrow, enclosed space was like a prison to the roving plains people. They could not talk or move around during the day for fear of attracting attention. At night they had to stay within the confines of the warehouse. Sengi brought them food and water, told them what news he knew, and gave them what he could to make them comfortable, but he could do little to ease their anxiety and restlessness.

Khan'di sent a message saying he was safe and still working on his plans. However, he could not come himself. Gabria worried about him and about all of her companions. The tension was wearing everyone thin.

She was particularly worried about Piers. The old healer spent most of his time drinking Sengi's wine and speaking to no one. He sat against the wall, his eyes staring at a place far away and his body sagging with the sadness of his memories. For his sake, Gabria prayed that their wait would soon end.

On the evening of the third day Khan'di finally returned, soon after the last laborer had left the warehouse. He brought with him a map of the palace and an old, ragged man wearing only a goatskin tunic and rough leggings.

Once again the travelers stared at Khan'di when he came into their hiding place. His rich court robes were gone, replaced by a shirt of chain mail, leather pants, greaves of steel, and a bright blue surcoat embroidered with his dolphin emblem. His normally controlled features were alive with anticipation. He held out his arms and cried, "Tonight, we go to war!"

The travelers gathered around him, everybody talking and asking questions at once. Piers rose from his place at the wall and came to join them.

"Please! I will explain," Khan'di called over the noise as he waved them to silence. Concisely, he told Gabria and the warriors of his plan to attack the palace and free Branth from the fon's clutches. When he was finished, they stared at each other and then at him in shock at the sheer audacity of his plan.

"Are you serious?" Gabria asked.

"Absolutely. The pieces have all fallen into place."

"You are relying on a great many pieces," Piers remarked dryly.

Khan'di's eyes blazed. "This plan will not fail."

"Can you trust him?" Athlone demanded, pointing to the old man who had been standing silently through the discussion.

"He is a hillman from one of the ancient tribes that live in the Redstone Hills. He has given his word that what he knows is true and that he will lead you where you need to go. He will die before he breaks his vow," Khan'di replied.

Athlone rubbed his chin. "Fair enough." He paused. "Will you give us your vow, as well?"

The nobleman locked eyes with the chieftain. "I swear to you before my god," Khan'di said, "and upon the honor of my family, I will raise the people and create the biggest riot this city has ever seen."

The chieftain studied Khan'di's face and was satisfied with what he saw. Gravely he responded, "Then I swear before our gods that we will follow your plan and do our best to find Branth."

"And kill him if you have to," Khan'di added. "Do not leave him in the fon's hands."

Athlone nodded. "Agreed."

"What about the fon?" Gabria asked.

"If all goes well, you won't have to worry about her. She'll be too busy fighting an uprising."

Piers looked dubious. He was the only one who completely understood the risks Khan'di was taking by trying to bring a city like Pra Desh into an armed revolt. "Are you so certain the army will mutiny?"

Khan'di slapped the hilt of the sword hanging at his belt. "Enough will. The fon's regulars won't, but the mass of the army is conscripted and they want no part of a war with the other kingdoms."

Piers shook his head. "My old friend, your audacity is astounding. Elaja be with you this night."

"And you, Healer." Khan'di looked around at them all. "Tomorrow we will meet again. Until then, good luck, my friends." He started to leave, then turned and squeezed Gabria's arm. "Thank you, Sorceress," he murmured.

When he was gone, the clanspeople gathered their weapons and their gear. They packed everything they did not need and stacked the bundles by the wall.

Piers exchanged his long healer's robe for a tunic and a pair of Athlone's woolen pants. He strapped his healer's bag to his belt. He was standing, staring at the floor when Gabria touched his arm. He nearly jumped out of his skin.

"Are you all right?" she asked, for his face was sickly pale. He seemed to have aged ten years the past three days.

The healer licked his dry lips. "I never thought I'd go back there. To the palace. Did I tell you my daughter died in that dungeon?"

Gabria's heart went out to him. "You only told me the fon had killed her."

"Tortured her," he corrected bitterly.

"We have Khan'di's map. You don't have to go."

Abruptly Piers's head snapped up. "Yes, I do, for both our sakes. Besides, a guide works better than a map."

"I am glad you think so, too," she said with relief and gratitude.

"What about Tam and Treader?" Sayyed asked. "Do we

leave them with Sengi?"

The words were barely out of his mouth when Treader start-ed barking madly. Tam sprang forward and wrapped her arms around the Turic's waist. Gabria, Athlone, and Sayyed clamped their hands over their ears to stifle the racket, but they could not silence Treader's frantic pleas ringing in their heads.

"He's trying to tell us that Tam is terrified to be left alone," Gabria cried over the barking.

A strange, sympathetic look came over Sayyed's face, and he bent down to pry Tam from his side. The girl transferred her grip to his neck, and he lifted her easily, whispering something in her ear. Treader's barking immediately stopped; the big dog's tail wagged. Sayyed glanced at Athlone and shrugged. "When I was small, I did not like to be alone either. I'll keep her with me."

The chief agreed, and Tam shyly smiled her thanks.

When they were ready to go, Athlone signaled to the hill-man to lead the way. The old man could not speak their lan-guage or even the polyglot language of the wharves and streets. He merely grunted and loped out of the warehouse, expecting the others to follow.

The moment the travelers stepped out of the warehouse, they sensed something was different in the warm spring night. The city seemed to crackle with the tension of a coming storm. A strange brightness from thousands of torches glowed in the market streets and guild houses. An angry murmur was heard in the distance—the blending of thousands of feet marching on stone, the shout of angry voices, and the clash of weapons. On the hill above the warehouses, horns blared from the bar-racks and the palace.

The company had to hurry to keep up with their guide. Al-though he was old enough to be Athlone's grandfather, the hillman was as wiry and agile as a mountain goat. He led them down into the dark maze of warehouses, wharves, and custom houses. Several times the travelers had to press back into the shadows as groups of shouting, angry people, brandishing knives, pikes, or homemade weapons, marched past. Khan'di's uprising had begun.

Before long, however, the noise and activity were left behind. The hillman led his charges out of the harbor district and up into the hills behind the old city wall.

Gabria glanced up as they hurried through the darkness and was surprised to see the sky was clouding over. Lightning flickered far out over the sea. She hesitated. A strange feeling teased the edges of her senses, but whatever it was, it was too faint for her to recognize. Putting the feeling aside, she hurried after Athlone.

The hillman was leading Gabria and her companions up the southern end of the Redstone Hills, a place where the steep slopes were weathered by harsh seas. Deep gullies slashed down between the hills, and rock-strewn crags reared up over the stony vales. Not many people came up into the hills, for the inhospitable slopes made traveling difficult. Only the ancient tribes lived in the rugged lands, raising their half-wild goats, unimpressed by the vast city that lay at their feet. And only the hill tribes knew the extensive honeycomb of caves and passages that riddled the heart of the hills.

The night was completely dark by the time the party came to a narrow ravine about half a league behind the city wall. Clouds had totally obscured the moon and stars; the only illumination came from the distant lightning and from the torches and fires in the city below. The travelers turned to look back at Pra Desh and were surprised to see rivers of torchlight flowing up the streets toward the old city. The mobs were on their way to storm the gates.

Gabria knew the success of this part of Khan'di's plan depended on the fon's army; if enough men mutinied, the gates could be seized and held open, and the citizen mob would spend their rage against the palace. It was too difficult to see what was happening around the barracks and walls, but it seemed obvious from the noise and the blowing horns that there was a great commotion going on. Gabria could only pray that Khan'di's plot was proceeding as hoped before she followed her companions down into the night-dark ravine.

They stumbled along the rocky bottom for a time before the hillman came to a stop in front of a huge fallen boulder. The massive piece of granite was half-buried in the side of the ravine and camouflaged with brush and rock debris. Without a word, he began to pull the brush away to reveal a narrow, black hole behind the boulder. Quick as a squirrel, he darted in, leaving the others standing outside.

"Is this it?" Gabria asked suspiciously.

The old man poked his head out and waved angrily for them to follow him. One at a time, the warriors, Gabria, and Treader squeezed through the hole. Tam kept her hand glued to Sayyed's, but she followed without a complaint or a whimper into the pitch-black cave.

The party crowded together. The cave was barely high enough to allow them to stand upright and so lightless they could not see the walls, the floor, or each other's faces. No one dared to take a step.

Suddenly a tiny light flared in the back of the cave, where the hillman crouched over his flint and steel. To everyone's relief, he lit several rush torches and passed them on to the men, then he gestured again and vanished into the darkness.

"I think I'd rather be back in the warehouse," Bregan said, staring up at the low-hanging ceiling.

Athlone gripped the warrior's arm as he started after the old man. "So would I," he said. "So would I."

In single file, with Athlone in front and Bregan bringing up the rear, the party followed its silent guide down into the depths of the earth.

* * * * *

Not far away, in a small, dark room beneath the palace, the fon stood with her back against a wall, watching Branth through narrowed eyes. She was not certain he was ready to attempt the spell again. She would have preferred to wait a few more days to summon the gorthling and launch her army at Portane, but only a short time ago she had received word that a mob had risen in the streets and was marching toward the palace. The army, the soldiers she herself had levied, had betrayed her and opened the city gates to the rabble.

She gritted her teeth, and a snarl of hatred twisted her thin mouth. Oh, heads will roll for this treason! The streets will run with the blood of traitors, she swore to herself. Already the mob and the rebellious factions of the army were fighting the guards still loyal to her. The battle raged in the streets near the palace, too close for complacency.

The fon slammed her palm against the wall. It was that damned Khan'di Kadoa's doing. She could sense his hand in this treachery. She should have disposed of that conniving vermin before this, but he had the support of the powerful merchant guilds and she had not been ready to face them in an outright confrontation.

Well, after this night the Kadoa family would cease to exist and the merchant guilds would come groveling. This night she would have her gorthling.

In front of her, Branth leaned over the big, leather-bound tome on the table and emotionlessly recited the words of the spell. An aura of power was building around him. Even the fon could see the faint greenish glow. Yet the man seemed unaware of anything but the book and the small golden cage on the table before him.

His voice intoned unceasingly through the long, complicated spell. In the light of the small lamp the fon could see a sheen of sweat on his forehead, and a faint trembling begin to shake his frame. Then, to her delight, a tiny pinhole of light appeared, hovering in the center of the cage. She knew from reading the book that the pinhole was an opening to the immortal world of gods, dreams, and powers unlimited. Slowly Branth straightened and began the second part of the spell: to widen the door and call a gorthling out of his realm.

The fon watched impatiently. She wanted to rip the hole wider with her own hands and snatch the gorthling into her domain, but she had learned enough to know the evil creatures were dangerous and had to be handled with care and cunning. She curbed her frustration and watched as the hole began to open bit by bit. When the hole was a handspan wide, Branth suddenly stopped.

"What's the matter, you fool?" hissed the fon. "Go on!"

Branth appeared to struggle within himself, ready to say something. His mouth worked, and his hands tightened into fists. "No," he groaned between clenched teeth. "Not this."

The fon stepped forward, her eyes blazing. "Do it!" she screeched.

The exiled chief blanched. The days of drugs and mind control slowly destroyed the feeble vestiges of his will. Like a living corpse, he turned back to the tome and the cage.

As he resumed the spell, the green aura grew brighter. The magic about him increased, widening the hole of light in the cage. The light grew so dazzling that the fon had to shield her eyes.

She blinked once before she saw it.

A small, wizened face peered through the hole. The fon held her breath. Branth had lost control of the creature at the same point during his previous attempt at the spell. This time, however, he did not fail. He chanted the incantation, slowly drawing the gorthling out of his world and into the cage.

The creature came cautiously. He climbed out of the hole one limb at a time and finally crouched, snarling, in the corner of the cage. Branth said a command, and the hole of light snapped shut.

The fon's eyes took a moment to adjust to the faint light, then she stared in horrified fascination at the thing in the golden cage. The gorthling resembled a small, incredibly ancient monkey with long, twisted limbs and the face of a mummified child. The fon suppressed a shudder as the creature turned his inhuman eyes toward her. Before he could look her in the eyes, she turned away and snapped to Branth, "Put the collar on the thing."

This was the most dangerous part of the spell, for the sorcerer had to put a collar of gold on the gorthling in order to properly control him. However, the tome stated in no uncertain terms that the gorthling could not be touched by human hands. The fon did not know why, and she did not want to find out.

Branth reached for a long-handled clamp and the golden collar. He had practiced many times with the clamp upon various small animals; he was now quite deft at snapping the collar around creatures in the cage. But neither he nor the fon had counted on the cunning and agility of the gorthling.

He zipped around the small cage, avoiding the collar and Branth's best efforts with ease. Time and again the sorcerer almost had the collar about his neck only to have the gorthling slip away. The fon grew wild with frustration. "Collar the thing!" she screamed.

At that moment, the collar dropped off the clamp and fell to the cage floor by the edge of the bars. Branth, his consciousness numbed by the fon's poisons, simply reacted. He stuck his fingers through the bars to retrieve the collar.

"No!" the fon shrieked.

Even as she sprang to grab the man's arm, the gorthling pounced on Branth's fingers and sank his teeth into the man's skin. Branth howled in agony and tried to yank his hand through the bars, but the gorthling clung to his fingers, ripping off chunks of flesh and gulping them down.

The taste of blood drove the creature into a frenzy. He screeched and clawed and tore Branth's hand to shreds. The man writhed and screamed so violently, the fon could not get near to help him.

All at once, the gorthling fell quiet. The fon stepped back, her eyes wide in dread, for the creature was beginning to grow. His body pulsed with a lurid red light and blood dripped from his mouth. In just a moment he was as big as the cage.

Appalled, the fon backed to the door, leaving Branth to his doom. She hoped the creature would remain confined in the cage, yet even as her hands fumbled for the latch, the gorthling burst the bars of the gilded prison. Branth and the fon froze.

Still clinging to the sorcerer's bloody hand, the gorthling turned his eyes on the fon. Across the room, the fon caught his gaze and was drawn into the black depths of his eyes. She found herself gazing into an evil she never knew existed, an evil so powerful and destructive it swallowed her rational thought and emptied her mind of everything but total terror.

Her shriek filled the small room. Somewhere in the shreds of her consciousness a tiny spark of self-survival remained and guided her hand to the door latch. The gorthling reached his clawed hand for the oil lamp on the table. Instantly he flung the lamp at the woman as she wrenched the door open with a desperate heave and fled screaming down the corridor.

The oil lamp smashed against the wooden door, its oil bursting into flames on the wood and running in fiery rivulets down to the floor. The gorthling curled his lips in malicious glee, then he turned his eyes to Branth.

The clansman had not moved. His face was racked in fear and pain; his hand and lower arm were in bloody shreds. Still he could not force himself to move against the horror of the gorthling.

The creature stopped growing the moment he burst out of the cage, and now he crouched like a big cat on the table, clutching Branth's arm. "Where did you learn your spell, Sorcerer?" the gorthling rasped.

Branth shook violently at the sound of the dry, vicious voice. He gasped an answer and pointed to the book on the table.

The gorthling looked. "The *Book of Matrah*? No wonder you failed." He cackled. "Who are you?"

The sorcerer forced himself to answer, "Lord . . . Branth of Clan Geldring."

"A clansman. You would be. Only clansmen have ever called for my kind." He sank his claws deeper into Branth's arm. "Where are we?"

Branth whimpered. "A palace. In Pra Desh."

"You are not in your own land. Why is that, little chieftain?"

"I was exiled."

"Oh ho!" the gorthling sneered. "Your people have banished you. How sad. Perhaps I shall change that. It might be interesting to visit your clans." He laughed, the sound as bitter and raw as acid.

The creature's laugh was more than Branth could bear. He collapsed to his knees, sobbing and shrieking for mercy.

"Mercy!" the gorthling screeched. "I know nothing of mercy. But I know that you, little chieftain, are mine!"

Without warning, the creature sprang for Branth's face. The man fell over backward onto the stone floor, gibbering in terror and clawing at the thing on his head. The beast clung with grim determination. Smoke swirled about them, and the gorthling's eyes blazed in the light of the fire.

The gorthling's body began to pulse again with a lurid red glow. The being forced Branth's mouth open. The Geldring shrieked one last time in despair before he fell deathly still. Inch by inch the gorthling worked his way into Branth's mouth. The creature looked out once from between the chieftain's teeth and chuckled with satisfaction, then the man's mouth snapped shut and the gorthling disappeared from sight.

The room was quiet except for the crackle of the fire on the burning door. The fire had spread across the floor and now touched the pile of straw on Branth's pallet. The flames leaped higher. Smoke swirled out into the corridor.

Within Branth's body, the gorthling began his metamorphosis. Swiftly the creature melded his form into the sorcerer's body, joining his life to Branth's heart, muscle, and bone in a symbiosis that could be broken only by death. Once the union was complete, the gorthling had total control of the man's body and brain.

In the process, Branth's soul was destroyed. The gorthling stripped his victim's mind of all thoughts, memories, and dreams and inserted his own cunning and intelligence. As Branth's brain was emptied, the gorthling retained a very superficial knowledge of the chief's memories and emotions. One emotion in particular caught the gorthling's interest: hatred. There was a vestige of a very powerful hatred and resentment for one particular magic-wielder. Unfortunately, the gorthling could not clearly understand the jumbled human memory. Perhaps in time he would learn the identity of that magic-wielder. For now the gorthling had other things to think about.

Branth's body flinched and jerked upright. The gorthling opened his eyes. Branth's normal arrogant gaze was gone, consumed with his mind and soul. In its place was a glint of inhuman evil.

The gorthling stood up, slowly testing the muscles of the new form he had invaded. Other than the injured hand, which the gorthling could heal over time, the body was basically fit and healthy. The creature grinned. In his normal shape, the gorthling had no power of his own, only the ability to enhance other forms of power. However, once he tasted blood, he was able to inhabit a mortal body and add his powers to the new host's own abilities. This body had potential, especially with its inherent ability to wield magic. A great deal of damage could be done to this world before anyone became aware of his true identity.

First, though, the gorthling had to find out more about the people who lived here. In the immortal world beyond the realm of the dead, he had been distantly aware of this world and the human beings who trampled the earth. He had noted the course of their history in a faint, disinterested fashion, paying only slightly more attention to the clanspeople who had the unique ability to wield magic—a talent granted to them by Valorian, the Hero-Warrior and rumored half-human son of the goddess, Amara. Only a magic-wielder could have called the gorthling to the mortal world, and only a magic-wielder could sent him back. If he was going to stay here in this big, powerful body, he would have to find all of the clan sorcerers and destroy them. Particularly the one that caused his host, Branth, such hatred. That magic-wielder had piqued the gorthling's curiosity.

Something crashed behind the gorthling, causing him to

whirl around. The wooden door was lying on the floor, consumed in flames. The gorthling looked around at the spreading fire. Usually fire did not bother him, but this body did not
like it; the creature coughed and drew back from the heat.

Then he remembered the woman. She had been standing
by the door and had seen him arrive. She knew what he was.
There was no other option; he would have to find her. Gleefully snatching a torch stub from a bracket on the wall, the
creature lit it. Branth's ruined hand was painful, but the
gorthling had experienced worse pain before. He grabbed the
Book of Matrah from the table, darted past the burning door,
and sprang out into the corridor.

A staircase lay ahead. Laughing aloud, he ran up the stairs
and through the corridors of the lower palace levels, setting
fire to everything that would burn.

*   *   *   *   *

"Oh, gods," Gabria gasped. "Did you hear that?"

At the sound of her voice, the party stopped dead in the
black tunnel. They had lost track of how long they'd been
stumbling, crawling, climbing, and scrambling after the old
man through the endless maze of crevices, tunnels, and ca-
verns. The cold, damp blackness was wearing on them all.
They looked around nervously.

"Hear what?" Piers whispered.

They remained frozen, their ears straining through the impenetrable darkness. The old man looked back impatiently.

Gabria clamped her hands over her mouth to stifle a scream
as a wave of terror engulfed her. She sagged back against Piers,
trembling and light-headed. She heard Tam begin to whimper.

Sayyed and Athlone said together, "What was that?"

"What was *what*?" Bregan said too loudly.

Gabria felt her heart thudding in her chest. She was breathing heavily from the shock, but the unknown terror was sub-
siding as quickly as it had come. "I don't know. Something

happened. Close by. Something horrible."

The chieftain held up the wavering torch. "Did you hear a sound just then, Sayyed?"

The Turic shifted nervously. "I sensed it rather than heard it. It was hideous!" He bent down to reassure Tam and to hide the tremor of fear in his face.

Gabria drew herself up and tried to shake off the terrible remnants of her horror. "Athlone, we'd better hurry. I think that may have been Branth."

The party went on, faster now, driven by the urgency of Gabria's fear. The old man led them through another narrow passage, around a rock fall, under a stone ceiling so low they had to crawl on their hands and knees, and into a tiny, rough chamber that seemed hardly more than a wide crack in the earth.

The hillman said several incomprehensible words and pointed to the back of the cave, then he turned and disappeared into the darkness before anyone realized what he was doing.

"Wait!" Athlone yelled, springing after him, but the man had already ducked down another crack and was gone.

"By Surgart's sword, I'm going to strangle that little rat if he left us lost down here," Athlone cursed. He strode to the back of the chamber to the spot the hillman had indicated and found another slender fissure on the rock wall. Carefully he squeezed through. There was a long moment of silence before his voice came back to the others.

"Come this way."

Gabria and the others pushed through the narrow crack, came around some boulders, and found themselves in what seemed to be an enormous cavern. They could not see very much of the lightless space, for their feeble torchlight was swallowed by the towering blackness. A cold silence surrounded them. With great care they edged out across the floor. Only Piers remained frozen to his place, his eyes staring sadly into the dark.

Although she did not have a torch, Gabria walked forward a

pace to see what she could discover. Her shin abruptly slammed into a very sharp rock. "This is ridiculous," she snapped. Raising her hand, she called out a command and a ball of bright light formed over her head.

Every man there jumped like a stung horse.

"Good gods, Gabria," Athlone yelled. "Don't startle us like that!"

The four Khulinin warriors stared at the light and at Gabria in mixed disbelief and alarm. She looked back at them apologetically. She regretted being so precipitous with her spell, but the frustration of near-blindness and the pain in her leg drove her to act without thinking of what anyone's reaction might be. They were not used to her sorcery, and the sudden ball of light had been a shock.

Bregan finally shook his grizzled head and tossed his torch to the ground. "Have you got any more of those lights, Lady Gabria?"

Her smile to him was dazzling, and in just a few moments four balls of light hung in the air over the mens' heads. Their glow revealed the details of the entire cavern.

Their first impressions had been right; the cavern was huge. As they looked around, it became obvious that, while most of the cavern was natural, a great deal of human labor had been spent smoothing the floors and enlarging the walls. Some unnatural features had been added, too: cages, stocks, chains on the walls, a huge wheeled rack, a forge, and several other unidentifiable machines—all thankfully empty.

"Gods," Athlone shuddered. "It's a torture room."

Without warning, Piers gave a grief-stricken moan and ran forward. In the center of the cavern was a hole, and the healer stumbled to the very edge. He fell to his knees and leaned precariously over the rim.

"Oh, Diana," he groaned.

"Piers!" Gabria cried. She ran to him and tried to draw him away. The hole appalled her. It was a smooth-sided pit that fell away into a terrifying blackness. A faint, putrid odor rose from the unseen bottom.

"She's down there," the healer said, his voice sinking in despair. "The fon's executioner took great delight in telling me. Diana wouldn't confess to poisoning the old fon—even when they tortured her. They condemned her anyway and threw her down there. My poor Diana." He leaned against Gabria, covered his face with his hands, and wept. "All these years," Piers cried. "All these years. I never truly believed she was dead . . . until I saw this pit."

Gabria finally understood. So many things he had said and done fell into place: his flight from Pra Desh, his refusal to talk about his family or his past, his abiding sadness. She knew how he felt. For the healer, looking into the pit must have been like standing on top of a burial mound and saying goodbye to those buried there. She held onto her friend and let him cry.

"There's nothing down there any more," she said softly. "Diana is gone."

He wept until the worst of his grief had waned, then he was quiet for a very long time, his gaze lost in the depths of the pit. Gabria could hear the others moving around and searching the cavern for an exit, but she stayed with Piers while he faced the phantoms of his past.

When at last he wiped his eyes on his sleeve and stood up, Gabria knew his grief was under control. The slow, painful process of healing his old wounds had finally begun.

"Was this why you went back to Corin Treld?" he asked, offering her his hand.

She nodded, took his hand, and rose to her feet. "The dead must lie in peace."

"And so they will," Piers answered wearily. Then he added, "Now, let's seek the living. I would still like to face the fon."

"Do you know the way out?" she asked.

"Yes. I was here years ago as a healer, but I've never had to stay in this place of torment."

Piers led her around the pit and headed for a wall where a rack of tools and instruments hung. The others followed. He found the door latch, which was cleverly hidden in the stone, and pulled the rack aside to reveal the door. They filed out, with Gabria's lights bobbing overhead, and found a staircase leading up to the next level. When the last warrior left the torture chamber, Piers looked once more into the black cavern and gently shut the door.

The party went upstairs to the prison level and paused to wait for Piers to take the lead. The travelers stared about them in horror. There were two corridors, one on either side of the stairs, lined with lightless stone cells. The walls were wet with moisture, and the floors were ankle deep in muck and excrement. The smell was horrible.

The noise was even worse. The sight of the lights had excited the prisoners, and they screamed and cried and shouted behind their bars in a hideous cacophony of misery and fear. Surprisingly, there were no guards.

Piers slowed as he came up the stairs, and his eyes widened. "I know some of those people," he exclaimed. "They don't belong here!"

Secen started toward a door, but Athlone stopped him. "Not now. We don't have time."

They hurried on, leaving the dungeon and its tormented prisoners behind, and ran up to the next level. Khan'di's map did not include the deep underground levels of the palace, only the fon's wing, where Branth was supposed to be. The party had to rely on Piers's eleven-year-old memories of the extensive storerooms, wine cellars, and cold storage rooms underneath the main floors.

The healer was surprised by how much he remembered. Released of his grief, his memories flowed out as clear and sharp as yesterday's hours. He was able to lead his companions up through the levels to a corridor just below the fon's wing of the palace.

Khan'di had told them that, according to spies, Branth was being held in one of the fon's personal storerooms. The healer took his companions through a large room full of vats and up a winding staircase. At the top, a solid oak door blocked their way. Piers reached for the door handle, but Treader began barking furiously and shoved himself between Piers and the door.

"Piers, be careful!" Gabria cried. "Treader says there's fire."

The healer looked skeptical, but he stood back from the stout oak door and very carefully opened it just a crack. A dark cloud of smoke billowed out, and the voracious roar of a fire out of control sounded clearly through the slight opening. Piers slammed the door shut.

"By the gods, what happened?" Athlone exclaimed.

Piers glanced around worriedly. "I don't know, but we'll have to go another way."

The travelers raced down the stairs and through the storage room. From there they took a different corridor, one that led up the main stairs to the palace's banquet hall. There they stopped and gazed about them in frightened astonishment. A few torches were still burning in the sconces on the walls of the ornate room, giving off enough light so the party could see the expanse of the entire hall.

The banquet hall was in the central block of the palace along with the waiting rooms, the fon's throne room, and audience chamber. To the north was the fon's wing of private apartments, chambers, and servants' quarters. Already the fire from below was spreading through the first floor of that wing. It was eating through the timbers and the north wall of the banquet hall. As it climbed to the floor of the second story, the blaze consumed everything in its path. Even as the travelers came to a stop and Gabria banished her lights, the banquet hall was filling with smoke. A muted roaring echoed through the room.

Palace guards, servants, and courtiers ran back and forth, carrying items out of the fon's wing; some were running in panic, others screamed or yelled orders. No one seemed to be doing anything to control the fire, and no one paid attention to the clanspeople in the hall.

"Lord!" Keth called. "Look at this." He was standing in a deep embrasure looking out a rare glassed window.

Athlone and the others joined him and crowded into the space. They followed Keth's gaze out to the high wall that encircled the palace. The fon's guards were struggling to keep the mob from the massive wooden gate that blocked the entrance. But while the travelers watched, the gate was forced open by a well-disciplined troop of men who pushed through and attacked the guards. A huge group of people flooded through the breached gate behind them. A roar of triumph rose outside, then the mob came to a stunned halt. A pale flash of lightning illuminated the hundreds of faces staring at the burning wing of the palace.

Thunder and a distant crash reverberated through the building. The smoke grew thicker.

Gabria turned back to the dim, smoky hall. A boy rushed by her carrying an armload of jeweled goblets. The sorceress coughed and stared through the open double doors into the fon's wing, where the dancing red and yellow glow of fire revealed more and more people fleeing with the fon's valuables.

Athlone drew back from the window. "Where is the fon in all of this madness?" he yelled above the noise.

"And where is Branth?" Gabria shouted.

12

iers." Athlone grabbed the healer's arm. "What are the chances Branth could still be alive if he is in those lower storerooms?"

The healer tore a strip off his shirt and tied it over his nose and mouth to filter out the thickening smoke. "None, Lord. The whole corridor was on fire."

"If the fon had moved him, where would she have taken him?" Athlone had to shout over the noise of the people and the increasing roar of the fire.

"If there was time?" Piers lifted his hands. "He could be in her apartments or in the guardrooms of the other wing. He could be anywhere."

The chief thought fast. "Then we'll have to split up. Search what you can, then get out fast. If anyone finds Branth, either bring him or kill him. Everyone understand?" They nodded. "Piers, you know this place. Take Gabria and Keth. Look where you think he is the most likely to be. Bregan, you come with me. We'll go upstairs to the fon's rooms. Secen, Valar, and Sayyed, you take Tam and the dog and check the other wing."

They hurried into their groups and started to leave. Only a few of the fleeing palace inhabitants glanced their way before rushing on.

"Don't wait too long to get out," Athlone shouted after the men. Gabria was about to follow Piers when the chieftain took her hand. He wanted to say something to her before they parted in the smoke and fire, but sensible words failed to come to mind.

Gabria looked into his face, still bruised, bearded, and smeared with mud and dirt. She pulled off the strip of cloth tied over her nose and mouth and lightly kissed his cheek. Then she ran after Piers and vanished into the smoke.

Athlone looked after her in surprise before a quirk of a smile touched his mouth. He gestured to Bregan and left the banquet hall to find the stairs leading up to the next floor.

As Athlone and Bregan disappeared in one direction, Piers led Gabria and Keth through a set of doors, down another dim corridor, and into the audience hall where the fon usually held her large public festivals, court functions, and celebrations. A few lamps were lit in the room despite the late hour, and Gabria looked around in amazement at the rich furnishings. The walls of the vast room were covered with tapestries, colorful banners, and hangings of silk embroidered with the ship emblem of Pra Desh. Padded benches and chairs lined the walls, and a huge fireplace dominated one end of the room. Gabria noticed the big room was empty and was already filling with smoke.

Piers came to the center of the room and slowed down to get his bearings.

Gabria grabbed his sleeve. "Where are we going?"

The healer continued to study their surroundings as he answered. "The fon should know where Branth is. If we can find her, maybe . . ." He paused as another crash reverberated through the palace. Screams echoed down the corridor. "Floor gave way," he muttered. He glanced at the stone walls. "It won't be long before enough floors collapse to bring down all the walls."

"Then let's hurry," Keth suggested nervously.

"Do you know where she might be?" Gabria asked.

Piers curled his lip. "If I know that woman, she's in the vaults trying to save the treasury." He hurried his companions out of the audience hall and into the first of the fon's two waiting rooms. These rooms, where supplicants waited for personal interviews with the fon in her throne room, were even more luxurious than the hall. They were filled with precious rugs, wallcases of delicate porcelain, handsomely carved furniture, and shelves of valuable books.

This room was empty of people, so Piers walked through to the next. That room was much like the first. Here, her personal secretaries usually screened the people who would be allowed in the fon's presence. At that moment, the only people in the room were two noblemen and one palace guard. The courtiers were older men in various stages of night dress, and they were shouting and frantically pounding on an arched wooden door. The guard was beside them, trying to hack at the door handle and frame with the point of his sword.

Piers came to a quick halt and cursed under his breath. The men had obviously been there for some time, because the door handle was splintered from the guard's blows.

"What is it?" Gabria whispered behind the healer.

"The vaults are behind the throne room and that door is the only way in."

The guard shouted angrily at the clanspeople, "What are you doing here?"

"Quit yelping and *help* us," one of the noblemen ordered, ignoring the newcomers.

The guard gave a sharp laugh. "You'll never get that door open. She's barred it from inside."

"She?" Piers demanded. "The fon?"

The guard glared at him. "Who else? Now, get out of here!"

Piers shoved past the guard, ignoring his sword, and shouldered into the group of noblemen. "I'll help," he said, adding his weight to the door. The courtiers looked startled but they wanted badly to reach their ruler, so they moved over to include him. All three threw their strength at the door, but the wood did not budge.

One of the noblemen sagged against the door. He was breathing heavily, perspiration dripping down around his round face, and his eyes were wide in fear. "I can't believe this!" he cried. "A riot in the streets, a fire in the palace, and she hides in her throne room. What are we going to do?"

More crashes sounded upstairs. Cries and screams filled the corridors beyond the audience hall, and the distant rumble of thunder sounded outside.

The frightened nobleman shoved himself away from the door and ran for the other room.

"Wait!" His companion shouted after him.

"You save the shrew," he cried and dashed out.

The other men looked at one another. The courtier gave Piers an odd glance before turning away.

"There is no other way in?" Gabria asked.

They shook their heads and bent to try again.

"Look out!" the guard bellowed, leaping sideways as a smoldering chunk of the ceiling collapsed where he had been standing. Smoke billowed through the hole, and the room was lit by the lurid glow from the flames in the timbers above the false ceiling.

"We'll never get this door open this way," the old nobleman shouted over the crackling of the fire.

"Are you sure she's in there?" demanded Piers.

The guard replied, "She ran by here a little while ago, before we knew of the fire." He shivered and gripped his sword. "It was strange. She looked wild! Just slammed the door and barred it."

Gabria stared at the door while the guard was talking, and in her mind she formed the words of a spell. "Piers, get out of the way," she ordered.

Before the two Pra Deshians could argue, Piers hustled them aside. Gabria raised her hand and concentrated on focusing her magical energy. In that moment she sensed again the strange feeling of growing power, and this time she recognized what it was: the latent magic in the area was increasing. The phenomenon was still not strong enough that she could identify the cause of the increase, so Gabria set the puzzle aside for now. She spoke the command for her spell. In a breath, the door collapsed into a heap of splinters and wood dust.

"Oh, Elaja!" the guard wailed, and he, too, took to his heels out of the room toward the audience hall.

"Nicely done, Gabria," Piers said thankfully.

"The sorceress?" the remaining nobleman gasped.

Gabria tried to reassure him. "We're here for Branth, nothing else. Do you know where he is?"

"Dead, I hope," the man snarled. He thrust his body into the open doorway and blocked their path. "I thought I knew you from somewhere," he shouted at Piers. "You're the healer whose daughter was condemned for sorcery! Well, you helped kill one fon, but you won't get this one."

Keth leaped past Gabria and lifted his sword. Piers held him back. He finally recognized the man. "Ancor, I had nothing to do with the poisoning and neither did my daughter."

The courtier would not listen. "Her own husband admitted it!" he yelled.

Piers shouted fiercely in reply. "And where is he? Keeping the prince of Calah company in the bottom of the pit?"

The old man blanched as if that thought had occurred to him in the past. "The fon told us his ship went down with no survivors," he said defensively.

Another chunk of burning ceiling crashed to the floor, setting rugs and a tapestry alight.

"Healer," Keth called, "we've got to get out of here."

"Not without the fon," Piers answered harshly, and he tried to push past the nobleman.

The danger of the fire and the anger on Piers's face made the old man frantic. "No! Leave this place," he shouted. "You are a traitor and your daughter was a murdering heretic!"

Gabria was watching her friend and saw something break in the normally quiet, gentle man. All of the fury, the guilt, and the sense of injustice he had been carrying within him for eleven years had been stirred up by the sight of the dungeon and by the flood of memories that engulfed him. That this insulting old man would dare call his beloved daughter a murdering heretic was more than Piers could bear.

With a roar of fury, the healer balled his fist and hit the nobleman in the face. The man fell like a poleaxed cow. Piers sprang over his body and dashed into the throne room with

Gabria and Keth close on his heels.

No sooner were they through the door than they all skidded to a halt. Their attention was drawn to a large, canopied throne that sat on a wide dais against the opposite wall. The fire had already reached this small, opulent room through the ceiling. Sparks and flaming chunks of wood were raining down, starting more fires on carpets, tapestries, and on the red canopy over the golden throne. Beneath the flaming canopy sat the fon of Pra Desh, her eyes staring horribly at the intruders.

Piers's fury still burned in his blood. Without a conscious plan, he snarled a curse and ran toward the fon, ignoring the smoke and flames.

"Piers, no!" Gabria shouted.

The healer lifted his hand as he raced up the marble steps of the dais, and he was about to grab the fon when she looked up at him.

The healer faltered. He hardly recognized the woman. Her face was twisted into such a mask of horror that he realized instantly she had slipped beyond the edges of sanity. Her eyes were empty of reason and filled with insensible fear. When she saw him, the fon cowered down into her seat, moaning and trembling in terror.

Piers stared at her with pity and astonishment. What had happened to turn this strong-willed woman into a crazed, fearful wreck?

He was about to take her arm when a large piece of the ceiling crashed down to the floor behind him. Piers whirled around and cried out. The wreckage had fallen on Gabria and the warrior. Frantically the healer ran back, dodging small fires, and dragged Gabria's body out from under the smoking chunks of timbers and paneling. Keth was still conscious and able to move. He crawled out by himself and dazedly helped Piers smother the smoldering sparks on Gabria's clothes and drag her to the slim protection of the stone doorway.

Piers breathed a silent prayer of thanks as he examined the sorceress. She had a bump and a cut on her head and was dazed, but she was already coming around.

"Piers," Keth yelled, steadying Gabria. "If we don't go now, we'll never get out."

The healer agreed. The rooms behind them were already burning, and the throne room was almost intolerably hot.

"I'm going to get the fon," he called. He started forward, when something caught his eye. He half-turned, and a man burst through the doorway, slamming into Keth and knocking the warrior sideways. Gabria cried out and fell. The man rushed past Piers, his eyes hooded in smoke and shadow and his mouth twisted in a maniacal smile. He had a large book under his bleeding arm.

There was something familiar about that man, Piers thought, then all sensibilities fled from his mind. Horror-struck, he stared at the fon. She had risen from her throne and was watching the stranger, terror warping her face into a hideous grimace. Just as the man reached her, she screamed a heart-tearing wail of despair. Piers saw the flash of a dagger blade in the man's hand. Before the healer could move, the man had grabbed the screaming fon by the hair, hauled her off the dais, and slashed her throat. Laughing gleefully, he flung her bleeding body to the floor.

In the waiting room behind the clanspeople, the Pra Deshian nobleman regained consciousness. He gazed at the body of his ruler for one horrified second before he fled.

The murderer saw the movement and raised his head.

"Branth!" Piers whispered, shocked to his soul.

The exiled clansman ignored him. Still clutching his bloody dagger, he bolted past Piers for the door. Keth tried to block him, but the man slashed wildly, cutting through Keth's tunic into his arm. The warrior fell back, and Branth ran, laughing, out of the throne room.

Piers pulled himself together. There was nothing more to do but get out fast. He and Keth took Gabria's arms and helped her out of the room. Behind them the blazing canopy collapsed over the golden throne.

Gabria was still woozy from the bang on her head, but she was able to walk. With the aid of Keth and Piers she hurried past the fires in the waiting rooms and into the audience hall. The hall, too, was hot and filled with smoke. They rushed through the hall and entered the corridors. The roar of the fire in the fon's wing assailed their ears.

"This way," Piers said, and he led them away from the sweeping flames. There was no sign of Branth or anyone else. The people had long since fled that part of the palace. Bending low, the two men and Gabria ran, coughing and gasping, along the dark corridors to the spacious front entrance hall in the center of the palace.

The huge double doors were open, and a strong draft blew in through the hall. Outside, Gabria could see hundreds of people milling around the gates and the wall, watching the great fire.

She and the men were about to go to the doors when a new sound caught their attention over the roar of the fire and the crack and groan of the dying palace. They heard a thud and a clash of blades by the opposite wall in the shadows of a broad staircase.

"Branth!" someone shouted in fury.

Gabria's heart froze. It was Athlone's voice.

The sorceress and Keth leaped forward at a run to find the source of the noise. They dashed across the wide, dark hall and found three men locked in battle in the shadows at the foot of the stairs.

Just as Keth shouted the Khulinin war cry, one figure broke away from the other two and raced for the door. What looked like a large book was tucked under his arm. A pale flash of lightning filled open doors, and the light revealed the man's face for only an instant. In that instant, Gabria recognized him.

"Branth!" she hissed furiously. Her hands rose instinctively, and she fired a bolt of the Trymian Force at the fleeing man. The blue bolt seared toward him, but Branth dodged around the door. Gabria's arcane force exploded on the wooden frame.

The gorthling's step hesitated when he realized a magic-wielder had attacked him. Unfortunately, it was too late to do anything about it. The gorthling's new powers were untried and there were too many people around. He had to get away from this place as quickly as possible.

By the time Gabria reached the door, Branth had already disappeared into the crowd of onlookers.

"Gabria!" Sayyed shouted behind her. She turned to see the Turic and his group running into the hall from a corridor in the south wing. She went to join them, and the whole party converged at the base of the stairs.

Gabria took one look at Athlone and Bregan and stifled a cry. Bregan lay on the bottom step, a bloody dagger buried to the hilt in his chest. Lord Athlone was leaning against the wall, coughing and groaning. No one said a word. Sayyed and Valar picked up Bregan, Secen put his arm under Athlone, and the whole party fled the burning palace.

They crossed the courtyard and took shelter on the far side of the wall. Somewhere in the north wing, a section of the roof collapsed and a huge portion of the front wall slowly crashed into the raging inferno. Sparks and flames soared high on the night wind.

For a moment, Gabria leaned gratefully against the cold stone and gulped in the clean night air. She was sick, dizzy, and utterly exhausted. Her head felt as if a stone mason was pounding on her temples. She ignored the curious onlookers and wished desperately for a drink. Tam pressed against her, trying hard not to cry.

Beside her, Athlone had sagged against the wall and was taking deep racking breaths to expel the smoke in his lungs. She reached over and clasped his hand.

"What happened?" she asked.

For a long time he could not answer. Finally, he croaked, "We searched upstairs as far as we could and found nothing. The palace was a bonfire."

Gabria took a close look at him and winced. His face was black with soot, his clothes were riddled with burns, and the soles of his boots were charred.

"We came down the stairs to get out and saw Branth in the hall." The chief struggled to stand straight. "We tried to stop him, but he was . . ." Athlone tried to find the right word. "Wild. He just leaped at us like a mad wolf. Bregan saw his dagger and threw himself in front of me." The chief's voice cracked, and he shook his head in grief and anger.

Gabria glanced at Piers, who was bending over the old warrior. The healer caught her eyes and shook his head. Gabria wanted to weep.

At that moment, Khan'di came through the crowd. The nobleman's clothes were spattered with blood, and his face was strained with worry and weariness. His smile lit up when he saw the travelers by the wall. "Praise Elaja, you are safe," he cried. His expression fell when he saw Bregan, but he had little time for sorrow then. Urgently he turned to Gabria. "Sorceress, we desperately need your help."

Gabria groaned. She did not feel well enough to help herself, let alone Khan'di. Nevertheless she stood up, hanging on to Tam for support, and followed the noblemen back around the wall to the entrance gate.

For a long time they simply stood and stared at the monstrous fire that was consuming the fon's magnificent palace. The city's fire brigade was frantically trying to protect what was left of the central block and the south wing, but the blaze was too much for their bucket lines.

Khan'di cleared his throat. "Sorceress, the fire is far beyond our control. Is there any way you can put it out?"

Gabria was stunned. The fire was so big, so powerful, she had never considered such a thing. It was easy to form globes of light or make a door turn to dust, but to quench such a vast inferno? She doubted that she had the skill or the strength.

Lightning flickered overhead, and she looked up at the sky. "There's a storm coming. The rain will put it out."

Khan'di followed her gaze. "I know," he said, "but it's moving too slowly. Right now the wind is whipping up the fire." He pointed to the burning roof where a strong gust swept sparks and burning debris into the air. "If any of that lands in other parts of the city, it could start more fires. Some areas are so old and full of wood that a single spark could start a conflagration that even a hurricane could not put out."

Gabria understood his fear, but still she hesitated. "Isn't sorcery still against the law in Pra Desh? What will all of those people do if I start using magic?"

The nobleman tapped his sword. "You still have my promise of protection. No one will dare touch you as long as you are under my care."

Gabria was silent. If there was only something she could do! She pushed her weariness and headache aside and tried to think. How does one put out a fire? Water was the obvious answer and water was coming, but not fast enough. She knew from her teacher, the Woman of the Marsh, that human magic-wielders were not strong enough to control something as powerful and unpredictable as the weather, so she could not manipulate the storm. Nor did she think she should try to direct the tremendous fire itself. What she needed was a spell that was uncomplicated and foolproof that she could keep under control, even in her weakened state.

The sorceress rubbed her temples with one hand and held on to Tam with the other. What was another way to put out a fire? Blow it out with a great wind. Dump dirt on it to smother it. . . .

Her mind focused on an idea. She knew fire needed air in order to burn. If the air was cut off by dirt or a wet blanket, the fire died out. Gabria realized she did not need dirt, all she needed was an airtight, arcane shell over the fire. The flames would fade, the sparks could not fly, and the city would be protected. All she would have to do is hold the shield until the storm broke.

The storm.

Gabria stared up at the black sky, and the strange feeling of growing power that she had sensed earlier burst into understanding. The thunderstorm was enhancing the powers of magic!

Magic existed in every person, animal, and thing. It lay

everywhere to be tapped by a human with the talent to utilize the power. Gabria realized, as the thunderstorm bore down on the city, that the magic around her was intensifying as if the vast forces of the storm were heightening the magical energy already present.

She looked back at the walls of the palace and wondered if she could make use of this increased power. She would need a lot of strength to hold a shield so big—strength she did not want to needlessly waste with Branth still on the loose.

"All right," she said forcefully and dropped Tam's hand. She heard Athlone and Sayyed come up behind her as she faced the palace and concentrated on the enhanced magic around her. The splinter in her wrist suddenly blazed with a ruby light from the power that coursed through her body. Slowly Gabria formed her spell.

She began her shield on ground level, at the corners of the two four-story wings on the north and south sides of the palace. Using every fiber of her skill and concentration, she created a protective arcane ward at each corner and carefully lengthened the wards up until they resembled glowing pillars of red light. She raised them higher—past the first floor; past the second; up to the eaves of the palace. Gradually the wards arched upward and joined over the center of the roof. Their red light was almost lost in the fiery glow of the inferno.

The crowd behind Gabria stood in amazement and watched the scene in awe. Sayyed's mouth hung open, and Tam stared wide-eyed in fascination.

Lord Athlone stood transfixed by the spell Gabria was creating. He knew she could draw on the invisible magic around her and shape it to her will, but this was the first time he could clearly see and understand what she was doing. To his amazement, none of his old fears and superstitions rose to hinder him. Instead, he was filled with a budding fascination and a desire to reach out and test the magic with his own hands. He could feel the power around him and within him; it coursed through his veins as naturally and cleanly as his own blood. The Khulinin chieftain stared at the sorceress and felt the grip of his doubts and reluctance for his own talent begin to weaken. Without intending to, Athlone edged forward until he was standing just behind Gabria.

Meanwhile, Gabria spoke quietly to herself to fix her intent in her mind. She raised her hands to complete the spell. The red pillars of energy began to glow brightly. They spread out, wider and wider from top to bottom, rapidly stretching out to encase the entire palace in an airtight, glowing veil of magic. In a matter of moments the shell was complete. The edges joined, overlapped, and sealed, and suddenly the noise of the fire was gone. The shell began to fill with smoke.

The courtyard, streets, and gardens around the walled palace erupted with noise as everyone began talking and gesturing at once. Ignoring the uproar, Gabria fought to concentrate and maintain her spell. Even with the help of the increased magic of the storm, she could feel her strength slowly draining away. She held on and prayed the rain would come soon.

Time dragged by. Although the trapped smoke made it difficult to see within the shield, it soon became obvious that Gabria's spell was working. No sparks or burning debris escaped, and, without fresh air to feed its monstrous energy, the fire was dying. Little by little the flames sank down and went out as the air within the shield burned away.

Gabria closed her eyes and forced her concentration to hold steady. She was growing weaker by the moment; the red light of the splinter in her wrist wavered.

Lightning burst overhead, and the thunder boomed only a heartbeat later. The wind gusted, the smell of rain heavy upon its blast.

"Here it comes," Khan'di said with a quiet note of triumph.

A raindrop spattered on Gabria's nose. More drops fell, and lightning seared the sky. The sprinkle soon turned to a deluge. Khan'di shouted in glee and raised his fist to the pouring rain.

Slowly, so as not to restart the fires with a burst of air, Gabria dissolved her shield, allowing the rain to wet the red-hot stone walls. Steam boiled out of the wreckage where the rain drenched the remains of the fire. The light and the intense heat were gone. Gabria took a deep breath of the cold, wet night air. She did not care if she was soaking wet, she was only thankful to be cool and alive.

All at once her dizziness and exhaustion caught up with her. She sagged into Khan'di and felt his arms catch her. She heard Sayyed and Athlone around her and managed a weak smile before her eyes closed and she sank into welcome sleep.

*   *   *   *   *

Gabria woke up suddenly and bolted upright on the bed. Something was wrong. Her heart was racing, and her eyes stared wildly around the room. Nothing about this place was familiar. It was big and airy and comfortably full of dark furniture, elegant wall hangings, and thick rugs. An embroidery stand sat by the far window, where sunlight poured into the room. A table near the bed was covered with bottles of perfume, combs, and boxes of jewelry. Even the big bed Gabria was in was different from anything she was used to. This room was obviously not in a treld.

Gabria took a deep breath. Wherever she was, she could not help herself by panicking. She tried to think. The last thing she could remember was the storm. She had no idea how she came to be in this strange place or how long she had been there.

She was about to get up when a small girl and a large dog burst through the door. They saw Gabria was awake and threw themselves at the bed in delight.

Gabria, laughing with relief, grabbed them both in a hug. "Hello, you two! Where is everyone?"

Treader barked, *They're eating. They say if Gabria awakens, she should come eat, too.*

Gabria thought that eating sounded like a wonderful idea. She hopped out of bed and looked down at herself in surprise. Her dirty, burned, wet clothes had been replaced by a soft nightdress, and her body and hair had been washed.

Tam bounced off the bed and twirled around to show Gabria the blue dress she was wearing, then she danced to a chair where a red outfit was draped over the padded leather arm. She brought the dress back to Gabria.

The woman was astonished. "For me?" She ran her hand down the fine, soft red wool. The dress was fashioned in a style she had never seen before: it laced at the sides so the bodice fit tightly over her figure, then fell from her hips in a loose, swirling skirt.

Delighted, she slipped the dress over her head and pulled the lacings tight. The dress fit her well. When she was ready, she followed Tam and Treader along a passage past more rooms and down a staircase to the main hall.

Unlike the fon's palace, which had a separate dining hall, most of the houses in Pra Desh were built with a large central room that was used for dining, entertaining, and family gathering. At that moment, Khan'di, Athlone, Sayyed, two of the hearthguard, Sengi, and several members of the Kadoa retinue were sitting at a large table, eating what Gabria guessed was the midday meal. Everyone sprang to their feet when she came down the stairs. She was secretly pleased to see Sayyed's grin of pleasure and Athlone's open look of relief and admiration.

Tam and Treader ran over to join Sayyed, while Khan'di strode forward to escort Gabria to his table.

"Gabria, I am pleased to welcome you to my house."

She could not help but twirl around to display her dress. "Do I thank you for this? It's lovely."

Khan'di smiled in paternal appreciation. He had not realized until now how pretty this woman could be. "We had to throw out your singed clothes. I merely replaced them. It was the least I could do." He led her to a chair and heaped her plate with spiced meat, cheeses, fruit, and fresh bread. Sengi poured a cup of light, fragrant wine.

Gabria waited until she had eaten her fill before she asked any questions. The men were glad to answer.

"Much has happened the past two days," Khan'di began.

"Two days!" Gabria exclaimed. "I slept two days?"

"A day and a half really," Sayyed corrected. "It was almost dawn when the storm came. You slept yesterday, and it is noon now."

The sorceress was amazed. She had not known the spell would exhaust her so much. "What about the palace?"

Khan'di said, "The fire is out completely. The north wing is totally destroyed. The south wing has smoke and water damage, and the roof has been burned in places, but it is salvageable. We plan to rebuild."

Gabria caught a note of suppressed excitement in his voice. "We?" she repeated pointedly.

Athlone replied for his host. "Khan'di Kadoa has been chosen by the guilds and the noble families of Pra Desh to be the new fon."

Gabria's face lit with a smile. "That's wonderful!"

Khan'di's satisfaction showed in every movement of his body and in every line of his face. "We are going to rebuild the palace as soon as the economy of the city has recovered. The fon's army has been disbanded, and her supporters are in prison. Luckily, her treasury was still intact in the vaults. We have already sent peace delegations to the other kingdoms. And—" he leaned forward and his hand slapped the table in glee "—we found the prince of Calah unharmed in the dungeons."

"How is that possible?" Gabria asked in surprise.

"The fon must have been too cautious to kill him immediately, so she kept him handy."

"But what about the fire?"

"The fire did not reach down very far. The doors protected the underground levels and enough air leaked in from the cracks and fissures in the dungeon to keep all the prisoners alive."

Sengi added proudly, "The prince will be restored to his rightful throne."

"And the feuding will begin again," one of the other noblemen chuckled.

Gabria took a sip of her wine. "What about the fon?"

"The courtier, Ancor, and Piers told us what happened." Khan'di curled his lip in distaste. "The remains of the fon's body were found in the throne room. She and her monstrous tools of torture were dumped in the pit. The dungeons have been emptied and sealed."

"What of Bregan?" she asked softly.

Athlone frowned. The loss of his friend still pained him deeply. He could hardly believe the old warrior was gone. "He will be buried this afternoon. He has won back his status and honor as a Khulinin warrior."

She nodded and looked away to hide the blur of tears in her eyes. "Has anyone found Branth?"

There was a long silence; Gabria guessed the answer.

"The city guard did not recognize him in time," Khan'di said heavily. "He stole a horse and slipped out of the city. He was seen riding north."

The sorceress leaned back in her chair and stared at the far wall. Her responsibilities to Khan'di and Pra Desh were fulfilled with Branth's departure from the city. Everyone would have preferred to have him in chains and ready to face the city's judges, but despite their best efforts, the man had slipped away.

Gabria chewed her lip as she thought. She had two choices now: she could let Branth go and return home in time for the clan gathering, or she could pursue him and run the risk of missing the important council of chieftains. Her first inclination was to let Branth escape. She was tired of traveling and ready to go home. She wanted to settle her problems with Sayyed and Athlone, then attend the council and persuade the chiefs to change the laws against magic. The clan gathering was the only time in the year that all eleven chiefs met to create or change the laws that governed the clans. If she was not at the gathering this year, the chiefs could easily ignore the matter of sorcery or even vote against it.

Unfortunately her better judgment disagreed with her first inclination. The King Stallion had warned her that someone was experimenting in evil magic, and her vision had confirmed it was Branth. Back in the caves two nights ago, when she had sensed that great terror, she felt Branth had done something horrible. But what? A fearful, nagging doubt pricked her mind, and she remembered the look of bestial cruelty on his face in the throne room. The exiled chief was gone from Pra Desh, but he still had the *Book of Matrah* and was still very dangerous.

Gabria swallowed her disappointment. She rose and said to Athlone, "My lord, I have to go after him."

For a moment, the Khulinin chief did not answer. He had already guessed how she would choose. Although he was proud of her determination and courage, a small cloud of foreboding darkened his thoughts. The feeling of terror he, too, had sensed in the cave had lodged in his mind, and he was badly frightened for Gabria. Worse, he knew that the only way he could help her against Branth was to learn sorcery himself.

To Athlone's surprise, the idea did not unsettle him. When he had watched Gabria standing alone, smothering the fire and protecting Pra Desh, he had realized that he had made a mistake. Athlone had known for a year that he had the talent to wield magic, a talent that could be used for great good, and he had ignored it.

The chieftain stood and bowed slightly to their host. "Thank you for your earlier invitation, but we will be leaving as soon as possible."

Khan'di's shrewd glance went from the chief to the woman as he said, "I did not expect anything less."

*   *   *   *   *

They buried Bregan that afternoon in the hills above the city. The travelers and the new fon escorted the warrior's body up the steep trail to a high peak that overlooked the grasslands far away in the purple haze.

They built a bier of logs and arrayed the warrior's body in his mail shirt, his golden clan cloak, and his finest clothes. The hearthguard laid his weapons by his side; Lord Athlone put a gold armband on his forearm as a symbol of Bregan's restored honor, and Gabria and Tam brought the bag of salt, the loaf of bread, and the water bag that the warrior would need for his journey to the realm of the dead.

They doused the bier with oil and set it ablaze. As the flames climbed toward the sun, Gabria sang the women's prayers for the dead. It took several hours for the fire to die to embers. Only then did they cover the ashes with a high mound of dirt and mark the grave with a spear and helmet as befitting an honored clan warrior.

It was almost dark when the party rode back down through the hills, leading Bregan's horse. Halfway to the city, they paused while Gabria slipped off her horse and walked ahead a few paces into the twilight. She put her fingers to her lips to whistle a piercing call, but Tam's shrill call sounded before Gabria had drawn a breath.

The little girl's whistle was enough. Three Hunnuli cantered out of the darkness. They gathered around Gabria, nickering their pleasure, then Eurus went to greet Athlone and the colt trotted to Tam.

"It is safe to come to the city," Gabria told Nara. "Khan'di has granted us safe passage." She clambered up onto the mare's back and threw her arms around her neck. "I missed you," she murmured.

And I you, Nara replied. *But it's not over, is it?*

"No," Gabria answered sadly. "Not yet."

13

wo days later the travelers rode with Khan'di and an escort through Pra Desh to the outskirts of the city. They passed the guardpost at the city limits just after daybreak and stopped in front of an inn to make a final check of their baggage and to bid farewell to Khan'di. Everyone was rested and ready to go. The packhorses were fully laden, and all of the gear had been retrieved, cleaned, and repaired.

When Piers dismounted to tighten his saddle girth, Khan'di approached him.

The new fon looked ill-at-ease, but he came straight to the point. "I should have asked you this before, Piers. Now is my last chance. I would like you to stay in Pra Desh. I need a healer in the palace. Please come back."

Gabria and Athlone, overhearing the fon, looked at one another and held their breath.

The healer did not answer immediately. He was startled by Khan'di's offer and, for just a moment, he was tempted. He had spent his three days in Pra Desh in the houses of healing, helping with the wounded from the fighting and the injured survivors from the fire. In that time he realized he missed the big city and all it had to offer. He had much to learn of the new medical advances the Pra Deshian healers had made in the past eleven years.

Then he thought of the clan that had become his family, of the lovely valley where his own tent overlooked a shining river, and of the sorceress who had helped fill the aching loss left in his heart by his daughter's death. He settled his clan cloak over his shoulders and shook his head. "I can't."

Khan'di gripped his arm. "Piers, I know you're angry with me, but I did not know what the old fon's wife was planning that night. Please believe me! I found out later that the woman had given me something to make me ill in order to get you out of the way. By the time I learned of this, you were already gone from the city. I'm sorry!"

Piers clasped his old friend's hand in his own. For eleven years he had been plagued by uncertainties about Khan'di's deliberate involvement with the old fon's murder. Hearing the truth at last healed a few more of his lingering scars. "It's not that," he said, his thin mouth smiling. "I have finally put my daughter to rest. It's just that I have made a new home with the Khulinin. I want to go back."

Khan'di searched the healer's face, judging the sincerity of his words, then he nodded. "A few years ago I would have called you a fool to leave Pra Desh for the barbarian outlands." He shot a glance at Gabria and Athlone mounted on their Hunnuli. "Now I know better. Long life, my friend. Come visit when you can."

The nobleman stood back as the healer mounted. The clan horses shifted restlessly, pawing and sidestepping with excitement. They knew it was time to go.

Khan'di strode over to Gabria. He laced his hands behind his back and looked up at the woman with fondness. "I promised you a reward. Are you sure you won't take it?"

"We have no need of it. Your generous supplies are enough." She gestured to the hills beyond the city. "Just watch over Bregan's mound, will you?"

"With pleasure, and thank you, Sorceress. May Elaja go with you."

The woman nodded sadly. In spite of her earlier reservations, she had come to know and like this man in the two months they had traveled together. She would miss him. "And with you, Fon Kadoa."

Khan'di went to stand with his escort. "Don't forget," he called. "Take the north fork two leagues from here. My scouts said Branth is following the river."

Athlone raised his fist in salute to the fon, then he waved his arm to his own party. Eurus half-reared and leaped forward. His huge hooves pounded the paving stones. Nara and the other horses fell in behind, following the stallion down the caravan road. Khan'di raised his hand in farewell and watched until the horses disappeared.

* * * * *

From the shadows of a deep copse of trees, the gorthling watched the farm through Branth's eyes, his anticipation growing with each passing moment. It was one of the large communal farms that were common throughout the Five Kingdoms. Early morning sunlight washed the three white-walled cottages and their outbuildings in a pale golden light. Smoke rose from the chimneys, and chickens clucked around the yard.

As far as the gorthling could see, all of the men had gone to the fields, leaving four women, a girl, and several children in the houses. He licked his lips. For five days now he had avoided human contact while he learned the uses of his new body and studied the basic spells in the *Book of Matrah*. His ruined hand still bothered him, but it was healing well. Now he was ready to try out his new skills.

The door opened in one of the cottages, and a slender young woman walked out, carrying a bucket. The gorthling felt the bloodlust stir his thoughts and his body. He avidly watched the woman carry her bucket to the well and lower it down to fill it. The stirring grew to an urgent desire, and he stepped out of the shadows. His eyes began to glow with a vicious red gleam as he slid his dagger into his sleeve and began to walk toward the farm.

* * * * *

Gabria watched the plumes of smoke rise from the smoldering ruins of the farmhouse and tried not to look at the scorched bodies lying in a row under the apple tree. She was horribly shaken by this destruction. This was the third communal farm along the river that she and her companions had found in this state. The first farm in Calah had been appalling. There had been four men and a boy murdered by what Gabria immediately recognized was the Trymian Force. The horribly mutilated body of a woman was dumped in a wagon, and neighbors located the remains of the rest of the three families in the burned and gutted cottages. Even the outbuildings had been put to the torch.

Since that afternoon six days ago, the travelers had tracked Branth out of Calah and through neighboring Portane from one destroyed farm to another. They had ridden as fast as possible, but Branth stayed tantalizingly out of reach. Secen, one of the best trackers in the Khulinin, estimated the exile was only a day in front of them. However, Branth stole a horse whenever he needed a fresh one, and he never stopped long enough for anyone to catch up with him.

Gabria leaned forward to rest her arms on Nara's mane and let her head drop. She was tired and felt wretched. She could hear Athlone nearby, talking to the farmers who had found the smoking ruin earlier that morning. Piers and Tam were waiting by the road, while Sayyed, Treader, and the warriors searched the surrounding fields for some sign of Branth.

The woman let her eyes wander toward the charred cottage. It looked so hideously incongruous against the backdrop of the flowering orchard and the warm, bright spring day.

Athlone returned to her side. "It's the same as the first two," he said grimly. "No one saw anything. They think it happened late last night, but they don't know how or why. There is sign of only one man, and no one can believe only one man could do all this." The chief began to pace angrily between the two Hunnuli. "That's what I don't understand. I can believe Branth would steal a horse, food, or gold, and he would kill a man or two who stood in his way. He is a vindictive, arrogant brute, but he never did anything violent that did not serve his own ambitions." Athlone gestured at the ruins. "This kind of cruel, senseless destruction is not like him."

Gabria agreed. "Something happened to him in Pra Desh," she said. "Something changed him."

"Any ideas?"

"I wish I knew."

Athlone turned on his heel and mounted Eurus. "We'd better find him before he burns every farm in Portane."

Just then they heard a shout, and Secen came running toward them from the fields north of the burned barn. "Lord Athlone," he yelled, "we found his trail."

"Still heading for Rivenforge?"

"No, he's turned west. He's going toward the river."

"Sacred gods," Athlone cried, "please lead him to the plains!"

Branth's move away from the heavily populated farmlands was what the chieftain had been hoping for. Branth was exiled from his people and condemned to death for the murder of Lord Savaric and the part he had played in Medb's war. Nevertheless, Athlone thought the familiarity of the plains and the lure of home would lead Branth away from the Five Kingdoms. Athlone had no authority in the kingdoms or any experience with their laws and customs. He would prefer to be in clan territory when they caught up with the renegade.

Gabria, however, accepted Branth's move west with mixed feelings. She wanted him out of the Five Kingdoms, but if he entered the Ramtharin Plains and clan jurisdiction, her use of her arcane powers would again be problematic. She could not use her sorcery without breaking her vow to the clan chiefs. If she and her companions caught up with Branth and he fought them with his magic, she would have to dishonor her vow and face the wrath of the clan chieftains. It was not a pleasant prospect. With a sigh, she grasped Nara's mane and sat back while the big mare trotted after Eurus to find the other riders.

The travelers found Branth's trail and followed it across the farmlands and vineyards of Portane. The trail remained clear—Branth was making no effort to hide his tracks—and it continued west to the Serentine River. At the riverbank, the tracks turned north, parallel to the river, then, at the first ford, the tracks vanished into the water. Secen checked and found the trail on the far bank. Branth had crossed the river into the plains.

The travelers forded the wide, muddy river easily, struck the trail, and hurried on. Gabria looked out over the rippling plains with pleasure. The season was ripening to summer, the time when the plains were the most beautiful. The grass that clothed the treeless hills grew thick and green. Wildflowers of yellow, red, and white bloomed on every slope and in every hollow. The few trees close to the creeks that wandered here and there were in full leaf, and arching above it all was a clear, glorious dome of azure.

For five days Gabria and her companions trailed Branth, drawing no closer to the elusive exile. To Secen's annoyance, the trail remained clear, but it meandered all over the region. Branth backtracked, circled around, and wandered back and forth as if looking for something.

At one point he skirted very close to Bahedin Treld before turning northwest. Most of the Bahedin would have left for the gathering at the Tir Samod by this time of year, but the elderly and the very young often remained behind. Athlone pushed his party on without rest; they could not afford to lose Branth's trail.

After a day of running west, Branth angled north. His trail did not falter from that path, as if he had finally decided on a destination. The pursuers followed, but the farther north they rode, the more nervous they became.

"I don't like this, Lord Athlone," Secen said as he knelt to study the tracks left by Branth's horse. "If he keeps on this way, he'll ride straight into—"

"I know what lies to the north," Athlone interrupted sharply. "Moy Tura."

Just the name of the infamous ruined city sent a shudder down the chieftain's back. He looked north over the open plains, as if he could see across the leagues of grass to the ancient city of the sorcerers. He had heard many tales of the fabulous metropolis, and those tales were enough to keep the heartiest of clan warriors away from the place.

"How far is Moy Tura?" Sayyed asked uneasily.

"Seven leagues, perhaps. Enough distance that Branth might veer off and miss the ruins," Secen replied.

"I hope so," said Keth. "I don't want to find out if the tales about that place are true."

"Maybe we'll be lucky, Lord," Secen said as he remounted. "Maybe one of those legends will eat Branth for an evening meal."

The others laughed, and they set off again on the exile's trail, everyone hoping that the man would go anywhere but Moy Tura.

* * * * *

Far to the north of the Khulinin hunting party, a lone rider kicked his weary horse into a trot and rode up the slope of a high tableland. "It has to be here somewhere," the gorthling hissed. He had been searching for days for the sorcerers' city and so far, had not even seen a road that might lead to it.

He cursed his vague memory. The gorthling knew Moy Tura was the center of arcane learning. All of the clan magic-wielders went there to study their craft. If any man knew who and where all the magic-wielders were, he would be in Moy Tura. The only problem was the gorthling did not know exactly where the city was located, and Branth's memories strangely did not include anything about Moy Tura.

The gorthling curled a lip. He was growing tired of this fruitless search over empty land. He wanted to find Moy Tura and its sorcerers and destroy everyone who could possibly ruin his plans. He still wanted to locate those clans who had exiled his host's body—there would be perverse pleasure in wreaking revenge on them—and there was also the mysterious magic-wielder who had kindled such hatred in Branth's memory. It would be interesting to track that one down, too. But first, he wanted to find Moy Tura.

The gorthling urged his horse on, faster and faster, until it finally reached a decent vantage point. He reined the animal to a stop and sat looking at the view before him. There was not much to see. The huge, treeless plateau stretched away for leagues without features or landmarks to break its level expanse. The gorthling rode on. His instincts told him the city was close by, but he could see nothing that looked like a well-populated metropolis. There was only grass and sky.

A little while later the gorthling rose in his stirrups and caught sight of something rising out of the plain far ahead. He rode toward it. As he drew closer, he saw more details and features. There was a high, crumbling wall, and behind it he could see buildings, towers, and parapets, but they were all in ruins. What was this place?

It was not until he rode to the enormous entrance and saw the two huge stone lions laying in the rubble that he realized where he was. They had guarded the city since its birth, or so the stories said.

Viciously he reined his horse to a stop. What had happened? The gorthling could see now that Moy Tura had been destroyed. The entrance gates had been shattered by a tremendous explosion and most of the buildings had been razed. The streets were full of rubble, wind-blown debris, and weeds. As far as he could see the only life here was a rat, some magpies, and a swarm of flies. Even the land around the city was empty and barren. Where were all of the magic-wielders?

The gorthling cursed and urged his reluctant horse into the ruins. There was still time to search the place before dark. Perhaps he could find some clue to the whereabouts of the sorcerers. There had to be a few left to pass on the inherited talent or his host body could never have summoned him. The gorthling rode forward and disappeared into the dead city.

*   *   *   *   *

"Are you sure he went in there?" Gabria asked as she stared at the broken walls casting shadows in the early morning light.

Secen nodded, his face pale under its tan.

The travelers were silent as they gazed about them in nervous curiosity. They had arrived at the plateau late the night before, but they had not tried to enter the city for fear of losing Branth's trail in the dark. Now it was the dawn of a warm, breathless day, and Branth's tracks led directly into the old ruin.

Just in front of the riders, the entrance lay open, its gates in pieces. A stone lion crouched nearby, cracked in two, resting on the rubble.

Piers studied the lion curiously. "I thought there used to be two," he muttered. "The stories always mentioned a pair."

Athlone took a deep breath. "Let's go," he called. Eurus, his ears pricked and his nostrils flared, walked warily into the city. The others came behind, keeping close together as they passed the fallen lion and the piles of rubble at the gateway. The ruins closed in around them.

The party silently followed the tracks of Branth's horse through weed-choked streets, around crumbling houses and wind-torn towers, past empty shops and decaying walls. Grass grew in every available chink, and piles of broken stone lay everywhere. Here and there a few fallen statues or shattered fountains could be seen in the ruins, attesting to the grandeur of the once-proud city.

Gabria was amazed by the remnants of beauty that still survived in the desolation. Moy Tura had not been a large city, even by the standards of two hundred years ago. It had been a close community of people dedicated to the art of sorcery. They had built what they thought was the greatest, most magnificent city in the known world.

That was the tragedy, Gabria thought to herself. All of their beauty, wisdom, and power had not protected their homes from the jealousy, greed, and anger of the outside world. The sorcerers who had lived here had been too isolated from their kin. They had put themselves on a pedestal and had ignored the warning signs when the pedestal started to crack.

According to legend, the city was betrayed by a sorcerer, a bitter man who had told the clans of the secret ways into the city—ways that skirted Moy Tura's deadly magical defenses. The man was, in turn, betrayed by a chieftain. He, along with all the other sorcerers, were massacred. It took the gathered clans only one day to destroy the city. For two hundred years it had lain, slowly sinking into dust, hidden behind a shroud of fear and terrifying legends.

Gabria's thoughts were still on the past when Sayyed rode close beside her and drew her out of her reverie.

"I hope all the tales about this place aren't true," he said. His horse snorted at a rat that scurried past.

Gabria shivered and watched Treader chase the rat into a pile of stones. "So do I. There are some particularly nasty ones: ghosts, a guardian, a sorcerer's curse, hidden traps for unwary looters, and evil beings that lurk in the city at night."

"That guardian," the Turic said, looking nervously around. "Even the Turic tell the story of Moy Tura's guardian."

"The Korg?" Piers said behind them. "No one has proven that it exists."

"What's the Korg supposed to be? Doesn't that word mean lion?" Gabria asked.

"Yes, it was an ancient breed of large lions that once lived on the plains. That lion at the front gate was supposed to be a korg, one of two that guard the gates," Piers explained. "But the guardian of the legends was a sorcerer originally—a shape-changer. He altered his shape to avoid the massacre and remained here after the city was destroyed. It is said he went mad and lost the power to revert to human form."

Gabria thought of the desperate sorcerer and stared sadly over the ruins around her. Living here would drive anyone mad. Even in the sunlight the shattered city was bleak and desolate. So much wisdom gone to waste.

The riders fell quiet again. Their voices seemed jarring and unnatural in the dead city. It was better to ride in wordless haste and get through there as fast as possible.

Before long they found the remains of Branth's night camp in an empty house. His tracks, still clear in the dust, continued from there deeper into the city.

The travelers were over halfway through the ruins when Nara and Eurus threw up their muzzles and tested the air.

Branth is close, the mare told Gabria, *and so is something else*. She sprang forward.

"What is it?" Gabria cried. All the horses broke into a canter along the road.

I do not know. It is strange. It is near Branth.

Treader suddenly erupted into a furious barking, *Ahead! The man is close.* He bolted into the arched entrance of a courtyard. The riders followed him at a run. They burst through one of four gateways into what had once been a spacious, stone-paved courtyard in front of a multi-columned temple. Now the court was full of debris, and the temple was a pile of collapsed walls and shattered columns.

"There!" Athlone shouted, pointing toward a horse and rider in the shadow of the temple.

The rider glanced back at them in surprise, then he whipped his head around and stared at something in the temple ruins. His horse reared violently.

The travelers raced across the courtyard, led by Treader and those riding the Hunnuli. They saw Branth more clearly now. He was trying to regain control of his terrified horse. He savagely yanked its head around and whipped it forward into a frantic lunge just as a strange, fearsome beast sprang out from the fallen stones of the temple. A huge paw swiped at the horse's rump and missed. Branth wheeled his horse around a pile of stones, screeched in triumph, and sent his mount bolting out of the courtyard through another gate.

Snarling with rage, the beast turned to face the oncoming riders. Its body was half again as large as a Hunnuli's, but it had teeth like curved daggers and a great, tangled mane tumbling about its hideous face.

"The Korg!" Piers cried. "It's the missing stone lion."

Athlone reacted instantly. "Split up! Get out of here!"

The riders obeyed, for everyone could see that no weapon of theirs would make a dent on the stone flanks of the huge lion that faced them. They turned and rode desperately for the several gateways behind them. The beast roared in fury; its eyes glowed with an uncanny yellow light as it raced after the fleeing horses.

Before Gabria realized what he was doing, Sayyed slowed his horse and turned in the saddle. His hand raised, he fired a very pale blue bolt of Trymian Force at the lion. The feeble energy bounced off the beast's face, stinging it into a greater frenzy. It leaped forward faster.

"Sayyed, get out of here!" Gabria screamed.

The Turic's expression turned to horror, and he fled after the others. The warriors and Piers were already riding through the entrances. Gabria and Tam on Nara, Athlone on Eurus, Treader, and the colt were together in the courtyard when the lion finally caught them.

Gabria immediately created a wall of magic around her companions. The lion slammed into the invisible barrier and rocked back on its haunches. For just a moment, its yellow eyes blinked in stunned surprise, then it roared and paced along the front of the barrier, looking for a break in the wall.

In the brief respite provided by the shield, they made a dash for the gateway from the courtyard. In that time, Gabria also made up her mind to stop the creature, but without endangering Athlone. Quickly she told Nara what to do. "Hang on!" she yelled to Tam. The girl's arms tightened around Gabria's waist.

Just as Eurus reached the edge of the courtyard, Gabria dissolved the wall of force. Nara swerved sideways with Treader and the colt beside her, and Eurus galloped through the arch before Athlone realized what had happened.

The stone lion did not hesitate. It turned after the mare and followed her as she galloped back toward the temple. Gabria fired a powerful blast of Trymian Force that exploded on the lion's chest. The energy knocked the beast back, but it did no real damage. The lion was up and after the horse in a heartbeat.

Nara lured him on. She dashed out of the courtyard through the arch where Branth had gone and led the stone lion on a frantic chase through the ruined city, farther and farther away from their companions. Gabria kept the beast enraged with arcane blasts, but she could not kill it.

At last, the colt and Treader began to tire, and Nara looked for a place where they could hide and rest. They ran faster to put more distance between themselves and the lion, then they ducked into a maze of tumbled buildings and clogged streets. They lost sight of the lion for a moment, but its roar of frustration echoed behind them. Nara kept going until they saw another, smaller temple. The place was half-buried in the rubble of the fallen building beside it.

"In there!" Gabria cried. "The gods will protect us."

Nara stopped at the entrance to let her riders dismount, and the little group hurried into the cool shadows of the temple's interior just as the lion bounded into the street behind them. It snarled furiously, a grating sound that overwhelmed the silence of the ruins.

Tam and Gabria held their breath. They and the animals pressed back into the shadows of the small room while the hideous lion stalked by. The beast's weight made the stones of the temple tremble. It hesitated near the entrance to the ruined building, yellow eyes staring malevolently, then passed on down the street. The thud of its footfalls slowly faded out of earshot.

Gabria threw her arms around Tam and hugged her tightly. They settled back into the dim, dusty temple, their ears straining to hear any more noise from the Korg. Time passed slowly. Now and then Gabria heard the lion roar in the distance, and she prayed to Amara that her companions had made it out of the city safely.

While they rested, Gabria had a chance to look around their little shelter. The temple was bigger than the one in which she had spent the winter, but it, too, was simple and unadorned. The only real difference between the houses of worship—apart from their state of repair—was a magnificently carved stone altar. Even under the dirt and cobwebs, Gabria could see the detailed design. One large figure on the front of the altar caught her eye in the pale light filtering through the doorway. She scraped off the dirt from the stone and smiled to herself.

"Look at this," she whispered to Tam and Nara. The girl and the mare picked their way to her side. She showed them her find—a large relief of a man mounted on a Hunnuli stallion. From the lightning bolt in his hand, Gabria knew the man was supposed to be Valorian. The clans' Hero-Warrior had used the power of the lightning to give the Hunnuli their remarkable resistance to magic.

Nara moved around Tam to get a better look. As the mare did so, her hind hoof slipped on a loose slab of rock. She lost her balance, fell sideways, and crashed into the altar.

"Nara!" Gabria cried in alarm. To her immense relief, the mare staggered to her feet and shook herself ruefully.

I am bruised but unhurt, the mare reassured her. *I should watch where I am stepping.*

Tam grabbed Gabria's sleeve and pointed to the altar. The big stone altar had appeared to be a solid chunk of white marble, but the Hunnuli had knocked one side loose. With an exclamation, Gabria scrambled over to look. The whole side of the altar was a cleverly hinged door.

Gabria pulled the door open and peered inside. At first she saw nothing but dust in the dark interior. She reached gingerly into the cavity, feeling the cold stone and dirt beneath her fingers. She lifted the only thing hidden in the altar's interior with great care and laid the object on the floor. Whatever it was, it was heavy and wrapped in a stained piece of fine linen.

Gabria looked at Tam and the two grinned at each other like children with a present. The colt pushed close for a look.

Nara snorted. *Are you going to unwrap it?*

Her fingers trembling slightly, Gabria pulled back the fabric to reveal a mask of solid gold. She dropped the linen and stared. It was the face of a man, beautifully wrought and polished to a brilliant shine. In wonder she reached out to touch it. A strange tingling tickled her fingers, and she froze, her fingertips still resting on the golden surface. A faint pulse of power vibrated out of the mask into her hand. She had sensed power like that in the healing stone Piers sometimes used and in a brooch Lord Medb had once given Lord Savaric. It was the power of magic.

Without a second thought, she wrapped the mask back in its linen cover and tied it to her belt. "It's time to go," she said.

Do you know what the mask is? Nara asked as the little group moved to the door.

The sorceress shook her head. "No. But it is a prize too precious to leave here."

They slipped outside, and, after Treader and Nara made sure the area was safe, Gabria and Tam remounted. They tried to head back the way they had come. It was not long, though, before Gabria realized they were completely lost.

Gabria glanced worriedly at the sun. The day had passed to late afternoon. She did not relish spending the night in the old city with a living stone lion, Branth, or any other evil creature that might be loose.

She was lost in thought, pondering their unsettling situation, when Tam tapped on her shoulder. The little girl pointed to a magpie flapping overhead. She closed her eyes and raised her hand toward the bird.

To Gabria's amazement, the magpie fluttered down to Tam's hand. It squawked loudly. *Go to the next street. Turn at the broken statue,* the bird said in her mind. The sorceress turned to the little girl and grinned proudly before she passed the information on to Nara.

They followed the magpie's instructions and wound through the ruins to a broad avenue. Far ahead they saw a high wall with an open arch. There was no sign of the Korg or Branth, but to Gabria's endless relief, she heard a shout and saw two riders come out of the shadow of the wall. A few moments later three more riders, Athlone among them, came out of the ruins and galloped toward the mare, whooping with relief. The entire party met near the wall and greeted one another in joy.

Secen, who had been scouting the area, came riding in

through the open arch. The warrior beamed with pleasure when he saw Gabria. "You're safe! Praise Surgart." He turned to Athlone. "I've found him, Lord. Branth left the ruins through another gate. The trail leads west."

"Let's be after him," Athlone said. "I have no desire to stay and see that Korg again."

The others wholeheartedly agreed, and they thankfully rode out of Moy Tura behind Secen. Somewhere in the ancient ruins, the lion roared a cry of anger and hopelessness. Gabria glanced back in sadness for the magic-wielders who had been lost in blood and violence. She prayed that such a thing would never happen again. Tightening the knot that held the mask to her belt, she followed her companions as they resumed their hunt for the renegade chieftain.

14

abria did not show the mask to her companions until the next day, when they were away from the desolate ruins of Moy Tura. The party stopped at noon to eat and rest the horses, and she brought out the stained linen bundle and laid it on the grass in front of her. The men and Tam gathered around to watch as she peeled the fabric away.

Gabria's heart pounded. She could hardly believe the beautiful, magical object was real until she could see it again in the light of day. She lifted the last linen fold aside to reveal the golden mask. Drawing a deep breath, she held the mask up to the sun. It sparkled and shone as brilliantly as it had on the day it was made.

"What is it?" Athlone asked in a hushed voice.

"It looks like a death mask," Piers said.

The sorceress ran her finger over the mask's cheek. Piers was right, it did look like a death mask. If that was the truth, then this man had been very important. The clanspeople only made death masks of those they deeply revered.

It was a handsome face, Gabria thought. Even in the rigid lines of the metal she could see the character of his features. There was strength in the planes of his jaw and forehead, stubbornness in his long nose, and humor in the lines around his mouth. When she looked closer, she could see the cleft of his chin, the trace of a scar on his forehead, and the arched lines of his eyebrows. The eyes were closed, but Gabria fancied the irises would be brilliant blue if they were open.

"It's magnificent," Piers said.

"What are you going to do with it?" Sayyed inquired.

Gabria shrugged and turned the mask over in her hands. "I don't know. It holds some kind of arcane power, but I can't tell what the spell is supposed to do."

The Turic rose to his feet and flashed his grin. "Too bad it can't talk."

The young woman nodded absently. She studied the gold mask while the others ate their meal and watered the horses, yet she discovered nothing that was useful. There were no inscriptions, etched designs, or markings of any kind on the metal. It was simply a man's face with an enigmatic expression. Finally she wrapped the mask back in its cloth and packed it with her belongings. For the rest of the day she mulled over the puzzle of the mask and still could find no answer.

*   *   *   *   *

The party trailed Branth for seven days after leaving Moy Tura and drew no closer to the elusive exile. He was moving faster now that he knew someone was following him, and the travelers were hard pressed to keep pace with him. To their dismay, he seemed to be pulling ahead of them as he trekked south across the plains. All of them wondered where he was going and what he would do next. On the eighth day they found part of their answer.

That morning dawned clear and warm, hinting of the hot afternoon to come. A light breeze blew about the hills, and meadowlarks dipped and fluttered after grasshoppers. The party was riding south, following Branth's trail along the flank of a long, low ridge, when the Hunnuli abruptly stopped and neighed an alarm.

Gabria, deathbirds! Nara warned her rider.

The sorceress saw the birds then—a large flock of black vultures circling low over a place beyond the hills ahead. "Look," she cried, pointing them out to everyone.

They galloped urgently toward the place, rode to the top of

a high hill, and looked down upon a small valley lined with trees. The birds were swinging over a clear space not far from a meandering creek.

"Oh, gods," Athlone breathed.

Gabria bit her lip to stifle the sick feeling that rose in her stomach. The scene in the clearing below looked hideously familiar to her.

"Keth, stay here with Tam and the horses," Athlone ordered. The warrior was glad to comply.

The rest dismounted and walked down the long slope to the clearing by the creek. Several vultures squawked and flapped into the trees.

Twelve people lay scattered in huddled, lifeless heaps—five men, four women, and three children wearing the orange clan cloaks of the Bahedin. Their carts and belongings were torn apart and thrown carelessly among the bodies. The horses and other animals were gone.

Piers hurried to examine them, but as he turned the mangled bodies over and checked their pallid faces, it became very clear they were all dead.

While the healer was occupied with the corpses, Athlone and the others looked for signs of Branth. They had little doubt that he was responsible for the massacre.

"They were traveling with full carts and their tents. They must have been latecomers trying to catch up with their clan on the way to the Tir Samod," Athlone said bitterly as he examined the wreckage of a cart. This slaughter sickened him. The Bahedin had long been allies of the Khulinin, and they had stood with Athlone's father against Lord Medb at Ab-Chakan.

Gabria's face was pale under her tan. "On their way to the gathering." She turned away from the body of a young woman and swallowed hard. Flies were swarming around the dead girl's face, and vultures had been pecking at her eyes.

Secen joined Athlone and said, "Lord, I can only find sign of one man other than the Bahedin. It is as we suspected."

The chief cursed. "Branth."

"The hoof prints are from the same horse we have been following, and the boot prints seem to match the ones we saw in Moy Tura."

Piers hurried over, his face strained and white.

"They're all dead," Athlone stated rather than asked.

The healer nodded. "Yesterday. They were tortured."

Secen looked sick. Athlone raised his fist and brought it down on the side of the cart. "Why! Why is he doing this?" he shouted.

Treader began to bark furiously. *Come! I am at the creek!* his barks told the magic-wielders.

At the same moment, Sayyed yelled, "Gabria, Lord Athlone, over here. Quick!" Something in his voice spurred Gabria and the men into an instant response. They ran toward the sound of the Turic's shouts and Treader's excited barking. As they passed beyond a copse of trees sheltering the riverbank, they came to a sudden halt.

Sayyed stood on the bank, holding the frantic dog by the scruff of the neck. In shocked silence, he stared at a corpse that had been impaled on a sword against the trunk of a tree. The man's body hung so high his feet did not touch the ground, and they could tell his death had been painful by his wide, staring eyes and the hideous grimace twisting his features. He was an older man, with a lined, weathered face. His filthy, bloodstained tunic had a golden horse, the emblem of a herdsman, embroidered on the left breast.

"I tried to loosen the sword," Sayyed said, his voice tight with fear and wonder. "But he . . . moved."

"That's impossible," Athlone snapped. "He's dead."

The chieftain reached out to grasp the sword pinning the dead Bahedin. He yanked at it several times, then, as Sayyed had warned, the man jerked to life. As Athlone fell back in horror, the hersdman lifted his head. His lifeless eyes stared down at the travelers, and the pain-racked mouth groaned a horrible, bubbling sound of agony.

The warriors backed away, their eyes wide with shock. Treader cowered down against Sayyed's feet. Only Piers stepped forward. He reached up to find the man's pulse.

"By the holy gods," Piers exclaimed, snatching his hand away. "This man *is* dead. His skin is as cold as stone. He has no heartbeat. Look, he's not even breathing."

"Greetings, hunters. I know you are following me."

They turned back to the corpse, who spoke again, his voice raspy and hollow. "I have left this message for you so you will know with whom you are dealing. If you are smart, you will turn back while you are still able."

The dead man looked from one clansman to another. "I was brought here from the realm of Sorh by one of your kind— Lord Branth. I intend to remain here. I have learned from the people who lie dead nearby that there is only one magic-wielder left in the clans, and only she *might* possess the power to challenge me. I intend to seek her out."

Gabria gasped, and Athlone moved closer to her.

The corpse added, "If you wish to find me, I am going to the gathering of the clans." The dead man emitted a harsh, hideous laugh. "I have plans for the people of Valorian."

Abruptly the herdsman's head jerked, his voice stopped, and his body sagged against the sword. There was a long, silent pause before Piers tentatively reached up and closed the dead man's eyes.

"Good gods, what was that?" Secen murmured.

"A spell," Gabria replied, her voice as hollow as the dead man's. She was staring at the corpse. Her skin had gone deathly pale, and her knees were weak. "Branth, or whatever he has become, put a spell on this man to speak that message."

"Whatever he has become," Athlone repeated. "What do you mean?"

Gabria's shoulders sagged. "It claims to be from the realm of Sorh. I'm not sure, but I think there is only one such creature that can be summoned by sorcery: a gorthling."

"What's a gorthling?" Sayyed demanded.

When the woman did not answer, Athlone said, "They're monsters from our ancient stories. They're supposed to be creatures of immortal evil."

"They're not just stories. Gorthlings exist," Gabria whispered. "The Woman of the Marsh warned me about them." Her eyes held a faraway look. She crossed her arms over her chest and took a deep breath.

The men were silent as they tried to absorb the meaning of what they had heard. Athlone and Piers moved to the tree to take the dead Bahedin down. This time when the chieftain yanked at the sword, the man remained lifeless, his soul forever lost to death. They pulled the sword free and gently lowered him to the ground.

They carried the dead herdsman to the spot where his fellow Bahedin lay. A vulture squawked as they approached the bodies, and a few others that had landed nearby sidled away from the Khulinin.

"What do we do with them?" Sayyed asked, indicating the dead clanspeople.

"Bury them," Gabria said flatly.

"We don't have time. That will put us farther behind Branth," Athlone reminded her.

She looked down at the dead herdsman. "Someone buried my clan when I could not. Maybe it was the Bahedin. We could at least burn them. Someone else can build their mound."

The chief nodded. As badly as he wanted to catch up with Branth—or the gorthling that had sided with him—he knew she was right. They could not leave the slain clanspeople to the scavengers.

The task took Gabria and the men the rest of the morning. Using wood from the Bahedin's carts, dead tree limbs, dried brush, or anything that would burn, they built a bier and laid the thirteen men and women side by side with their tools, weapons, jewelry, and the necessities for their journey out of man's world. Keth and Tam brought the horses down, and the little girl watched solemnly as Gabria sang the songs of the dead and lit the fire under the bier. The smoke rose high above the plains, its acrid smell driving the vultures away one by one.

By noon the party was on Branth's trail again, heading south. They rode hard, their anger and worry following at their heels. They found a place to camp at sunset in a hollow between two hills. Gabria built a fire, and everyone gathered around the bright warmth. No one felt like talking.

It was Gabria who finally broke the silence. She lifted her head and stared up at the brilliant stars overhead. "Athlone, I want to go see the Oathbreakers."

The men started in surprise.

"No," the chief said automatically.

Gabria continued to look at the sky, her mind busy behind her eyes. "I will go without you if I have to."

Athlone closed his eyes and swallowed the anger he felt at her defiant tone. "Why? Why them?"

"They may be the only ones who can help me."

"Help you what?" he demanded.

Gabria lowered her eyes and shook her head. "They have a few books from the days of the old sorcerers in their citadel. I think Seth might be able to help me find something I could use to fight the gorthling."

"How can you be sure this *is* a gorthling? All you have are the magic words of a dead man," Athlone said angrily.

"I'm not certain, but everything fits. Branth summoned something evil and now he is slaughtering every human in his sight. He has changed, we have all sensed that. I think he has been overcome by a gorthling. That's how they work; they possess a host body and wreak havoc using it as a tool."

"So why don't we kill its host body?" Sayyed suggested.

"We could do that, but a gorthling is immortal. It would simply take another body as host."

Athlone leaned forward. "Then how do we destroy it?"

Gabria threw her hands up in the air and cried, "I don't know! The gorthling is a creature of magic and must be fought with magic. That's why I must see the Oathbreakers."

The Turic gestured to himself and Athlone. "*We* are magic-wielders. We can help."

The woman shook her head wildly. "I can't teach you

enough to fight something as powerful as a gorthling. Look at what it did to all of those people. It would slaughter you. I couldn't bear that."

"And what if it kills you?" Athlone said. "Who will fight it then? Do you expect us to just stand by and watch you face it alone?"

Gabria felt her heart leap. This was the first time Athlone had spoken to her about using his talent. Nevertheless, she forced her excitement down and shook her head. She did not want him learning sorcery just so he could die at the hand of a gorthling. "Athlone, let's start by learning how to fight this creature. Then we will worry about who will destroy it."

Athlone drew a deep breath. "All right. We'll go talk to the Oathbreakers. Just you and I. The others will follow Branth so we won't lose his trail."

The hearthguard warriors protested. They feared the Oathbreakers, as did any sensible man of the Dark Horse Plains, but they were equally intent on fulfilling their duty to protect their chieftain.

"That's an order," Athlone told them. "There's no sense angering Seth and his fellow cultists by bringing all of you. Gabria and I will be all right. You'll have enough to worry about just keeping up with Branth."

The three warriors agreed reluctantly, and Gabria nodded with relief. She knew Sayyed was not happy to be left with the other warriors, but he, too, had to accept the decision.

Later, as she packed the death mask in the small bag of belongings she would take with her, the sorceress wondered if Seth could tell her something about the golden artifact, too. She dismissed that hope immediately; it was possible that the Oathbreakers would refuse to talk to her at all.

*　*　*　*　*

The Khulinin left their camp shortly after sunrise the next morning. Secen led his group south on Branth's trail while Athlone, Gabria, and the three Hunnuli turned west to seek the citadel of Krath in the northern tip of the Himachal Mountains.

Athlone estimated it would take almost four days to reach the citadel, talk to Seth, and catch up again with the rest of the party. He hoped with all his heart that this trip to see the Oathbreakers was worthwhile. He had his doubts. The cult of Krath guarded their secrets jealously. They had gained the title Oathbreakers by forsaking their vows of fealty to clan and chieftain and shunning their own people for the desolation of their mountain temple. Even if they had the information Gabria sought, they would not help her out of loyalty to the clans.

Athlone could not stifle a cold feeling of dread at the thought of the Men of the Lash, as the cultists were known. A cloak of suspicion born of whispered rumors and stories of heinous deeds hung on the Oathbreakers' shoulders. Unlike the men of the clans, who worshiped two male gods, the Men of the Lash worshiped Krath, the dark sister of Amara. But where the goddess Amara embodied the positive aspects of femininity, her sister represented the dark, less predictable facets. Krath was the ruler of unbridled passion and violence, of secrecy and jealousy. Her power to destroy lay in ways that were either slow and subtle or sudden and unexpected.

Accordingly, Krath's followers became highly trained killers whose religious goals were to perform perfect murders in the service of their bloodthirsty mistress. The men used no metal in their arts. Their only weapons were their bodies, their whips, and their finely crafted killing instruments of leather and stone. It was said an Oathbreaker could snap a man's neck with his bare hands or remove a head with a flick of a vicious black whip.

The clanspeople looked on the cult with aversion and fear. It was not the Oathbreakers' bloodlust that the clans despised, but the subterfuge they practiced. Their silent, furtive, deliberate style of killing was incomprehensible to the men of the clans. The cultists, for their part, preserved their secretive ways. They had scorned the clans for generations and held themselves aloof in their secret stronghold.

As he approached that stronghold, Athlone missed Bregan's strong, solid presence more than ever. The loss of the warrior was a real blow. Athlone would have appreciated Bregan's level head and experience when the time came to deal with the Oathbreakers. The chief's hand tightened unconsciously around his sword hilt. If he had to, he would tear down the citadel of Krath stone by stone to get the help Gabria needed to destroy Branth. That murderer had too much clan blood on his hands to remain in this world.

The next day, Gabria and Athlone saw the gray-blue humps of the Himachal Mountains rise above the horizon. The Himachals were a much smaller mountain range than the mighty Darkhorns. They did not have the tall peaks and snow-covered summits, and they rose only to a modest height above the plains, yet their slopes were steep and rugged with an almost impenetrable wilderness of heavy timber and underbrush.

Fortunately Gabria and Athlone did not have to enter the wildness of the mountainside. The citadel of Krath was located in the northern end of the range, in the foothills not far from Geldring Treld. The citadel was not hard to find, but almost impossible to enter.

The weather had been clear and warm for several days, but that afternoon the wind shifted and began to pile clouds together. The horizon to the north turned iron-gray, its line edged with towering, white-capped clouds. Gabria and Athlone did not need to urge the Hunnuli faster to avoid the storm. The animals sensed the coming rain and picked up their pace. By late afternoon the riders spotted the citadel of Krath on a promontory a few leagues to the south in the tree-clad flanks of the mountains. They altered their route and hurried south ahead of the rain.

Before long, they came to an old stone road that paralleled the mountain peaks. Gabria and the chieftain recognized the stonework immediately as that of the ancient men, the Sons of the Eagle, who had conquered the plains long before the clans had arrived. The men from the west had also built the fortress

of Ab-Chakan, which lay only a few days' journey to the
south. The road ran past Ab-Chakan and the Isin River, then
vanished somewhere near Dangari Treld in the southern end
of the mountains.

For much of its length, the road was very old and concealed
beneath a net of grass and shrubs, but it was clear and easy to
follow in the rough foothills. Gratefully the Hunnuli took to
the road and hurried on.

Gradually they drew closer to the citadel. The horses came
to a stop at the foot of the mass of rock upon which it rested,
and Gabria and Athlone looked up in dread at the black towers. The two riders could not help but shudder. Neither of
them had ever been there before, for the clanspeople avoided
the stronghold like a plague camp. Few men who dared enter
the confines of the citadel survived to tell of the adventure.

The citadel sat on top of a rocky promontory overlooking a
wooded valley. A trail forked off the main road and wound up
the precipitous slope to the only visible entrance into the
closely guarded stronghold. As far as the travelers could see,
the citadel consisted of a massive central keep topped by
needle-sharp towers of black granite and surrounded by a
high, crenelated wall of the same dark stone. The whole edifice crouched like a brooding, malevolent beast over the road
and cast its shadow into the valley below.

The riders stared up at the citadel silhouetted against the
lowering clouds until the colt grew restive. The wind suddenly
swooped out of the north, whipping the trees and snapping at
the riders' gold cloaks. The sun disappeared behind the heavy
gray clouds.

The Hunnuli started up the trail at a trot. As they made
their way along the winding path, Gabria looked closer at the
towering citadel and realized it was not as finished as it appeared from a distance. Part of the keep was still under con-
struction and scaffolding surrounded several towers. She
remembered that Lord Medb had sent an army to destroy the
stronghold the previous summer, when the Oathbreakers had
refused to give him their books and manuscripts on magic.

The citadel had fallen, and the high priest and his surviving followers had fled to Ab-Chakan to join Savaric. After Medb's death, they returned to rebuild their home. Gabria was impressed despite her nervousness. The men of Krath had accomplished a great deal of work in a short period of time.

The sky was completely overcast by the time Athlone and Gabria reached the top of the rise. The mountains before them were lost in gloom, and the two riders could see dark curtains of rain hanging from the clouds to the north and west. Gabria shivered and pulled her cloak tighter.

The Hunnuli trotted up the narrow path to the massive front wall of the citadel. A single, round-arched gateway, barely wide enough for a wagon to pass through, was built into the wall. It was blocked by a thick oaken door and an intricately carved stone portcullis. The Hunnuli stopped; Eurus pawed the ground.

The citadel loomed over them, silent and menacing, but no one challenged the riders from the walls. In fact, the stronghold seemed strangely lifeless. There were no banners or flags on the towers, no smoke from cooking fires, and no lights or torches. There did not seem to be any guards on the battlements, and there was no sound of life within the walls.

All the same, Gabria sensed she and Athlone were being watched. She looked up at the high walls. "They know we're here," she said.

"What are we supposed to do, knock?" Athlone made a sound of irritation deep in his throat and slid off Eurus. He found a chunk of rock and strode to the gate. "Seth!" he bellowed, banging the rock on the portcullis. The noise rang around them, but nothing stirred behind the gates or on the walls. A few drops of rain spattered in the dust.

After shouldering the sturdy door, Athlone shook his head and returned to Gabria's side. "Those doors have the same type of arcane wards as Ab-Chakan—you know, those small inscribed tiles. We couldn't batter them down if we had one hundred men." He shrugged and added facetiously, "Maybe they're not answering because they're hiding from the rain."

Gabria jerked her head angrily. "Seth!" she shouted at the walls. "The sorceress seeks your help."

Still there was no response from the citadel, and the rain began to fall heavily. Gabria's expression grew angry. She knew that the Oathbreakers were there and that they were aware of her presence, but she had no time to waste on playing their games. She leaned over Nara's shoulder and said to the chieftain, "They're testing me. If we want in, we shall have to invite ourselves."

Athlone cast one last look at the walls and nodded. Only the gods knew how the Oathbreakers would react to two outsiders breaching their door, but if the cultists would not answer, there was no other real alternative. As an afterthought, he removed his weapons and put them in the meager shelter of the wall. No need to seem too antagonistic.

Gabria saw the sense of his move and handed him her dagger. The Oathbreakers despised metal, so it would be best not to insult them by carrying steel into their stronghold. Besides, Gabria knew full well that if the Oathbreakers wanted her dead, no weapon—save magic, perhaps—could protect her.

She waited while Athlone remounted, then threw her hood back and stared intently at the heavy stone portcullis. It's too bad there is no thunderstorm, she thought, since mere rainstorms did not seem to enhance magic. She could have used the added power to help shatter the arcane wards. Gabria wondered briefly if any of the cultists were magic-wielders. Someone had to have set the wards.

But as she studied the small tiles inset into both sides of the gateway, she realized the wards were very old. Seth had told her once that the Oathbreakers had a collection of old spells and relics left by the ancient sorcerers. These wards were probably from that collection. They would work well against normal humans, but they were too old and weak to withstand a full arcane attack.

Ignoring the heavy rain that soaked her neck and shoulders and plastered her hair to her head, Gabria raised her hand and began her spell. Once again the diamond splinter glowed under her skin. She did not notice that Athlone was watching her with a fascinated intensity. She spoke a command, pointed to each ward, and concentrated her magic on them. They held for only a few moments, then the old wards cracked and the tiles fell out of the wall. Gabria spoke a second command, and the heavy portcullis began to slide up in its grooves. There was a cracking noise behind the oak door and, suddenly, the entire door fell back and crashed heavily to the ground.

Gabria glanced back at Athlone with a faint smile of satisfaction. She was pleased when he nodded with approval and gestured to her to enter first.

Nara snorted and stepped carefully over the fallen door. Eurus and the colt came close behind. The three Hunnuli walked into a dark, empty courtyard that lay before the keep. Gabria held her arm high so anyone watching could see the glowing splinter in her wrist. She and Athlone strained every sense to catch any movement or hidden danger.

Though no attack came, a tall, black-robed figure did emerge from the deep shadows of the keep. A long hood hid his face, and a black whip hung at his belt. He stopped on the steps in front of the Hunnuli and slowly pushed back his hood. In the fading daylight the two riders recognized the gaunt, hawk-nosed face of Seth, brother of Lord Savaric and high priest of the Cult of the Lash.

"Welcome, Sorceress, to the citadel of Krath," he said coldly.

The woman nodded in reply. She did not dismount at once, but sat on Nara and returned Seth's deadpan scrutiny. It was said of the followers of Krath that they could look into a man's heart and find the hidden evils that were buried there; they pried into secrets and opened guarded emotions that were secreted behind masks. Because of this, few men dared to look an Oathbreaker in the eye, but Gabria was different. She had faced horrors and tragedies, trials and triumphs, until the facades of her life had been worn away, and she had learned to face herself for what she was. She had no fear of what Seth would find in her heart. She knew herself well and had nothing to hide.

After a moment, the high priest seemed to reach the same conclusion, for he nodded once, pulled his hood back over his face, and gestured for them to follow. Gabria tied the bag with the golden mask to her belt, then she and Athlone dismounted and hurried after the priest. The Hunnuli went to stand in the shelter of a nearby shed.

The priest led his visitors up the stairs of the keep, through a wide door, and into the central hall. The big room was dark except for a fire burning in the large fireplace against the opposite wall.

The flames gave off just enough light for Gabria and Athlone to see around the empty room. Unlike the rich luxury of the son's main halls, this one was stark and barren. There were no rugs or wall hangings, just bare stone. The only furniture in the room was a long, stone table set before the fireplace. On the right wall, a staircase went up to a gallery that ran the length of the hall and half hid a series of arched doorways.

A huge, painted statue, the height of several men, sat in the shadows against the far wall and leered down on the visitors. Gabria recognized the red-painted face and the multi-armed body of the goddess, Krath. The goddess was in a sitting position with her six arms reaching out. Her tongue lolled out of her mouth, and her eyes were wild and malevolent.

Gabria stifled a shiver and turned away. Praying silently that Amara would come into this house of Krath and protect her, the sorceress hurried on after Seth.

The priest moved to the fireplace and stood before the flames for several minutes. He did not offer his guests food or drink. When he spoke again, he simply said, "Your need must be urgent for you to break our door."

"If you had answered us in the first place, Uncle, she wouldn't have had to do that," Athlone snapped.

The high priest turned toward the chieftain. The man's face was still hidden by the hood of his robe, but his eyes burned in the firelight. Athlone gritted his teeth and met his uncle's stare. He had turned away from Seth's merciless eyes once, a

year ago, but he would not do it this time. He forced his eyes
to remain steady on the unblinking, penetrating glare. It was
like looking into the eyes of a cobra.

Seth suddenly threw back his hood. Athlone and Gabria
were surprised to see a sardonic smile twist up the corner of his
mouth.

"You have grown stronger since last summer, Nephew,"
Seth stated. "Now, why are you here?"

"We think Lord Branth used the *Book of Matrah* to summon a gorthling," Gabria stated flatly.

To her dismay, Seth's emotionless, hard-lined face actually
blanched. "How do you know?"

Gabria described her vision, the events at Pra Desh, and
Branth's subsequent actions. When she repeated the message
spoken by the dead man, Seth's mouth tightened.

"From what we know of gorthlings, I believe you are right,"
he said. "The creature has invaded the man's body."

The sorceress nodded. "I was hoping something in your library could help us. We have to find some way to destroy it."

The high priest was silent, as if caught up in some internal
debate. Then, without a word, he took a torch from a bracket,
lit it in the fire, and strode toward the stairs. Athlone and
Gabria hurried after him.

The woman glanced up at the gallery overhead and gasped;
shadowy forms stood in the arched doorways. The figures
melted back into the darkness as the high priest walked up the
stairs, and by the time Athlone and Gabria reached the top,
the gallery was empty. Nevertheless, the two clanspeople sensed the wary, watchful presences that lurked just out of sight in
the lightless corners.

Seth paid no heed to his men nearby, but walked on
through a maze of halls and corridors, past closed doors, down
stone stairwells, and deep into the heart of the citadel. Everywhere they went, Athlone and Gabria felt, rather than heard
or saw, the constant attendance of the unseen watchers.

At last Seth came to a stout door that was bolted with a brass
locking mechanism. The two clanspeople watched in fascina-

tion while the priest drew a key from his sash and deftly undid
the myriad bolts. He pushed open the door and walked in.
Athlone and Gabria stepped inside and looked about in wonder. The large room was lined with shelves. Though many of
the boards were empty, about one hundred books and manuscripts lay piled in various places around the room.

Books were a rarity to the clans, for they were difficult to
obtain and a nuisance to move from place to place. Normally
only healers, priests, and clan chieftains could read, although
occasionally the wer-tains, the chieftains' families, or the
priestesses of Amara learned the difficult skill. Gabria had
never been taught, and as she looked over the Oathbreakers'
precious volumes, she thought she would one day like to
learn.

"I thought Medb's men destroyed your books," she said to
Seth.

"Some of them, yes. But we were able to hide the most important ones." He set his torch in a bracket on the wall and
gestured to a table and benches in the middle of the room.
Silently he searched through the priceless collection of books.

"I'm afraid there is very little here that will help you," he
said, studying the tomes.

Gabria's heart sank. She had hoped desperately that the
Oathbreakers would have some useful information. She did
not know where else to turn. "Do you know of anyone else
who might know?" she forced herself to ask.

The high priest pulled out several volumes and shoved them
back. "I've read all of these. They are just general essays on
magic. The problem is that there was never much written
about gorthlings. All we know is that they are easy enough to
summon, but they are treacherous, cunning, and vicious. If
they taste blood, they can inhabit any body they choose. Once
that happens, it becomes extremely difficult to send them
back."

"Send them back where?" Athlone asked.

"A gorthling cannot be destroyed or killed, it must be sent
back to Sorh in the realm of the dead."

"How?" Gabria cried in exasperation.

Seth's reply was chilling. "I don't know how. The only ones who ever summoned a gorthling successfully were Matrah and Valorian. Matrah's spells are probably in his tome."

Gabria sighed. "That doesn't help us much."

"What about Valorian?" Athlone suggested.

"Valorian never wrote anything down. He did not wish those spells concerning the gorthlings to be remembered."

The chieftain threw his hands up and paced restlessly to the shelves. "So now we are stuck with a bloodthirsty creature bent on destroying Gabria, and we have no hope of getting rid of it."

Seth turned his basilisk stare on his nephew. "I did not say there was no hope. The gorthling's human body is vulnerable like any other flesh, and its ability to use sorcery is limited by its own knowledge and its body's weaknesses. It can be destroyed, but you will need strength, ingenuity, and courage."

"A few words of instruction would be better," Gabria muttered. She half-turned to say something to Athlone when the heavy weight of the bag banged against her leg. She remembered the mask. "Perhaps you could tell me what this is," she said, unwrapping the mask and laying it on the table before her.

Seth's cold expression did not change, but he reached out and touched the gold surface. "Where did you get this?"

"I found it in Moy Tura."

The priest's head snapped up, and he stared at Gabria. "You were in Moy Tura? Is the Korg still there?"

"Yes," she replied with a half-smile. "It was because of him that we found the mask. It was hidden in a temple."

"The gods were leading your steps," Seth declared.

"Do you know what that is?" Athlone asked.

"It is the death mask of Valorian." The high priest studied the gold mask on the table. "If anything could help you fight the gorthling, this mask might."

"How?" Gabria demanded.

"The mask was once a powerful talisman. It was used in secret ceremonies for the worship of Valorian. When the clans destroyed Moy Tura and the magic-wielders, the mask and everyone who had used it disappeared."

Athlone crossed his arms. "How do you know about it?"

Seth gestured to the books. "It was described in those several times."

"But you don't know how to use the mask's power," Gabria said.

"Unfortunately, no. That was a secret that was only passed on to the priests of Valorian. Nevertheless, if the magic is still viable, you might be able to discover the artifact's purpose and put it to your own use."

Gabria nodded halfheartedly. She was very disappointed. The high priest had not given her much useful information, only puzzles, hints, and more questions.

Seth, sensing her frustration, wrapped the mask in its cloth and gave it back to her. "I am sorry I cannot be much help, Sorceress. Yet you should not abandon your quest. The gorthling is powerful, even more so housed in a human body endowed with magic. It must be sent back or it will wreak havoc in this world."

The sorceress nodded again, without reply. There was nothing more to say. Silently the priest led his two guests back to the main hall and escorted them to the front door. Despite the rain and the darkness he did not invite them to stay, and they did not ask.

Before Gabria walked down the steps toward the waiting Hunnuli, the high priest stopped her.

"If you are successful in defeating the beast, sorceress, come back. We have other books and relics from Moy Tura. They belong to the heirs of magic. I will teach you how to use them."

"Thank you, High Priest," she answered. "I will."

Under the wary gaze of the hidden cultists, Gabria and Athlone mounted their Hunnuli and rode out of the citadel to rejoin the hunt for Branth.

15

thlone and Gabria did not stop after leaving the citadel of Krath. They rode through the night, letting the Hunnuli follow the old stone road that ran south along the flanks of the Himachal Mountains. The man and woman traveled silently, each lost in his or her own thoughts and weariness.

At sunrise the Hunnuli came to the Isin River and the fortress of Ab-Chakan sitting on its ridge at the opening of the defile of Tor Wrath. The riders paused for a brief time at the edge of the valley, and their eyes turned to the crumbling old fortress and the two burial mounds nearby. The larger mound contained the bodies of the fallen clan warriors; the smaller mound was the grave of Lord Savaric.

Athlone was very quiet as he looked on his father's mound. The memories of many words and deeds passed through his mind. When he and Gabria were ready to go, the chieftain raised his fist in salute to his dead father and rode on. For a long while after leaving Ab-Chakan, Athlone's expression was very thoughtful.

The horses continued to follow the old road south beside the Isin River. The Isin was a natural guide to the Tir Samod and the clan gathering, and the two riders hoped to find their party somewhere along the banks. At midmorning the three Hunnuli stopped for a drink of water from the shallows under a shady tree.

Gabria and Athlone dismounted and stood staring at the water rippling by. They had not said much to each other during the journey to the citadel. Now they realized their time alone would soon be over.

They looked at one another self-consciously. They did not want to waste this precious time, but neither of them knew what to say. Athlone cleared his throat; Gabria hugged her arms to her chest.

Finally the sorceress broke the silence. "Whatever you may think of me, Athlone, I want you to know that I did not break the vows of our betrothal. Nothing happened in my tent at Jehanan Treld between Sayyed and me."

Athlone's heart was pounding like a drum. He put his hands behind his back and clenched his fingers hard. He felt in the core of his being that she was telling the truth. "Sayyed makes it easy to jump to conclusions," he said. "I'm sorry. I should have trusted you more. I should have listened."

The woman was quiet again. She remembered her vow to avoid confrontation with Athlone or Sayyed until after her quest was complete, but she could not let this chance for reconciliation go by. Athlone meant too much to her. "We still have a lot to offer one another," she replied hesitantly, turning her armband on her arm. "I don't want to give that up."

He watched the sunlight glint off the gold band, and he marveled that she was still wearing his gift. "Neither do I. Your friendship is too precious to lose."

"Perhaps if we start over again . . ."

He grinned. "If the gods will give us some time."

Gabria glanced up at him. "Is it worth a try?"

"What about Sayyed?"

"I don't know. He is my friend, too."

"Then we will see what happens. Many things may change in the days ahead."

Smiling, Gabria held out her hand, and he clasped it tightly. She felt the strength of his fingers and the warmth of his skin; her heart sang with pleasure and relief.

They mounted their Hunnuli and continued south beside the rippling water. At noon Eurus and Nara saw the rest of the party on the riverbank far ahead. The Hunnuli neighed their greetings.

Sayyed, with Tam behind him, rode out to meet them. Tam jumped off the horse before Sayyed brought it to a stop and threw her arms around the colt's neck. He whinnied in delight. The girl happily waved to Gabria and Athlone, then, to Gabria's surprise, Tam did not reclaim her usual seat on Nara but climbed back on behind Sayyed. The Turic ruffled her hair.

"While you were gone, I acquired a new partner," he told Gabria as the group trotted on to rejoin the other men.

The sorceress smiled. "That's wonderful. How did it happen?"

"I'm not sure. She's been staying close to me since I took her through the caves in Pra Desh, but I think she really needed someone while you were away. She seems to have stuck to me."

Gabria looked at the girl who was hanging on to Sayyed's waist. "Just be careful with her feelings," she warned the Turic. "Tam has lost a lot in her short life."

He nodded once just before they reached the other men, and any further conversation was lost in a storm of greetings, questions, and answers.

"You were right, Lord," Secen said to Athlone after the welcomes were past. "Branth has followed the river for two days now. He's still heading south, about a day ahead of us."

"Toward the gathering," Athlone said. He shivered slightly. The thought of the gorthling loose among the unsuspecting clanspeople was appalling. The chief turned to see Gabria come up beside him. He gestured downstream. "I don't suppose we could use magic to catch up with him or to move ourselves to the gathering ahead of that beast."

She was startled that he would ask such a question, and it took her a moment to answer. "Unfortunately, no. It is too dangerous and uncertain to transport people by magic. Too many things could go wrong. Besides, we could lose Branth's trail. There is no real promise that he is going to the gathering. And—" she stopped to pat Nara's neck "—we could not move the Hunnuli. I will need Nara when I face the gorthling."

The chieftain shaded his eyes and looked toward the south, where the green plains rolled beyond the horizon. He knew Branth was far out of sight, but an irrational hope still made him study the hills for any sign of the gorthling. At last he pulled his gaze away and ordered everyone to their horses.

The company rode for the rest of the day as fast as they could go. It was late into the evening when they finally stopped to eat and rest.

Immediately after their hurried meal, Athlone took Gabria a short distance away from camp to a sandy bank beside the river. For a while he said nothing, but stared thoughtfully into the water. The night gradually settled down around them, warm and comforting, rich with the sounds of crickets and the rush of the river.

At last Athlone drew a long breath and released it in a rush. "You asked me once," he said to Gabria, "if I thought Father would have been disappointed in you and your power."

The woman tilted her head to look at him, touched by the sadness and regret in his voice.

"And I told you that he would have been proud of your courage." Athlone hesitated. He wanted to touch her badly, to bring her close and draw on her wonderful inner strength, but he could not do it. He knew he had to face the reality of his decision by himself or he would never be able to wield magic with the honesty and power of his own will.

He had decided in Pra Desh to use his talent, but it was not until he had passed his father's grave at Ab-Chakan that he had fully accepted his irrevocable choice. He sensed now some of the fear and dread Gabria must have faced when she had made her decision to use her talent. Yet, even as he tried to still the cold trembling in his hands, he felt an effusive glow of elation pour out of his mind and release the heavy weight of guilt and remorse that had hung over him from that first moment when he had known of his power and had been ashamed of it. At last he was accepting the truth of his being.

"Father would have been disappointed with me," he went on. He held up a hand to stop Gabria's protest. "Savaric always taught me to use my strengths and abilities to my utmost." Athlone's teeth flashed with a grin in his dark beard. "Once he got over the shock of having a magic-wielder for a son, he would have been furious at my refusal to use my power. I want to change that, Gabria," he said forcefully. "I am a magic-wielder. I am going to learn to use my power."

Gabria gasped. Her breath was taken away by the conviction in his voice. Her thoughts leaped with a jolt of mixed emotions, and she clasped his hands in hers.

He held on, interlocking his fingers with hers. "I need your help, Gabria. Teach me your sorcery."

Her fingers tightened their grip, and she swallowed hard. "No," she replied, her voice firm.

"I have the talent. I only need to know how to use it."

She stared at him, torn between delight and fear. She knew why he was asking now as clearly as if he had said the words; he wanted to help her fight the gorthling. Her mind cried out in protest. If she tried to teach him and Athlone battled a gorthling with untried, poorly trained powers, he would be slaughtered. On the other hand, the chieftain was a stubborn man once his mind was made up. If she did not teach him something, she knew he would try to learn on his own and probably destroy himself in the backlash of a poorly controlled spell.

"Athlone," she cried in exasperation, "please wait! I can't teach sorcery. I don't know enough yet, myself."

He let go of her hands and stepped back. "Then I'll figure it out by myself. Is it like this?" and he snapped a command, the same words Gabria had used in the dungeon to form a globe of light. To her surprise, a soft ball of light did begin to glow just over their heads. In seconds, though, it went out of control and blazed into a furious sphere of brilliant, hot white light that hummed with unleashed magic. The two people shrank back from the heat.

Gabria heard shouts from the other men, but she ignored them and kept her attention fastened on the light. "All right," she cried. "I'll teach you what I can."

"Good," he yelled. "Then would you show me how to put

this thing out?"

The woman sighed. She could put it out herself, but if he really wanted to learn, this was as good a time as any to start. "Concentrate on your spell," she shouted to him over the rising noise of the globe. "Fix your purpose in your mind, then speak the words of your command." She watched the chieftain while he closed his eyes and lifted his hand toward the sphere. The blazing ball wavered, dimmed, then it flared again brighter than before.

"Concentrate!" Gabria demanded. "Feel the power within you. Bend the magic to your bidding."

Athlone tried again. A sheen of perspiration glistened on his forehead, and his face went rigid from his effort. This time, instead of thinking about the sphere and wishing it would go out, he concentrated on the feel of the power that surged within him. He had felt that power before, when he had rescued Gabria from the Woman of the Marsh and when he had fought the duel with Gringold. However, in those two instances, the magic had flowed through him uncontrolled and unconsciously. Now he drew it forth willingly and shaped it. When at last he stopped and opened his eyes, the light was gone and Gabria was smiling.

"I did it!" He grinned like a small boy and picked up Gabria by her waist and whirled her around.

The other men appeared out of the darkness, their swords drawn. "What's going on? Are you all right?" they asked as one.

The chieftain waved his men to a stop. "We're fine."

"What was that light?" Sayyed demanded.

Athlone did not hesitate. He had made his decision to wield his power no matter how his clan would react, but he badly wanted his companions' support. The healer and the warriors were his first and most important test of the clan's willingness to be ruled by a chieftain-sorcerer. He cocked an eyebrow and said, "I tried a spell to create a globe of light. It went a little wild."

Piers did not seem surprised. He nodded in approval. The

three warriors looked at their lord speechlessly. Secen glanced at Gabria, then back at Athlone. Both his and his fellows' jaws hung slack.

Valar cleared his throat and said slowly, "But Lord, the laws forbidding sorcery have not been removed. What if you are exiled or put to death?"

The Khulinin chieftain replied, "I have thought about that and about many things. I realize I am endangering my position as ruler, but I can no longer turn my back on this power I was born with. The time is coming when we will have to face the gorthling's threat to the clans, and swords will not be enough."

The three warriors stared at him for a long, painful minute until, one by one, they sheathed their weapons and turned back to camp.

Athlone watched them go. They had not jumped into an instant acclamation of his decision, but they had not condemned him, either. He released his breath in a long, silent sigh. It was one thing to demand obedience from a warrior on the field of battle, but Athlone could not in good conscience order his men to accept his talent as a sorcerer. He could only hope their loyalty and respect for him as a chieftain would eventually win them over. Their acceptance would mean a great deal to the rest of the clan.

Sayyed had been watching the exchange with deep interest. He was very aware of the significance of Athlone's decision to wield magic. He slid his sword back into its leather scabbard and stood arms akimbo, his body tight with anticipation. "Good! Gabria, you can teach us both to use our powers."

"Not now," she said hastily. "The night is late."

"This is as good a time as any to start," Athlone said.

Gabria groaned inwardly. She could hardly bear to teach Athlone for fear of what he wanted to do. Now she had to include Sayyed. The men were watching her expectantly, so she gritted her teeth and marched back to camp. Athlone and Sayyed were not going to let her wiggle out of this; it was clear she would have to teach them something—a few of the basic premises she had learned from the Woman of the Marsh. Perhaps if they knew more of the dangers of wielding magic they would have enough sense to leave the gorthling alone when they found it.

Gabria settled down by the fire and waited while Sayyed and Athlone came to join her. Tam came, too, and curled up beside Sayyed, her large eyes glittering in the firelight with a strange excitement. The other men went to their own tasks, but Gabria noticed they stayed close enough to hear her voice.

She paused briefly and cast her mind back to the mangrove tree in the swamp and the ancient sorceress whose rasping voice still spoke clearly in her memory.

"Will is at the center of sorcery," Gabria forced herself to say. "With every spell you create, you are attempting to impose your will on the fabric of our world. Magic is a natural force that is in every creature, stone, or plant. When you alter that force, even with the smallest spell, you must be strong enough to control the effect and the consequences. The forces of magic can destroy you if you cannot control them," she told her fascinated listeners. "The strength of will is the most important trait of a magic-wielder. Therefore, you must know yourself, every measure and degree of your own soul so you can recognize your limitations and know when the sorcery has begun to leach strength from your being."

"Is that what happened to Branth?" Athlone asked.

Gabria nodded. "I think so. I think the fon pushed him too far and his mind was not clear enough to recognize his danger. All magic-wielders must be very careful not to overextend their powers."

"What else does a magic-wielder need?" Sayyed demanded.

"Desire, concentration, and imagination," the sorceress continued. "Not all spells are rigidly defined. You can often create your own. The reason you need spells is to clarify your intent in your mind. The words help you focus your powers on the magic. You must know exactly what you want to do or the magic will go awry."

"Like my sphere," Athlone said.

"Exactly."

Sayyed leaned forward. "What about the Trymian Force?"

"The force is drawn from the power within the wielder. You can use it at will and change its intensity, but you must be careful not to overuse it or it will seriously weaken you."

"Can you show us how to control it?" he requested, his excitement sparkling in his eyes.

Alarmed, Gabria shook her head. "No. It's too soon. You nearly got us killed when you tried to use the force against the Korg."

"But Gabria," Sayyed protested. "How can we help you fight the gorthling if you don't show us how to use our power?"

All at once, Gabria's fear and reluctance broke loose, and she rushed to her feet. "Don't you see?" she said forcefully. "You can't help me. There isn't enough time to teach you to defend yourselves, let alone fight something as powerful and evil as the gorthling. You will be killed if you try. So don't learn. Don't try. Let me fight it, and if I win, I will teach you later, when there's time."

"And if you don't win?" Athlone asked quietly.

"Then you'll have to find another teacher."

Sayyed sprang to his feet, his long black hair flying like a stallion's mane. "Gabria, you are being unreasonable! You can't fight that thing alone."

"I most certainly can," she cried. "I won't be responsible for your deaths."

Athlone looked up at her, his voice cold with anger. "You will jeopardize the clans and endanger yourself."

"I'll endanger myself far more by taking two unskilled sorcerers into an arcane battle they have no chance of surviving. Without you, I won't be distracted, worried, or terrified for your safety. No! No more. Stay out of this, all of you." She swept her cloak onto her shoulders and strode out of the firelight.

Athlone and Sayyed looked at one another, and for once their thoughts were in perfect accord.

"She is not going to fight it alone," Sayyed muttered.

"No." Athlone arched an eyebrow. "If we work together, perhaps we can learn enough to surprise her."

Sayyed held out his hand, and the Khulinin clasped it to seal the vow.

Tam watched them with her bright, eager eyes and, unbeknownst to the men, she made her own vow to herself. They were not going to leave her out of this.

Meanwhile, Gabria hurried into the darkness. The night was warm and dry, so she went to sit on a nearby hill. Long after the distant campfire had burned out, she sat on the grassy slope while her thoughts spun through her mind. She was frightened of meeting the gorthling alone, but she was terrified of losing Athlone or Sayyed to the beast through their lack of skill or hers. She knew she could never forgive herself if they died in a situation they had no business being in at all.

"No," Gabria whispered to the stars, "they must not fight. It is my duty, not theirs." Within her heart she vowed to fight alone, even if it meant leaving her companions and seeking the gorthling herself. Athlone would be furious, but at least he would be alive.

At one point a doubt crept into her mind: what if they were right? Was she being arrogant and selfish to think she could handle the gorthling alone? What would the clans do if the creatures did kill her? Gabria immediately banished those doubts. She could think of no other way to destroy the gorthling. The creature had to be fought with magic, and she was the only one who had any hope of succeeding.

16

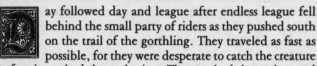ay followed day and league after endless league fell
behind the small party of riders as they pushed south
on the trail of the gorthling. They traveled as fast as
possible, for they were desperate to catch the creature
before it reached the gathering. They pushed themselves and
their horses hard and stopped to rest only when necessary. To
increase their speed, they dumped most of their gear, using
the pack horses as spare mounts.

Gabria worried at first that Tam or the Hunnuli colt would
wear down under the rigors of the rough travel—the journey
had already been a long, hard one for everyone. To her relief,
the Reidhar girl and the colt managed very well. Tam stayed
close to Sayyed, riding with him and keeping him company in
the evenings. She still had not said a word, but she smiled
more and pampered Sayyed with her constant attention. The
Turic, for his part, was pleased to have her friendship and
treated her with the humor and affection of a protective big
brother.

As for the Hunnuli colt, the months of travel had strengthened him as no time in a pasture could have. He was as big as a
Harachan yearling, well developed and feisty. He remained in-
separable from Tam.

Five days passed, and the travelers gained very little on the
gorthling. Secen estimated they were still about a day behind
him. Although he was moving very fast, he still made no attempt to hide his tracks. He seemed to be deliberately luring
the hunters after him.

On the fifth day the company passed close to Dangari Treld,

so Athlone sent one of his warriors to check on the camp. The
Dangari had grown sedentary over the years and left many of
their people at home during the gathering. They bred and
trained superb horses and usually took their breeding stallions
and brood mares to cooler pastures in the mountains for the
summer. Athlone prayed the gorthling had not found any of
the Dangari.

To his relief, the warrior returned with some gifts of food
and greetings from the Dangari in the treld. They were unharmed and had seen no sign of Branth. Lord Koshyn and the
main body of the clan had left many days before and were
probably already at the gathering.

The travelers rode on beside the Isin River as quickly as they
dared go. They managed to draw a little closer to the gorthling
until he was perhaps only half a day ahead, but he remained
infuriatingly out of reach. The pursuers did not dare force
their Harachan horses any harder for fear of killing them and
losing all hope of catching the gorthling in time.

The long, hard days of riding were frustrating to Gabria.
She spent the endless hours studying the death mask of Valorian and trying to think of ways to destroy the gorthling. Unfortunately the mask gave her no answers, and her knowledge
and experience were so limited that she had very little idea of
what she might have to face when she finally confronted the
creature.

The only two things of which she was certain was that she
had to fight the creature and that she would do it alone. Athlone and Sayyed had not brought up the subject of sorcery
again since that night, and Gabria did not care to remind
them. Nevertheless, she knew the two men well enough to realize they had not put aside their eagerness to use their
powers. At any other time she would have been overjoyed to
help them and would have done anything she could to learn
more and teach all her companions, including Tam. But not
now. Not so they could face a gorthling.

If only she knew how to convince them of the deadly folly of
their desire to help. She sensed they had not given up their

wish to learn. Athlone and Sayyed were spending an unusual amount of time talking together out of her hearing. For two men who barely spoke to each other only a month ago, they had suddenly become very friendly. Gabria did not know what they were up to, but it only increased her determination to slip away at the best opportunity and confront the gorthling herself.

If she was going to succeed in leaving the men, she knew she would have to plan her departure just right. She was not a good tracker and she did not want to risk losing Branth's trail. It was possible that he could detour from the Isin and not go to the gathering at all. Therefore, she wanted to stay with the men until they were close enough to the gorthling for her to find him, yet far enough away so the men could not easily catch up with her. Nara was not going to like the idea, but Gabria trusted the Hunnuli mare to help her.

The woman sat on Nara's broad back and forced herself to be patient. The waiting was difficult. It gave her imagination ample opportunity to run wild—an exhausting luxury she could ill afford. They were still many leagues behind the gorthling and had a long way to go. She clenched her jaw. It was time to find the gorthling and finish the ordeal. Branth was not going to slip away from her again.

*   *   *   *   *

As the gorthling and its pursuers headed south, the eleven clans of Valorian were making their way across the grasslands to the Tir Samod. For as many years as the clanspeople had inhabited the Ramtharin Plains, the clans had gathered together each summer at the junction of the Isin and the Goldrine rivers to renew their ties and worship their gods as one.

The gathering gave the chieftains the opportunity to meet in council and establish the laws that governed the clans. Through their efforts, they carried on the traditions handed down from their fathers, maintained clan unity, and enhanced their own authority.

While the chiefs met in council, their people were also strengthening clan unity. The gathering gave everyone a chance to renew old acquaintances, visit family members in other clans, strike up new friendships, and arrange betrothals. It also gave the clanspeople an excellent outlet for competition and entertainment.

One of the most popular attractions of the gathering was the huge bazaar and livestock market that sprang up even before the last clan arrived. Merchants and traders from the Five Kingdoms and the Turic tribes came early and set up booths to trade with the enthusiastic clanspeople. Along with the foreign merchants, the clan artisans added their own specialties to the market, so the people had a wide and richly varied supply of goods from which to choose. They loved to trade and barter, and they pitched into the haggling with great delight.

The days of a gathering were usually wild, noisy, and exciting. This year, however, the people were restrained. Too much had happened at the gathering the summer before for the clans to reunite peacefully. Clan had fought against clan in a bloody war that was still fresh in people's memories.

With that danger in mind, Lord Koshyn of the Dangari and Lord Sha Umar of the Jehanan made certain that their people arrived at the gathering first. The two lords, the Khulinin's oldest allies, made it a point to welcome every arriving clan and chieftain as if all the troubles of the past year had been forgotten. Their attitude spilled over onto their people and helped soothe the barely suppressed anger many still harbored. Unfortunately, they could not make the clans forget everything.

When the remnants of Lord Medb's old clan, the Wylfling, came on the fourth day, the whole gathering nearly shattered in rage and old grief. Only the Wylfling's new chieftain, Lord Hildor, held his clan together and forced them to stand their ground before the anger of the other clans. His courage and the timely arrival of the Khulinin helped defuse a potential tragedy. The Khulinin wer-tain, Guthlac, remembered his orders from Athlone and had the entire Khulinin clan come forward to greet and embrace the Wylfling. Gradually the heated emotions cooled down, and the clans warily got down to the business of the gathering.

The chiefs then discovered another real problem: Lord Athlone was missing. The Khulinin chieftain had not been seen or heard from since he had left Reidhar Treld almost two months before. The Khulinin reported that he was going to Pra Desh with Lady Gabria to find Branth, but they did not know when he was coming back.

The chieftains were alarmed. They did not want to start the serious proceedings of the council without him, yet they could not wait all summer for him to appear. Lord Sha Umar finally suggested postponing the council for at least five more days and offered to send scouts out along the clan trails to try to find Athlone.

The other chiefs readily agreed, and Lord Koshyn and Wertain Guthlac sent their scouts out as well. While the chiefs settled back to wait for some word of Athlone, speculation ran rampant through the camps about his disappearance. Rumors spread like flies. Some people whispered that Gabria's sorcery had destroyed him, while others thought perhaps Branth had killed him. No one knew what to believe.

On the evening of the fifth day, there was still no sign of Lord Athlone or his party, and the clans were growing tired of waiting.

Lord Koshyn tried to curb his own impatience during the day, without much success. Immediately after his evening meal, he retrieved a flask of redberry wine he had left cooling in the river and walked downstream along the bank to the camp of Clan Jehanan. He found Lord Sha Umar relaxing on a rug under the awning of his tent. The chieftain's maroon banner flapped idly overhead. The Jehanan leader welcomed the young Dangari gladly, and they sat down to enjoy the cool wine.

For a while they rested in companionable silence, watching the evening activities of the clan. The women were cooking over campfires while the children tumbled in the dirt with the dogs. Some warriors lolled in the shade of the trees. A piper was playing nearby, making his music light and capricious to match the fitful wind that blew through the camp, swirling the dust and tugging at the tents.

Koshyn suddenly sat upright. "That man is a nuisance!" he said in annoyance.

Sha Umar followed his friend's gaze and saw Thalar, the Khulinin clan priest of Surgart, talking vehemently to a crowd of onlookers at the Bahedin camp just across the river. The priest had been using his time to preach against sorcery to all the clans. He knew, as well as everyone else, that the chieftains were going to discuss magic during their council and debate on the possibility of altering their laws. Thalar took full advantage of his lord's absence to try to influence the other chiefs and their people against sorcery.

"He has certainly been making his opinions known," Sha Umar replied dryly.

Koshyn looked away, his blue eyes vivid with anger. "And too many people are listening to him. If Athlone doesn't get here soon, he may find the entire gathering ready to exile Gabria and turn against sorcery forever."

Koshyn had fought beside Athlone at Ab-Chakan and was his close friend. He liked the young woman, Gabria, too. He recognized the truth of her arguments to reinstate sorcery in the clans and did everything he could to forward her cause. The fact that his friend Athlone had the talent to wield magic only increased his determination to rescind the law that forbade the use of sorcery on pain of death.

"We can't put the council off much longer," Sha Umar said, his tanned face lined with worry.

"What do we do if he does not come at all?"

The Jehanan chief scratched his beard. "If he and Gabria both disappear, the people will think the problem of sorcery will simply vanish."

"No, it won't," the Dangari said vehemently. "Too much has happened for everyone to forget." He gestured to the teeming camps along both rivers. "Somewhere out there are other magic-wielders who know of their talents and are afraid, or those who will learn of their powers by accident and will be killed or exiled. Those people are not freaks. There is a reason some clanspeople can wield magic. We can't keep turning our backs on that power."

Sha Umar's mouth widened into a grin, and he held up his hand. "All right! You don't need to convince me." He passed the wine flask to Koshyn. "We should push to change the laws whether Athlone is there or not."

"Absolutely. We don't need another tragedy like the one Medb brought down upon us."

"Agreed."

Koshyn leaned back on a cushion and stared out beyond the camps to the far hills darkening in the purple of twilight. "I just wish I knew where Athlone was."

"And Lady Gabria. Without her, our task will be much harder," said Sha Umar.

"They must have run into trouble."

The Jehanan chief snorted. "Probably Branth. That fool has been nothing but trouble. I wonder where *he* is."

"Dead, I hope," the Dangari said honestly.

Sha Umar raised his cup to that hope.

At that moment, in the low hills at the edge of the river valley, the subject of the chieftains' annoyance was lying on a flat rock and looking out over the busy gathering. Branth's eyes glowed red with satisfaction and anticipation. The gorthling had not known the clans were so numerous, but that did not bother him. To the contrary, he was delighted. The clanspeople he had found days before had told him there was only one sorceress left on the plains. He had realized then that she must be the hated magic-wielder in the memory of his host body. All he had to do was destroy her and an entire population would be his to do with as he pleased.

The gorthling laughed to himself. There were such fascinating possibilities for revenge against the people who had been so harsh to Lord Branth. With his arcane powers, he could destroy these people one by one, slaughter them all at once or, better yet, enslave them and keep them for his own use.

He studied the gathering carefully. The sorceress was supposed to be at this place, but it was quite large and he did not know exactly where to look for her. The individual clans were camped on their traditional sites along the banks of both rivers. The huge market was on the east side of the Goldrine River, and to the south of the camps was the wide, flat stretch of the valley used for racing and competitions. On the point of land between the two rivers was an open tent crowned by the colorful banners of the ten chieftains present at the gathering. The holy island of the Tir Samod and the temple stood empty in the middle of the confluence of the two rivers. There was nothing anywhere to indicate the presence of a magic-wielder.

The gorthling finally shrugged. The light was fading, making it difficult to see. Besides, at this distance he could not distinguish one woman from another in those busy camps. He moved back into the shelter of a rocky outcropping and settled down to wait for daylight. He would simply go down to the gathering in the morning, when the clanspeople were the most active, and find the sorceress. Even in those sprawling camps, she could not escape him for long.

* * * * *

A few hours later that same night, Athlone brought Eurus to a halt in the shelter of a small copse of trees beside the river. The two Hunnuli were still fresh and willing to go on, but the Harachan horses stumbled to a grateful halt and stood drooping under their saddles. Their riders were just as exhausted. The Hunnuli colt pressed close to his mother, and Treader flopped on the ground and panted. Although they were only half a day's ride from the gathering and everyone wanted to keep going, even Gabria knew they had to stop and rest.

Wordlessly the travelers dismounted, rubbed down their horses, and hobbled them to graze. No one lit a fire. The men dug into their packs for some nuts and dried meat, and they ate a cold meal. Before long, Tam and the men were wrapped in their blankets and sound asleep under the watchful guard of the Hunnuli. Only Gabria remained awake.

The time had come to leave. Athlone had hoped the gorthling would wait a while before starting trouble with the clanspeople—at least long enough for the weary horses and riders to catch up with him. Gabria did not want to give the gorthling a chance to be loose among the clans. She wanted to stop him immediately.

She lay in her blankets for a time to let her body rest. Staring at the stars, she listened to the subdued sounds of the sleepers around her. She was thankful for the nervous, queasy feeling in her stomach and the cold clamminess of her hands, for without those to keep her awake, it would have been very easy to fall asleep in the warm summer night.

Just after moonrise, she slipped out of her blankets, tied the golden mask in its bag to her belt, and went to Nara. The three Hunnuli gathered around her in the darkness and listened as she told them what she was going to do.

Nara's reaction was immediate. *Gabria! You can't fight that monster alone. It is too strong for you!*

The sorceress reached out and laid her hand on the Hunnuli's neck. "I have to try. Are you coming with me?" As she had suspected, the mare could not refuse. Nara would never betray her rider or let her go into such danger alone.

Gabria turned to Eurus. "Please, do not wake Athlone. Let me go alone or he will follow me and die at the gorthling's hands."

You do not know that, the young stallion replied.

"I know enough to not take a chance. Please, Eurus."

The Hunnuli bowed his head. *I will do as you ask.*

"Thank you," she said gratefully. Then she turned to the colt. "Don't worry, little one, your mother will be safe." Gabria sprang to Nara's back and pinned her cloak tightly around her shoulders. For just a moment, she looked back at the sleeping forms under the trees.

While the woman was occupied with her own thoughts,

Nara turned to Eurus and sent her message only to him. *We cannot stop her. She is too determined for her own good sometimes.*

What do we do? the stallion asked.

My son can wake the men in a short time. That will allow you to keep your word to Gabria. Bring them as fast as you can. She will not be able to avoid them if they join her at the gathering.

Eurus tossed his head, and his nostrils flared.

Nara turned to her colt. *I must give you a mighty task, my son. Are you willing to try?*

Yes, Mamma!

You are strong enough to carry the girl. After you have awakened the men, take Tam toward the mountains and seek the King Hunnuli. The two of you together can call him. Ask him to come. The sorceress needs his help.

The colt nickered softly in reply, his broom tail whisking in excitement.

Unaware of the Hunnuli's thoughts, Gabria bid farewell to Eurus and the colt. Like a shadow, Nara moved out of the trees and turned south toward the Tir Samod. As soon as she was out of earshot from the camp, she broke into her smooth canter, and she and Gabria vanished into the darkness.

Athlone stirred in his blankets. A strange feeling of alarm disturbed his exhausted sleep, and he tossed and turned. Something was not right; he could sense it even in his sleep, something was missing. He was on the verge of waking when something warm and soft nudged his face. Athlone bolted upright with a yell, grabbed his sword, and came nose to nose with the Hunnuli colt.

Gabria is gone, the young horse told him.

Athlone was on his feet and yelling for Eurus before the other men awakened and realized what was happening.

"Where is she?" the chief demanded when the stallion came to his side.

She left to find the gorthling alone.

"Why didn't you stop her?"

The other men were climbing to their feet, looking confused. "What is it, Lord Athlone?" Sayyed asked. He looked around. "Where is Gabria?"

Athlone snarled, "She's left without us. I'm going after her." He sprang to Eurus's back.

Before the Hunnuli could move, Sayyed ran in front of the big horse. "Not without us, you're not."

"Get out of the way!" the chief yelled. "I've got to get to her before she attacks that beast alone."

"I'm going with you!"

"Your horse can't keep up with a Hunnuli."

"He can try! You cannot go alone," Sayyed insisted.

Piers stepped forward, his demeanor calm. "Athlone, he's right. You and Gabria will need him. Take him on Eurus, and the warriors and I will follow."

Athlone looked down at the old healer, and something in his friend's quiet, reasonable voice calmed his wild impulse. Some of his father's cool, deliberate cunning surfaced in the chief's mind, and he nodded. "All right, Sayyed. You ride with me."

The Turic whooped with relief and went to collect his weapons and burnoose.

As the Turic and the chief were about to leave, the three hearthguard warriors stepped up to Eurus. They were not happy about being left behind, even though they understood the reasons. Nevertheless, they looked up at Athlone and gravely saluted. There was a short pause as they glanced at one another, then Keth said, "Be careful, Lord. The clans need you back."

Athlone said nothing. His hand tightened on Eurus's mane in expectation.

Secen, his strong, plain face clear in the moonlight, said quietly, "We were afraid at first when you told us that you were going to wield magic. But Lady Gabria's mask reminded us that Lord Valorian had once been a chieftain and a sorcerer. If his people could accept that, so can we."

"We'll support you before the clans, too," Valar added.

Lord Athlone raised his fist and returned his warriors' salute. He was proud of his men and vastly relieved for himself. Their acceptance would give him strength in the days of controversy ahead—provided, of course, that he survived until then. "Come as fast as you can," he ordered.

With Sayyed behind him on Eurus's back, Athlone yelled the Khulinin war cry and urged the Hunnuli into a canter. The two men and the stallion were gone from sight in the blink of an eye.

During that moment of departure, no one noticed that Tam quietly slipped onto the colt's back, and she, the colt, and Treader trotted away into the night.

17

he sun rose orange above the plains into a cloudless sky. Its early heat baked the dust, stirred the flies, and gave the promise of a hot day ahead. In the camps of the eleven clans, the people rose early to take advantage of the cool morning before the day turned uncomfortable.

The food vendors selling meat pies and fruit rolls did a thriving business. The bazaar merchants pulled aside their curtains and opened their booths to the women who came early to haggle. Several bards in the camps brought out their instruments to practice for the storytelling competition to be held before the clans that evening. Children ran and played among the tents. Some of the older boys went out to hunt, while others rode their horses along the river. Five of the chieftains met under the trees by the council tent to enjoy a cup of ale and discuss the possibility of starting the council without Athlone.

No one paid attention to the lone man, wearing a Bahedin cloak, who walked across the fields past the empty site where Clan Corin once camped, and sauntered into the market. For a while he walked aimlessly about, simply looking at the women and the booths. His hood was pulled up to hide his face—a common enough practice on a hot, sunny day. He did not stop to talk to anyone, and no one bothered him.

After a time, the stranger wandered over to the river. Every year the clansmen and the merchants erected a simple, temporary bridge across the shallows of the lower Goldrine River to simplify the crossing from many of the camps to the bazaar.

The stranger crossed the bridge easily and walked up a path between the Bahedin and the Dangari camps, heading toward the shady point of land where the council tent stood.

He was about to pass the Bahedin camp when he realized someone was behind him. He walked faster, but the clansman caught up with him and put a hand on his shoulder to stop him. The stranger's fingers curled in anger.

"Excuse me," a man's voice said. "Have you seen . . ." The speaker hesitated as the stranger turned and looked down at him. The man, an old weaver from the Bahedin, felt a strange shiver run down his back. "Oh, I thought you were someone else." He looked curiously at the tall, silent man, then took a closer look. His eyebrows drew together with consternation. "That cloak. Where did you get it? The embroidery on the hem looks like my son's."

The stranger did not answer. He shoved off the weaver's arm and started to walk away.

"Wait!" the Bahedin called loudly. Alarmed now, he caught up again with the man and yanked him around. "Answer me! You're not Bahedin. Who are you?"

The stranger clamped his hand around the weaver's neck and snarled, "The sorceress. Where is she?"

The old man's eyes bugged out in fear. He tried to pull away, but the merciless grip only tightened around his neck.

"Where is the sorceress?" the stranger hissed. He lifted the struggling weaver into the air with one hand. The Bahedin's face went red, then blue.

Someone screamed close by. All the people in the vicinity turned to stare and several came out of their tents. A short, elderly woman charged up the path, flung herself at the stranger's back, and pummeled him with her fists. She was screaming with fright and fury, and her cries brought people running.

The gorthling cursed. He was not ready yet to draw so much attention to himself or his powers. He wanted to find the sorceress first. Annoyed, he threw the weaver to the ground and backhanded the woman with a stunning blow that sent her reeling into a wicker corral. His violent motion knocked his hood off, and the sun shone full on his face. He paid no attention to the shocked clanspeople who gathered around the fallen couple. He ignored the shouts of the people behind him and continued walking down the path. Close by, a voice cried in stunned disbelief, "Branth! That's Lord Branth."

Other clanspeople stared at the gorthling in open disbelief as he strode by. A loud, angry commotion was building in the two camps and spreading outward in ripples of outrage and disbelief as word of Branth's arrival flew from tent to tent.

The gorthling's lips curled in a wicked grin. Let them yap, he thought. Perhaps the uproar would attract the sorceress and bring her to him. He was growing impatient. Although he studied every female he saw, he did not see any that matched the description of the clan's only magic-wielder. He passed the fringes of the Dangari camp and went down to the banks of the Goldrine.

He glanced back and saw armed men advancing on him from the Dangari camp, sunlight glinting off their blades. Across the river, where the council tent stood in its grove of cottonwood trees, several clansmen were attracted by the loud commotion and gathered on the bank.

Branth hesitated, looking up and down the river where other camps were clustered along the shores. Several women were standing in the shallows nearby, staring at him, their washing hanging from their hands. He was about to turn and head for another camp, when the armed warriors jumped him.

Jubilantly they bound his hands behind his back and searched him for weapons. To their surprise, all they found was a heavy, leather-bound book in a pack slung on his shoulder. A huge crowd gathered, and many of the people shouted threats. Here at last was a scapegoat for some of their pent-up anger, grief, and resentment for the previous summer's bloodshed.

The gorthling watched them with an ugly sneer on his face. He would go along with this farce for a little while longer, just to see if these noisy humans would take him to those who commanded their tribes. Their leaders might know where the sorceress was hiding.

The Dangari warriors shoved Branth down the bank and hauled him across the river to where their chieftain stood, framed by the open entrance of the council tent. Much of the crowd followed, trampling through the water like a herd of horses. The Dangari brought their prisoner to stand before Lord Koshyn, Lord Sha Umar, Lord Wortan of the Geldring, old Lord Jol of the Murjik, and Wer-tain Guthlac. Together, the men faced the bound prisoner while the crowd pushed around in a shouting, gesturing ring.

Lord Koshyn held up his hand for silence. The onlookers gradually fell quiet as their curiosity got the better of their hostility.

Koshyn studied the man before him and tried to quell a growing uneasiness. He did not like Branth's strange arrival. No exiled man under penalty of death just wanders into a clan gathering without a powerful reason. Then, too, if Athlone went to Pra Desh to find Branth and Branth appeared at the Tir Samod—what did that say of Lord Athlone's fate? The Dangari narrowed his eyes. There was a strange aura of menace about the prisoner that made the hairs rise on Koshyn's neck. Something about Branth was very different.

The chieftain turned to his men. "Was he armed?"

"No, Lord. He only had this with him." One of the warriors handed the leather bag to the chief.

Koshyn felt his hands grow cold when he looked in the bag. "The *Book of Matrah*," he said aloud. His uneasiness boiled into full alarm.

Lord Jol drew a sharp breath and edged away from the book. The other chiefs looked at one another with mixed expressions of suspicion and confusion.

After he handed the bag back to his warrior, Koshyn squared his shoulders. "You are under penalty of death," he said to Branth. "Why did you come back?"

The gorthling sneered. Death? That was a joke. He drew himself up to Branth's full height and stared out over the crowd, looking for the sorceress. He still wanted to find her before he blasted these annoying mortals to burned bits.

"Branth," Sha Umar said sharply, "you are condemned to die for conspiracy, treason, and murder. You can choose your own manner of death if you answer the question. Why are you here?"

The gorthling had had enough of their questions. He turned his inhuman glance on the chieftains. "To be your master!" he said with cold, deliberate malice.

The clanspeople reacted immediately. They surged closer, jostling and grabbing at the prisoner. The Dangari warriors struggled to keep them away until the chiefs could decide what to do.

Koshyn's face flushed with rage. Yet even as his fury mounted, a warning cry sounded in his head. Branth had had the *Book of Matrah* in his possession for almost a year—plenty of time to learn sorcery. If that was the case, then the only way they could render him defenseless was to kill him, or at least knock him unconscious. While he could think, he could cast spells; someone would have to deal with him, and quickly.

Everyone's attention was on Branth, and the gorthling's attention appeared to be on the Dangari warriors that crowded around him. Without warning, Koshyn snatched a battle axe from the belt of a warrior beside him and brought it swinging toward Branth's head.

It never landed.

The gorthling saw the blurred movement out of the corner of his eye, then barked a spell that froze the chieftain in mid-motion. The clanspeople around them fell still, their eyes strained wide, their faces caught in expressions of disbelief and shock. The silence spread outward into the crowd until the entire council grove was quiet.

The gorthling laughed and snapped the bonds around his wrists. "Now, worthless little man," he hissed to Koshyn, "perhaps you can tell me where the sorceress is." He raised his hand and sent a powerful burst of energy sizzling into Koshyn's body.

The excruciating pain ripped through the young Dangari. He screamed and fell to the ground in a writhing heap, unable to fight the torturous magic.

The sight of the vicious arcane spell broke the crowded clanspeople's stunned lethargy. They backed away to put a wide space between themselves and Branth. The chieftains, even Lord Jol, drew their swords, and they and the Dangari warriors leaped in to try to save the young lord. The gorthling blasted them aside as easily as swatting flies, killing three of the warriors. He continued to torture Koshyn.

"The sorceress!" Branth shouted furiously. "Where is she?"

"She's not here," Lord Sha Umar answered desperately. He picked himself up from the ground, his eyes pinned on Koshyn's writhing body.

The gorthling's face twisted into a frightening mask of delight, hate, and rage that sickened the watchers. "Where is she?" He made a jabbing motion with his hand, and Koshyn screamed in agony.

Sha Umar stepped forward, his hand raised in a pleading gesture. "We don't know. She went to look for you."

"She went to Pra Desh to find you," Lord Jol cried. The old chief was on the verge of panic. "But she'll be here soon."

Branth pounced on Jol's words. "Soon? When!"

Wer-tain Guthlac spoke up. "No one knows."

"Tell me, you worms, or this man dies!" Branth screamed. "I want the sorceress."

"Then look behind you," a new voice called from the edge of the grove.

The men started in surprise.

The gorthling whirled around and saw a young woman sitting astride a great black Hunnuli. He forgot about the men around him. His cruel mouth laughed in triumph, and his eyes began to glow red as the horse slowly paced toward him.

Without hesitation Sha Umar and Guthlac grabbed Koshyn's arms and dragged the chieftain's body out of sight, behind the council tent. The other clanspeople fled hastily out of the way. In the chaos, no one remembered the ancient tome in its brown leather bag lying in front of the council tent among the fallen stools, the scattered personal belongings, and the three dẹad Dangari warriors.

The gorthling sneered. "I've been looking for you, Sorceress."

"And I you," Gabria replied. Nara stopped twenty paces away, and the woman and the gorthling studied each other. Even in the warm morning Gabria felt a chill. The man before her looked like Branth physically: tall, brown hair, muscular build, everything perfectly normal and human. Only his presence was different. There was a cold glint of merciless cruelty in his eyes and an aura of hostility in his every move.

"We don't want you in this world," Gabria said.

The gorthling smirked. "Some people did."

"Go back to your own realm," she retorted. "You don't belong here."

"It's too late, Sorceress. I am here to stay." Even as the words left his mouth, the gorthling fired a bolt of the Trymian Force at the woman.

It came so fast Gabria was taken by surprise. However, the Hunnuli had been waiting for just such a move, and she reared high to protect her rider. The blue bolt struck her full on her chest, burst in a cloud of sparks, and evaporated harmlessly in the air.

The mare snorted.

Shaken, Gabria patted Nara in thanks and quickly formed an oblong clan battle shield with her arcane power. The magic shield was not as effective as a full force field, but it needed much less energy to maintain and would provide some protection. The gorthling came at her again and fired another bolt. This time she caught the force with the shield. Again and again Branth attacked, his barrage of sizzling blue blasts almost constant. He circled the Hunnuli to catch the woman from every angle, but either she or the mare blocked each blow.

In the back of her mind Gabria prayed that a stray bolt would not hit some of the clanspeople hiding among the trees of the council grove or any of the onlookers across the rivers. The uproar of the battle had brought people running from all directions. They were crowding on the banks of both rivers and watching Gabria and the gorthling with mixed amazement and horror. Many of them had never seen an arcane battle before. Fortunately for Gabria, no one dared cross the river to the council grove, and those people who hid among the trees and around the tent stayed very low.

Gabria made no move to take the offensive. She knew the gorthling's ability to enhance human powers would make him a formidable opponent, a sorcerer far stronger than Lord Medb. She hoped that by letting him expend his strength in this attack on her, she could wear him down enough so her powers would have an effect on him. Until then, she and Nara had to stay alert.

Strangely, the gorthling had so far only used the Trymian Force against her. Either he was too arrogant to bother with other spells, or he had not had enough time to study the more complicated spells in the *Book of Matrah*. Gabria prayed his reason was the latter.

The gorthling hurled bolts of the Trymian Force at Gabria and Nara, but he soon grew weary of the attack. He seemed to realize Gabria's intent was to simply avoid him, for he suddenly changed tactics. Instead of bolts that the woman could easily deflect with her shield, he threw balls of fire at the mare's feet that set the grass ablaze. Then he launched a spell that wrenched deep, wide cracks in the earth all around the horse.

Nara was forced toward the gorthling while Gabria frantically tried to put out the fires and seal the cracks. Before she had time to snuff out all the flames, the gorthling fired at her again with the Trymian Force.

Nara reared and caught one blast, barely avoiding a huge crack at her feet. The second hit Gabria's shield at a bad angle and nearly blew her off the mare.

Out of desperation, the sorceress formed a complete protective shield around herself and Nara just long enough to recover her seat and get the mare away from the fires. To Gabria's relief, the gorthling did not try immediately to shatter her defense. He had hesitated and seemed to be breathing heavily. Gabria wondered if he was tiring at last.

"What do I do?" she whispered frantically to Nara. "I can't hold this shield much longer."

The big mare leaped over a crack in the ground and angled around Branth to safer ground. *He is immortal, but his body is human. He is most vulnerable there,* the mare suggested. *He may not know all of his weaknesses.*

Gabria thought fast. Perhaps she could use his human frailties to destroy the gorthling's human body. If he was separated from Branth, it might be easier to trap or banish him. When the gorthling raised his arm to attack her again, she dissolved the arcane shield and formed her spell.

Not knowing the intricacies of the human body, the gorthling had no defense against her magic. Black boils suddenly erupted on his flesh. The gorthling hesitated; a peculiar expression came over his face. His skin faded to a bilious yellow, and he doubled over in excruciating pain. "Sorceress," he bellowed. "What is this?"

Gabria did not answer. She breathed deeply to relax and regain her strength. Now it was her turn to use the Trymian Force. She drew the power from within herself and fired a searing blow at the gorthling.

He was so sick and weakened by the unfamiliar fever that he barely avoided her blow. Time and again Gabria carefully attacked him with the Trymian Force and other missiles— daggers, fire, rocks—anything she could think of to make him move and react and use up his strength.

Finally the gorthling understood the sickness she had given him and cured his symptoms one by one. He staggered to his feet, his human face full of wrath.

Gabria hesitated. She did not think another sickness spell would be effective, because the gorthling was beginning to understand how the illness affected him. He would be better able to defend himself against a second attempt. But now she was at a loss over what to do next.

During that brief pause Gabria and Branth faced each other. The creature curled his lip and said, "You are better than I believed, Sorceress. You have withstood the usual battle spells I use." He raised his hands. "Now try this one."

Gabria stiffened to face the blow, but when it came, it took her completely by surprise. Her mind went abruptly blank. Then the world seemed to explode into a fiery maelstrom of whirling winds and searing heat. She felt herself being pulled helplessly into a giant vortex of tornadic winds and swirling fire.

She rolled and tumbled in the funnel of air and fire, screaming in pain, helplessness, and beneath it all, fury. The heat charred her skin, the winds flayed her face and limbs. Somewhere in the winds she heard wailing voices of other humans in torment, but she could see nothing in the yellow and orange fires. Gabria felt herself drawn deeper into the storm toward a place where the funnel fell into a mindless chasm of madness and everlasting emptiness. She fought back against the winds, clawing and writhing with a desperation strengthened by her powerful will to survive.

Suddenly, out of the roaring chaos she heard a beloved voice reach out like a lifeline to her mind. *Gabria, hear me! It is only a vision. Come back!*

The words rang like a sweet bell in her thoughts and awoke memories of another time and of another sorcerer, Lord Medb, who had also tried to defeat her with visions. She closed her eyes to the winds and fire, and out of the depth of her soul, she laughed.

The roaring winds abruptly ceased. The heat and the pain vanished. When she opened her eyes, she saw the glorious blue sky, the green cottonwood trees, and the muddy brown rivers. Her skin was whole, her arms and legs healthy, and the magnificent Hunnuli still carried her across the council grove. Gabria felt weary to the bone, but she was alive and still able to fight.

She jerked her head up and saw the gorthling standing near

the council tent. A flicker of surprise crossed his face. His arcane shield was down, and he was sweating. He looked as tired as she felt.

Gabria knew she did not have the strength at the moment to call upon the Trymian Force, yet there were other spells she knew well that did not need as much effort. She snapped a command, and the bits of rock and gravel around the gorthling's feet were transformed into a swarm of wasps.

The insects buzzed around the gorthling, stinging his human body and infuriating him. He felt his strength waning. He had seriously misjudged this sorceress. She had taxed his power with her unexpected human diseases and her determined counterattack, then he had foolishly drained his own strength to destroy her mind only to have her rescued by the Hunnuli at the last moment. She surprised him with her intelligence and self-will. The gorthling knew he was too weary to continue the fight at the present time. He needed a short time to rest until he could think of a way to destroy this woman and take his revenge on the clans. He vowed he would never leave until he had fulfilled his lust for their blood.

With a furious word, he dispelled the wasps into dust and looked around for some means of retreat. His eyes found the ring of stones on the holy island. For the first time, he noticed the clanspeople clustered on the far banks, and an idea took shape in his mind. Humans had a weakness for the safety of other humans. This woman was likely no different.

A furtive movement out of the corner of his eye caught Branth's attention. Before Gabria knew what he was doing, he ran a few steps toward the council tent and pounced on two men trying to peer around one wall. Both men carried swords, but the gorthling stunned them into immobility with a spell and disarmed them.

Gabria choked back a cry when the gorthling shoved his prisoners in front of him. They were Lord Wortan of the Geldring and Wer-tain Guthlac.

"Do not come near me, Sorceress," the gorthling shouted. "Or these men will die . . . horribly!" He slowly edged around the tent and began to back toward the river, keeping Wortan and Guthlac between himself and Gabria. Nara paced his movements step by step.

At the water's edge he grabbed the two men and hauled them in with him. Both were dazed and could barely stumble through the shallows. He forced the men on through the Goldrine toward the holy island. The Hunnuli and her rider stood on one shore following his every move; the clanspeople stood along the other banks watching what was happening.

The gorthling raised a hand. A lurid red glow ignited over his body, and before everyone's horrified gaze, he began to grow. His body grew taller and larger until he towered higher than the trees and his shadow fell on the people on the west bank. His face warped into a huge mask similar to the gorthling's original wizened features. The beast roared his fury and reached toward the nearest crowd of people. Those by the water's edge screamed in panic and tried to flee, but the press of people blocked their way.

Gabria screamed a warning. She tried to block Branth's hand with a spell, but she was too late. The gorthling grabbed seven people with his enormous hands and dragged them, struggling and shrieking, into the river to join his other hostages. As a diversion, he sent several blasts of the Trymian Force into the fleeing crowd.

Gabria was able to destroy all but one of the blasts. The last searing bolt struck a group of clanspeople, killing six and injuring many more.

"Stay back, Sorceress!" the gorthling bellowed. "Or I'll kill all of them."

Wordlessly, Gabria watched the gorthling shove his hostages together. Even as she racked her brain for a useful idea, the gorthling took his nine prisoners into the circle of stones and sealed the ring with a protective arcane shield, then he shrank back to normal size to conserve his strength.

Gabria gritted her teeth. She had failed. On the far riverbank, screams, wails, and cries of grief and pain blended into a lament that cut Gabria like an accusation. This disaster was her fault. She had not been strong enough to defeat or even contain the gorthling, and now the problem of fighting the creature was worse than ever.

She lifted her gaze to the island, her eyes glittering like cold gems. The gorthling had out-maneuvered her this time. She swore she would not let that happen again. Somehow she would find a way to defeat the beast and send it back where it belonged.

abria!" someone shouted. "What's going on?"

Lord Sha Umar ran to Nara's side and stared at the holy island where the gorthling had retreated. "What is Branth trying to do?" he asked.

"That isn't Branth any more," Gabria replied wearily. "Lord Branth summoned a gorthling in Pra Desh, and the creature invaded his body."

Sha Umar was horrified. "What's he doing here?"

"Trying to kill magic-wielders."

The chieftain looked over at the woman for the first time and noticed how wan and tired she appeared. "Where is Athlone?" he asked.

"North of here. Half a day's ride." She glanced at the sky and saw with surprise that the sun had barely risen to its midmorning height. Her battle with the gorthling had seemed interminable to her, but it had taken little time.

The island was quiet for the moment. Gabria could make out the group of prisoners huddled together in the center of the stone circle. Branth was sitting on a flat rock nearby, watching his hostages and resting. Of course, Gabria knew he was not resting completely. He was still using power to maintain the faint red force field that glimmered around the circle of stones.

On the opposite banks of the two rivers the camps were in chaos. More people gathered on the banks, their horrified curiosity getting the better of their fear. Relatives and friends grouped around the dead and wailed their grief. Others carried the wounded to the clan healers. No one was entirely cer-

tain what was going on. There was a cacophony of frantic
shouting, crying, yelling, and excited talking as everyone tried
to learn what had happened.

Four other chieftains came running toward the council
grove and forded the river. They met Sha Umar and Gabria
with a barrage of questions.

The Jehanan chieftain deftly maneuvered them away for a
moment to let Gabria collect her thoughts. The woman
slipped off Nara and rested thankfully against the mare's
strong shoulder. Her moment of quiet was over in a heartbeat.

Lord Caurus pushed past Sha Umar and shook his fist under
her nose. "I knew it! I knew you'd be trouble. It was only a
matter of time. Two of my people are dead, and it's your
fault."

Gabria let his anger wash around her like a wave. She understood his rage and fear, and in part, he was right. She had
let the gorthling snatch the hostages and slip away.

Lord Bael, the new chieftain of the Ferganan, butted in past
Caurus. "What is Branth doing here?"

"And where is Lord Athlone?" Young Lord Ryne called over
the noise.

"How did you get here? I thought you went to Pra Desh?"
Caurus added.

The Shadedron chief, Lord Malech, demanded, "What are
you going to do about this disaster?"

Gabria answered their questions as best she could and hurriedly explained her long journey to and from Pra Desh. The
men's anger and confusion cooled somewhat as they listened.
Gabria was pleasantly relieved that the chiefs heard her out
with a measure of respect and concern.

The only question she avoided was Lord Malech's. She did
not know what to do about the gorthling or his hostages. Even
after their battle, she was no closer to sending it out of the
world than when she had started. All she had succeeded in
doing was tiring herself and forcing the gorthling into a strong
defensive position.

She was still trying to explain the battle to the men when

Lord Jol pushed through the group and took Gabria's arm. "Lady Corin, would you come and look at Koshyn?"

Koshyn! She had forgotten about him. She broke off and hurried after the old Murjik chieftain. The others followed silently in their wake.

Sha Umar and Jol had laid the Dangari in the big council tent after the gorthling had left the grove. The chief was resting, unconscious, on his blue cloak. Three of Koshyn's hearthguard were dead, but two others stood by their lord, their faces showing their concern.

Gabria knelt down beside the wounded chieftain. Koshyn had suffered no obvious external injury from Branth's torturous spell, yet everyone could see there was something dreadfully wrong within him. He twitched and writhed and moaned in pain; his muscles jerked spasmodically, and his hands were clenched in knotted fists. When Gabria touched him, his skin was hot with fever.

"There is nothing I can do," Gabria said sadly. "Only our healer, Piers, can help. He has a stone of healing that will remove the harmful magic from Lord Koshyn's body."

The Dangari exchanged glances. "Where is your healer, Lady?" one of them asked.

"He will be coming soon, I hope." She glanced out the open tent flap. "Lord Koshyn is not the only one who will need the stone of healing. There are other people who were sorely injured, too."

At that instant, Nara spoke gladly in her mind. *Gabria, the men are coming!*

To the chiefs' mutual amazement, the sorceress jumped to her feet and dashed outside. She ran out to the edge of the trees and saw them coming. Athlone and Sayyed were doubled on Eurus, and the Hunnuli was galloping across the valley toward the gathering.

At that moment, Gabria did not know which of her emotions was stronger, her dismay that they had come when the gorthling was still a danger or her joy at their arrival. She knew she had disappointed them by leaving, but they had come to her aid anyway.

Gabria yelled and waved. They saw her and veered toward her. Athlone nearly fell off the big Hunnuli in his haste to reach the woman. His anger and worry were abruptly doused in the flood of relief that swept through him when he saw her alive and well. He caught her in his arms, crushing her close.

She said nothing, just wrapped her arms around him and held tightly.

Athlone did not say anything, either. He let her go, and she turned to greet Sayyed. The Turic, too, hugged her fiercely.

"I'm glad you're safe," he said, somewhere between laughter and tears.

"Where are Piers and the others?" she asked.

"On their way. The other horses could not keep up with Eurus." Sayyed flashed his charming smile. "I was nearly left behind, too."

The other chiefs caught up with the three just then, and they greeted Athlone with undisguised relief. They immediately bombarded him with questions and several versions of the events of the morning. He talked with them just long enough to hear them out and answer a few of their questions, then he excused himself and went to join Gabria and Sayyed.

As Gabria looked into Athlone's eyes, she could not trust herself to speak. She had tried to decide the men's fate by leaving them, convinced that the fight with the gorthling was hers alone. She knew now that she had been wrong. The creature was too strong for her to face by herself. She had to admit that she needed the help and the support of these two men. However, the decision to use their untrained sorcery in a battle against a much stronger foe was theirs to make. She was still desperately afraid for them, but she had to let them choose their own path.

"I will say only one thing before we talk about the gorthling," Athlone said. He cupped his hands around Gabria's face, and his brown eyes bored into hers. "Don't ever leave me like that again."

The intensity of his quiet words meant more to her than

anything he could have said in anger or any statement of his concern for her safety. Warmed to the center of her being, Gabria raised her hand palm up and said, "I promise."

His fingers interlaced with hers, and the vow was made.

They stood in the shade of the tree near the council tent, and Gabria told the two men what had happened from the moment she arrived. They could hear the noise still going on in the camps; the voices of some of the chiefs rose above the cacophony as they tried to assess the damage and calm their people. The council grove bustled with activity, but Gabria, Athlone, and Sayyed were left strictly alone.

Suddenly they heard a voice close by. "I demand to see Lord Athlone. My right as a Khulinin cannot be denied."

The chieftain groaned when he saw Thalar, the clan priest. Lord Sha Umar was trying to distract the priest, but Thalar grew louder and more insistent by the moment.

"I will not leave," Thalar shouted, "until I speak with my chieftain!"

Athlone nodded to Sha Umar, and the Jehanan stood aside. The priest came striding over. "What is it, Thalar?" the chieftain asked, the irritation clear in his voice.

The priest ignored his tone and planted himself before his chief. "Lord Athlone! You have finally come. I'll have you know that the gods-cursed heretic, Branth, has invaded the holy island, destroyed the sanctity of the gods' temple, and slaughtered people of our clans. I demand that you remove him from the sacred ring before the gods curse us for allowing this sacrilege to occur."

Lord Athlone tried to hold his temper. Although the priests and priestesses of a clan did not have as much authority as the chieftain, even the chiefs did not deliberately insult or antagonize a representative of the gods. Thalar, however, made self-control difficult.

"We're trying to—" Athlone began, but Thalar turned away before he could complete the sentence.

The priest faced Gabria, and his color turned as red as a beet. "As for her," he shouted, pointing a trembling finger at the woman, "that evil-tainted sorceress has destroyed this gathering! The moment she appeared, all the fury of Sorh broke loose."

Gabria tried to stifle a smile. Thalar did not know the truth of the gorthling's identity, so he had little idea how close he was to the truth.

Unfortunately the priest noticed her half-hidden expression and misread it for ridicule. "See how she laughs? Does she care that six people lie dead, that many more are injured, that nine are hostage, including a chief and your own wer-tain? Does she care for the sacrilege that is being done to our holy temple? Lord Athlone, that woman is a menace, and I demand that you banish her from this camp before she destroys us all."

"No," Athlone replied simply.

Thalar rose to his full height and bellowed, "Then kill her! Root out her evil!" His voice thundered across the grove. Anyone nearby who was not already listening to the harangue turned to watch. "Put an end to this vile stain of magic or by Surgart, I swear I will bring down the wrath of the gods upon this clan. I will—"

He went no further. Lord Athlone had had enough. The chief raised his hand, spoke a single word, and the priest's voice caught in his throat. Thalar's face turned from red to a sickly white, and his eyes bulged as he attempted to speak. Sha Umar and Sayyed grinned; the other chiefs looked stunned.

"No," said Athlone calmly. "As you can see, the stain of magic is spreading."

Thalar gasped and gagged with a mighty effort to say something, but the words would not come.

"You will listen now," Athlone ordered, a bite of steel in his tone. "I am a magic-wielder, too. I intend to help Lady Gabria as best I can to remove that gorthling."

Thalar abruptly stilled, and his body stiffened.

The chieftain saw his reaction and pushed the point home. "That's right. That creature is not Branth, but a beast of Sorh, and Lady Gabria was trying to save the clans from its evil. Do you understand?"

Thalar nodded, his eyes narrowed.

"Good. If you wish to remain with the Khulinin, I suggest you think about your position on sorcery. There are two sides to every argument." Athlone spoke a second command, and the priest put his hand to his throat. He cleared it a few times to make certain that he could speak again.

"So," Thalar said, his tone low and cold, "you, too, have succumbed to the heresy. Are you here to fight the gorthling or help it?" He glared ferociously at Athlone and stalked away from the group.

The men standing nearby stared at Athlone in amazement. "That was very interesting," Sha Umar said.

Gabria touched Athlone's arm. "You have been practicing," she said reproachfully.

"A little," he admitted. "Enough to get a feel for the way magic works."

She turned to Sayyed. "I suppose you have, too?"

He grinned. "Of course."

"How? You two don't know enough to teach yourselves."

Athlone replied, "By listening and watching you."

"You're lucky you did not destroy yourselves with an uncontrolled spell," she said.

Sayyed lifted his hands and shrugged. "You can't show us a feast and expect us to be happy with crumbs."

Gabria was about to reply when a shadow passed over the council grove. Nervously she glanced up, but it was only a cloud passing overhead, formed by the growing afternoon heat.

The sorceress was still gazing at the sky when an agonized scream tore through the camps. Everyone within hearing froze in their tracks. As the scream died away, Gabria, Athlone, and the others ran to the riverbank and stared at the island where the gorthling was standing. He had dissolved his force field and had dragged a woman out of the circle of standing stones to the graveled bank. The other eight hostages still huddled in the ring.

"Sorceress!" Branth yelled. He yanked his prisoner to her feet and held her out at arm's length. "Come to me or this female dies!" He shook the young woman viciously to make her scream again.

"Let her go!" Gabria shouted. "Let them all go, and I will come."

"You come *now*!" he screamed. "I will not wait." So saying, he shoved the sobbing woman toward the water. She ran frantically to escape, but the gorthling's spell caught her before she had taken five steps. The magic seared through her. The creature did not kill her with a quick, explosive burst of Trymian Force. Instead, he used an agonizing power that arched through the woman's body in a slow, massive, disintegrating wave.

Scream after scream ripped from her throat as she thrashed and writhed in the shallow water. The clanspeople watched, motionless with horror. The woman gave a final shriek, then sagged face-first into the water. The current tugged gently at her lifeless body and swirled her fair hair.

Branth did not give the clanspeople time to react. Instantly he shouted a command, and the nearest hostage in the circle stumbled to his feet and began to walk helplessly toward the gorthling. It was Guthlac, the Khulinin wer-tain.

Gabria's eyes blazed with green fury. "Athlone . . ." she began to say, but something interrupted her.

A man stepped off the council grove riverbank into the water. His robes swirled around his short legs, and his face was red with righteous fury. He held his priest's staff over his head like a spear pointed at the gorthling.

"Begone, foul heretic! Beast of Sorh, leave this holy place!" Thalar shouted with all his rage and indignation as he waded toward the island.

"Thalar!" Athlone yelled. "Get back here."

The priest did not hear him. His mind was focused on driving the evil from the blessed island. The Tir Samod was the gods' holy temple, the sanctuary of the priests and the sacred heart of the clans, not a hiding hole for a creature of profane powers. If no one else was going to rid the island of this evil, Thalar swore he would do it himself.

He raised his staff higher. "Go, you gods-cursed worm. By the power of Surgart, I command you to leave."

The gorthling laughed and, without a word, struck the priest with a brilliant blue bolt of Trymian Force. Thalar shrieked once, threw his arms up, and toppled into the river. The rippling water caught his scorched body and carried him gently downstream.

"That's two, Sorceress," the gorthling yelled. "Do you want more bodies to clog the river?"

Gabria spun on her heel and whistled for Nara. Both Hunnuli came at her summons. "That beast must be stopped," she said as she sprang to Nara's back.

Athlone immediately mounted Eurus, and the big stallion blocked Nara's way. "We're going with you," the chieftain said calmly.

Gabria looked from Athlone to Sayyed and saw the same look of determination on both faces. She could not leave them behind this time, even if she wanted to. She inclined her head once in gratitude and shoved her fear for them out of the way. Now, however, she hesitated, for she was uncertain how to mount an attack that would use the skills of the two men. Sayyed had no mount, and neither man was very proficient with the Trymian Force.

She was still trying to think of a way when Nara perked up her ears. Eurus lifted his head high, and his nostrils flared. On the edge of her senses, Gabria felt something, a faint vibration like distant thunder, or . . . horses' hooves. She raised herself up on Nara's back and saw a plume of dust on the ridge of hills to the west. The vibrations grew louder. A dark form appeared on the horizon, then another, then many more. Nara and Eurus suddenly neighed a joyful greeting that pealed through the gathering and was echoed by every horse in the valley.

A herd of horses galloped down the hills and across the valley, their black coats shining in the sun. A small rider on a little Hunnuli ran just behind their leader. The clanspeople saw them, shouted in awe and delight, and stood aside to let them pass.

The gorthling, too, stared at the approaching horses, and for the first time since he had taken his mortal guise, he felt a pang of apprehension.

The herd thundered down to the river and plunged in with a tremendous, sparkling splash. They ran through the water as easily as air until the entire herd had encircled the island, cutting off the gorthling from the clans. Then the Hunnuli stopped, their heads turned toward the island. Sunlight glistened on their wet coats; their lightning marks gleamed on their shoulders. They pawed the water and snorted in anger.

Five of the horses charged toward the island, their hooves flashing and their teeth bared. The gorthling clasped his hostage in front of him like a shield. He backed away to the shelter of the temple just as the enraged Hunnuli burst up on the shore, then swiftly revived his protective shield of magical energy. The five horses circled the temple warily and waited for their king's command.

Finally the King Stallion cantered up to Gabria on the riverbank, his deep, wise eyes glowing with a golden light. He bowed his head to her. *Sorceress, you needed us, so we have come.*

For a moment Gabria was utterly speechless. She gazed up at the magnificent old stallion, then transferred her amazement to the beaming, dark-haired girl sitting astride Nara's colt.

"I won't ask now how you did this, Tam," Gabria said softly. "You can tell me later, but I am deeply grateful."

The little girl blushed under her tan, and her shy grin grew even wider. Sayyed strode over and pulled Tam off the colt into a huge hug of relief and pride. Tam wrapped her arms around his neck.

The King Stallion snorted angrily. *Tam has told us a gorthling has been released in the world.*

Gabria gestured to the island where the gorthling was pacing back and forth within his defense shield, studying the new arrivals. "Do you know of any way to send him back?"

Sadly, no. That knowledge was never passed on to us. The King Stallion swung his massive head toward his herd. *His magic cannot affect us, however. We will try to keep him confined to the island so he does not harm any more of your people. The rest you must do yourself.*

Gabria was disappointed that even the King Stallion did not know how to dispel a gorthling, but she appreciated his help enormously. She would not have to worry about the clans with the Hunnuli herd to protect them.

I see that you have one sorcerer unhorsed. That will not do. The King Stallion neighed, and another stallion left the ring of Hunnuli. The new horse came to stand in front of Sayyed. He stretched out his muzzle to gravely sniff the Turic.

This is Afer. He will be your mount for this confrontation, the King Stallion told Sayyed.

For once the young Turic was nonplussed. He was torn between delight and awe as he ran his hand down the big Hunnuli's nose. Gingerly he mounted the stallion and settled down on the broad back.

Gabria nodded her thanks to the King Stallion before she turned to the two men. "Remember, Eurus and Afer are immune to magic," she said rapidly. "Stay on them at all times. If you need protection, form a shield between you and the gorthling." After a pause, she added, "Please try to use spells as little as possible. I will attack the gorthling, but I'll need you two distract him. We will try to wear him down until he is too weak to use his power."

"What about the prisoners?" Sayyed asked.

"If we can cut the gorthling off from them and keep him occupied, maybe they'll escape on their own. Perhaps the Hunnuli will help them."

"Have you tried the mask yet?" Athlone wanted to know.

Gabria shook her head. "I still don't know what to do with it."

"Sorceress!" the gorthling suddenly yelled. "I see you brought some help." He laughed maliciously. "These useless beasts will avail you not. Come. I grow tired of waiting. You or these mortals must die!"

Gabria curled her lip in a feral grimace. "We *will* find a way to destroy him." She turned and called, "Lord Sha Umar, the Hunnuli will try to protect the people from any destructive magic, but please keep the warriors and priests away from the island. Will you also watch over Tam?"

"With pleasure, Lady Gabria," the Jehanan answered, coming forward to stand beside the little girl. "The gods go with you."

Gabria turned away so quickly she did not see the stricken look pass over Tam's face. The sorceress signaled to Athlone and Sayyed, and the three magic-wielders rode down into the river. The gorthling laughed with glee as they came.

19

hile the King Stallion rejoined his herd, Gabria, Athlone, and Sayyed separated and spread out so they could approach the island from different angles. Their mounts passed through the ring of Hunnuli horses and carefully waded toward the island. The five Hunnuli on shore held their positions and waited.

The gorthling, wary but confident, watched the riders come. There were three humans now. That was an interesting development. There was only supposed to be one magic-wielder in the clans. Curious, he formed an opening in his defense field and fired a blue bolt at the nearest man. He was amazed when the clansman formed a shield and deflected the energy harmlessly into the air. For just a second, the gorthling felt a twinge of fear. Then it passed, and he snarled. What was another magic-wielder or two? He would simply have to strike fast and kill them before they could wear down his strength with their greater numbers.

He glanced at the Hunnuli, too. They were another problem. He knew the five on the island were only waiting to break through his shield and chase him out into the open. No magic would stop them. What he needed was a spell to frighten the humans and a weapon untouched by magic to drive off the horses.

His eye lit on the tall, upright monoliths of the temple, and a cunning grin curled his mouth. He spoke the words of his spell, and once again his body glowed red and began to grow. Soon he towered over the temple and could straddle his hostages. His defense shield dissipated. With a great laugh, he tore a stone from the sacred ring and swung it like a club at the nearest horse. The animal barely dodged in time.

The King Stallion neighed to call his horses back. Magic was a weapon they could avoid, but the horses had no riders to defend them against stone clubs. The five Hunnuli reluctantly withdrew, leaving the magic-wielders and their mounts to their duty.

Before the three sorcerers reached the island shore, the battle was joined. The gorthling fired at Gabria and the two men with a rapid-fire assault of the Trymian Force and other destructive bolts of power. Fortunately for all three, the gorthling was using so much strength to maintain his tremendous size, his bolts of magic were not as powerful as before. The greatest danger lay in the gorthling's stone club, which he swung at the riders whenever they got too close.

The riders quickly discovered another danger. The land around the temple was uneven and rough underfoot. Rocks, boulders, tough shrubs, vines, and small saplings covered the island and made movement on horseback difficult. The gorthling made full use of the uneven ground, forcing the Hunnuli to constantly maneuver over the stony island.

The gorthling himself did not try to move, for the little group of hostages was clinging together in a terrified huddle between his huge legs. They did not dare run, and neither the Hunnuli nor the magic-wielders could reach them as long as the beast stood over them.

It was not long before the gorthling noticed that only the sorceress was offering any real counterattack. She fired her own spells at him while the men only tried to distract him with awkward feints whenever possible. They were rank beginners, he realized gleefully. That noted, he began to concentrate his attack on Athlone and Sayyed, forcing Gabria to expend more and more of her energy to defend her companions.

As time went on, the battle grew more desperate. Gabria silently thanked the gods for the Hunnuli herd. She knew she and the two men would not have lasted so long against the gorthling if they'd had to defend the crowds. The horses stopped several bolts of magic, and their presence kept the gorthling penned on the island.

But even with the help of the Hunnuli, the struggle was telling upon the three humans. Athlone's and Sayyed's inexperience was beginning to show. Their shields were weakening, and several times the gorthling nearly knocked them from their horses. Gabria's fear for them intensified.

Gabria, too, was tiring. She had faced the brunt of the gorthling's attack, and she knew her strength would not last much longer. She pressed the gorthling harder with the Trymian Force, with fireballs, smoke, and flights of arrows. She tried everything she could think of, yet her magic had no effect. The gorthling's size and greater strength helped him ward off her blows with ease. Gabria was running out of ideas.

Then, in the blink of an eye, everything changed.

Sayyed's Hunnuli, Afer, was near the sacred ring when he abruptly slipped on a mossy stone and his front hoof slid down between a cluster of rocks. The stallion lost his balance and fell heavily to the ground. The snap of his foreleg was heard all over the island.

Sayyed was thrown over the stallion's head into the rocks. The Turic lay dazed while his Hunnuli tried frantically to free his broken leg and defend his rider. The other Hunnuli neighed in strident, ringing calls, and Eurus and Nara sprang forward to help the fallen horse and rider.

The gorthling moved faster, grabbing the dazed Turic with one huge hand. Sayyed was bleeding heavily from a cut on his head and was too stunned to try to escape. Nara and Eurus started toward the giant in the stone circle.

The gorthling laughed, and his eyes glowed red. "Now," he bellowed, brandishing his stone club with one hand and Sayyed's struggling form in his other, "watch one of your own die."

To the watchers' horror, Branth hoisted the young Turic over his head. Sayyed fought back weakly, his face working with fear when he saw the ground far below.

Across the river, Tam stood by the Hunnuli colt and Lord

Sha Umar, watching the battle. She had not moved from the riverbank since Gabria had left, and she had ignored Sha Umar's offer for food or drink. Her hand stayed on the colt's neck and her eyes remained on the island.

When Afer fell, Tam stiffened and her mouth opened slightly. She watched in growing apprehension as the gorthling grabbed Sayyed. A tiny whimper escaped her lips. When Tam saw the creature lift Sayyed into the air, she quivered with anger and fear. A fury that she had never known before exploded at the injustice and cruelty of losing another person she loved. No, her young mind cried, not again. No! No!

"No!"

Tam's voice rang out loud and clear across the water. At the same time, she instinctively used her wild talent to project her furious thought into the human brain of the gorthling.

The effect was stunning. The protest burst on the gorthling's unprepared mind like an explosion, sending him staggering back. He let go of the Turic and clamped his hands to his head. His concentration broken, he dropped his stone club and began to shrink back to normal size.

The magic-wielders reacted instantly. Before Sha Umar could stop her, Tam jumped on the small Hunnuli and galloped him toward the island. Gabria broke Sayyed's fall by transforming the stones beneath him into a thick pile of hay, and Athlone fired a bolt of the Trymian Force at the unprotected gorthling. The bolt was weak and uncontrolled, but it was enough to knock Branth onto his back and give Sayyed a chance to escape.

"Get to the other side of the river!" Gabria cried.

The Turic did not listen. Instead of retreating, he flung himself into the group of hostages. The gorthling screeched in rage. He fired a blast at the people huddled together, but Sayyed formed a shield over them all. The Trymian Force bounced harmlessly away.

The gorthling felt his twinge of fear return and grow stronger. He immediately revived his own defensive shield. Now he had no escape route, no hostages for safety, and no place to retreat. He was trapped, and while his enemies were tiring, so was he. He could no longer maintain his gigantic size or the full power of his Trymian Force. The thought occurred to him that he had seriously underestimated these humans. He paused for a moment, breathing heavily, and looked around the island for some means of turning this battle in his favor.

Gabria and Athlone took advantage of the brief respite to regroup. Nara clattered over the rocks closer to Eurus, and their two riders watched the gorthling warily.

"We seem to be in a stalemate," Athlone said between deep breaths. "What do we do now?"

Gabria frowned in frustration. "I really don't know. He can't leave the island, but I still don't know how to send him back to Sorh's realm. Nothing I do works!" She glanced into the temple. "Sayyed, are you all right?"

The Turic answered without his usual humor. "We are safe for the moment."

Tam and the colt trotted up the bank and hurried into the temple to join Sayyed. He seemed relieved to see her, so Gabria merely shook her head and let the girl stay for the moment. Tam was already slipping out of the temple to help Afer free his leg, and several Hunnuli from the herd were coming to join her. Tam would be well protected.

The gorthling saw the Hunnuli coming, too, and his anger rekindled. He could still slaughter these people and drive away the infuriating horses. Abruptly he ended the respite and fired a bolt at Athlone, hoping to catch the chief unprepared. To his fury, the man's big stallion stopped the magic on his powerful chest.

"Give up, you feeble humans. You will never defeat me," the gorthling taunted. "I will be here forever! As long as there are bodies to inhabit. No one has ever conquered the gorthlings of Sorh."

"You're forgetting Valorian," Athlone retorted, "and Matrah." He shot a blue bolt at the gorthling's defense shield.

His blast exploded harmlessly, but his words set off a small spark of thought in Gabria's mind. Like a streak of lightning, the thought burst into an incandescent inspiration.

She slapped the heavy bag at her side. "That's it! Of course. Valorian knows!" she cried. The diamond splinter in her wrist flared from her excited burst of energy.

Athlone stared at her sudden transformation. "What are you talking about?"

"The mask!" she said, trying to keep her voice down. "Quick, Athlone, Tam! Get into the temple and join Sayyed."

The little girl had just released Afer's broken leg from the rocks, so she patted the injured horse and hurried to obey, leaving him with the other Hunnuli.

Athlone hesitated. "What are you planning?"

"If Branth can summon something from the realm of the dead, so can I," Gabria replied excitedly.

"Not another gorthling."

"Of course not. I'm going to try to use the power in the mask to summon Valorian. If I am successful, *he* can tell us how to rid ourselves of that beast."

Athlone was awestruck by the simplicity and audacity of her plan. Valorian. My gods! Athlone thought. Without another word he took Eurus into the temple.

Gabria loosed two quick bolts at the ground by the gorthling's shield. As they exploded in a cloud of dirt and gravel, she and Nara hurried through the ring of stones after Athlone and joined the group of people in the center of the temple.

Before the gorthling could retaliate, Sayyed lowered his shield and renewed it around the entire group, including Nara, Eurus, and the colt.

"By the gods," Wer-tain Guthlac said to his chief, "I'm glad to see you!" He instinctively ducked when the gorthling fired a blast at the shield.

The other hostages stared at Gabria in confusion and hope. She gave them what she hoped was a confidant smile and untied the bag from her belt. The mask felt heavy in her hands. She turned to Athlone and said, "I will not be able to help you maintain the shield while I do this spell. You, Sayyed, and Tam will have to protect us all."

He grinned. "Gladly."

Her green eyes sparkled at his reply. "Two months ago I would never have thought you would say that."

"You've taught me well," the chieftain replied.

He went to stand by Sayyed and Tam, and the three joined their wills together to hold the magical shield around the beleaguered group. The gorthling shrieked in rage. He fired more arcane blasts at the shield to try to weaken it, but for now, the three magic-wielders held it firm.

Gabria slid to the ground and leaned back against Nara. The mare curved her neck around Gabria and nickered softly. *In the memory of my sires, Valorian was a tall man, dark-haired, proud, kind, and fearless. Bend your will toward him through the mask. Perhaps he will hear you.*

The sorceress bowed her head. She did not know a formal spell for summoning a being from the realm of the immortals, so she would have to create one of her own. Nara's suggestion sounded as plausible as any idea she might decide upon. She straightened and turned to face the flat stone altar on the eastern side of the temple.

The hostages watched her in growing amazement. The clanspeople on the riverbanks who could see her muttered among themselves, wondering what was happening.

The sorceress studied the stones still standing around her. Legends said that Valorian dwelled with the gods, beyond the realm of the dead. What better place from which to summon him than a sacred temple? If there was anyplace on the Dark Horse Plains where the world of man touched the unseen realm of the gods, the Tir Samod was it.

"Amara, give me strength," Gabria prayed.

Reverently, she held the golden mask up to the sky. As the sunlight sparkled on the enigmatic face, the mask tingled in her hands.

Gabria closed her eyes. One by one, she focused on the sounds around her—the curses of the gorthling as it struggled to break through their defenses, the murmur of the hostages behind her, the click of the horses' hooves on stone, the ripple of the rivers—and one by one, she shut them out of her mind until there was only a vast silence.

Into the silence she sent her plea to Valorian. She bent her will into the magic of the mask and called him with every fiber of her being. The world around her seemed to recede until she was floating in a limitless, lightless, ethereal realm beyond the bounds of her earthly senses. She went without fear into the darkness and continued to call Valorian with her heart, mind, and soul.

Time passed, although Gabria did not feel it. Her mind was wrapped around the image of a tall, dark-haired warrior with a cleft chin and the look of eagles in his face. She had to find him. The safety of his people depended upon it.

Her summons went on without pause until, far ahead in the horizonless distance, she saw a light appear like sunlight through a crack. Gabria moved instinctively toward it, staring at the brilliant, shimmering golden radiance until its power filled her being and tested the measure of her spirit. A warm sense of comfort and familiarity enveloped her.

The mask shifted in her hands. The light vanished, and the sounds of the world rushed back. Around the island the Hunnuli horses neighed a trumpeting welcome. Gabria was so surprised she opened her eyes and looked at the mask.

The most vivid pair of blue eyes she had ever seen looked back at her.

The death mask twitched, stretched, and the mouth suddenly lifted into a smile. "I have come, Daughter. As you have asked." The golden face spoke in a voice both powerful and kind. Its words rang out over the island and were heard as far away as the riverbanks.

Gabria nearly dropped the mask in astonishment. She had not known what to expect when she tried to summon Valorian. She had only used the mask as a focal point for her spell. She raised the mask up again.

A question formed in her mind, but she could not bring herself to ask if this truly was the Hero-Warrior from the clans' distant past.

The mask glowed with a pure radiance, the same light Gabria realized she had seen in her mind. "I am he whom you have called. I am the essence of the man once named Valorian."

For a moment, Gabria was overcome with joy and awe and an overwhelming desire to cry and laugh at the same time. "I can't believe you have come," she said, trying to calm her shaking hands.

"Your power is strong, my daughter. Your need must be great."

"Forgive me, Lord. I have to ask you something that only you can tell me."

"I will listen. But ask your question quickly. I cannot stay long in this world."

Gabria shot a glance at the three magic-wielders. Sayyed, already weary and injured, was concentrating fiercely on the spell, and it was obvious to her that he was tiring fast. Tam was ashen, and even Athlone was beginning to look strained. The shield was a difficult spell to maintain, even without the added strains brought on by the gorthling's constant barrage of destructive magic.

Quickly she turned back to the death mask and looked boldly into the eternal blue eyes. "My lord, one of the Geldring men has summoned a gorthling."

The mask frowned. "How?"

"With a spell from the *Book of Matrah*."

"Those spells should be stricken from all human knowledge. There are some things best left alone by man. Where is this gorthling now?"

"Here. It possessed the man's body and came to our clan gathering. My lord Valorian, I am the only magic-wielder with any training to speak of, but I don't know how to destroy it."

Valorian gazed at her with compassion. "No human, no matter how skilled, has enough power to force a gorthling back through the portal between the world of mortals and the eternal world."

Gabria turned cold. "It has to be done," she cried. "How

do we get rid of him?"

"Only one thing in your world has the power to open a passage and force the creature back through."

"What?"

The mask lifted its eyes to the sky. "The power of the lightning," he said simply.

Gabria's mouth dropped open. She was aghast. "Lightning? But no one can withstand the fury of the gods' thunderbolts."

"You are a magic-wielder, a daughter of my blood. Do you travel with a Hunnuli?"

She nodded.

"Astride a Hunnuli, you will be protected. They bear the mark of the lightning for good reason. Their sire, my stallion, was transformed by the lightning into the first of that noble breed of horses."

"Lord Valorian," Gabria said, trying to stay calm, "I cannot create a storm. Where do I find lightning on a clear day?"

"If there are more than one Hunnuli with you, they can summon a storm and its lightning."

The golden light began to fade from the mask, and the blue eyes dimmed. Valorian's expression relaxed, then stiffened into the one the mask had worn when Gabria found it.

"Valorian, my lord," Gabria begged desperately. "What do I do with the power of the lightning?"

"I must go, Daughter," Valorian said sadly. "Use the lightning to send . . . it . . . back."

A faint echo followed the final words, as if they had been spoken across a great and hollow distance. Then the mask was still and lifeless once more. Gabria stared at the golden face and willed it to speak again, but it was too late. Valorian was gone, beyond her reach.

"How do I wield lightning?" she called in despair to the voiceless stones. There was no answer here, she knew, and now there was no more time. The gorthling was using a fierce blue barrage against the shield protecting the little group. Already the force field was beginning to waver. Sayyed looked ready to pass out, and Athlone's teeth were clenched as he concentrated.

"Hold on!" Gabria cried to her friends. "Nara," she yelled over the noise of the gorthling's attack. "Call the King Stallion. Tell him to summon a storm."

Beyond the island, the King Stallion replied with a strident neigh. *We have not called the lightning in generations of our kind. We will try.*

The ring of black horses abruptly lifted their muzzles to the sky. The Hunnuli on the island, even the colt and the wounded Afer, joined their silent communion with the air. Only Nara and Eurus did not include themselves in the call, deciding instead to keep alert in case their riders needed their aid.

To the Hunnuli's advantage, the afternoon was perfect for a storm. The day's heat and a humid wind had already formed billowing clouds in the blue sky, and several little rain squalls patterned the far horizons. As the Hunnuli herd concentrated their power, darker clouds began to gather overhead; the rain squalls moved closer. The horses strained, but the ability they had inherited from their sires served them well.

Gradually the sky grew dark, and a tremendous thunderhead reared out of the forefront of an angry mass of gray clouds. The sun was blotted out, and lightning flickered in the storm's turbulent heart.

The gorthling looked up, and fear shone clearly on Branth's face. That fear did not distract him long, though, and he did not miss the events unfolding in the circle of stones.

"Gabria," Athlone suddenly yelled. "Sayyed passed out. The shield is failing!"

The sorceress jumped on Nara's back just as the gorthling shattered the magic field. With a wild screech of triumph Branth fired a blast at the chieftain through the breach.

Athlone was too exhausted to defend against it. He saw the bolt coming and leaned into Eurus's side. The stallion reared up and took the blast on his shoulder, but the violent movement of the stallion and the explosion of power slammed Athlone backward. He crashed to the rocky ground where he lay motionless.

Tam, exhausted beyond bearing, mentally called the Hunnuli that stood by Afer, and two of them immediately joined Eurus to defend the fallen men.

The gorthling turned away. He could not get near the fallen chieftain or the Turic as long as the Hunnuli stood over them, but that did not matter. Neither man would be any more trouble.

Gabria had not moved from the temple. She and Nara stood between the gorthling and the hostages. Behind her she heard Lord Wortan and Wer-tain Guthlac trying to calm the terrified prisoners. Gabria kept her gaze pinned on Branth. The wind was starting to roar through the temple, and thunder rumbled across the sky. The herd of Hunnuli stirred from their motionless concentration and neighed their victory to the oncoming storm.

The gorthling began to edge warily into the temple, his cruel eyes fastened on Gabria and her mount.

The sorceress stared at him implacably and made no move to attack. She had only one idea for what she would do with the lightning. If that did not work, she would not have a chance to try anything else. She sat still on Nara, feeling the powerful heat of the Hunnuli warm her legs; her fingers touched the jagged white mark on Nara's shoulder.

As it had in Pra Desh when Gabria had fought the fire consuming the palace, the magic around the sorceress was intensifying with the power of the storm. She knew the enhanced power would help her, but it could also aid the gorthling. Quickly and precisely she began to form her spell in her mind, waiting for the right moment to strike.

The gorthling stepped between two stone pillars. "Valorian was wrong, Sorceress," he hissed. "Nothing can send me back. Get ready to die!"

Gabria did not reply. Lightning flashed overhead, and she felt the split-second surge of power in the air. Lightning happened so fast, she would have to act instinctively. Branth took another step forward and raised his hands to the sky.

Gabria! Nara cried in the woman's mind and leaped sideways not a moment too soon. A sizzling bolt of Trymian Force slammed down on the spot where they had been standing. The gorthling was using the intensified magic to his full advantage.

Gabria threw herself to the right as another of the gorthling's bolts seared past her. Another blast and another. They were so fast, hot, and deadly that Gabria could not concentrate on her own spell; it took her full attention to dodged the wicked bolts. The sorceress did not dare form a defense shield for fear of using too much of her depleted strength. She could only rely on the agility and protection of her mount.

Big drops of rain spattered on the warm rocks nearby. A lightning streak exploded on a tree across the river near the Jehanan camp, followed instantly by a deafening clap of thunder. The storm was moving, and Gabria knew she only had a brief time before the lightning was too far away. Yet the moment to attack was still not right.

The gorthling fired another bolt at her. It struck the ground at Nara's feet, shattering the rocks and sending gravel and splinters flying. The mare reared away, her motion nearly unseating Gabria.

The gorthling began to laugh, a rude, wicked sound that reflected his arrogance. The sorceress would never destroy him, for in a moment she would be dead.

Frantically Gabria struggled to regain her balance. She saw the gorthling draw his hands back. At the same time, a tingling skittered across her skin and the hairs on the back of her neck rose. She felt more than saw the power that surged around her, concentrating its energy on the tallest stone pillar near the altar to her right. This was even better than she had hoped for. The woman closed her mind to all but her spell and let her instincts guide her.

Lightning struck the top of the great stone monolith, its incredible energy searing the very air. The gorthling flinched away, but Gabria put her trust in the natural protective powers of the Hunnuli and reached out for the streaking energy.

In one fluid movement, she snared the lightning bolt and wrenched it from its natural path into her hand. She felt the incredible power surge through every fiber, bone, and hair of both her body and Nara's, and she saw the mare glimmer with a greenish white glow. Surprisingly the bolt felt warm and soft in Gabria's hand. She swung around and threw the lightning like a javelin, using every bit of strength she had left.

The blue-white bolt split the air to the gorthling and struck his body in a blinding explosion of light, sparks, and heat.

Gabria's vision went black and red with pain. She heard the gorthling's high-pitched screech of despair and hatred, followed by a tremendous crash of thunder. At that same instant, the backlash of the lightning's energy slammed into her and Nara. The Hunnuli staggered under the explosive force, and Gabria was flung to the wet, cold ground.

he sound of thunder faded from Gabria's ears, and she became aware of a persistent, needle-sharp pain behind her eyes. It brought her out of her state of shock and back to reality. She opened her eyes for just a moment and saw nothing but blackness and red shooting streaks. A tremor fluttered in her chest. She was blind!

She forced down her terror and concentrated instead on a small, calm voice that was speaking softly near her ear. The voice was unfamiliar, but something about its gentle tone was soothing.

"Tam?" she whispered out of the dark. She tried to sit up, but every bone and muscle in her body sent up a painful protest.

The quiet voice replied with intense relief. "Yes, Lady, I am here. No! Don't move yet. Help is coming."

Gabria obeyed willingly. She lay still on the cold, hard ground and felt the rain pounding on her body. Tam had to be shielding her face, but Gabria could not see.

The sorceress reached out for the girl's hand. "Tam, where is the gorthling?"

"He's gone," Tam answered excitedly. "The lightning you threw disintegrated him! There isn't even a finger left."

Gabria could not help but smile. Tam had certainly found her tongue in the midst of all the chaos.

Another person joined them, and a familiar voice said, "Gabria, let me help you." The clan priestess of Amara wrapped a warm cloak around the sorceress and very carefully eased her to a sitting position. "Can you stand?" the priestess asked.

Gabria swallowed hard and shook her head. Pain and nausea coursed through her head and her stomach. Every muscle she had was trembling. She felt as weak and blind as a newborn kitten.

"Never mind. Sit here a moment," the priestess told her. "I will tend to the others."

Gabria heard her walk toward the place where Athlone had fallen. Nara came to stand upwind of the sorceress to block some of the wild wind and rain that lashed across the island. Tam still held her cloak over Gabria's head.

"Nara, are Athlone and Sayyed badly hurt?"

They are exhausted, but will recover, I believe.

Gabria turned her sightless eyes toward the mare. "Your thoughts are strained. You sound weary. Are you all right?"

I am very weak. The strength needed to protect us from the lightning was almost more than I had.

The woman reached out and felt the mare's strong foreleg. "Thank you, Nara."

The mare nickered like a gentle laugh. *It was a good battle. The gorthling is gone, and we are still here.*

Gabria sighed. "What is going on out there? Is a healer coming to help Athlone and Sayyed? Afer's leg is broken. Is anyone coming to help him?"

Tam answered, her young voice high with anger. "The priests and priestesses will not allow any more uninitiated onto the island, but they won't cross the river themselves to help. Only the priestess of Amara from your clan had the courage to come."

Gabria's anger stirred sluggishly in her thoughts. She and her companions had faced death to save the clans, but now that they needed help, the people would not even come to their aid. Her nausea faded a little, and she sat up straighter, stirred by resentment.

Before she could think of a suitable angry response, an image of what she had done came to her mind. Her anger retreated while she considered how the entire arcane battle must have looked from the clans' point of view. They were probably terrified out of their wits.

Gabria realized she had an excellent opportunity to make a positive impression on her stubborn, skeptical, suspicious people. They had seen the horror of the gorthling's cruelty and the terror of his magic. Now she could show them the other side of magic: the pleasure of victory and the comfort of healing.

Strengthened by her resolve, Gabria painfully pulled herself up Nara's iron-strong foreleg until she was standing, dizzy and gasping, by the mare's shoulder. The cold rain poured down her face, but she did not care. She concentrated on staying upright, gritting her teeth against the exhaustion that rocked her, and held on grimly to Nara's mane.

A strong arm was laid across her shoulders and steadied her. The priestess's calm voice said, "Gabria, please. You need to rest."

The sorceress refused. "Not yet. Where is Athlone?"

"I'm here." Lord Athlone's voice was strained, but steady. It sounded wonderful to Gabria. He walked wearily around the big mare to say something more and hesitated when he saw Gabria and the strange expression on her face. Her eyes were closed tightly, and her head was tilted to one side in a concentrated effort to hear.

"Are you hurt?" Gabria asked the chieftain.

"Just a knock on the head, but I feel exhausted." He rubbed his temples and looked around, bleary-eyed. "What happened?"

Tam replied, "The sorceress destroyed Branth with a lightning bolt."

"Good gods," he exclaimed.

At that moment, the King Stallion cantered through the water to the island and pranced up to the small group. The Hunnuli herd gathered behind him, their black coats glistening in the rain.

"Athlone," Gabria whispered. "Help me up."

Willingly the chieftain gave her a leg up onto Nara's back

and stood aside to watch as the tall, slim woman turned to face the huge stallion.

The black Hunnuli shook his mane. *You have done well, Sorceress.*

Gabria gestured to the herd. "Thank you for your help. It means more than I can ever say."

Valorian would be proud. Suddenly he lifted his great nose to her face. His nostrils flared gently. *Are your eyes hurt?*

"I cannot see," she said simply.

Athlone felt his heart grow sick.

The lightning's brightness burned your eyes.

"Will they heal?" Gabria asked with more hope than conviction.

The stallion snorted softly. *Perhaps. In time.*

She nodded once and changed the subject. "What about Afer? Is there anything we can do?"

At that the King Stallion bowed his head. *We Hunnuli can withstand the greatest arcane powers in the universe, but we are as vulnerable to bodily injury as any other horse. Your magic will not affect him, for good or ill, and your healers cannot mend a horse's broken leg.*

Gabria felt her voice choke, and she had to force herself to ask, "Then we must put him out of his misery?"

"No!" Sayyed's cry echoed through the circle of stones. The tribesman, a rag tied to his bleeding head, was trying to put a temporary splint on the stallion's broken leg.

Tam quickly went to help her friend as he stepped forward in front of the horse.

"You can't kill him," Sayyed said forcefully.

"Sayyed, his leg is broken," Athlone said, trying not to be harsh. "You know no horse can recover from that."

"One has! My father's prize mare. She broke a leg in a race, and my father could not bear to kill her. He suspended her body from a sling until her leg healed enough to bear her weight. It's not easy, but it can be done. Please," Sayyed cried, "give him a chance."

They were silent for a long moment as they thought about

the enormity of that task. However, to Gabria and Sayyed, the effort was worth the chance if it would save a Hunnuli.

"We'll try it," Gabria said.

Thank you, Sorceress. Then we will gladly leave Afer in your care. The King Stallion lifted his head and neighed a call that rang to the hills and shook the stones of the temple. He lifted his massive body up high to paw the air in a salute of honor to the magic-wielders. The other Hunnuli reared also. Every human watching thrilled to see the majestic Hunnuli at the height of their pride and glory.

As one, the black horses followed the king up out of the river and west toward their home in the mountains. The thunder of their passing faded away into the storm, but the wonder of their presence stayed with the clanspeople for many days to come. Nara, Eurus, and the colt neighed a long farewell.

Gabria's fingers clenched her pantleg, and tears slipped out of the corners of her closed eyes. She could not see the Hunnuli leave, yet she felt the aching loss of their disappearance. Abruptly she shook her head to clear her mind. The pain shot through her eyes, and she gasped.

"What is it?" Athlone asked, the worry plain in his words. "Are you truly blind?"

Gabria tried to push the pain aside and smile. "For the moment. It should pass. Can you ride?"

He looked up at her and was not reassured by her off-hand reply. He decided not to push her and merely answered her question. "Yes."

"Then, come. Tam, Sayyed, you come too. We have to face the clans."

The others obeyed. Athlone quickly understood what Gabria was trying to accomplish, and he helped Sayyed onto Nara's back with no further questions. He mounted Eurus, with some difficulty, and waited while Tam scrambled onto the colt. Afer hopped painfully over the short distance to stand between Eurus and Nara.

"Priestess," Gabria called. "Will you bring the mask?"

The priestess of Amara went to find the death mask of Va-

lorian. At the same time, the eight hostages stopped in front
of the magic-wielders. Guthlac saluted his chieftain with respect; Lord Wortan stepped forward and blinked into the rain
to look up at Gabria.

"Thank you, Lady," he said with sincerity. "Is it all right if
we go?"

She nodded in his direction.

The eight clanspeople gratefully started out for the river.
They walked at first, then their joy and relief broke loose, and
they ran through the muddy water to the far bank where the
crowd of onlookers and their families welcomed them back
with open arms.

The priestess of Amara found the golden mask of Valorian
lying on the stony ground of the temple, its handsome face
still and lifeless. Her hands trembled as she picked up the
heavy gold mask. She carried it to where the magic-wielders
waited and stopped before Gabria.

"Truly," she said, her voice ringing with gladness and respect, "you are the blessed of Amara. Go now, Sorceress. The
clans are waiting." The priestess raised the golden mask high
above her head and began to sing a hymn of praise to the
Mother Goddess. Her song reached out to the watching people
on the riverbanks and stirred their hearts with a strange feeling
of reassurance.

The watching clanspeople did not understand exactly what
had happened on the island. They had seen and heard many
strange things, things both wonderful and horrifying. Now it
seemed that Branth, or whatever he had been, was gone; there
were four magic-wielders instead of one, all apparently alive
and well; the entire Hunnuli herd had honored them before
all the clans; the hostages were free; and a priestess of the
Mother Goddess was offering her oblation of song to praise
their deeds.

The clanspeople did not know what to think. This spectacle
of good and evil, courage and cruelty, honor and treachery was
hardly what they had expected from magic. Magic was supposed to be entirely evil, corrupting, and heretical. Many peo-

ple had been willing to accept Gabria as an aberration. Yet here were three other magic-wielders, two men and a child, who had the same decency and courage and the willingness to lay down their lives for their companions and their people. That was not supposed to be the way of magic.

Emotions were mixed as the four riders and the four Hunnuli waded across the river. The group came very slowly, for Nara and Eurus were supporting Afer between them as he hobbled painfully through the water, so the people had ample time to study the strange party. No one knew whether to cheer or throw stones at them.

The crowd silently watched as the horses angled toward the cluster of chieftains gathered at the tip of the council grove. At the edge of the shore in front of the lords and warriors, the Hunnuli stopped. They stood before the wall of men, their fetlocks deep in the swirling brown water and their manes hanging limp with rain.

There was an uncomfortable pause as the chieftains looked up at one of their own peers and at the woman who had captured the lightning. Quiet hung over the camps while the people waited and watched to see their lords' reactions. Thunder rumbled far to the east, the wind slowed to wayward gusts, and the heavy rain faltered to a drizzle.

Gabria saw nothing of the gathering around her, but she sensed the tension and confusion as surely as if she could see the peoples' faces. She had hoped to influence the clan chieftains to change the laws against sorcery, but she had never thought to go so far.

She heard the men shift reluctantly, then a voice said, "Welcome to the gathering, Lord Athlone. I did not get a chance to see you earlier." It was Lord Hildor, the chieftain of the Wylfling.

His pleasant words and genuine welcome broke the tense stand-off. The chiefs stood aside to allow room for the four Hunnuli to pass, and every lord came forward to voice his greetings to the magic-wielders. The crowds of people broke apart, too, into talking and wondering groups that made no move to go back to their camps.

With a sigh of relief, Lord Sha Umar came to Nara's side and helped Gabria dismount. Like the others, he wondered at her closed eyes, but he made no comment. He only put her hand on his arm and led her to the council tent. The others followed.

Secen, Valar, and Keth had already arrived and were waiting at the tent. The three warriors saluted the magic-wielders with obvious pleasure and relief. Secen told Gabria that Piers was already at work with his healing stone.

Athlone watched while his hearthguard raised his golden banner beside the other chiefs' flags above the tent. He had to swallow hard to fight down the strange mix of relief, pride, and nervousness that rose within him.

The battle with the gorthling was won, but the battle for the survival of sorcery would continue. Athlone and Gabria both knew the clanspeople were too stubborn and their beliefs were too ingrained to be wiped out in a short time. They might be grateful for the defeat of the gorthling, but they were not going to forget two hundred years of hatred and suspicion.

At the entrance to the council tent, Lord Sha Umar, the chieftains' council leader for the year, raised his hand and shouted for attention. "Tomorrow, if Lord Koshyn and Lord Athlone are able to attend, we will begin the council of chieftains. My lords, we have a great deal to discuss this year."

A loud murmur of assent met his suggestion.

He continued. "If all of you are willing, I would like to call a special meeting in the afternoon to learn more about sorcery. Lady Gabria, the Turic, and the girl, Tam, should be allowed to attend."

The other chiefs readily agreed, and so it was decided. Gabria felt weak with relief. She curled her arm up around Nara's throat and pressed her face into the mare's warm cheek.

She nearly jumped when someone said beside her, "Lady Gabria? Lord Koshyn asked me to find this and give it to you. He thought you would need it."

She felt a heavy leather bag being pressed into her hand. "He's awake?" she asked, feeling into the bag.

"Only a short time ago. Healer Piers says he will be . . ." The Dangari warrior's voice faded away at the expression of disbelief and rueful dismay that settled on the sorceress's face.

Gabria began to laugh. She did not need her vision to recognize the old, faded smell, the heavy leather binding, or the faint tingle of power that tickled her fingers from the ancient tome. Now, when she could use it the least, the *Book of Matrah* was in her hands.

The chieftains recognized the book, too, and they stared at her apprehensively. That book had been the cause of strife and death. They wondered what Gabria would do with it.

"Thank you," the sorceress said gently to the warrior. "Would you please give this to Lord Sha Umar until the chiefs can decide what to do with it?"

Sha Umar met Athlone's grin with a shrug and a chuckle of relief. He put the book under guard for safekeeping.

* * * * *

Shortly after the *Book of Matrah* had been passed to Sha Umar, Gabria went to find Piers. She found the healer among the people stricken by the gorthling's arcane blow. He had just finished using the healing stone on the last victim and was talking to the overjoyed relatives when he saw Gabria. He took one look at her, bustled her off to his newly erected tent, and put her to bed.

For that night, the next day, and the following night Gabria slumbered in a peaceful, recuperative rest that not even the uproar in the camps around her could disturb. When she woke in the afternoon of the second day, her first reaction was fear. The world was still completely dark. Her hands flew to her eyes and grabbed at a cloth bound around her head.

"Easy. It's all right," Pier's calm voice soothed her panic. His hands took hers and gently laid them aside. "I've bandaged your eyes for now to let them rest."

She drew a long breath and slowly relaxed. "Is it possible my eyes will heal?"

"I really don't know if you will see again," he told her sadly. "I've never had any experience with this kind of blindness." Piers frowned. He did not like being so unsure about something so important. "I have examined your eyes and I can find no damage. We'll just have to wait."

"I hear voices," someone called outside. "Is she awake?" Sayyed sauntered in, bringing in the smells of sun, wind, and horses. He smiled at Piers, then strode over to Gabria's pallet. "I was beginning to wonder if you were going to sleep through the whole gathering," he said, sitting beside her.

"Before you two talk all day, I have something for Gabria to drink." Piers handed her a cup. "Nara said it is for strength and healing."

The sorceress sat up and raised the cup to her lips. She smiled. The cup was full of the Hunnuli mare's rich, warm milk. Gabria drank every drop and felt her energy flooding back. "What has been happening?"

With pleasure Sayyed and Piers told her everything that had occurred the past two and a half days. Sayyed immediately began with Afer, and with delight in his voice said, "No one expected my idea to work." He laughed. "They kept saying no horse would tolerate being slung by his belly for days on end. They didn't take into account the intelligence of a Hunnuli. We have him supported in a special framework under the cottonwood trees. His leg is splinted, and Tam is spoiling him with treats and handpicked grass. He seems to be doing very well. Even your herdmasters are shaking their heads and saying the sling just might work."

Gabria was delighted to hear that news. The men went on, telling her that Lord Koshyn and the clanspeople Piers had treated with the healing stone were doing well. The chieftains' council had met as planned, and Lord Athlone had explained the details of the gorthling's vicious nature to them all.

"I don't think they fully comprehended what we were fighting until Lord Athlone told them about the massacre of the Bahedin," Sayyed told her. "When they came out of the council tent yesterday, every man among them was as white as the moon." He slapped his knee. "I wish you could have been in the camps last night. The tales of Branth, the gorthling, and our journey to Pra Desh spread from one end of the gathering to the other."

Piers chuckled. "Hardly anyone but you slept last night. They were too busy talking."

"And gawking. The Priestess of Amara and Athlone put the mask of Valorian on display. Every man, woman, and child stood in line to see it." Sayyed shook his head. "No one quite knows what to make of all this—a gorthling, arcane battles, Valorian's mask, the Hunnuli herd—your people have enough to keep them thinking for years."

Gabria smiled. "I hope so. What about the council, have they had their meeting on sorcery?"

Piers answered, "Not yet. They're waiting for you."

"Athlone is at the council tent now, trying to convince Lord Caurus that sorcery is not going to destroy the clans," Sayyed said.

"He'll have a tough fight with that man." The mention of Athlone sobered Gabria. She had something important to tell Sayyed, but she was not certain where to start. The young Turic was so dear to her soul, it was very difficult to tell him what her heart had been trying to tell her all along. She loved Sayyed as a brother and a friend, as someone who filled the aching void left by her twin's death. She wondered sadly how he would react when she told him the truth. Would he stay or would he leave in a cloud of hurt feelings?

But Sayyed surprised her. The Turic took her hand. "It is good to have you alive and well, Gabria," he said. "When you left us to find the gorthling alone, we feared the worst. Lord Athlone was like a stallion heading for battle. He would have left by himself if Piers hadn't talked him into taking me. I've never seen a man so wild." He nodded his head. "If you don't take that man for your husband, he will go berserk one of these days."

Gabria inhaled sharply. "You understand?"

Sayyed gently rubbed her palm with his fingers. "I've known for many days. I just didn't want to see the truth because I wanted you so much, but his feelings and yours are undeniable. You are destined to be together."

"Thank you," she whispered. She touched her bandages with her hand, wishing she could see his face. Despite his words, she would hear the sadness and disappointment in his voice.

"I hope this doesn't mean you won't teach me more sorcery," he said.

Her fingers tightened around his. "You'll stay?"

"Gabria," Sayyed said earnestly, "my love for you is undying. I must simply change it so it does not burn so hot. I came to learn sorcery, and if you will still have me by your side, I want to stay."

"So do I," Athlone said from the tent's entrance. The Khulinin chieftain strode in and joined Gabria and Sayyed. Piers quietly withdrew, leaving the three magic-wielders in the privacy of the tent.

Lord Athlone sat down beside Gabria. He was nervous about her reaction to what he was going to say, and it took him a moment to find the words. "Sayyed and I have talked a great deal the past few days," the chief said slowly. "We have settled a few of our differences, and I have come to understand many things about sorcery and myself. You asked me once if I was willing to live with magic and all of its difficulties. Now I can tell you with all my heart, yes, but only if you are with me. Would you consider renewing our vow of betrothal?"

Gabria sat still, her thoughts swept away by her emotions. "If my eyes do not heal, can you live with my blindness, too?"

"I love you for who you are," he answered simply.

There was a breathless pause, then she raised her hand palm up and said, "I give you my pledge from this moment."

His fingers interlaced with hers, and the vow was made.

Athlone shot a glance at Sayyed. The tribesman nodded once in satisfaction, and the chieftain held out his other hand to the Turic. Sayyed grasped it firmly. He knew then that he had lost a woman, but he had found two new friends. Perhaps, he thought, that was a good exchange on the wheel of life.

The next morning Gabria slowly dressed to attend the council meeting. As she sat waiting for Athlone, Piers unwrapped the bandages around her eyes to replace the cloths with clean ones.

To his astonishment, her hand suddenly grasped his arm in an iron grip. The sorceress was squinting at the entrance where sunlight was leaking through the untied tent flap. "I can see the light," she gasped.

Piers was delighted. He quickly checked her eyes and, against her protest, wrapped them again in the cloths. "Your eyes need rest!" he insisted. "Tonight I'll let you try them, after the sunlight is gone."

When Athlone, Sayyed, and Tam came to get her, they found Gabria in a state of euphoria. Her smile was brilliant, and her joy radiated from every line of her face. The four magic-wielders took her healing as a good omen, and they went to the council of the chieftains with hopeful hearts.

Gabria would never forget that council meeting. After listening to her speech in defense of magic, the chiefs debated for hours over the fate of sorcery and the fate of Gabria and her friends. Athlone, Sayyed, and Tam sat around her through the long, often angry speeches and did not move once to defend themselves. The final decision was up to the chieftains now, and no one could say with certainty what their choice would be.

At last, late in the afternoon, Koshyn and Sha Umar won a major victory. Lord Caurus rose from his seat and said grudgingly, "I see I must cast my lot with the rest of you. I agree to remove the death penalty for the use of sorcery. However, I demand that strict limits be set on the use of magic and on the actions of the magic-wielders. The use of sorcery must be contained to those we deem responsible enough to use it!"

Lord Sha Umar raised his hand. "It is done. I suggest that

we extend the gathering a few more days and use that time to establish the new laws for sorcery. This is too important to put off for another year."

The chieftains and the magic-wielders agreed. When Sha Umar gave Gabria the *Book of Matrah*, she and Athlone found the dangerous spells of summoning gorthlings, tore them from the book, and burned them.

"There are some things," she said, repeating Valorian's words, "best left alone by man."

News of the council's decision spread through the camps even before the meeting was over. Emotions were widely mixed throughout the clans, but no one was greatly surprised. The clanspeople were beginning to understand that magic was part of their heritage, a part they could no longer deny.

* * * * *

Three days later, on a gloriously clear, warm summer evening, Lord Athlone of Clan Khulinin married Lady Gabria of Clan Corin in a ceremony witnessed by all eleven clans. The Khulinin Priestess of Amara, clad in flowing green robes, performed the rites of marriage and blessed the couple with prayers of harmony and fertility.

Gabria wore the red dress Khan'di had given her and a golden veil from Athlone's mother—the red to represent the clan she was leaving and the gold to symbolize the clan she was finally officially joining. Lord Athlone was resplendent in his finest clothes and his golden torque. Piers and Tam were there to represent Gabria's family, and Sayyed stood as Athlone's witness.

When the ceremony was over, Athlone removed Gabria's veil and tied it around his waist like a sash. He took his new bride into his arms and sealed their happiness with a long and very thorough kiss.

The three Hunnuli beside them lifted their heads to the evening star and whinnied their joy over the vast Ramtharin Plains.

A Short Glossary

THE CLANS	CHIEFTAIN	CLOAK COLOR
Corin (massacred)	Dathlar	Red
Khulinin	Athlone	Gold
Geldring	Wortan	Green
Wylfling	Hildor	Brown
Dangari	Koshyn	Indigo
Shahedron	Malech	Black
Reidhar	Caurus	Yellow
Amnok	Faltor	Gray
Murjik	Jol	Purple
Bahedin	Ryne	Orange
Jehanan	Sha Umar	Maroon
Ferganan	Bael	Light Blue

Hearthguard: The chieftain's personal bodyguard. These men are the elite warriors of the clan and are honored with the position for their bravery, skill, and loyalty.

Herd-master: The man responsible for the health, breeding, and well-being of the horse herds.

Holdings: Land granted to a clan for its use while in winter camp.

Outriders: Those werod riders who guard the herds and the camp or act as scouts.

Treld: A clan's permanent winter camp.

Weir-geld: Recompense paid to the family of a murdered person in the form of gold or livestock, or by death in a personal duel.

Werod: The fighting body of a clan. Although all men are required to learn the rudiments of fighting, only those who pass certain tests make up the werod.

Wer-tain: The commander of the werod. These men are second only to the chieftain in authority.

for 1992

Thorn and Needle

Paul B. Thompson

When two intriguing travelers journey to a perfect city to destroy a strange new god, two powerful forces collide. Available February 1992.

Kingslayer
L. Dean James

In this sequel to *Sorcerer's Stone*, young Gaylon Reysson, the new king of Wynnamyr, must learn to use the magical sword Kingslayer. Will he capture a glorious victory for his people--or destroy himself and the world he hopes to save? Available May 1992.

The Nine Gates
Phillip Brugalette

Gopal, the prince of Goloka, sees his teacher burst into flames, then the many-armed Virabhadra go on a rampage. Gopal decides he must perform a sacred test but needs help from a centuries-old mystic to survive. Available August 1992.

Half-Light
Denise Vitola

Commander Ariann Centuri's betrothed is killed by the bat-faced Benar, and she is stricken with a terminal mind-bending disease. Suddenly she finds herself wedded to the Viceroy of the Galactic Consortium of Planets . . . and fighting for her life. Available December 1992.

Prism Pentad
BOOK TWO
The Crimson Legion
Troy Denning

A dream born from tyranny . . .

After a millennium of sorrow, the city of Tyr cast off the yoke of the brutal despot who reduced its fields to dust and its citizens to bondage. The new king, Tithian of Mericles, has liberated the slaves . . . and plunged the city into chaos. Only the man-dwarf Rikus, the gladiator slave who sparked the rebellion, can save the city from the mighty army sent from Urik to destroy it. Available April 1992.

Book Three: *The Amber Enchantress*, October 1992.

FORGOTTEN REALMS

Fantasy Adventure

COMING IN 1992

Druidhome Trilogy

Douglas Niles

***At last,
the long-awaited
sequel to
the Moonshae Trilogy.***

Prophet of Moonshae

March 1992

The Coral Kingdom

October 1992

The Druid Queen

Spring 1993

■ THE HARPERS ■

A Force for Good in the Realms!

Red Magic
Jean Rabe
One of the powerful and evil Red Wizards wants to control more than his share of Thay. While the mage builds a net of treachery, the Harpers put their own agents into action to foil his plans for conquest.

Elfshadow   Elaine Cunningham
Harpers are being murdered, and the trail leads to Arilyn Moonblade. Arilyn must uncover the ancient secret of her sword's power in order to find and face the assassin before he finds her.

The Night Parade   Scott Ciencin
Myrmeen Lhal, the seductive ruler of Arabel, enlists the aid of the Harpers to rescue her long-lost daughter from the Night Parade, a shadowy group of creatures that feeds off human misery and fear. Available May 1992.

The Ring of Winter   James Lowder
Harper Artus Cimber travels to the jungles of Chult to find the fabled Ring of Winter, but the Cult of Frost also seeks the ring, which contains the power to bring a second Ice Age to the Realms. Available October 1992.

**Coming in 1992
A New Dimension in
Outer Space Adventure!**

Invaders of Charon Series

*An uneasy alliance is born as NEO and RAM
join forces against a formidable foe.*

The Genesis Web

C. M. Brennan

Follow the adventures of Black Barney, from his
birth in a RAM laboratory to his daring escape
from his evil creators and beyond, into a world of
danger and intrigue. Available April 1992.

Nomads of the Sky

William H. Keith

The mysterious, dreaded Space Nomads take
Vincent Perelli prisoner, forcing him to fight a
ritual battle for his life before he can seek
The Device, a missing RAM artifact that may save
Buck Rogers. Available September 1992.